Please return/renew this item by the last date shown
on this label, or on your self-service receipt.

To renew this item, visit **www.librarieswest.org.uk**
or contact your library.

Your Borrower number and PIN are required.

LibrariesWest

Anna Smith has been a journalist for over twenty years and is a former chief reporter for the *Daily Record* in Glasgow. She has covered wars across the world as well as major investigations and news stories from Dunblane to Kosovo to 9/11. Anna spends her time between Lanarkshire and Dingle in the west of Ireland, as well as in Spain to escape the British weather.

The Rosie Gilmour thrillers

The Dead Won't Sleep
To Tell the Truth
Screams in the Dark
Betrayed
A Cold Killing
Rough Cut
Kill Me Twice

DEATH TRAP

Anna Smith

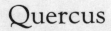

First published in Great Britain in 2017 by

Quercus Editions Ltd
Carmelite House
50 Victoria Embankment
London EC4Y 0DZ

An Hachette UK company

A CIP catalogue record for this book is available
from the British Library

PB ISBN 978 1 78429 483 0
EBOOK ISBN 978 1 78429 484 7

10 9 8 7 6 5 4 3 2 1

Typeset by Jouve (UK), Milton Keynes

Printed and bound in Great Britain by Clays Ltd, St Ives plc

For Tom and Marie Brown.
Old friends, bookends, inspirational.

'I didn't write. I just wandered about.'

Martha Gelhorn, novelist and journalist

Near Lennoxtown, August 2000

Tadi watched, frozen with fear, as the dark blue pickup truck screeched into the yard and came to a shuddering halt, sending up swirling clouds of dust. He knew what was coming. He'd been here before. He wiped the sweat off his brow with an oily rag and shoved it back into the pocket of his dungarees. Then he turned back to the engine he'd been cleaning and kept his head down. Across the yard, where the sweltering heat rose in waves, the old man he knew as Jake was buffing the bonnet of the red Jaguar til it gleamed in the sunlight. He looked back nervously, polishing faster. They both knew there would trouble, even before they heard the shouting from the boss man as he came storming out of the house, kicking over a bin and ranting as he strode towards the pickup. Tadi kept one eye on the scene as it unfolded.

'Get the fucker out!' big Rory O'Dwyer bellowed, his beer belly shaking as he roared, his Irish accent as strong as the day he left Limerick twenty years ago.

Tadi watched as O'Dwyer's son, Finn, and his brother, Timmy, dropped open the hatch on the back of the truck and climbed in. They roughly grabbed the limp body and heaved it over the side. It hit the dust like a sack of potatoes.

'I hope you've not killed him yet.' O'Dwyer glared at his sons, who shook their heads as they jumped back out.

The body on the ground moaned and shifted in the dirt.

'Get up, you cunt!' The boss stood over him.

'I . . . I c-can't.'

O'Dwyer glanced at his sons and jerked his head. They bent down and dragged the man to his feet. Tadi had to strain his eyes to recognise the skinny figure – it was Bo, and he'd been here for seven years. His face was bruised and bloodied, his eyes puffy slits. His shirt was half ripped off, and crimson welts raged across his puny chest. The brothers must have given him a good kicking when they found him. He knew how that worked. He'd been there too.

'What the fuck did you think you were doing?' The boss took a step closer to Bo, whose legs were buckling as he tried to stand. 'Going to the bizzies, were you? Going to report us to the fucking cops, you shitebag!'

Bo started to cry.

'I'm sorry, boss. I'm sorry. I won't do it again.'

'You've fucking tried to get away twice, you prick. You're fucking right you won't do it again.'

From where Tadi was standing, forty feet away, he could hear the sickening crack as O'Dwyer's fist crunched into Bo's face. Blood and teeth flew through the air, and he slumped to the ground. But Finn hauled him up, grabbed his hair and jerked his head back, so the boss could punch him again. Then they let him go and he collapsed and gurgled on the ground, curling into a defensive ball. The boss laid into him, the force of his kicks moving Bo's skinny frame along the ground like a burst football. He lay there limp and still. O'Dwyer nodded to Finn, who climbed into the back of the pickup and brought out a petrol can. Tadi glanced at Jake, who had stopped polishing and stood open-mouthed. Two of the other workers who'd been cleaning the path and tending the garden also stopped and watched. Timmy, O'Dwyer's youngest son, wore the same wide-eyed, crazed expression he always did, grinning like the psycho he was as he doused Bo in petrol. As the fumes filled the air, there was a slow, sickening realisation of what was going to happen. Nobody spoke. The only sound was the hysterical barking and growling of O'Dwyer's Dobermans, straining behind their high wire fence, as though sensing the drama. Tadi looked away, feeling sick to his stomach. He didn't want to see this.

Suddenly O'Dwyer turned to the workers and shouted. 'You fuckers take a good look at this . . . and learn!'

He took a box of matches out of his trousers pocket and sparked one, holding it up like a torch.

'You hear me?' he snarled.

Then he dropped the match onto Bo, and his body burst into flames. There was only one piercing scream, but by that time Bo's entire body was engulfed in flames, black and red and sending plumes of smoke up to the sky, quickly filling the air with the smell of burning flesh. Tadi blinked and looked at the ground. He couldn't watch this. He thought of his Ava and their little boy, Jetmir. Wherever they were being held, at least they weren't here to witness this.

'Tadi!'

The boss man's bark made him jump and he straightened up.

'C'mere.' He curled a beckoning finger.

Tadi walked towards him, hesitantly.

'Get the digger and move this piece of shit from here. Then you and the lads bury him.' He pointed to a field beyond the yard. 'Go over there to where that clump of trees is and bury him there.'

Tadi swallowed, looking from the boss to the brothers to the smoking pile of what was left of Bo. He swallowed the urge to throw up.

'Bury him?'

The boss man looked at him, incredulous, his lip curling to a sarcastic smile.

'Well, unless you want to eat him, if you're fucking hungry enough.'

The brothers sniggered like the halfwits they were.

'Now get moving, don't be standing there like a stupid cunt.' He shouted over Tadi's shoulder so the others could hear. 'This is what happens if you fuck with the O'Dwyers. So make sure all your dipshit mates understand that.' He hawked and spat in the direction of Bo's body. 'Now get to work, or I'll fucking barbecue the lot of you.'

Tadi said nothing, but found himself nodding as he turned and walked slowly away, his legs like jelly. The others were standing next to old Jake, their faces a mask of fear and disbelief. Tadi couldn't help but notice that Jake had wet his trousers and was snivelling, wiping his tears with the duster he'd used to polish the car.

'They're going to kill us all. I know it, Tadi.' His voice trembled.

The others shuffled from one foot to the other and looked to Tadi for an answer. He looked at their lean, unshaven faces, hollow cheeks from hunger, not knowing what to say. He barely knew these middle-aged men. All he'd learned from his three months here was that they were prisoners, just like him. They'd been homeless down-and-outs, living rough on the streets of Glasgow, when they'd been offered a place to live and a job by Finn O'Dwyer. They were alcoholics, they had no family they could remember, and were totally alone in the world. Tadi was nothing like them, yet he too was a prisoner here. He'd been a mechanic back in Kosovo, before the war made him flee to the UK as a refugee. His wife and baby son were here – out there somewhere. The O'Dwyers had taken them in, offered him work and board in return for fixing their machinery and vehicles. He'd accepted, because he had overstayed his time in UK. If the authorities had found him he would have been sent back to Kosovo, where the country was still in ruins from the war. But he didn't know that he wouldn't be allowed to leave. An image of Ava and Jetmir came to him, and his chest hurt. Where were they? Every day he didn't see or hear from Ava, his heart broke. It was punishment, big O'Dwyer had told him, for his own attempt to escape. Three weeks on, and Tadi was still pissing blood from the beating Finn and Timmy dished out to him. He couldn't afford to try to escape again. They would kill Ava and the child, they told him. He would live with what he had for the moment. He had no choice.

'Come on,' he said to the men. 'We must do this. We have to be strong. Bring some spades.'

He walked away from them to the digger at the far side of the yard, climbed onto it, and started the engine. The O'Dwyers passed by without looking in his direction, and went into the big, long, low bungalow that was their home. Tadi could smell the food being cooked for the family lunch and his empty stomach groaned. He hadn't eaten since yesterday. He drove the digger towards where Bo lay, his body still smoking in the dust. The men followed him, afraid not to. Then between them they picked up Bo's body and placed it carefully into the dumper bucket. As they did, Bo's head slumped to the side, his face an unrecognisable mass of burnt and singed flesh. Tadi looked at the others as he climbed onto the digger, and jerked his head, beckoning them to follow on foot. They did, and he drove on slowly with them walking briskly at his side. When they got to the clump of trees, the sun had disappeared behind some clouds and the place was suddenly darker.

'I think he means here,' he said. 'Wait. I open up the ground first before you dig.'

He lowered the digger and it clawed at the ground, dragging back moist, black earth. The engine roared as it scraped more and more earth, digging deeper. The men stood watching helplessly, waiting to be told what to do. Then Tadi stopped suddenly. He saw something white in the ground. He switched off the engine and jumped off the digger.

'Give me a spade,' Tadi said to one of the men.

He stabbed the spade into the earth and there was a sharp sound as it hit something solid. He stepped closer, clearing the muck. Then he gasped and stood back. It was a long bone, like a thigh or a shin bone. He carefully scraped away more earth. A skull. Not a whole skull, but one that looked as though half had been caved in. He could feel his heart beat faster as he carefully dug around the bones. Then he saw it. A much smaller skull. Like that of a small baby. It couldn't be. A baby? He stopped, his whole body trembling, then he turned to the men, who stood, their eyes wide in shock. Jake started to cry again, then the other two began blubbing.

'Stop!' Tadi snapped at them. 'Stop it now! Don't let them see you. Do you hear me?' He threw away the spade and shook Jake by the shoulders. 'Listen to me. We didn't see this. Okay? We saw nothing.' He looked at all three of them. 'Come. We bury Bo.' He threw down the spade and walked to the dumper bucket. 'Is all we can do for him now.'

CHAPTER ONE

You could have heard a pin drop in the crowded courtroom as Thomas Boag got to his feet, handcuffed between two policemen. Rosie Gilmour studied him intently from the packed press benches, where reporters shuffled their feet impatiently, desperate to see him led downstairs to the cells so they could get out and hit the phones with their colour pieces for tomorrow's front pages. In the flesh, Boag – stocky, balding, his face pallid – looked a harmless figure, the kind of individual you wouldn't give a second glance to if he sat next to you on the train. There was nothing remarkable about him. That was the beauty of the deception. He didn't look threatening. Rosie scribbled the word 'invisible' in her notebook. That's what he is, she thought. Nobody suspected him, because nobody saw him. The big uniformed sergeant turned his head around and they exchanged a look somewhere between relief and satisfaction. They were old pals during the many years she'd covered trials in the High Court as a young reporter. She knew he was retiring in a few weeks, so he'd be glad to have this one to tell his grandchildren. It wasn't over yet though. Boag had been captured, charged and remanded in custody in the past few days. In the next couple of hours he'd be on his way to HM Prison Barlinnie to await his trial. The hard men in the jail were already baying for his blood and word was out that he wouldn't even make it to the end of the day, let alone his trial. Boag was a beast and he'd get what was coming to him. He had butchered a young gay man he'd picked up in a late-night bar, and the hunt for the killer had gripped the entire country. The twenty-year-old's hacked-off body parts, strewn between beaches and woods, had been pieced together like a forensic jigsaw. Detectives were still hunting for one missing teenage boy, as well as the young female tenant from the flat below Boag's, who hadn't been seen for months.

But the young student he'd butchered wasn't just anybody. He was Jack Mulhearn. His father was Jonjo Mulhearn, the notorious Glasgow gangster, who'd been banged up for the past twelve years, but was due out any day. He'd been given the news of his only son's brutal murder while in jail, and the media had watched in droves when he came out in handcuffs for the boy's funeral. The fact that one of the hardest men in Glasgow's son had been frequenting gay bars was a talking point, but someone had murdered Jonjo's boy, and that person would pay. The tabloids loved the sensationalism of a murder story, but grisly details of this one were turning stomachs, and Rosie was glad that the end game was in sight. In the past few months, she'd interviewed the traumatised families of the missing woman, and the parents of the other young gay man who never came home from a night out and whose body had never been found. Jack Mulhearn's mother had never spoken – and friends had said that both she and Jonjo were completely broken.

It was Rosie's exclusive in the *Post* that led to Boag's eventual arrest, and for that she'd be remembered as the journalist who helped put a suspected serial killer behind bars. But right now she felt an icy chill as Boag turned to the press benches and scanned the faces of the reporters, until he finally stopped at hers. It was only a fleeting moment, but his dead eyes met hers and she stared back, defiantly, as she held her breath. She thought she saw the slightest curl of his lips before he was prodded on the back by the other policeman and led downstairs to the cells.

'Fuck's sake, Rosie! You got the cold stare there, all right.' Bob Burke, an old rival and friend from the *Sun* newspaper, gave her a nudge as the reporters squeezed their way out of the courtroom doors. 'He obviously read your piece on him. Did you see the way he looked at you? You'd better not go home in the dark!'

'Yeah. Gives me the bloody creeps,' Rosie said. 'I hope some of the lags cut his throat before the week's out.'

'Me too. Don't know about you, but I might need a drink after that. Are you coming to the Ship?'

'I'll maybe call in, Bob. I've a couple of contacts to see here first.'

Rosie stood in the corridor as the press pack filed out and made their way through the big swing doors and into the street. She took a long breath and massaged the back of her neck to take the tension out of her shoulders.

'Do you want me to get that for you?'

Rosie spun round, recognising the voice of the Strathclyde Police detective who was her close friend and informant.

'Hey, Don. How you doing? You'll be glad to see that bastard getting huckled downstairs then?'

'You bet, pal. Beyond evil. You can quote me on that. Was it you he was staring at before they took him down? Weird as fuck that was.'

'Yes.' Rosie grinned. 'This is actually my nervous smile.'

'Come on, I'll buy you a drink.' He gestured to the lawyer beside him. 'You know Brian McCann, don't you?'

'Sure.' Rosie smiled at the young lawyer, whom she'd met once before. He worked in the firm of one of her solicitor pals, who'd told her that McCann was a rising star. 'How you doing, Brian? Keeping busy?'

They walked together towards the swing doors.

'Oh yeah. A lot on the go. But it gets stranger every day. You'll never believe what I was just doing this morning in here. A fucking asylum-seeker charged with trapping a seagull.'

'A seagull? You kidding?'

'No. Honestly. How the hell it ever got into court, I'll never know. Poor bugger said he was hungry, so caught the seagull to eat.'

'Christ! To eat? How did he trap it?'

'Some kind of contraption with a rope and a tin tray, from the window of his flat.'

'Did he actually eat it?' Rosie was intrigued.

'Well, not exactly. But it was in the oven when the police arrived.'

'I can't believe someone phoned the police and they actually went to investigate! No wonder you can't get a cop when you're being battered to death.'

'Tell me about it.'

'So what happened to him? Where's he from?'

'Kosovo. Came here and was supposed to go after a year, but stayed on, working in the black market. A wife and kid. You know, the usual story.'

'Yeah, too well. A lot of them stay on and disappear into the black economy. Can't blame them, really.'

They went through the doors and onto the street, where photographers were waiting around to snap anyone connected with the Boag appearance. Don and Brian stopped and lit up cigarettes, both of them drawing in the smoke as if it was their last. Then Brian suddenly looked across the street, straining his eyes.

'Wait a minute! There's my man there – my refugee! What the fuck's happening?'

Rosie looked across the street and followed Brian, who was walking briskly. There was a skinny man, dishevelled, being strong-armed towards a waiting red Jaguar.

'What's going on, Brian? Who's that with him?'

'Christ knows. I was only the duty solicitor today, so I don't know much about the guy. The case was put back to a later date, because the sheriff wanted to get the Refugee Council to give him more information. So I might not see him again. But what's this guy doing slapping him?'

Rosie watched as the bigger man smacked the refugee on the back of the head and bundled him into the car. She rushed forward, beside Brian who stood next to the car, battering on the window. The Kosovan looked up with that look she'd seen in the faces of refugees in camps, or limping across borders. Desperate, lost, helpless. The car screeched off. She managed to get the number plate, repeating it to herself as she jotted it down in her notebook.

'Who's the guy, Brian? Any idea?'

'Nope. He didn't mention anything about anyone. Said he knew nobody and was just living hand to mouth.'

'Well, he's being abused there. That's for sure.'

Don caught up with them.

'Come on, guys. Let's have a pint.'

Rosie watched the car as it sped out up High Street and out of sight in a line of heavy traffic.

'There's something not right about that.' She turned to Don as they crossed the road towards the pub. 'That bastard was slapping the poor guy around. I need to find out more.'

'Did you clock the number plate?' Don pushed open the door of the bar and allowed Rosie to go through.

'I did.'

'I'll get one of the lads to run it through.'

'Can you do it soon, Don? Like now?'

'Christ! Can I order a drink first, sweetheart?' he joked. 'We've just banged up what might be one of the country's most twisted serial killers. Take a breather, Gilmour – for Jesus' sake.'

Rosie smiled and put a friendly arm around his shoulder.

'I know. You're right. But you know what I'm like. I can smell trouble out there.'

Don grinned.

'Out there? Look around this place, pet. You can smell trouble in here any day of the week.'

Rosie smiled as they sat down and she took in the surroundings of the famous Old Ship Bank pub – yards from the High Court in the rougher end of town. If you sat here long enough on any given day, the stories just kept unfolding. In one corner there would be murderers freed on a not-proven verdict holding impromptu parties, karaoke at full tilt, celebrating sticking it up the arses of the cops. Or, across the bar, a few lawyers and QCs imbibing with their clients, or the victims, traumatised after going into court in search of justice. Sometimes they got it – often they got a pie, a pint, maybe drunk. Rosie opted for a mug of tea instead of alcohol. It was too early in the day for a gin and tonic, and the Ship wasn't known for its red wine. It was one of the few places that still sold Lanliq, Eldorado and Buckfast by the glass. Don brought over three pies on a plate, which they proceeded to tear into with their hands. It's how it was done. Don's mobile rang, and Rosie watched him speaking, then winking at her.

'Get your pen out, Gilmour. Here's the sketch,' he said.

'Already?'

'Yeah. Like you were sitting there not bothered. Your arse was making buttons to get started. I know you.'

'So I'm ready.' Rosie took her notebook out.

'O'Dwyer. Gadgie. Well . . . settled gadgie, but gippo nonetheless.'

'Your political correctness is astounding, if I may say so, sir,' the young lawyer piped up between mouthfuls of pie.

'Fuck that! I know of this bastard. He's not a major player as such, but a gangster, and worse still, one of the big faces in the travelling community. They own some farmland out towards the Campsie Hills. But word is they're also fences, moving stolen gear, plus they dabble in drugs. Nobody's ever been able to get a handle on them because the last thing anyone does in the gadgie community is grass.'

'So what is he doing with my asylum-seeker?' the lawyer asked.

'No idea, mate. He's your case.'

'We need to find out,' Rosie said. 'That poor bloke looked distraught. I hate to see that. He was being bullied into that car.' She looked at Don and the lawyer. 'I'm going to have a look at this O'Dwyer character. I've never heard of him.'

'Well, just be careful,' Don said.

'Will you be able to give me some details on the Kosovan – his name and a bit of background?'

'I don't have much, but no problem. His name is Tadi. Married with one young son. I'm curious myself. I didn't like what I saw there either.'

They went back to their lunch and ate in silence.

Don's phone rang again and he pressed it to his ear. Rosie watched as the colour drained from his face.

'You are fucking joking me,' he whispered. 'Tell me you're not serious.'

Rosie and the lawyer exchanged glances. Then they heard the sirens. They watched as Don listened, rubbing his forehead in frustration, alarm and shock.

'Right. I'm on my way.' He put the phone back into his pocket.

'What is it, Don?'

'It's Boag. Fucking Christ almighty! The fucker's escaped. He's slashed a cop's throat on the way out.'

'Jesus! B-but how? He was in handcuffs. What the Christ happened?'

Don was on his feet.

'No idea. Seems to have kicked off when he was going into the cells. All hell broke loose. There are another three cons missing as well in the mayhem. But fuck them! Boag is out! Holy fucking shit!'

Rosie looked out of the window where the blue lights of a police car flashed as it sped past. A shudder ran through her. Boag was out. It was her story that led the police to arrest him over a week ago. And he knew it.

CHAPTER TWO

Martin Black opened the tailgate of his jeep, and with a swift clap of his hands, the springer spaniel leapt in, tail wagging.

'Good boy, Rex!' He turned to his girlfriend as she opened the passenger door. 'Let's hope he's tired out. I'm knackered after that walk.'

He got in and pulled on his seatbelt, then eased the car out of the lay-by and back onto the road. In his rear-view mirror he could see the light beginning to change over the Campsie Hills, giving the sky an almost lilac tinge. He thought of getting out to take another photograph, but he knew Katie would only moan at him.

'No more pictures,' she grinned. 'I can read your bloody mind, Martin. Come on. We've enough pics for the day. Let's get settled somewhere and get the tent up. I'm starving.'

It was mostly farmland around the Campsies, and Martin

had already sorted out a spot close to where they had turned off the main road to go up with the dog for a hike in the hills. There was a house in the distance, and he knew they should probably go and ask permission to camp, but they hadn't done it so far, while they'd been travelling up from the Borders over the last few days. It was his idea not to pitch their tent in campsites. That was for the people who were kid-on campers, he said. They were going to be real survivors, he'd told Katie, when they'd left England. They'd be pitching the tent where they could, bathing in rivers, cooking on their small gas stove. Three days into the trip, and Katie had already been bitching that she longed for a long hot shower and a meal in a restaurant. Tomorrow night, he'd promised her. We'll stay in a campsite and do what the rest of the herd does. He knew the only way to keep her onside was if he toned it down a little. They were hoping to go all the way up to Oban in the Highlands, so he had to make some compromises along the way.

'I've already seen a place we can camp,' he said. 'It's close by, so we can have the tent up and dinner on before it's dark.' He rolled down the window and stuck his head out, scanning the sky.

'I'm just hoping it doesn't bloody rain. I can't cope with another night, waking up with the dampness going right through me.' She shook her head and smiled. 'Why the hell did I let you talk me into this bloody trip? It was all right when the sun was shining.'

'Me Tarzan. You Jane.' Martin reached across and ruffled her hair. 'Tarzan going to make Jane feel good later tonight.'

'Yeah. Well Tarzan will be struggling to keep Jane awake, if we don't get started soon.' She giggled, running a hand up his thigh.

They'd only been going out six months, after meeting at Durham University, but Martin already knew he was never going to let Katie out of his life. They'd hit it off at a party in a bar close to the university, and by the time the night was over they had sat up all night talking of their dreams, lives and plans. This was as good as it gets, Martin had told himself. They became instant friends. In less than a month they were lovers.

Martin pulled the car into the side of the road and opened the gate to the field.

'Are you sure we should be doing this?'

'Of course. Don't worry. The Scots are an easy-going crowd – someone will probably come down and offer us a whisky later.'

'Yeah. Or shoot us for being on their land.'

'But we don't know whose land it is. Look.' He spread his hands out. 'There are two farms. One closer, but the other one has things growing in it, so maybe this is their field. So rather than make a scene, let's just pitch here. We'll be off before they're even up in the morning.'

Martin got out of the car, slung his rucksack over his shoulder and dragged the tent out of the back seat, then headed up towards the clump of trees at the edge of the field, with Katie following. He stepped an area out.

'Here will be great. There's a bit of shelter from the trees in case the wind gets up in the night. And look – there's some papers and stuff. Like someone's been camping here before. Probably kids.'

The two of them went to work pitching the tent and had it up in minutes. Katie took the sleeping bags inside and Martin set up the stove and brought some food out. In twenty minutes they were sorted and dining on sausages and powdered mashed potatoes washed down by a couple of cans of beer.

'Food fit for kings.' Martin winked at Katie.

'It's great, actually,' she agreed. 'But tomorrow can we go to a cafe and get fish and chips?'

'Definitely. I promise.'

When Martin was finished eating, he got up and brought the dog out of the jeep and put food and water into his bowl. Then they got into the tent.

Under the flickering light of their lamp, they snuggled in and the dog lay sleepily outside the tent. A couple of times earlier, Martin noticed it had been over at the clump of trees, sniffing and scratching. He'd commanded him to come and lie down, threatening to tie him. The dog had looked at him, a bit resentful, but was finally settled. They finished their beers, switched off the lamp, and lay back in their sleeping bags.

'I'm knackered,' Katie said. 'Can we put off this Tarzan and Jane lark til tomorrow night?'

Martin leaned over kissed her on the lips.

'Okay, pet. Tarzan's a bit done in too, as it happens.' He lay back, pulled the sleeping bag over him, and seconds later felt himself drifting off to sleep.

It was still pitch black when Martin's bladder woke him up. He tried to turn over and ignore it, but he could feel the pressure. Shit! Shouldn't have drunk all that beer, he muttered to himself. He slipped out of his sleeping bag and crept out of the tent, turning for a second to see Katie's face in deep, contented sleep. Outside he got to his feet, and could hear the dog sniffing and breathing, but couldn't see him. Then he looked around, his eyes adjusting to the darkness. He spotted Rex, clawing at the earth, just yards away beneath the clump of trees. The dog was digging furiously, agitated.

'Rex,' Martin rasped. 'Get over here, you stupid mutt.'

The dog turned around and barked twice, then went back to digging.

'Christ almighty! You'll wake up the whole place.' He glanced back to the tent, where Katie was already poking her head through the flap.

'What the hell, man? It's the middle of the night.'

'Sorry, Katie. It's bloody Rex,' he whispered. 'I got up for a pee, couldn't see him, and then found him over there digging like mad. You know what he's like. Go back to sleep.'

But Katie was already on her feet and stumbling in the darkness. The dog barked again.

'Shit! Go and bring the bugger over here,' Katie said. 'The farmer might come.'

In the distance they heard the barking of at least one more dog.

'See! He's bloody wakened the whole of the countryside.'

Martin took his torch and went over to the dog, shining light over him. He glanced back at Katie.

'Bloody hell. He's only gone and dug a great hole in the ground.' Martin took a couple of steps, but his dog wasn't even looking up, just scraping with his paws.

'Rex! What the hell you looking for, you daft dog?'

Martin shone the torch into the hole. There was a faint smell of burning and he thought he could see a blackened, torn shirt. Then, suddenly, he realised it was a body. He stood rooted, his head swimming with shock. Don't panic, he told himself. Just calm down. Just go back and get Katie to get into the tent, wrap things up and get to hell out of here. They didn't want to be part of whatever was in that hole. They shouldn't be here.

Then the dog growled as it turned and looked beyond Martin. It happened so fast. Martin was barely conscious by the time he had slumped to his knees, felt the numbing sensation in his head and warm blood run down his face. Then a sickening thud as something smashed his head again, as though it had cut him in two. Katie shone the torch into the darkness. All she could see was the ski mask on the man's face, and Martin on the ground with what looked like an axe in his head. The dog lay whimpering at his side, the white patches of its coat stained and wet. She opened her mouth to scream, but it was too late.

Tadi stood under the shower until the water ran cold, then stood for a few moments longer, hoping the icy water would bring him to life. It had been a sleepless night, but he had to be sharp. Yesterday, when Finn was driving him back from court, he had told him that the boss wanted to talk to him in the morning. He didn't want to ask why for fear of another tirade of abuse from Finn, so he said nothing. During the journey back to the farm, he'd sat in silent dread. Finn had asked him what the hell was he playing at, trapping a seagull. He was planning to eat it, Tadi told him. He was hungry. Finn shook his head in disbelief, but never once asked him why he was hungry. Tadi wanted to tell him that the three pounds a day wages he paid wasn't even enough to have one square meal, never mind three. Especially with the way they were working him back at the yard. He was constantly hungry ever since he'd gone to live with them, and the other men were the same. He noticed how slack his trousers had become and how his clothes hung on him, his cheeks sunken. He'd stopped looking in the mirror because the last time he did, he saw an old man looking back. He prayed that wherever Ava was, at least she and his boy weren't going hungry. That would be too much for him to bear. But he'd been surprised yesterday when Finn drove out of town and stopped at a fish and chip shop, handed him five pounds, and told him to go in and eat something while he sat in the car. Tadi had wolfed the fish and chips down with bread and butter, vaguely aware of the other people in the cafe watching how he was eating the food, barely chewing it. It had lain in his stomach all night while he was in bed, staring in the blackness, trying to work out why Finn was suddenly being so nice to him. When he'd dropped him off, Finn told him to be bright and early in the morning, that there might be a surprise in store for him. Tadi was nervous, but also excited. He dared not even hope that maybe they were bringing his wife back. He feared that it was bad news, maybe big O'Dwyer was going to give him a kicking for ending up in court.

He turned off the tap and stepped out of the shower, drying himself with the threadbare towel. He put on the only clean dark T-shirt he had, and pulled on a V-neck sweater over it. Then he looked in the cupboard to see if there was anything to eat. He cut the mould off a hunk of bread and ate it with some ketchup. As he sat drinking a cup of tea, he looked out of the window and could see the pickup truck coming up the street, one of the other workers already outside waiting. He picked up his rucksack and went downstairs into the bright sunny day, glancing around as people left their homes, going to their jobs in the city, kissing loved ones on their doorsteps. It under-lined his loneliness, and his chest ached to see Ava and his son. He looked down at the truck and Timmy was sitting smoking, the usual mad expression on his face. He climbed into the back of the truck and blinked a hello to the other worker who lived in the flat below him as they drove away.

CHAPTER THREE

'We should get some protection for you, Gilmour. It makes sense. It's two days now and this bastard is still on the loose.'

The implications of the stark fact that Thomas Boag was out there didn't need to be spelled out to Rosie. She'd been looking over her shoulder ever since she left the Ship pub, minutes after Don had taken the call that Boag had escaped. Even in her flat, three floors up in St George's Cross, she'd found herself casting glances into the shadows as she'd stood on the balcony last night watching the lights twinkling across the city. It was madness, she knew – stupid to be spooked by the cold stare Boag had given her as he was being led down to the cell. She told herself that, realistically, he was now a prisoner on the run, and his priority would be to stay out of jail – not to seek revenge on her for helping put him there. He wouldn't come after her. It was just paranoia. But her gut still twitched every time she walked down the street or left the office. She did feel a bit exposed, but there was no way she wanted a bloody minder.

'Mick. You know I can't live like that. We've done this before, moved me out of my flat or sent me away, but I hate all that crap. They'll probably catch him in the next few days anyway.'

'Yeah, well, don't hold your breath. The plods will still be tearing their hair out wondering how the Christ this happened in front of their bloody noses. What a bunch of dicks! What were they thinking of? Did they think he would just go quietly to jail and serve out his sentence? Security? They couldn't fucking spell it.'

Rosie couldn't disagree with that. The *Post* had been giving the cops pelters for the last two days that a serial killer had managed to be armed with a switchblade all the time he was sitting in court. All of the newspapers were the same, and the Chief Constable of Strathclyde Police had already appeared, ashen-faced, at a press conference yesterday declaring that they were carrying out a full inquiry into what happened. Lessons will be learned he'd said. But the *Post*'s TOO LATE headline trashed his comments and accused the police of being inept and not fit for purpose. It had spiralled into a political row over cutbacks and outsourcing of the court security, now run by a private company. From what the papers had already gleaned, Boag had got out as he was leaving the cells to be taken to the waiting van. He'd suddenly struck out, slashing one of the workers accompanying the prisoners, and then, as all hell broke loose with other cons running around, it was the police who intervened. The big sergeant who'd been Rosie's pal for years tried to tackle him. But by the time Boag was finished, he lay with his throat slashed on the steps outside the back door. He was only two weeks from retirement.

McGuire was on his feet.

'I hope the plods are not disappearing up their arses working out who to blame instead of finding this fucker before someone else gets murdered.'

'The city feels like it's on lockdown, Mick. The streets are swarming with police, especially at night. They've even brought in reinforcements from Lothian and Borders. I'm told the Met have also offered their services. They'll get him. I mean, where can he go?'

'That's what I'd like to find out. How are we doing with that forensic profiler you were trying to get – the shrink?'

'I talked to him this morning and he seems well clued up. He's been doing this for ten years, digging psychos out for the cops. Hopefully it will be a good interview when I see him.'

'Well, while you're at it, ask him if he thinks Boag will come after you.'

Rosie rolled her eyes to the ceiling.

'I mean it, Gilmour.'

'Sure. I'll ask him.'

McGuire folded his arms and looked at her. 'Is that big Bosnian ghost you use still in the country?'

Rosie shifted in her seat a little uncomfortably. The last time she'd seen Adrian was when she'd fallen asleep in his arms. When she awoke, he was gone without a word, and she hadn't heard from him since. That was months ago. She hoped it didn't show on her face that Adrian had become more than a friend and an occasional minder, both in Glasgow and abroad. He had saved her life not once but twice. She'd never intended anything to happen between them, but their relationship had exploded into passion on a warm night in Sarajevo when Adrian had been looking after her. They'd become lovers, in a series of unplanned trysts that were never going to go beyond what they were. But she hadn't contacted him since the morning he left her bed. It was probably best if she left well alone – though she was ashamed to admit that it was Adrian she immediately thought of when Boag escaped.

She shrugged as if it didn't matter.

'I haven't heard from him in a while. I suppose he's back home in Sarajevo. Why don't we just leave this to the cops? They're all over it. Boag will be back in jail within the week. He has to be. They can't afford to fail on this one.'

'Well. We'll see. What are your cop contacts saying? Any inside info?'

'Only that they are covered in shame, but we already

know that. I'm hoping to get an early heads-up on developments from my detective contact.'

'Okay. Between you and Declan, get the copy pulled together for tomorrow's paper. I've got a conference in five minutes.'

The meeting was over. But Rosie turned to McGuire as she was leaving.

'Mick, I want to take a run out to an address later. Nothing to do with Boag, just something I'm looking at. A travelling family. Settled travellers. Gangsters. When I was coming out of court the other day, this bloke was taking a guy – a refugee, Kosovan – away in a car. He'd been up in court for trapping a seagull to eat.'

'A seagull? He was in court charged with trapping a seagull?'

'Yeah. I met his lawyer and he was telling me. The court put the case back.'

'What the hell was it doing in court in the first place? What were cops doing even investigating the case?' He shook his head. 'No wonder we've got a fucking serial killer on the loose. I might want a bit on that to illustrate how these bastards prioritise their days. Jesus wept! A seagull!'

'We'll see. But I want to tread softly on it first – see if I can find out what's going on.'

'Okay. Let me know if it flies.' He grinned. 'See what I did there? If it flies?'

'Yeah. You should have your own show.'

Rosie shook her head and walked towards the door.

Tadi was in the pit, below the car he was fixing, when Jake called down to him.

'You've to come up, Tadi. Finn wants you.'

Tadi looked up from the darkness where he could see old Jake staring down at him. He had his usual worried expression on his face, and Tadi wondered if he already knew what was going on. His stomach niggled as he wiped his hands and climbed up the ladder. The workshop was deserted.

'Where's Finn?' He turned to Jake.

Jake shrugged. 'You've to go over to the house. To the kitchen, he says.'

Tadi ran a hand across his chin, shrugged back at Jake but said nothing. He left and walked across the yard where the others were working on the garden and painting the fence. They nodded and continued with their work. Sometimes, Tadi tried not to look at their faces, because their fear depressed him. Especially over the last few days since they'd buried Bo. They'd all looked at him as though he was their leader for some reason, and that put him under even more pressure. He was the same as them. They were all prisoners, and he couldn't afford to take everyone's worries on his shoulders. He was desperate to find a way out of here, a way back to Ava and his son, and he didn't have room for anyone else – even though that thought sent pangs of guilt through him. He walked on, up towards the back door and automatically wiped his feet on the mat as he knocked gently on the door.

'Come in.' It was the voice of O'Dwyer's wife.

Tadi slowly opened the door, his body tense, prepared for some onslaught, terrified of what may be behind it. Then as he stood in the doorway, his jaw dropped.

'Ava!' His head swam. 'Ava!' was all he could say as he saw his wife sitting at the kitchen table with his son on her lap.

'Papa!' Jetmir's face lit up and he struggled off his mother's lap and ran towards him with outstretched arms. 'Papa!'

Tadi fell to his knees and scooped him up, hugging him so tightly he was afraid he would break him. He could smell the shampoo and the washing powder on his clothes, the fresh smell of a child who was loved and cherished. He kissed him and buried his face in the boy's shoulders, trying to compose himself before he looked up.

'Ava.' His lip trembled.

'Tadi.' Ava stood up and went towards him. Then she put her arms around him and they stood like that, holding each other tight, Ava snuggled into his chest. He caressed the back of her head, her soft curls, and the nape of her neck, so smooth and tender. He couldn't speak.

O'Dwyer's wife smiled, and somewhere behind that hard face she wore every day was someone who recognised what this was: the longing, the love.

'I've made you some lunch, son. Sit down, the pair of you. The boss said you've to relax for a while.' She put a pot of tea and a plate of sandwiches on the table. 'I'll leave you now for a bit.'

She backed out and Tadi caught her eye again.

'Thank you, Mrs O'Dwyer.' He sniffed. 'Thank you so much.'

They sat for a long moment, looking at each other, their hands entwined on the table, unable to speak. Tadi's throat felt tight as he scanned Ava's face, noticing the dark shadows below her eyes and how pale her skin was. He ran a hand over her hair and leaned across to kiss her on the lips.

'I miss you so much. It hurts me every day, Ava, like a physical pain in my chest.' He touched her cheekbones, remembering how he'd fallen in love with her face the moment he saw her.

'I know, Tadi. I miss you. We both miss you every day. But we have to be strong.'

'Yes. I know. But it's so hard not to see you. It's my fault, for trying to escape. They are so cruel to everyone.'

Jetmir climbed up on the chair and reached across for a sandwich.

'Mama!' he said.

'Come on, Tadi,' Ava said. 'We must eat. You must be hungry. How thin you are! Do they not give you food?'

'Yes,' Tadi lied. 'It's okay. I think I'm just thin because I miss my girl.' He turned to Jetmir and ruffled his hair.

'And this little monkey.' He pushed the plate towards Ava and poured two mugs of tea and juice for the boy. 'Come on. Eat everything they gave us. I don't know how much time we have.'

'All they said this morning was they are bringing me to see you. That's all.' She touched his hand.

Tadi ate hungrily, but tried to restrain himself from gorging, pretending he was well fed.

'How are you? Where are they keeping you? Are they bad to you?'

'No.' Ava shook her head. 'It's all right. I clean the house for people, that's all. I have a small room to sleep in with Jetmir. And there is food.' She poked his ribs. 'Not like you, I think. You are not telling me the truth. I think you're going hungry. I know how you like to eat. Something is wrong. Tell me.'

Tadi shook his head and smiled between mouthfuls of food.

'No, no. Nothing is wrong. It's okay. I promise. I work hard. Maybe now the punishment is over and they'll bring you back. Maybe even give us a caravan to stay in together. Who knows? Even for a couple of days.'

They sat for a moment in silence.

'I just want to go home, Tadi,' Ava sighed. 'This country makes me sad now. I want to go back to Pristina. See our families. I heard in the news how things are getting better – some families are going home.'

Tadi swallowed hard and took her hand.

'I know. I want to go home too. And soon. I think soon we will be okay and maybe they will have had enough of us here. We must believe that.'

Ava smiled, but Tadi could see the fading hopes and dreams behind her eyes. He'd promised her that they would find a new life free of war and conflict, somewhere he could work and make money for his family. But he had taken them to a place where he was bullied and beaten. Where he was a slave like all the others in the yard, with no escape. He smiled back at her, and held her hand tight.

CHAPTER FOUR

'I lost my virginity out here, you know,' Matt declared as he drove out of Lennoxtown and towards the foot of the Campsie Fells.

'I'm glad you shared that, Matt. I feel I know you better now.' Rosie shook her head, gazing out of the windscreen. 'I can see how easy it would be to get caught up in the romantic beauty of the countryside. How old were you, by the way – twenty-three?' She chuckled.

'Aye, very good, Gilmour. I was sixteen, actually. Out here camping with a few mates and we met these birds. Swedish they were. Her name was Greta.'

'Greta?' Rosie lapsed into a Scandinavian accent. 'Hello, my name is Greta. The bigger the betta for Greta.'

'You can laugh, but it was magic. She was eighteen, blonde, gorgeous. I mean, it doesn't get any more wet dream than that – for a wee boy from the tenements who only saw blonde birds in scud books.'

'Yeah, all right, Matt,' Rosie laughed. 'I get the picture. But enough of your pubescent reminiscing. Where exactly are we? I don't mind wide open spaces, but are we going in the right direction? The O'Dwyer farm is meant to be down here somewhere.'

'We're on the right road. I checked the address before we left. There are two farms about two miles outside Lennoxtown. I reckon we've come that far.'

'Well, go easy. I don't want to be in O'Dwyer's driveway before I realise it.' She flipped back a page of her notebook. 'Can you believe he named the farm Tara, like the plantation in *Gone with the Wind*? He obviously thinks he's some big-shot landowner, but I'm told he's just a two-bit gangster.'

'Look,' Matt said. 'In the distance. I see a farm on the left, right across the field there. See it? The big bungalow?'

As they drove down the country road, Rosie could see another farm on the horizon to her right, but the one closer to them had tractors and a couple of steamrollers in the yard.

'That might be it. O'Dwyer does the tar on roads and driveways. Family business, I'm told. He's got a couple of sons working with him. He's made a lot of money, but it's not all from digging up driveways, according to my cop contact. He shifts stolen goods and is involved in all sorts of skulduggery.'

'How come he's not been caught?'

'Don't know. Maybe he's not big enough in all the different scams? But the cops know him as a hard bastard – a notorious bare-knuckle fighter in his day, apparently, and that earned him the respect of all the travellers.'

'In that case, we'll be driving right past his house.'

'Of course,' Rosie said. 'But slowly. Look. There's the sign "Tara" up on the pillar at the entrance. Just take your time going past, Matt. I want to see what I can clock.'

Matt slowed down yards from the entrance and Rosie lowered her window. Across the yard there looked like some kind of workshop at the far end, with a couple of cars parked. An old man was hunkered down with a contraption at one of the wheels. A couple of men worked in the stretch of garden going all the way out to the back of the house, and one of them was emptying the contents of a lawnmower. Then, from the workshop, a figure emerged in a blue boiler suit, wiping sweat from his forehead. Rosie recognised him immediately.

'That's him, Matt. Slow right down. That's our seagull man.'

Matt slowed to a snail's pace.

'You sure?'

'Yep. I know that face. It was the look in his eyes that has stayed with me for the past couple of days. He looked frightened and helpless as they drove away from court. I caught his eye for a few seconds.'

'So what do you want to do? There's nobody around. Do

you want to chance stopping for a minute? I could snatch a pic from here and we'd have it in the bag.'

'Okay. Do it. But be quick.'

As the car stopped, Rosie bent down to look in her bag, so as not to attract any attention. Matt pushed on a long lens to his camera and focused.

'Well done, son,' he murmured to himself as he clicked away. 'He's looking over. That's it, mate. Right down the lens. Done.'

Rosie looked up and she could see the man looking across at the car, but he wasn't making any moves to come towards them.

'Let's go. Come on. I'll buy you a coffee in Lennoxtown and we can get a look at the pictures. Maybe you can tell me more tales from your lusty youth.'

Matt chuckled as they picked up speed and drove past the farm. Rosie flipped down her visor and looked in the mirror, where she could see the man picking up a piece of equipment and disappearing back into the garage. She sat back in the seat, enjoying the cool breeze on her face. She watched as they drove past a field, the road so narrow she could hear the wheat rustling in the breeze. For a moment she was transported back a lifetime ago, when she was shoulder high on the unspoilt field, running barefoot with her mother on a trip out to these very Campsie Hills. She could almost hear herself giggling as her mother chased her until they both stumbled and fell down, then lay gazing up to the sky, making shapes and pictures out of drifting clouds. A perfect day.

'You're lost, Gilmour. What are you thinking?' Matt asked.

She turned to him and smiled, then looked back out to the wheat field.

'Just thinking, Matt. Sometimes, when we look back on a great day as a kid, I wonder was it really as perfect as that, or have I just made it that way in my head . . .'

Matt said nothing for a moment, then sighed.

'I think it was that perfect, Rosie. Some days as kids were just like that. And it's good if you can go there sometimes and remember that. It's what I do, when I see something that pricks my memory.'

Rosie smiled. 'Yeah. Like the Swedish girl.'

Matt smiled, but said nothing.

Rosie's mobile rang, crashing in on the moment. It was Don.

'Don. Have you caught Boag yet, so I can rest easy in my bed?' Rosie's bravado was just that, and Don probably knew it, but it was important to keep up a front.

'Not yet, pal, but we'll get him.'

'Nothing new on it?' She hoped he was calling her with a new lead. It had been the same stories the past few days, the horror and outrage revisited, but nothing to take the story forward.

'No. Not yet. But I'm giving you a heads-up on something.

It'll be out on a press release later. A car has just been recovered from the Carron Valley Reservoir.'

Rosie had to think for a moment to place it.

'Carron Valley? Out towards Stirling?'

'Yep. A couple of guys were fishing yesterday, spotted it and called in.'

'So what's the story? Bodies?'

'No. That's the mystery. The plates check out to an address down over the borders, but no sign of the owner. He's a student. It seems him and his girlfriend went camping in Scotland about a week ago. But nobody's heard from them in a couple of days. Their parents are obviously frantic now that the car has been found.'

'Any suggestions of suicide or anything?'

'Nope. They're a couple of students, doing well at uni and taking a holiday. No sign of anything being wrong before they went missing. In fact, the guy has been phoning home every night as his father is having treatment for cancer, but he dropped off the radar two nights ago and they can't raise him on his mobile.'

Rosie felt the cold chill run through her.

'Are you thinking Boag?'

'Trying not to, Rosie. I hope to Christ this couple aren't his latest victims. But we've nothing at all to suggest that – because we've got absolutely nothing, except a car fished out of the reservoir. Forensics are all over it. Looks like it's only been in the water for a day or so, but there will be nothing much to find from it. Their camping equipment is in the car, as though it's been stuffed in there in a hurry.'

'Does it look like the work of Boag? Is it not gay men he picks up? What would he want with a young couple?'

'That's anybody's guess. And another thing. The couple had a dog with them. No sign of that either.'

'That's weird, Don. It's giving me the creeps.'

'You and me both, darlin'. Look, I'll give you a shout and we'll have a drink at O'Brien's. I'll know more later this evening or the morning.' He hung up.

'What's that all about?' Matt asked.

'Missing couple. Young students on holiday, and their car has been fished out of the reservoir at Carron Valley.'

'That doesn't look good, does it?'

'No, definitely not. One of these ones that you just know in your gut is not going to end well.'

Rosie punched in McGuire's number as they headed back to Glasgow.

Tadi waited anxiously in the kitchen, having been summoned from the workshop. He could hear voices behind the door, but O'Dwyer's was the loudest. He couldn't work out why he had been asked to a meeting. Any instructions they gave to him were usually issued with the usual snarl from Timmy or Finn, and he rarely met the big man himself. His head flooded with worrying thoughts. Had he stepped out of line giving Ava a lingering kiss in the kitchen before she left? He hoped that whatever they wanted him for, it wasn't to tell him that he couldn't see his family again. That would be too much for him to bear. He wiped his sweaty palms on his dungarees and stood waiting. Then suddenly the door opened and Timmy appeared. He jerked his head for him to come inside, and Tadi approached sheepishly.

'Come in, Tadi.' O'Dwyer looked up from his desk, a mug of tea clasped in his big hand. 'Sit down.'

He motioned him to sit on a leather armchair. Finn and Timmy both sat on the sofa opposite him and all three faced O'Dwyer.

'So, Tadi.' O'Dwyer looked at him. 'You enjoyed your little visit from that lovely wife of yours, eh? And the nipper?'

Tadi nodded and half smiled. He didn't want to look too excited or happy, as he couldn't gauge what the mood was.

'Yes. Thanks, Mr O'Dwyer. Thank you.'

'Okay. That's good.' He paused, sniffed, and slurped a mouthful of tea. Then he leaned forward on the desk. 'So listen, boy. Here's the situation. You've been here now, how long? Three months, is it?'

'Th-thirteen weeks, sir. I'm here thirteen weeks tomorrow.'

O'Dwyer looked at him slyly. 'You keep track. Of course, I must remember you're a smart one. You know a lot of stuff, don't you? Clever with your hands and your mind. You've worked well here.'

Tadi wondered where this was going. O'Dwyer slowly looked from Timmy to Finn.

'Okay. Well, listen to this, lad. We've got a little job for you to do. What you might call a special job.'

Tadi looked at him but said nothing.

'Do you understand me, boy?'

'Yes. I understand. A special job.'

O'Dwyer eyed him.

'We're going to a house. The home of someone with a whole lot of money.'

Tadi swallowed the dry ball in his mouth. They were going to rob someone. He could feel his chest tighten.

O'Dwyer put the mug down.

'I'm not asking you to do it for nothing, Tadi. There is a big reward for you, if you do what you're told. Do you want to know what the reward is?'

Tadi looked at Finn, who stared back at him blankly. Timmy was lean and thin-lipped, his eyes in another world.

Tadi nodded his head slowly.

'Okay. Your reward is that you can walk out of here with your wife and the nipper and never come back. How do you like that?'

Tadi's gut felt like a hand had reached in and twisted it around. The very idea that he could walk out of here with

Ava and Jetmir at his side was almost making him dizzy with longing.

'I would like that very much, Mr O'Dwyer. Very much.' He could feel his eyes glazing and blinked twice.

'And we'll throw a few quid to you. Make your way in the world, or go back to that shithole you came from. Up to you. But you'll be a free man.'

Tadi was afraid to say anything. He didn't know how he was supposed to react. These men were vicious, edgy, and one wrong move could get him a beating.

'I . . . I would like that.'

'Okay. So you're in.' O'Dwyer got to his feet and came round the desk to stand facing him. 'You'll be told only what you need to know. You come with us, and you don't open your mouth unless it's to ask an important question on the job. You do what you have to do, and when we leave we come back here and that's it. Do you understand?'

Tadi nodded. O'Dwyer leaned down and he could smell the tea and cigarettes from his breath.

'If you open your mouth to any of these fucking morons out there now, or at any time, it won't be just you dead. Do you know what I mean?'

Tadi didn't need it spelled out. He meant Ava and Jetmir. He nodded his head vigorously.

'Of course, Mr O'Dwyer. I say nothing.'

'Good. Now fuck off, and we'll let you know when the job is happening.'

Tadi stood up and backed away. They looked at him as though he was supposed to say thank you, but he couldn't bring himself to speak. He turned and walked out of the room. He stopped briefly in the kitchen, where Mrs O'Dwyer gave him a sympathetic smile. He nodded in acknowledgement, then looked down as he slipped out of the door.

CHAPTER FIVE

Jonjo Mulhearn was awake long before the first glimmer of light spread across the sky. Today was the day. He lay with his hands behind his head, gazing around the prison cell that had been his home for the last nine years. As prison cells went, it wasn't a bad gaff, with satellite television, a desk and an easy chair. He knew people who lived in worse bedsits, he often told himself. Life in the Special Unit of HM Prison Shotts was all right. He'd been in a lot shoddier, from stinking Wormwood Scrubs to freezing his balls off up in Peterhead jail. It had been here, for the first time in Jonjo's considerable criminal career, spanning most of his life, he'd been able to look inside himself and see what he was. They provided shrinks and self-help groups where you could find out more about yourself than you ever imagined, if you really wanted to. And there were trades to be learned, not that he was ever going to use them. Jonjo still ran his crime world from behind bars, but learning a bit of metalwork, or how to use a computer, passed the time. He didn't feel like a caged animal. He'd made up his mind when he got sentenced to twelve years for shooting the two wasters who'd tried to muscle in on his turf, that he'd get through his time. It was the longest sentence he'd ever been handed down, but with good behaviour and all the rest of that crap, he knew he could manage nine years, until he'd be back home to his family. It was a mindset thing.

But all of that fell apart when the word came about Jack. His beloved Jack. Just the picture of him as a toddler still caught his chest when he thought about it. Butchered by some fucking psycho who'd picked him up in a gay bar. A fucking gay bar. He knew what people would say on the outside – Jonjo's boy is a fairy – but he also knew they'd never say it to his face. If only he'd come to him, told him, he'd have seen the kind of da he was underneath all that shit he had to build up to keep himself top of the heap. He looked at his watch. In fifteen minutes, he'd pick up his bag and walk out the door. His brother Tony was picking him up, and no doubt there would be some kind of celebration tonight with all the faces from around the city. But it would be muted. Jack wouldn't be there, and Jonjo would have to look his wife in the eye and tell her that life had to go on, even if he didn't believe it himself. There was to have been retribution, and it was meant to be swift. Thomas Boag was being held on remand and had appeared in court.

Jonjo had made sure all the arrangements were in place. The bastard wouldn't see daylight. His guilt was never in doubt, so why the fuck squander money giving the cunt justice he didn't deserve? Jonjo's boys promised him they'd see to it, and he'd be able to read in the papers how they made the fucker suffer. Then came the sudden news that Boag had escaped. In the name of fuck! The cunt cops couldn't even hold their own shite.

His door clicked open and he sat up.

'You right, Jonjo?'

'Aye.'

He got up and walked towards the door, taking one last look at his empty cell. He'd said his farewells to the lags last night before lights out, as they'd sat drinking tea in the recreation room. They'd been like family, or as close as you got inside. The Special Unit had been an experimental regime designed to house around eight violent and disruptive prisoners, and was first set up in Glasgow's Barlinnie jail. It had been so successful, they built one at the newer Shotts Prison twelve miles away. Prisoners were more settled in the relaxed regime. They were still violent men, even if they'd proved they could live together in some kind of harmony.

Normally, when one of the lifers was leaving the Special Unit, the guys would be lining up shouting their goodbyes: 'Get a ride, big man'; 'Knock yourself out'; 'Kill a cop for me . . .' But now, as Jonjo walked along the corridor, not a word was uttered, even though the boys were all there. The wee schizo, who'd cleaved a warder's head off as he escaped the State Mental Hospital in Carstairs thirty years ago, stood with that odd smile he had, where you never quite knew if he was going to cave your head in with an ashtray or offer you a cup of tea. Another two, sent to the unit for shotgun murders, stood with their arms folded. And two of the toughest men in the jail, who were also now a couple, stood silent, their faces set. Nobody had ever judged them. Rules of the Special Unit. Whatever went on within these walls, stayed within these walls.

Jonjo walked through the iron doors, the prison officer ahead of him, keys jangling. Then through another gate, another alarm. The crackle on the radio, then another gate opened. Then to the main area, where an officer behind a counter was waiting for him to sign for the bag of clothes he'd been wearing the day he was jailed for life. A black pinstripe suit and white shirt. He suddenly saw himself standing there in the dock that day. Now he was dressed in jeans and a sweatshirt, feeling fitter and younger – physically anyway. As he walked towards the huge prison exit door, it clicked open. He stepped outside into the thin morning, the sky pale grey. He was tempted to look back, but didn't. He looked across at the car park, and saw his brother Tony get out of the car. They resembled each other, but Tony was fatter, his face bloated with drink. He watched as he walked the few steps to meet him.

'You're looking good, Jonjo.'

'You're still a fat bastard.'

They embraced, big bear hugs that lasted long enough for their driver to be shifting around on his feet, not knowing where to look.

'C'mon. Let's get to fuck before they shout me back,' Jonjo said.

'You all right, big man?'

'Aye. As right as I can be.'

They both got into the back seat of the silver Mercedes.

'There's a wee do on tonight at the Tavern for you. Usual suspects. You okay about that?'

'Aye,' he sighed. 'Is Mary all right?'

Tony took a moment to answer. 'She's getting by. That's all. But she'll be glad to see you.'

Jonjo didn't answer. He'd be glad to see her too, thoughts of holding her in her arms and feeling his cheek next to hers. He'd only held her once – at Jack's funeral. But even then it was with one arm, the other handcuffed to a prison officer. Once in nine years. What a fucking waste. He'd wasted it himself, and he knew that. But it was how he lived, and the truth was it had brought them everything they had. He gazed out of the passenger window at the countryside flashing by, as they began to approach Glasgow. They passed Barlinnie jail, and the big external wall he remembered as a kid trying to climb . . . the big gasworks at the other side. Memories of a lifetime flooded through him. He pushed them away. Only one thing was on his mind now, and Tony hadn't even mentioned it. He was probably too scared to spoil the moment of freedom. But there would be no freedom for Jonjo. Thomas Boag. He was all that mattered now.

The driver pulled off Great Western Road and into leafy Kelvinside where huge sandstone villas had stood for generations, and you could nearly smell the success. It was only a ten-minute drive from the sprawling Drumchapel housing scheme where Jonjo grew up, but it was a world away. When he'd been sent to jail, he and Mary had just bought this big house and were in the process of moving in – so he'd never even spent a night in it. But during her visits Mary told him how they'd settled in, and she'd brought him pictures of all the rooms. But even now, it felt like going into a strange house. The car stopped and he opened the door.

'Nice looking gaff, isn't it?' Tony said.

'Aye. Feels funny though.' He looked up at the bay windows and thought he saw Mary fleetingly. He got out of the car.

'Right. See you later then.'

'You sure you're up for it? Just getting home and all that. Everyone wants to see you.'

Jonjo sighed. He wasn't up for it. Not in the slightest. But he'd be there all right.

'No problem. I'll be there.' He closed the door.

As he climbed the wide stone steps, he heard the door locks click and suddenly the big oak door was pulled open. Mary stood, her eyes a little crinkled at the side, the blue of them piercing in the daylight. Her blonde hair was swept back and she looked fresh and beautiful, her grief hidden somewhere behind the make-up. But Jonjo could still see it. She stepped back for him to come in.

'Jonjo.'

Now he managed a smile for the first time, stepped into the hall and dropped his bag on the floor. He glanced around at the high ceiling, the cream walls and all the brightness. He and Mary looked at each other for a long moment before he stepped forward and took her in his arms. They stayed that way for a while and he could hear her sniffing a little. He felt so choked he couldn't trust himself to speak. Finally, she composed herself and pulled back.

'You must be starving,' she said, as though feeding him would make all the pain go away. 'And you'll want a long, hot bath. And I've got a new suit for you, Jonjo. I hope it fits. I . . . I—'

'Sssh,' Jonjo said. He took her face in his hands. She was nervous. She'd probably longed for this moment as much as he did, but now she was talking on her nerves.

'All in good time, sweetheart.' He kissed her on the lips, a soft kiss, then a long lingering kiss, and he remembered how good it had been to lie with her from the very first time when they were fifteen and he stole her from the local hard man in his gang. He'd had to fight for her then and he'd fought for her all his life. Now there was just them. He held her tight.

'Okay. Let's start with the grub,' he joked, trying to find his old self. 'Then you can show me around our swanky house.' They walked into the massive kitchen and he let out a low whistle at how lavish it was.

After they'd eaten she'd shown him around and was running a bath for him while he walked around the top hall. He noticed the room at the end of the hall that she hadn't shown him yet. It must be Jack's room. They hadn't even mentioned his name. Too much, too soon. He was afraid to mention him in case he would explode. As they'd eaten breakfast, he'd been talking about his plans for coming home, and all the stuff they would do. But not a word about Jack. Nothing about Boag. Now, he took a few steps towards the room and quietly opened the door. He stepped inside and crossed the carpet, gazing at the posters on the wall. Celtic, Henrik Larsson, rock bands. A computer sat on the desk. Nothing had been touched – it was like a shrine. He walked around, seeing Jack in every corner – noisy, with his mates, studying, eating. All the things he'd missed out on when he was inside. He'd seen his son on visits, and at first he'd been shy and difficult, then as he got older he got used to it. If he'd been ashamed of his da he never showed it. But it was clear Jack didn't want *his* life, the life of a criminal, and Jonjo was glad of that. He was proud that he'd gone to university. He picked up a football medal from the shelf, and placed it back down. Then the blackness in his head came on, at how it had all been torn apart because of Boag. Suddenly he was aware of Mary at his back. He turned around and she stood there, tears running down her face. Jonjo went across to her, put his arms around her and held her close.

'I'm so sorry, sweetheart. I'm so sorry I wasn't here for you.'

'Oh, Jonjo. I miss him so much. When will the pain stop? I'm so sad . . . all the time.'

Mary wept on his shoulder and he held her, trying with every fibre not to break down himself. He should have been here when all this happened. He hated himself for that.

'We'll be all right, darlin',' he whispered. 'I promise you. I'll never leave you again.'

CHAPTER SIX

Rosie watched the missing couple story unfold with the same sense of dread as the rest of the country. Two days had passed since their car had been recovered from the loch. Police were saying it had been in the water at least one day. From her desk on the editorial floor, she kept an eye on the twenty-four-hour news channels on the three televisions mounted on the pillars. Each of them led with the same story. Declan, the talented young reporter who sat opposite her, had been sent to the hurriedly convened press conference at Strathclyde Police HQ, where the mother of missing student Martin Black sat alongside the father of his girlfriend Katie. They read out prepared statements, their faces etched with anxiety and disbelief. They looked down the camera lens and appealed for their children to get in touch. Rosie had seen those faces so many times over the years, and seldom did the story end in anything but heartbreak.

The DCI in charge of the case took over. The questions were routine, and Rosie watched as the reporters took notes. But the elephant in the room was the fact that a serial killer was out there somewhere. Who would be the first to bring it up? Rosie was glad when it was Declan's voice she heard.

'Detective Chief Inspector, I fully understand that this is a difficult question, but can I ask if there is growing concern for the couple's safety, given that there is a serial killer at large?'

Declan's words hung in the air, and Rosie watched as a muscle twitched in the DCI's jaw. Katie's mother's head went down and her hand went to her mouth. There was the sound of shuffling feet among the press corps who kept their heads in their notebooks, pens at the ready. The silence seemed to go on for ever. Rosie glanced at McGuire who had come across from the back bench to watch the press conference. She shrugged.

'Well done, Dec, for having the balls to ask,' she said, looking at the screen. 'It's the question on everyone's lips. But at least Declan asked it.'

'Good lad, that,' the editor said, arms folded as he continued to watch.

The DCI cleared his throat, and they could see a flush rising above his shirt collar.

'Look. This is a difficult time for the family. At the moment, we are investigating a young couple who have gone missing in unexplained circumstances. We are hoping that by the family making this appeal, people will come forward who may have seen Martin and Katie while they've been camping. Any information, even if you think it's insignificant, please get in touch.' He glared at Declan. 'However, I don't think it helps to speculate or sensationalise matters in order to get a newspaper headline.' He paused, scanning across the rows of reporters, but by the look on his face, he knew he wasn't going to get away with just fobbing this off. 'Look,' he said almost apologetically. 'At this stage, this is a missing person case. Obviously there is grave concern that their car has been found where it was, and as the time goes on, we . . . well, there is growing concern. But it isn't helpful to start jumping to any conclusions, and we will certainly not be doing that.' He gathered up his papers. The press conference was over. 'Now, if there are no more questions, please excuse us.'

Rosie and McGuire walked away from the news desk.

'I'll be very surprised if this couple don't turn up dead,' the editor said.

'Me too. And I think the cops are probably thinking the same thing.'

'My morbid instinct tells me Boag will be at the end of this.'

Rosie half smiled.

'We don't even have any bodies yet, Mick.'

'We soon will have. Remember you heard it here first.'

Rosie looked at him, put her hand up. 'You're not thinking about throwing that out there?'

'No. But you can guarantee the *Sun* will take a flyer. And they'll only be saying what everyone is thinking.'

'That's up to them. But what about the families of the couple? They're probably thinking the worst – but the last thing they'll want is to see it all over the papers.'

'Well, our boy Declan asked the question, so it will be reported everywhere. But we'll do it with our usual measured restraint.' McGuire smiled wryly.

Rosie looked at her watch. 'Okay. I'm off to meet my forensic shrink. See if he can give us an insight into Boag's twisted mind. But to be honest, the big story right now is this missing couple. People don't just vanish like that.'

'Of course not. But you just don't want to be the bastard who says it in the paper. Don't worry, Gilmour. We'll play it straight from the press conference, bringing in Declan's question and all the rest of the stuff we've got. But ask your man about it, and see what he says.'

'Okay.' She shoved her notebook into her bag and headed for the stairs.

Rosie wasn't sure what to expect at her meeting with criminal psychologist, Dr Donald McLaren. She'd envisaged an office stacked with wall-to-wall books, and a desk groaning under the weight of folders bulging with case histories. So she was surprised when he had arranged to meet her in an old bar in Partick, in Glasgow's West End. He liked to escape from the office when he could, he'd told her. She was glad, though, as she always preferred the more relaxed atmosphere of a pub to an office, even if she wasn't drinking. She pushed open the swing doors of the Three Judges, and stepped inside. It was quiet, apart from a couple of guys in working clothes downing pints at the bar, and four old men playing dominoes at one of the tables in the far corner. The barman shot Rosie an enquiring look. It may have been the kind of bar some women stopped in for a gin in the afternoons, but they didn't look like her. The Three Judges was a rough-around-the-edges man's pub, and one of the few bars that still sold quarter-gill measures, so the serious drinkers came here. Rosie flicked a glance around the room, and recognised McLaren from library photographs. He was sitting at one of the tables close to the back, reading a copy of the *Post*, with a glass of what looked like whisky on the table. As she walked across, he looked up and smiled.

'Good to see you're a man who likes a tabloid read.' Rosie stretched out her hand. 'Rosie Gilmour.'

'Well, who else would you be?' His eyes twinkled in his round, ruddy face. 'It's not as though they get a lot of fine-looking young women in here.'

'Flattery will get you everywhere.' Rosie smiled at him. 'Well, it'll get you a drink, Dr McLaren. Good to meet you. Another?' She nodded in the direction of his glass.

'Call me Donald. Never mind all that doctor stuff,' he said. 'I'll have a Glenfiddich, please. I've escaped for the rest of the day, so I'm clear to have a couple of drinks. And to be honest, after listening to the questions of a bunch of psychology students all morning, I really need them.'

Rosie went to the bar and ordered another whisky for him and a soda water and lime for herself. She instantly liked this guy, who had a warm smile and an even warmer handshake. In his crumpled check shirt and tie, it was clear that sartorial elegance was not high on his agenda. She'd never met an academic yet who wore a sharp suit. She returned with the drinks.

'So, do you really read the *Post*? I'd have had you down as a *Herald* man, or even the *Independent*.' Rosie sat down.

'No. I grew up with the *Post*. My father worked in the shipyards, and he would come home in the evening with the paper in his jacket pocket, so that's where I got all my early reading. I take the view that if you want to know what's going on in the world then the tabloids are the best – short and to the point. I can't be arsed with all that overwriting that goes on in a lot of the broadsheets.'

'Here's looking at you.' Rosie raised her glass to her lips and sipped. 'A man after my own heart.'

'So. Let's get down to business, because I know what you reporters are like, and I know you'll be wanting to get back to the office. A lot of big stories on the go this week. Escaped

killers and now a missing couple. The plot thickens, eh?'
He swirled his glass and swallowed a mouthful.

'It does. Which brings me to my first question. Out of
interest more than anything, Donald: do you think this
couple are alive?'

He sat back, sighed, and shook his head slowly.

'No. Do you?'

'Well. No, I don't actually. It sends a shiver down the
spine that their car was found in that loch. Do you think
they've been murdered?'

He shrugged. 'It's not looking good, put it that way. And
I take it you reporters are choking to bring in Boag to the
equation? I saw the press conference earlier.' He jerked his
head in the direction of the television mounted on the
wall above the bar.

'I suppose it's kind of staring everyone in the face – even
though we don't have any bodies. So what do you think?'

He took a moment, lifted the packet of Marlboro Lights
and offered one to Rosie. She declined and he put one
between his lips and lit it, inhaling deeply, and she watched
the trail of smoke from his nostrils.

'It's hard to say. It's possible that Boag has been living
rough since he escaped and came across this couple and
their car by chance. But you have to ask why he would kill
them. If it was robbery, then why didn't he steal the car
and get away as fast as he could out of this area? Every
cop in Scotland is looking for him, so if he was living

rough, he'd stick out like a sore thumb. And what would he do with the bodies? Why dump the car and not the bodies?'

'So you don't think Boag has anything to do with their disappearance.'

'I don't think bumping off a random couple is his bag. The murder he committed was a homosexual young man – and one still missing so far as we know. We still can't be sure how the young bloke he killed came to be in his company. Only he knows that. Though from your piece in the paper, we know that Boag did cruise gay bars. But nobody seemed to see him leaving with anyone. Maybe they just didn't notice. I don't think people pay too much attention to what's going on in these places.'

'Do you think he's gay? Or one of these freak shows who wants to kill gay men?'

'Could be a bit of both. Maybe he's in denial or something. But then, what about the missing tenant below his flat? Do you have any more on her? She seems to have slipped off the radar. Nothing in the papers of late. If you ask me, I'm pretty sure he's killed her.'

'Why would he kill her? All of the information is that he was a loner who didn't talk to anyone in the building.'

'Maybe she heard something, saw something – you know, when he was dismembering the lad in his house. Who knows? It's strange she's disappeared, and I wouldn't be surprised if we find bits of her appearing down the line.'

Rosie wrote down his answers. This would make for a good sidebar piece for tomorrow.

'How do you think the police manhunt is going? Are they doing the right things? Are you involved with them?'

He smiled and blew out smoke.

'Ah, the intrepid Rosie Gilmour. On the hunt for an exclusive. I'm sure the police are using all their resources.' He leaned forward. 'Including me – but I'm not sure they're going about things the right way. Let me put it this way, and you can use a flavour of what I'm about to say – but for Christ's sake it didn't come from me.'

'I'm all ears.'

'For me, Boag is clever as well as warped. He's planned this over the years, including the worst scenario – that he might get caught. I'd be surprised if he hasn't got bank accounts, credit cards and stuff in false names.'

'Really? You mean he planned for this even before he started killing?'

'We really have no idea when his killing spree started. All we know is the body parts that have turned up so far match one individual. But he could have been doing this for years. How many gay men have disappeared in the last five years? Think about it. People go missing all the time, and police don't act. But it's time the police did start to think about this. They need to look back, trawl through the archives.' He paused. 'Which is all the more difficult, because they will be shitting themselves every day he's out there, in case he's already stalking his next victim. He'll kill again, Rosie. He's cunning as well as evil. But in answer to your question, I don't think he's got anything to do with the disappearance of that couple, so you might want to tell your editor that. Of course, I could be wrong.'

'I will. But I want to be able to use some of the things you tell me. For example, can I use the line that he'll kill again and that police should trawl back through the records of any missing gay men?'

'Yes. I've no problem with that.'

'And what about him planning ahead, the fake bank accounts, etc.?'

'Well maybe as I said, just a hint of it. Because I know the police are looking at that, so leave it for a couple of days. But he also might have taken a storage place, you know, like a lock-up?'

'What makes you think that?'

'It's what guys like him do. He's not just a nutter who picked up another man at a club and had a row. This is a proper maniac. He kills either because he likes killing, or he's on a mission; perhaps there is some religious attachment to it, or some deep-rooted childhood situation that has helped create the monster he is.'

They sat for a long moment as Rosie tried to picture Boag out there, planning, waiting. It gave her the creeps.

'By the way, you'd want to watch your own back, Rosie.'

Her stomach flipped over.

'I know. The editor wants to get me some protection. It does worry me. Boag gave me such a chilling look when they were taking him to the cells. I'm looking over my shoulder, I don't mind telling you.'

'And it's keeping you awake at night. I can see that from the shadows under your eyes.'

'Oh, cheers for that.'

'It's quite attractive actually, gives you character. But I've read a bit about you, Rosie. I've followed some of your stories. You sail a bit close to the wind, do you not?'

Rosie nodded. 'Yeah. Sometimes, I suppose. It just happens. I don't plan it that way.'

'Well, just be careful. You should get some protection until this bastard is caught.'

'Now you *are* making me nervous.'

He downed his drink and sniffed, then looked at his watch.

'Okay. I've got to move, if that's all right. I'm meeting a mate for dinner. And I'm taking a couple of weeks' holiday from tomorrow – going to the South of France to see some old mates.'

'Fine. You've been more than helpful, Donald. I really appreciate it. Thanks.'

He stood up and shook her hand, held onto it a little longer than was necessary and looked in her eyes.

'Take care of yourself. You can buy me a curry some time, if you ever want a chat about things in general. Life's hard sometimes. Jobs like yours – you walk in and out, you move on. But not always, I'd say. Not in your case, I can see that.'

Rosie looked at him, a little surprised that he could apparently see into her head.

She smiled.

'Thanks. I'd love a curry with you some time. We can analyse the world over a bottle of good wine.'

'Now you're talking.' He winked as he turned and left.

Rosie watched as the small round figure made his way to the door.

CHAPTER SEVEN

Rosie stared in the bathroom mirror at the tired, pale blue eyes looking back at her. McLaren was right. The dark smudges under her eyes had grown worse over the past few months. She needed a holiday. It had been a long haul of recent stories and investigations – one or two of them full-on, leaving her with sleepless nights and bruised ribs. Now this. There was a serial killer on the loose, and she might be next on his list. She told herself that was a ridiculous notion, but her vivid imagination created all sorts of scenarios, particularly when she was in bed at night – alone, as she had been last night, after cancelling her dinner with TJ. Her phone conversation with him played out again in her mind, when she'd told him about the stories she was working on.

'I want to have an early night, TJ. I need to get my head around all this. I need to straighten it out in my mind, because I'm beginning to freak a little.'

'You need to listen to your editor, Rosie, and get some protection.'

'I just can't face that. If I keep running for cover every time someone makes faces at me, I'd never go out of the house. It's up to me to be able to handle it.'

'This is not making faces. This is a serial killer on the loose, and you helped get him arrested. The idea that Boag is out there, and you could be on his list, should freak you out. It makes me shudder. You need to look at some more security. Your editor's right. Maybe you should move out.'

Rosie sighed. 'We'll see. Right now, I just want to get it in some perspective in my mind. You know what I'm like.'

'Yeah, Gilmour. I know what you're like. Okay. Have it your way. Get some kip, and try to relax. We'll talk again tomorrow. But I do worry about you.'

'Don't worry,' Rosie said. 'I'll be fine. See you later.' She hung up, knowing TJ wouldn't believe her bravado any more than she did.

She'd relaxed in the bath and then in the darkness of her bedroom, waiting for sleep to come. It did, and brought with it the usual nightmares. The one that woke her was of a young couple drowning in a loch, and she'd lain there in bed in the throes of the nightmare, unable to catch her breath. It was her body gasping for air that had woken her. The morning light streaming in the window made her fully awake, but there were no traffic sounds outside, so it couldn't be any later than five. She got up, went into the living room and flicked on Sky News. The missing couple story was high on the agenda, with police saying they had received several calls from people who had seen the couple on their travels, and they could now map out where they had been. The last sighting was in a corner shop just before the Campsie Fells, where the newsagent had identified the young man when he came in and bought some cans of beer and a pint of milk. But there were no campsites around the area, so police were working on the theory that they had camped in a field. A search would begin today for any trace of the couple. The aerial view of the area around the Campsies was vast and pockmarked with smallholdings and farmland. They could have pitched their tent anywhere. A picture of their car flashed up and the reporter urged any motorists in the area to call in if they'd seen the vehicle in the country roads surrounding the Campsies, in case the couple had picked anyone up at any stage.

Rosie's mobile rang as she pulled into the *Post* car park.

'Are you in hiding, Rosie?'

It was Don.

'No, of course not. How you doing?'

'I tried to phone you last night, but there was no answer.'

Rosie tried to think back. She'd switched her phone off so she could relax in her bath, but forgot to put it back on again, after she flopped into bed, exhausted. It was unlike her. Even though the ring of her mobile in the middle of the night was never good news, she always kept it on.

'Sorry, Don. I must have switched it off. I was knackered last night. Don't tell me I've missed something?'

'No, no. Don't worry. I wanted to give you an early shout though. We got a call last night from a motorist who identified the couple's car on a road outside Lennoxtown. He said he passed them on a farm road about three days ago, and he remembered that the car was in a lay-by and that there was a dog with them. The couple were standing outside the car drinking bottles of water, and he assumed they'd just finished a long walk. So we've got a fairly narrow area we're going to be searching. We're taking dogs out this morning, and it'll go out on a press release but not for another couple of hours, so you might want to get yourself down there for some pictures before everyone else. They'll be keeping the press back.'

'So where is it?'

'It's a road about two miles outside Lennoxtown. Country road. Two farms on either side.'

Rosie stopped in her tracks. She didn't want to ask Don the name of the farms – he probably didn't know anyway. It might not be O'Dwyer's farm, but it sounded as though it was in the vicinity.

'Okay. I'll get a photographer and head out. Will you be there?'

'Yeah. For a while. I'll be with the DCI, so don't be

approaching me. He's not very happy with that boy of yours who asked about Boag at the press conference. He was spitting nails when he came out. The family were very upset.'

'I thought he'd not be happy, Don. But you have to admit, the question had to be asked.'

'Well, I'm not a reporter, so I can't admit that. I'll see you later.' He hung up.

When they got to Lennoxtown, Matt drove past the police station, where they saw a dozen officers piling into a minibus. He drove into a side street and turned the car around.

'Unless I'm mistaken, Sherlock, I'd say there's a very real chance they're going out on the search.'

Rosie watched as the van pulled out of the car park, followed by a police car.

'Looks like it,' Rosie replied. 'Okay. Let's follow them – but at a very discreet distance, because once we get into the country there won't be a lot of cars around.'

'No problem. There's bound to be a bit of a high spot where we can get a look across the fields.'

They drove out of the town, glad the police convoy was heading in the right direction. Matt pulled a left up a tighter dirt track road and onto a hill. When they reached the top, they pulled into a lay-by and got out of the car. Matt scanned the horizon with his binoculars.

'I can see where they're headed. Look. At the far end of

the road, there's a few cop cars parked. They're not far from O'Dwyer's place, actually.'

He handed Rosie the binoculars and she watched as the van they'd been following drove towards the parked cars. She could see the long, low bungalow on the O'Dwyers' land, and in the distance the other farm.

'I can get a picture from here with my long lens,' Matt said, 'but we'd want to be a bit closer, see what's going on. Let's head down there so we get our bearings, and then just go past them like we were out for a drive.'

'Okay.' She looked at her watch. 'They'll be putting out a press release shortly saying they're here, and the pack will descend. But swing past the O'Dwyer house again, just to see who's around.'

Rosie scanned the area with the binoculars, homing in on the O'Dwyer place while they were still a good distance away. She could see a pickup truck and two other cars in the yard. One of them looked like the red Jaguar she'd seen outside the court that day. She zoomed in as close as she could and could see the big, burly figure of an older man. He resembled Rory O'Dwyer, only older, so it could be him. The pictures she'd seen in the library were at least twelve years old, when he'd been cleared in court of the attempted murder of a man from another travelling family during an illegal bare-knuckle boxing match. But there was no mistaking the man who had been slapping the Kosovan around. He looked like a younger, fitter version of the pot-bellied man, and she assumed it was one of the sons. The other was a weedy-looking guy with collar-length, greasy hair, smoking a cigarette furiously and nodding as the older man spoke. Rosie looked across the yard and stopped when she spotted the Kosovan coming out of a workshop and walking towards the three men. As the older man spoke, the Kosovan turned around, towards the direction of the police cars in the distance. Then he moved away and she watched as he went across the back of the house and out of the field onto the road ahead of them.

'That's our man, Matt. The Kosovan. He's walking up in the direction of all the activity. Looks like he's been instructed to go there. I wonder why? Let's get up to that area before he gets there and watch him from the other side. See what he's doing.'

They drove on and pulled up close enough to see the police activity. Rosie watched through the windscreen as officers with tracker dogs took to the fields, accompanied by at least a dozen other cops with long sticks. She watched as the Kosovan crossed the field behind the O'Dwyer house and stayed close to a clump of trees that separated the field from the road.

'Our man is looking a bit shifty, Matt. Look.' She handed the bins to Matt, who looked through them, then put his camera up.

'I can see him better through this, and I'll get a picture

in case we need it. Yep. He's kind of hiding in among the trees, but watching what's going on. What do you think?'

'I don't know. He's obviously working for the O'Dwyers, doing what he's told.'

They watched for another few minutes, Rosie's eye trained on the Kosovan, intrigued by what his role was in among a family of gangsters. Especially as she'd seen him abused by one of the sons. Then, eventually, the Kosovan came out of the shadow of the trees and returned through the field.

'Drive back down a bit, Matt. Til we're nearer that field.'

'What for?'

'Just . . . I want to try something.'

'Oh, Christ! Here goes. Gilmour, don't do anything daft.'

'Would I ever?' Rosie said, as the car turned around and drove a few hundred yards. 'Here. Stop here.'

She opened the door and got out.

'What the fuck are you doing?'

'I'm going to approach him in the field. Before he gets within eyeshot of the house.'

'What if he's a nutter?'

'What if he's not?'

'Jesus! Will I come with you?'

'No. I'm sure he clocked my face that day leaving court. I just want to make contact. Better if I do it on my own. I'll only be a minute.' She turned around to climb the fence. 'Don't go away.'

Rosie was in the field and approaching the Kosovan

quietly from behind. When she was close enough to call out, she did.

'Excuse me? Hello?'

The Kosovan stopped in his tracks and turned around, bewildered. Rosie walked as briskly as she could through the field towards him, hoping she hadn't got it wrong, and that this was the same guy she saw in court. When she got up close to him, she was positive.

'Sorry,' she said, a little breathless. 'Sorry to disturb you.'

He looked at her, confused, then she saw a flash of recognition. He took a step backwards.

'Excuse me,' Rosie said. 'It's Tadi, isn't it?'

He looked at her, then over his shoulder, frightened. She took in his hollow cheeks and the shirt open at the chest, exposing his puny body. He was underfed and weary-looking. Hard to say what age, but he could be anything between twenty-five and thirty-five. He shook his head.

'You're Tadi, aren't you? I remember you from court. The seagull case. I saw you being taken in the car that day. You remember. Do you speak English?'

He swallowed, his eyes full of fear.

'W-what you want? I am not Tadi.'

'But I saw you. A few days ago. You were with one of the O'Dwyer boys. I thought it was scandalous that you were even in court. You understand what I mean? I . . . I wanted to help you.' Rosie paused. 'I'm a reporter. From the *Post*. You know. The newspaper? My name is Rosie Gilmour.'

His face kind of crumpled and he bit his lip and shook his head. 'Please. You cannot help me.' He backed away.

'Please, Tadi. I can help you. Let me try. I can see you are worried. Do you work for the O'Dwyers? Listen to me. I have been in Kosovo, during the war. I saw people like you, frightened people. Will you talk to me?'

'No. Please. I . . . I cannot speak.'

'Can I come and see you at your house?'

He shook his head.

'Why are you up looking at the police here? Do you know what they're looking for?'

He shook his head vigorously. 'No. I don't know anything. Please. You must go away from me. I . . . I'm afraid. My . . . my family.'

'Your family? Are they here? On the farm? Do they live with you?'

He shook his head and his lip trembled.

'No. Please, I must go.' He backed away, then turned and almost broke into a run.

Rosie was tempted to pursue him, but it was too close to the house. She couldn't risk it. But she knew she was onto something. She had seen fear like that in the eyes of people who were afraid to speak because of what may happen to them. She had to find a way to get to him, but he was clearly terrified of the O'Dwyers. She watched as he scurried across the field, stumbling in potholes, eventually climbing the fence back into the yard.

CHAPTER EIGHT

The Tavern was jumping by the time Jonjo and Mary arrived in the Merc driven by Aldo, his oldest mate. They got out of the car and stood for a moment, the music blaring into the street. A young man came outside, then rushed back in when he clocked Jonjo. Another man came out and stood for a second, a smile spreading across his face.

'The whole place is turned out for you, Jonjo. I knew it would be.'

Jonjo took a deep breath and smiled at Aldo. They'd been pals since they were twelve years old in the Drum, robbing sweets from the local shops, before they graduated onto beating the shit out of the bullies. They'd started running their own little protection racket by the time they were teenagers. It was small-time, but it paid, and got them noticed. Aldo Jaconelli was small, Italian and looked like he belonged in the Sicilian village that his grandparents had left two generations ago in search of a better life. Aldo used to joke that they thought they'd got on a boat to America, so were well pissed off when they ended up in Ardrossan.

Jonjo took Mary's arm and ushered her in through the swing doors. As soon as they came in, the whole place erupted in cheers. The drummer played a three beats and clash on the cymbals for added measure. First up to greet him was Danny McLoughlin, another old buddy who he hadn't seen since his last visit to jail a few weeks ago. Big hugs followed more hugs and back-slapping among his closest associates. Other people who knew their place came up a few minutes later to wish him well, and Jonjo shook their hands. Danny and Aldo ushered him to the bar where a corner was cleared for them, and they were served large drinks. Jonjo declined all the drink, saying he'd been off it and was now teetotal, which was met with looks of disbelief. He drank water, shook more hands vigorously, and listened to the homage being paid to him. He scanned the room. The place was buzzing. Everyone here was either in the firm or knew someone in the firm, they were working in his bars, renting his property or running his security firm. All legit jobs, through the books, and only they knew what went on behind the scenes. Jonjo had made his big money back when he was a haulage contractor on paper, but in reality it was running container loads of cannabis through Morocco and Spain. It had set him up and made him a millionaire, but now he had moved on, and he invested in property, bars and security firms. He looked across and saw Mary sitting with friends who he knew had looked after her over the years. These people were the salt of the earth and he was glad to be home. Eventually he stood at the bar with just Aldo and Danny.

'So, Jonjo. How was it? I mean, coming back home. Into the house and all that. I . . . I know it must be hard.'

Aldo's mouth tightened, and Jonjo knew that he meant going into the house without Jack being there. Aldo was his godfather and had taken his murder almost as badly as Jonjo himself. He adored the boy and Jack, even though he was always going to be educated and never a gangster, adored his Uncle Aldo in equal measure.

'It was tough, Aldo.' Jonjo shook his head. 'It's fucking tough. But I'll tell you . . .' He looked over at Mary. 'It's been a lot tougher on her. Here on her own.'

'She's tried to be strong, Jonjo, but she just fuckin' loved that boy,' Danny said. 'We all did.'

All three of them stood for a long moment saying nothing, and for a second, Jonjo remembered them eighteen years ago at this very bar for Jack's christening.

'So,' Jonjo said, looking from one to the other, 'this Boag fucker. What do you think?'

'Hard to believe he was actually on his way to the Bar-L and now he's out there. Some poor bastard will be his next victim.'

'Not if we get him first,' Jonjo said. 'But how we going to

do that? Listen, boys, this is the only show in town for me. I'm telling you.'

'I know, man. If he was one of us, like a proper criminal, he'd be fucking easy to find. But he's not. He's just this anonymous wee guy and he's disappeared into the crowd.'

'We'll need to find a way. What about our cops? Any of them in the mood to give us a heads-up if they're getting anywhere near him?'

Aldo puffed.

'Not so far. They're in the same position as the rest of us. You'll not have seen the town, Jonjo. It's got cops on every corner. They're all over the place looking for him. But he's gone to ground. Christ knows where he is.'

'What about the papers? Have they had much on him?'

Danny shrugged.

'They've all been full of the usual stuff. Only thing was the other day, the *Post* had some bit from a police psychologist – you know like that Cracker guy off the telly a few years ago?'

Jonjo nodded but said nothing.

'Well, he was saying that he might have made contingency plans – like he's been planning for all eventualities in case he got caught. Like maybe he's got another ID and bank account. He might even have another house or something.'

Jonjo nodded.

'But somebody will see him eventually. His ugly face is everywhere.'

'I know.'

While they stood at the bar, food had been served, and an hour later an Irish folk band, who were friends of Danny's, got the party in full swing. Jonjo stopped in mid sentence when he heard the mandolin pick out the song, *Every time I hear a sweet bird singing, I think of you and I, my love, think of you and I . . .*

It had been their song. The band would know that and before the first line was up, the floor had cleared and Jonjo looked over at Mary. He remembered the first night they'd met in the Irish club when they danced to that song. Jonjo jerked his head towards the dance floor and Mary got up and came towards him. He held her in his arms and everyone cheered as he held her thin waist, feeling the warmth of her body. He was home now. This was what they expected. They knew he was grieving and unforgiving, but they needed Jonjo back and he had to give them this dance, the dance he'd been doing for nine fucking years inside. He held Mary close, and went through the motions. But only one thing was on his mind. Thomas Boag.

CHAPTER NINE

The single line of police officers poking the grass with long sticks had been slowly plodding across the fields for the past three hours. Rosie and Matt sat close to the press pack and TV film crews that had gathered once word went out that cops were searching a specific area. She'd phoned Don down at the scene to ask him why they were concentrating on these fields in particular. All he could say at this stage was that they were working on information from the motorist who had seen them in the vicinity.

'I hope we're not going to be here all night,' Matt said. 'I'm starving.'

Rosie looked out of the windscreen, where the sky was beginning to turn grey.

'Me too. I don't think so. It's going to rain, and the light is fading. They won't stay much longer.'

She was hoping the search would be called off for the night. There was nothing more dreary than staking out one of these police searches, because half the time they came up with nothing. But it was a stick-on that if you decided to disappear for an hour, that's when they would make some dramatic discovery. She scrutinised the action through the binoculars, and could see a couple of the dogs straining at the leash and becoming agitated.

'The dogs are barking, Matt. Maybe they've found something.'

'Maybe they're just hungry, like me.' He sat up and leaned out of the window, looking down the long lens.

'You're right. I can see the dogs pulling the cops towards that clump of trees in the distance. Can you see it?'

Rosie scanned the field.

'Yep. I see them now.'

'Shit,' Matt said. 'The rest of the plods have obstructed my view now that they've all arrived at the top of the field. All I can see is a wall of cops. We'll just have to wait.' He turned to Rosie. 'By the way, what are you going to do about the Kosovan?'

Rosie sighed. 'I don't know yet. But I can see he's terrified, as I told you. When I asked about his family, he freaked. I wonder if he means they're here or somewhere else, maybe still in Kosovo. I can't get anywhere on it unless he talks to me. I don't think he will though. He was too scared. It's depressing, because I know he's being abused by that O'Dwyer mob. I just don't know how I'm going to prove it.'

'What about his lawyer? Has he said anything?'

'No. He'll probably never see him again. He was only the duty solicitor on the day, and he'll have contacted the Refugee Council. I might talk to them tomorrow. I used to have a contact there. He must have been registered with them when he arrived, so they might be able to tell me about his family. But I've got to tread very carefully, because I'm not sure if it's a good idea to let the refugee people know where he is right now, in case there's something going on with his family. I want to see what I can find out. Maybe the lawyer's got no intention of reporting to them about the court case. I get the impression he's just disappeared off the radar – and not by choice.'

Rosie stared out of the side window across the fields, her mind drifting back to Emir, the Kosovan refugee she'd met during the demonstration in a Glasgow housing scheme where the residents were complaining that refugees were getting too many handouts. Emir had been standing close by in tears, and her encounter with him then led to a massive investigation that refugees were being murdered and their body tissue sold for profit. Poor, tragic Emir had been killed in the crossfire, helping Rosie unmask the international criminal gang. Nearly three years on, it still haunted her. Now this refugee, with the same desperate look, had nowhere to turn either. Her mobile rang, bringing her back from the gloom.

'Rosie. Are you still sitting up there?'

It was Don, his voice not much more than a whisper.

'Yeah. Still watching and waiting.'

'Well, hold onto your hat for this, pal. Our dogs have just dug up what looks to be the couple's dog.'

'Christ! Seriously? We heard your dogs barking and I saw through the binoculars that they were straining like mad.'

'Yeah, they were. Our boys have been combing the whole field, then when we get towards the end, the dogs start going mental. They dragged the handlers up to this clump of trees, then the dogs started digging. It's looking a bit grim. We've pulled them back now.'

'Why?'

'Listen. I can't say too much, but the lads started digging very carefully, and it's looking like there's more in there than the dog.'

'Jesus, Don! Are we talking the couple?'

'Don't know, Rosie, and that's the truth. It's possible. Everything's stopped and they've sent for forensics. Whatever they find, this whole place will be taped off soon. I have to go now, but things will start moving in the next hour, so this is an early shout. We'll have to put something out tonight, but it'll be very vague, so be careful.'

'Will the statement mention the dog?'

'Not sure yet. Once the real digging gets under way, we'll see what we find. But if it is the couple, then obviously we'll not be saying that – not til we get to the families.'

'Shit, Don! This is awful. Their poor parents. Talk later.'

Rosie hung up, and turned to Matt as she punched in McGuire's number.

'Looks like they've found the couple's dog.'

'Oh fuck!'

The editor answered his phone in two rings.

'Gilmour. I was wondering what the Christ was happening out there. It'll soon be dark.'

'Mick. They've found the couple's dog.'

'Fuck! When?'

'About ten minutes ago. The dogs were going mental and started digging under a clump of trees. I got an early call from my cop pal. But, listen. He's given me the nod that there might be more buried in there.'

'You mean the couple?'

'I think so.'

'What a fucking result.'

'Well, their families might not see it that way, Mick.' The professional in Rosie was already planning the story in her head, but she couldn't quite share her editor's delight.

'Yeah, right, but you know what I mean. Good shout though, Gilmour. I take it the cops will be putting out some kind of bland shite later in a statement?'

'I'm told they will. But don't know how much they'll say. Hopefully we can at least say the dog has been found buried – so we're looking at something very grisly here.'

'They've been murdered, haven't they?'

'I think so.'

'Are they in that grave?'

'I think so.'

'Poor bastards. Okay. Get something down and ping it over to copy when you can, then talk to me as it develops. We'll change the front page.'

Tadi stood in the kitchen, trying not to look as O'Dwyer's wife stirred a pot on the cooker. It smelled like beef stew, and he was so hungry, the aroma was almost knocking him dizzy. Usually, by this time of night, he'd have been back at his flat and would have eaten whatever meagre food there was in his fridge. But it was almost eight thirty, and after a long, hard day, he'd been waiting two hours to see the boss so he could tell him what he had seen up at the field. O'Dwyer's wife looked over her shoulder, then went back to the pot. She took a bowl out of the cupboard and ladled some food into it, then put it on the table along with a chunk of bread. Tadi stood, his mouth watering, assuming she was about to have her dinner. But to his surprise she looked at him and pulled out a chair.

'Here! Get stuck in.' She put cutlery on the table. 'He might not be too long now, so throw it down you before he arrives, or he'll shoot the boots off me.'

Tadi looked at her, not knowing what to say. He licked his lips and eyed the bowl.

'For me?' He went towards the table. 'Thank you, Mrs O'Dwyer. Y-you are kind.'

He sat down. He had barely spoken to the woman since he came here. She seemed to be in the kitchen cooking all the time, or coming back with shopping. Tadi assumed she was the same as the rest of them – cruel and bullying. But then one afternoon, while he'd been passing by the kitchen window, he'd overheard O'Dwyer shouting at her, and thought he could hear her crying. Then the other day, when he'd come to meet Ava and his son, her eyes seemed to soften. She was different from the others.

She cleared dishes from the worktop as Tadi wolfed down the food, dunking the bread and savouring every mouthful.

'This is the best food I have in months, Mrs O'Dwyer. Like the stew my mother used to cook for me back home.'

She turned around and stood, folding her arms.

'And where's home?'

'Kosovo.'

Tadi could see from the look on her face that she didn't really know where it was.

'Is your mother still there?'

'Yes, and my father. But he is very ill.' He paused. 'I . . . I miss them.'

Their eyes met, but she said nothing, and he ate the rest of the meal in silence. She picked up the bowl when he finished.

'You were hungry.'

He smiled. 'Yes. Thank you.' Tadi got up and stood back at

the door. They exchanged glances when they heard the truck coming into the yard.

Mrs O'Dwyer gave him a sympathetic smile, then she turned back to the sink. They heard the back door open, and in walked her husband, his two sons at his heels.

Rosie had phoned over her piece for tomorrow's front page, but there was nothing exclusive about it. The police had put out a brief statement saying that the police search had found a dog, with what appeared to be stab wounds, buried in a field outside Lennoxtown. The press office wouldn't take any questions or confirm that it was the couple's dog. They were continuing to dig the site and they would resume their search in the morning. She watched as one or two of the police cars began to drift away, leaving a patrol on for the night around the taped-off area.

'I think we can call it a night.' She turned to Matt, stretching her arms above her head and yawning. Then her mobile rang, and she saw Don's name.

'Rosie. Listen. Be careful how you use this, but it's looking grim here.'

'Jesus! Don't tell me they've found the couple too?'

Silence. She could hear Don's breathing.

'Not just the couple.'

'What?'

'I can't say any more. But it's looking like there are more

than two bodies. You should get here early in the morning. This is massive.' He hung up.

Rosie phoned the editor.

'I'm coming back to the office, Mick. There are more bodies in this grave out here. Not just the couple. I've had a nod from my cop pal. Nobody else knows yet, I've been told.'

'Oh fuck! Hurry up and get in here. We'll keep it for the main edition.'

CHAPTER TEN

Tadi sat on the floor in the back of van as it turned off a main road and up a narrow country lane. It was pitch black outside, and the last road sign he had seen was when they came off the motorway and went through Giffnock. He had no idea where that was. All he knew was that he'd been in the airless van for more than half an hour and was beginning to feel nauseous, partly from the motion, but mostly from nerves. Finn sat in the front next to the driver, and alongside him on the floor were Timmy and two other men he'd never seen before. They'd been laughing and joking most of the way, ignoring Tadi as if he was invisible. He was glad of that, because his mind was in such turmoil, and his mouth was so dry, he doubted he'd have been able to form a sentence if they asked him a question. He was exhausted. It was nearly midnight and he'd been up since six working on his usual job at the farm, when he'd been told that tonight was the night when the big job was on. He was also weak with hunger. Finn turned around to face them as the van slowed down. He threw something at each of them, but in the darkness, Tadi couldn't see what it was.

'Right. Get these on now, lads. And keep them on.'

As Timmy pulled one over his head, Tadi could see it was a ski mask. The two others did the same, and Tadi followed, adjusting his mask so he could see and breathe. But he still felt claustrophobic and tried to control his breathing as he looked at the others, feeling their eyes staring through the holes at him.

'Right,' Finn said in loud whisper. 'Timmy, Dan, Sean – you all know the score and what you've to do. You know where the alarm is, so disable the fucker from the outside at the back before we go in. Tadi – you just do exactly what you're told. I don't want anyone to speak unless they have to, and if you do, then make sure you don't use any fucking names. Got that?'

Tadi didn't answer or nod. He was almost choking with fear. He had to calm down, because if something went wrong, he knew it would be the end of everything for him, for Ava and for Jetmir.

They stopped the van at the edge of the driveway and everyone piled out. Timmy handed Tadi a rucksack.

'For the safe.'

Tadi slung it on his back, not knowing what else to do. They crept around the house, keeping close to the perimeter in case any of the sensor lights came on. They seemed to be moving fast, especially the other two men who'd been in the back, disabling the alarm, as though this was all routine. Finn and Timmy followed behind, with Tadi in between the two of them. Nobody spoke. Tadi's eyes were getting used to the darkness and he could see one of the men creep forward and quietly go towards the door. Then, almost silently, he pushed a jemmy on the edge and the door pinged open as though he'd used a key. Timmy and Finn looked at each other and smiled approvingly. Finn nodded Tadi forward, and he followed behind the other two men as they went in the back door. There was a stillness in the house, and the smell of old polished wood. Tadi glanced around – everything looked expensive and old – a carved hall table and elegant coat stand, and a heavy stained-glass door leading to a porch at the front. He crept behind the others as they stopped at the foot of a staircase and then moved stealthily up, like a team of storm troopers. Tadi felt his legs like jelly as they climbed the stairs, but the men in front seemed to know exactly where they were going. He wondered if they'd been in the house before, perhaps under false pretences, so they could find where everything was. They crept along the thick pile carpet at the top hallway towards a half-open door. The first man pushed it open and waved over his shoulder for the others to join. In the bedroom, as a shaft of moonlight shone through the window, he saw an old couple asleep. The man looked as though he could be in his seventies, and the woman with her high cheekbones and papery skin around the same. She slept, barely breathing. Then suddenly, one of the men went forward and there was a click as he pointed a gun at the bed. Tadi heard himself gasp.

'Get up!' the man said as he put the barrel of the gun to the old man's head.

It was the old lady who stirred first. Her mouth dropped open, her eyes wide in horror. Then her husband's eyes opened.

'Get up, before I shoot your fucking head off.'

The old man's face went whiter than the sheet he lay on, as he put one hand up and the other around his wife's shoulder, pulling her towards him.

'Please. Please don't hurt us. We will give you anything you want.'

'You're fucking right about that. Get up, you Yid bastard.'

He took a step back as the old man slowly pulled himself out of bed, holding his hands up above his head as though he were under arrest. Tadi stood shocked, watching the weak, old man in his pale blue pyjamas, his grey hair wispy, his skin sallow. The old woman stood up, but her legs went weak and she stumbled onto the bed again. Her husband made to help her from the other side, but he was hit by the butt of the rifle and almost knocked off his feet. Tadi swallowed the lump in his throat, as blood seeped from the side of the man's head. He glanced at the others.

Timmy's eyes were on fire, as though he was relishing the violence. Tadi had seen him like that before.

'Please . . . Please let me help my wife.'

'Aron. It's okay, my darling. I'm all right.' She looked at the gunman. 'Please let me go to my husband. He's not well. He has a heart condition.'

The gunman stood back and jerked his head towards her, and she stumbled from the other side of the bed. She put her arms around her husband as they sat on the bed, her hands trembling, tears running down her face.

'It's all right, Aron. It's all right,' she whispered.

Finn looked around the room and pulled a chair from the dressing table, then left the room, returning a moment later with another chair. He looked at one of the men.

'Tie them up. And make a fucking good job of it.'

The other gunman roughly dragged the old man onto the chair, then grabbed the woman as she stumbled and pushed her onto the chair next to him. Tadi watched as he and the other man tied them up, wrapping rope around their arms and legs, so tight the woman winced in pain. Finn pulled back a curtain and peered out of the window. Then he turned to the old man.

'The combination. What is it?'

'W-what combination? I don't know what you mean.'

Finn crossed the room fast and slapped the old man hard on the face. Blood spurted from his nose.

'Now don't make it fucking hard for yourself, old man.

The fucking safe combination. You think I'm fucking stupid? Give me the combination right now.'

The old woman was sobbing.

'Give it to them, Aron. Please! Just give it to them.'

'I will give it to you.' The old man's voice shook as he spoke. 'Please, but don't hurt us any more. Please. I beg you. Everything we have is in that safe. We have worked hard all our lives for everything we have. But take it all. Just please don't hurt us. We have a grandchild.'

'Hurry the fuck up, and don't give me your worries,' Finn spat, then he turned to Tadi.

'You. Get over there by the safe. Behind the picture.'

The old man's voice was shaking.

'Three, five, seven . . .'

He paused. The gunman raised his hand and was about to strike him.

'Please! I am trying to remember. Please . . . er . . . Three, five, seven . . . Yes . . . er, six, eight, two, zero, one.'

Tadi stood rooted, looking shocked.

'What the fuck are you doing, you idiot? Put the combination in, you thick fuck.'

Tadi's fingers trembled as he stood at the dial. He looked at Finn, who then turned to the old man.

'Again. The combination. Slowly this time.'

The old man repeated it slowly, and with each number Tadi turned the dial, and with each number he felt more and more sick. Then click. The door pinged open. His eyes almost popped out of his head. So much money stacked in bank notes, and an ancient-looking gold jewellery box, studded with diamonds.

'In the rucksack,' Finn said. 'Everything. Every single fucking thing. You hear me? Go!'

Tadi glanced over his shoulder at the old woman, sobbing, her husband shaking his head, his chin on his chest.

'Fucking go!' Finn spat.

Tadi stood for a second, then he opened his rucksack and began to empty the safe. The feel of the money, stacked inside, more money than he'd ever seen, made him feel dizzy and agitated. He glanced over his shoulder to see the two men shove something in the old man's mouth. He gagged as they put tape over his mouth. He wanted to tell them to stop, that he was suffocating, but he was too afraid. The woman whimpered and they did the same to her. He could hear the others mumbling while he kept loading the rucksack. Purses, wallets full of money and soft velvet bags which felt as though there was jewellery inside. Then a leather folder. As he took it to put it in the rucksack, a photograph dropped out of it onto the floor. Nervously, he picked it up. It was an old black and white image, cracked in the middle. But he recognised immediately what it was. It was somewhere like the ghettos he'd seen in TV footage or newspapers about Nazi Germany. People were standing in the background, loading up wagons. Others stood around the streets. He could see the star of David on their jackets and noted the pale worried faces of children. There was a woman with a small boy at her side, he couldn't have been any older than Jetmir. He was holding onto his mother's skirts, looking up to the camera, fear in his eyes. The woman looked young, gaunt and tired. But the resemblance between her and the woman who now sat across the room tied up and sobbing, was striking. He closed his eyes for a moment. Tadi didn't know what possessed him, but he stuck the photograph inside his shirt, and emptied the rest of the safe into the rucksack. Finn came over and for a moment he thought he'd spotted what Tadi had done. But Finn merely glanced inside the safe, then gave him a look.

'Right, come on. Let's go.'

As Tadi left he took one last look at the old couple, and he knew that the pleading in the old woman's eyes would haunt him for ever. He didn't look back as they all padded downstairs. In the hall the gunman pulled all the telephone wires out of the wall. They left by the back door and piled back into the van.

'Gimme.' Finn stretched out his hand to Tadi as he was about to get into the car.

Tadi handed him the rucksack, still trembling in case he'd seen him take the photograph. They got into the car and drove out of the estate, and once they were onto the main road, Finn opened the rucksack and rummaged around inside.

'My information was right. Old bastard was fucking loaded.'

Tadi lay in his bed, staring at the ceiling. Every time he closed his eyes, all he could see was the look in the eyes of the old woman, and her husband, his face deathly pale. Four hours had passed since they left the house. They could be dead by now. They wouldn't be able to free themselves, and if nobody came to their rescue soon, anything could happen. They looked so frail. They reminded him of old people he'd seen back in Kosovo when the Serb soldiers came, burning the villages and forcing people from their homes at gunpoint. The morning light was beginning to break through, and Tadi turned to his bedside table and picked up the photograph he'd stolen. Why had he done that, he'd asked himself again and again? He could have left it in the safe, but the chances were that Finn would have seen it, or that madman Timmy, and they'd have ripped it up. If it was in the safe, then it was treasured. He looked at the picture again, the little boy, in his shabby coat with the star of David, and he thought about himself and his family and friends and the constant movement out of Kosovo when the marauding Serbs butchered their way through. Their faces could have been the faces from this picture, the same haunted, tired, exhausted expressions. This boy could have been his boy, bewildered and clinging to his mother's skirts. Tadi turned in the bed and curled into a ball, the photograph under his pillow. His life could never be the same now, because of last night. He had been an illegal immigrant in a bad situation before, but now he was in so much more trouble. Now, he was a criminal. He was helpless, with nowhere to turn. And he felt cold fear run through him. He sat up on the bed. Finn had told him to be back at work as normal for half eight. Maybe today they would let him go as promised, but as he went into the kitchen, filled the kettle and stared out of the window at a train passing in the distance, he knew they would never let him go. There was no way back. He was trapped.

CHAPTER ELEVEN

Rosie and Matt were back at the farm long before the media pack who were turning up in even greater numbers than yesterday. There were a few outside broadcast units from BBC, ITN and Sky News. A couple of young students going missing, found in a shallow grave, was one thing, but the fact that it all happened days after a notorious killer escaped from custody made it a national story. Rosie's piece in this morning's *Post* pushed things a bit further, because of her inside information from Don. She revealed that bodies had been found in the grave, and that the police hunting for the missing couple had forensic teams all over the area. McGuire had been desperate to use the line that there may be more bodies, but Rosie had pleaded with him that it would land her police contact in the shit. She hoped it would keep til tomorrow. They'd driven past O'Dwyer's farm on their way to the crime scene, but there was no movement in the yard, and the blinds were still drawn in the house. She wondered if they would see the Kosovan again today.

Around mid morning, activity picked up at the police scene. The area where they were digging was tented off, but Matt's long lens allowed him to see people coming in and out.

'Something's rotten down there, Rosie. The guys coming out of the tent look sick – like they're about to throw up. Have a look.'

He handed Rosie the camera and she looked down the lens, at the white tent and the area around. Most of the officers had white forensic suits on, but the other officers and detectives were now pulling on masks. She spotted two ambulance men approaching with stretchers.

'Here. You'd better get that, Matt. Stretchers. They're bringing something out.'

'It *is* the couple, isn't it? It's them buried in there – you think?'

'We've not been told officially, but I'd say it is.'

Rosie's mobile rang and she could see Declan's name on the screen.

'Rosie,' he said. 'The cops have just announced a press conference up at HQ. Are you coming back for it, or do you want me to go? I think they're going to be saying they've found the students' bodies.'

Rosie thought for a moment.

'You go, Dec. I'm best to stay here. It'll be a short

conference. They might not even say officially it's the couple, as the bodies will have to be identified by the family. But, between us, I was told last night that there are more bodies. The editor knows, but we held it over because nobody has that line. Hopefully we can use it tomorrow. So keep quiet about that up at the press conference, unless, of course, they mention it. But I'm sure they won't.'

'Sounds pretty grisly.'

'Yeah. It's grim. Talk later.' She hung up.

Rosie got out of the car and walked along to where a few journalists she knew were standing having a chat. The usual suspects from the daily and evening papers hung around, chatting to each other. They'd obviously been phoned about the press conference, and some of them were preparing to leave. She listened to them speculating that if they'd found the dead students, it was beginning to look like Boag had claimed his first victims since his escape. One hack piped up that the only confirmed victim up til now had been a young gay man. Maybe that's just the one we know of, another said. But there was a definite feel among the press corps that this was the work of Boag. Rosie said nothing. She wasn't so sure. But right now, she'd be happy if all of the reporters disappeared to the press conference to air their theories, so she could wait here to see what other secrets the grave held. Her mobile rang and she walked away from the crowd. It was Don.

'Howsit going, pal? I had to hold the editor down last night so he wouldn't use your info.'

'Thank Christ you didn't. I'd have got lynched.'

'So what's happening now? We could see in the distance that more of your guys were wearing masks.'

'Yeah. That's because we pulled the young couple out. Christ, Rosie! Poor bastards! They couldn't have stood a chance. Looks like they'd been hacked with an axe.'

'My God! How awful! Those poor families coming up here to identify them.'

'I know. The bodies have been taken to the mortuary now. But listen. Believe it or not, we're in the process of digging out more bodies. One fairly recent. It's like something out of a fucking horror movie. I feel sick to my stomach.'

'What's happened?'

'There's the remains of someone who's been torched. Looks like a bloke, but he's horribly burned. And it's recent. So he's being carefully brought out now by our forensic team. But even worse – and this goes no further right now – there's another two bodies.'

'Are you serious? This *is* a horror movie.'

'I'm deadly serious. There's not much left of them, but it's looking like a woman and a baby.'

'Jesus Christ!'

'Yep. We're all completely numb down here. Nobody even speaking to each other. The bodies are at least a year old, and obviously there's been some decomposition. But it looks like a newborn baby.'

'Who would do a thing like that?'

'Not Thomas Boag, anyway. That's for sure. He's an evil bastard, but murdering a woman and a newborn baby is not his bag. Someone else is out there who did do this.'

'So, where do you go from here?'

'We'll have to start with the basics, ask around. But the murders could have been done anywhere, then brought here. It happens. But how likely is it that a guy's burnt body is buried on top of an older corpse of a woman and her baby? Somebody must be returning to this place.'

'But is that not the work of a serial killer?'

'I just don't know, Rosie. But I don't think so. Not Boag anyway. Christ! We don't know where to start. We'll have to try to identify the bodies, so they'll be going to the morgue soon − or what's left of them.'

'When are you putting it out?'

'The DCI says it'll need to be tonight. He was just talking to HQ. It will have to go to everyone. Sorry. But it'll be just the basics, that more bodies have been found, and one is thought to be a child. They won't have all the information you have.'

'I understand. But I want to be able to say that there may be a mother and her newborn baby.'

Don sighed. 'It's up to you, Rosie. You might be right if

you said that, but it didn't come from me. You'll have to say you took a flyer if you're asked.'

'You sound shattered.'

'I am. But on top of all that, we've just been told of an armed robbery in Glasgow. An old Jewish couple. Tied up and robbed in their home. The old man's probably going to die. Looks like a professional job.'

'Who found the couple?'

'Their cleaner came in this morning and found them tied up in the bedroom. The old guy was unconscious, and the woman was barely conscious. They're both in hospital. He's got a heart condition, so he's struggling.'

'Jesus! We'll need to have a look at it. I'll tell the news desk. By the way, if you're up for a beer later, give me a shout.'

'Will do.' He hung up.

Tadi had been functioning on autopilot since he got back to the farm, after his sleepless night. Coming in on the back of the pickup truck, he'd kept his head down, avoiding eye contact with the other workers. He didn't want to engage in any conversation, but most days it was the same, anyway. They knew very little about each other and even though they travelled together and lived in the same block of houses owned by the O'Dwyers, they seldom spoke. Tadi only knew that his neighbour was from Bulgaria and had been at the farm when he'd arrived. He guessed he must be a prisoner too, but it wasn't safe to discuss things with others, as you never knew how close they were to the O'Dwyers. People this desperate would do anything to survive. He had just committed armed robbery and the thought terrified him. He wondered if they'd used the Bulgarian for similar robberies, but he didn't dare broach the subject.

Tadi heard his name being called and climbed out of the pit where he'd been working on the exhaust of a car. It was the old man, Jake, and he looked agitated.

'Tadi. Did you see the newspaper today?'

Tadi shook his head and said nothing.

'The police. Remember yesterday, they were over at the field. Where we . . . where we . . .' His voice trailed off. 'The newspaper says they've found a dog or something. They're digging over there. That's what they are doing.'

Tadi listened, then shrugged, but didn't reply.

'What if they find the body? They'll come here. For us.'

Tadi took a step closer to him. 'We say nothing. Remember that. You must say nothing.'

'But what if the police come?'

'We say nothing. They won't come to us. We are only workers.'

'I'm scared.'

'Don't be, just keep quiet. Go back to work, old man.'

Tadi felt weak, his arms heavy. The police would be here

today. No doubt they would all be questioned. He looked around him. If he had been on his own, he would walk away now, break into a run and get on a bus and go somewhere. But he couldn't. Not with Ava and Jetmir being held somewhere else. He went back to work, his hands shaking as he climbed back into the pit.

Between the exhaustion and his mind being somewhere else, Tadi took longer than normal to fix the exhaust. He heard Timmy's voice from above.

'Have you not fucking finished that exhaust yet, Tadi? I could have done it quicker myself. Get up here. Rory wants a word.'

Tadi swallowed his contempt. He climbed out of the pit, wiping his oily hands on his dungarees. Timmy jerked his head and began walking towards the house.

'Wait here,' he said as he went in through the back door.

Tadi could see Mrs O'Dwyer working in the kitchen at the sink, and she turned and gave him a thin smile. He nodded in acknowledgement. The door opened and Rory came out, followed by Finn and Timmy. They walked past Tadi, Rory beckoning him to follow. He did and walked behind them until they reached the pickup truck. Then they stopped, and the boss turned to him.

'There's a lot of shit going on up at the field now, Tadi. More than yesterday, when you had a look. Do you know that?'

'No. I haven't seen anything. Yesterday, I couldn't see.'

'Well. Have you seen the paper?'

Tadi shook his head.

Rory snorted and spat.

'They found something. The cops. Bodies. More than one. Did you see anything when you were up there digging?'

Tadi shook his head. 'No.' He glanced at Finn, who stared back. Timmy seemed to shift around in his feet.

'Are you sure? You didn't see anything at all?'

Tadi shook his head. 'No. Nothing. I see nothing.'

'What about the other halfwits? Did they see anything?'

'No,' Tadi said, shaking his head again. 'Nothing.'

'Okay. Well fucking keep it that way. And if the fucking bizzies come down here asking questions, you'll tell them nothing. You hear? You were never in that field. You understand?'

Tadi nodded. He felt desolate. He just wanted it all to stop.

The boss went into his pocket and took out a ten-pound note. He thrust it in front of him. Tadi looked at him, then at the other two who were watching him, waiting.

'For last night,' O'Dwyer said. 'You did all right.'

Tadi could feel his head swim. What about the deal? he wanted to ask.

'B-but . . . you said . . . before I went . . . you said. I could be free now. With my wife and child. You said I could go back home, Mr O'Dwyer.'

O'Dwyer looked at him for a long moment, his eyes cold and angry, and Tadi braced himself for a punch in the face.

Then the fat man burst out laughing, a chesty cackle, his big belly shaking.

'I say a lot of things. Now get back to work, you stupid cunt.'

Tadi could feel his eyes stinging with anger and frustration, and he bit his lip. He had to turn away or he'd have broken down in front of them. He walked back to the garage, his shoulders slumped, his legs barely able to carry him. When he got in the door to the darkness he broke down, fell on his knees and wept.

CHAPTER TWELVE

Rosie slipped into the front row for the police press conference a few minutes before it was due to begin. The conference room at Strathclyde Police HQ in Pitt Street had been transformed over the past few days to accommodate the growing press pack in the wake of the student murders. On top of that, they'd been trying to keep the press briefed on the manhunt for Thomas Boag. That in itself was putting years on the police hierarchy and press office team, who looked like they were ageing every time they popped up on television to admit that Boag was still at large.

The *Post* was not the only newspaper to be asking questions. Most of the media had filleted the police in recent days, falling just short of calling them inept. MPs were jostling for political gain, demanding that an outside force be brought in to conduct an inquiry. If it hadn't been for the fact that there were so many other things going on,

McGuire would have been calling for resignations at the highest level. But the press had been so busy reporting the news as it unfolded, there was no time to stand back and take a breath.

And now, the armed robbery of the old Jewish couple – the Cimmermans – out in Giffnock, was the latest story everyone was chasing. It was this story that brought Rosie to the press conference – she'd normally have left Declan to cover it. But McGuire was incensed at the way the old couple had been bound and gagged in their own home and left to die. The husband, Aron, was clinging to life at the Southern General Hospital. Today, the police were putting the wife, Berta, up to make an appeal at the press conference. It was risky, brave, and McGuire wanted Rosie all over it. The couple were well known in the Jewish community, respected jewellers who had come here after the war. They were both refugees who had survived Nazi prison camps, but had never spoken publicly about it before, from what Rosie had been told. That they should survive all that and be brutalised like this had stuck in McGuire's throat, and he told Rosie he wanted every word that the old woman said during the press briefing.

The buzz of conversation came to a halt when the door opened into the room, and the Assistant Chief Constable came in with assorted high-ranking officers, and a woman police inspector assisting the old lady. Rosie watched the frail, diminutive figure limp in, clutching the police officer's arm. She looked up as the cameras whirred and the flashguns popped, and Rosie caught the panic in her face. She glanced anxiously at the policewoman for support, and was gently guided into the chair. The room fell silent as all eyes and cameras were trained on the old woman, her grey hair loosely pushed back into a bun. The ACC spoke first about the horrific attack, describing the details as everyone listened intently. He announced that Mrs Berta Cimmerman would make her own appeal, but would be taking no questions. Rosie saw a lump in Berta's scrawny throat, and her hands trembled as she tried to push back a strand of wispy hair. Then she spoke, gazing across the room full of journalists.

'Please. I want to appeal to the people who came to our house.' She paused, and swallowed, her lips tightening. 'I want to tell you that you took everything we have. All we have that is precious to us that we have treasured over the years. It was everything we had.' She swallowed. 'My Aron is very sick in hospital. I don't know why you do this to us. We are good people. We try to help people all our lives. Because we suffered so much in –' her voice broke off – 'in the camps. But we survived, and that is the most important thing.'

Rosie glanced around the room, choked, and could see hard-bitten journalists trying to be stony-faced. Then Berta went on.

'If taking our things makes you happy then keep them.

You need them more than us. But . . . but . . . please. In the safe was a photograph. This is what breaks our hearts. It is a very old photograph, and it is of no importance to anyone. It is a picture of our son.' She stopped, bit her lip, as the journalists looked at each other. 'It was back in the ghetto, before they took us to the camp. It was the last picture we had of us together. He was only four years old. They took all of us a few days later, but they split us up. I didn't see my husband for three years. And . . . I never saw my son again. I cried so much then. All my life I have been crying for my son. But like so many other people, we live with the pain.' She stopped for a moment and dabbed her eyes. The police inspector gave her arm a comforting squeeze, and she continued. 'All we have are the memories of our lives before they took my Saul . . . We only have the photograph. But it is gone. Why? Why you take a photograph? Is nothing to you? Please . . . please give it back. I ask for nothing else. Give me back all I have left of my boy. Please.' Tears streamed down her face, and the inspector put an arm around her shoulder and glanced at the Assistant Chief Constable.

He intervened.

'As you can see, this is a very difficult time for Mrs Cimmerman, and I thank her for her courage in coming forward today. We'll not be taking any questions under the circumstances, but you can direct them to the press office. Thanks for your patience and understanding. Please get in touch even with the smallest piece of information that could assist us in this investigation.'

He stood up, then Berta was helped to her feet by the inspector, and she shuffled out, dabbing her cheeks. A hush fell over the room. Normally after a press conference people would rush out, but everyone sat in respectful silence as the old woman disappeared.

'Christ, that was a choker, was it not, Rosie?' one of the grizzled hacks from the *Sun* puffed as he got to his feet.

'Sure was,' Rosie agreed. She wanted to be out of here.

McGuire shook his head in disgust when Rosie told him about Berta's photograph.

'What kind of bastard steals a family picture? A picture that would tear the heart out of you. It doesn't get much fucking lower than that.'

'Maybe they were just emptying everything from the safe and it ended up in the pile among the jewellery. The robbers probably don't even know they've got it. They might have chucked it away,' Rosie said. 'You should have seen the poor woman, Mick. It broke my heart to listen to her.'

'Well, I want you to bleed all over your copy, Gilmour, because these robbing bastards have to be found. There must be somebody out there who knew this was happening. What are the cops saying?'

'Not a lot. There were no questions, just the woman's

appeal. Guaranteed to get everyone's attention. But I'm not sure if they have a clue who's done it. I'm meeting my detective contact for a drink shortly, so I'll ask.'

'Well, while you're at it, tell him that the plods are beginning to look like the arse is falling out of the empire all around them. And that bastard Boag has disappeared off the face of the earth. I mean, what are they actually doing about it?'

'I think they're well aware that the heat is on them.'

McGuire stood up. The meeting was over. The cops weren't the only ones feeling the heat. She didn't need reminding that Boag was still out there. She went back to her desk and began writing about Berta's appeal while it was still fresh in her mind.

Tadi was surprised but glad to be in the O'Dwyers' kitchen again. He'd been working all morning in the garage, trying to keep his head together, trying to quell his growing anguish. Big O'Dwyer's laughter was still ringing in his ears and he'd hardly slept a wink last night, worrying about when he would see Ava again. He didn't even know if he *would* see her again. They were using her against him, pulling him deeper and deeper into their criminal world. And he could do nothing. It had taken him all his time to keep the other workers who had helped him bury Bo from going into meltdown, because they were freaking out at all the police activity in the field. Today, the O'Dwyers had gone to a machinery market and would be out for the afternoon. He'd been surprised when it was Mrs O'Dwyer who shouted him in from the garage when he dropped off the keys after fixing her car. She'd made a pile of cheese sandwiches for the workers, but told them to keep quiet and never, ever mention it. While they ate outside, Tadi sat at the table, eating the brown bread sandwich and drinking from a mug of tea. He'd been feeling sick and didn't think he'd be able to eat, but once he made the effort he realised how hungry he was. Mrs O'Dwyer was working at the sink, peeling potatoes. The television buzzed in the background as the BBC lunchtime news came on. Tadi glanced up at it. Then he froze when he heard the words 'the robbery of a Jewish couple'. He put his mug down and concentrated, trying to understand what they were saying. He immediately saw the old woman's face, and remembered the terrified look in her eyes. He could feel his hands shaking as he listened hard.

She said something about a concentration camp and then about a photograph. It was of her son, she said. Tadi felt sick. She described the picture. He heard her saying that she'd never seen her son again after they took them to the camps. That picture was now under his pillow. It had kept him awake last night. 'Please give it back. I ask for nothing else. Give me back all I have left of my boy. Please.'

'Terrible carry-on, that,' Mrs O'Dwyer declared without turning around. 'After everything they've been through.'

Tadi was only half hearing her, his head swimming, trying to stop himself from shaking. He pushed the plate away. But suddenly, he covered his face with his hands.

'Whatever is the matter with you, Tadi?' Mrs O'Dwyer turned around and wiped her hands on a tea towel. She stood looking at him.

Tadi couldn't tell her. He dare not. He shook his head, sniffing.

'I miss my wife,' he sniffed. 'My little boy. I miss them so much.'

Mrs O'Dwyer looked at him for a long time and then at the television, but said nothing. She turned back to peeling potatoes.

'Come on now. Eat your lunch. You'll be fine.'

Tadi tried to compose himself, nibbled at the sandwich, and lifted the cup with two hands. He felt weak, exhausted, broken. And now this. He sat for a while in silence, staring into space, then suddenly, the silence was broken. Mrs O'Dwyer turned and looked at him, her face like flint.

'It was you, Tadi, wasn't it?'

He looked up at her, bewildered. He said nothing.

'That robbery. It was bloody Finn and the others. You were with them. Weren't you?'

Tadi said nothing.

'Did you take the picture?'

He looked at her, then at the floor.

She sighed.

'Oh, Tadi.'

He stood up.

'I must go now. I have work. Thank you for the sandwich.'

As he was going out of the back door, he heard her calling after him. Then she came towards him and took hold of his arm.

'They'll see the news when they come back, Tadi. So they'll ask you if you took the picture. Listen to me. Don't tell them anything. Just deny it. Deny everything. You're in a lot of trouble now.'

Tadi glanced over his shoulder at her face, flushed with anger.

'Wait there,' she said.

She went into her bag and took out a piece of paper. She wrote down an address, then crossed to the door, handing it to him.

'Go and get your family, Tadi. Go now, before they come back. Run, Tadi. Take your family and run, and never come back here. Ever.'

He took the paper and left without saying a word.

CHAPTER THIRTEEN

Don was already in the bar when Rosie walked in. He looked even more craggy than usual, as though he'd been sleeping in his crumpled suit for the past couple of days.

'You look like you're on the run, Don,' Rosie joked as she gave him a playful pat on the shoulder.

'I feel as if I have been. I've had about four hours' sleep in the last two nights.' He sighed. 'Gin and tonic?'

'No. Glass of red wine will be fine.'

She was going for dinner later with TJ.

He signalled to the barman and ordered the drinks, then turned to Rosie.

'It wouldn't be so bad if we were actually getting somewhere, but we're not, just plodding along in the dark. Nothing on the murdered students, and fuck all on Boag.'

'What about the old couple?'

'Well, nothing much there either. Christ! But we'll get something on that, hopefully, once the robbing bastards try to shift the jewellery. Actually, we've got a wee snitch who keeps his ear to the ground for us, and he phoned one of the lads this afternoon saying he'll get a name for one of the guys involved. Says it's something to do with travellers. So not sure if it's someone up from down south or settled travellers here.'

Rosie was suddenly interested.

'Is it not settled travellers who live quite close to where you were digging the last couple of days, where the student bodies were found?'

Don looked at her, curious.

'I don't know, actually. How do you know that? You been sniffing around there?'

Rosie shrugged. 'Not really. Someone must have said it around the press pack. It's one of the farms nearby. They're these guys who build driveways and stuff. But the boss is Rory O'Dwyer. That's the guy you tracked for me when I gave you the number plate outside the court that day. Remember?'

She didn't particularly want to part with this information so soon, as she was still doing her own groundwork. But it was Don who had led her to O'Dwyer, so she knew she had to play fair. It might not have been much interest to him as the robbery, though cruel and brutal, wasn't number one on the agenda – Boag was. But Rosie held back on the fact that she'd met the Kosovan in the field the other day, and that he seemed to be lurking around, trying to see what the police were digging up.

'I'll get someone to poke around, see what's going on with them.'

'I thought the old woman's appeal would have flushed out something,' Rosie said.

'I think it will. Early doors yet. Our wee snitch saw the press conference and he said he'd pull out the stops for us. Some lowlife gangsters would literally rob their own granny, but most draw the line at hitting old people. So whoever did this has no scruples. We thought at first it was junkies, because they've got no qualms about kicking in the door of some blind pensioner and beating seven shades out of her for the few quid in her purse. But the robbery looked like it had been planned, more professional. We'll get them, Rosie. Same as we'll get the bastard who did the students. And Boag. We'll get him too.'

'But what about the other bodies in the grave – the woman and baby? We can't get any further with it in the paper unless we get a newer line.'

Don looked at her, and then leaned closer.

'Okay, listen. You didn't hear it from me, but there are no records of the woman. No dental records, nothing. We're thinking she might have been a refugee or people-trafficked. Maybe she was in Glasgow or something and was murdered and brought out here. Looks like the bodies have been there for over a year. The forensic people are try-ing to piece together some kind of profile, genetic or otherwise, to see if she was from here, but my guess is she wasn't. Surely someone would have reported a woman and a newborn baby going missing. It was a baby girl.'

'Do you really think she could have been trafficked?' Rosie asked. 'Why murdered though? Why kill her baby? And why bring her all the way out here?'

Don sighed, draining his pint.

'Your guess is as good as mine, Rosie.' He sniffed and ran a hand through his mop of greying hair. 'You up for another?'

'No. That'll do me.'

'Okay. I'm going home to my bed. I've to be back out by eight in the morning, so I need some kip.'

He gave Rosie a peck on the cheek and she watched as he went towards the door and out into the night. She sipped her wine, intrigued by what he'd told her about the corpse of the woman and baby. The Kosovan came to mind, the shifty way he was when she saw him. Was he frightened or guilty-looking? Rosie decided he was frightened, but that may have been because she always felt empathy towards immigrants. Nobody chooses to up sticks and leave their homeland with nothing unless they are in danger. And they end up here, like the Kosovan, trapping a seagull to eat because he was hungry. She finished her drink and left the bar to head home before going out to meet TJ. As she walked up the road towards Charing Cross, the early evening traffic was thinning and the sky looked a promising blue. Her mobile rang, and she assumed it was TJ. When she fished it out of her pocket, she stopped in her tracks. It was Adrian. She stood looking at it for a long moment as it rang and rang. The last time he'd rung, she didn't answer. She'd decided to let go of whatever it was they had. He would know that, so if he was phoning her now, it was to tell her something. Maybe a story. Without another thought, she pressed it to her ear.

'Adrian.'

'Rosie. I hope I am not disturbing you.'

'No. Of course not. Great to hear from you. Are you okay? I mean, is everything okay with you? We haven't talked in a while.'

The silence seemed longer than it was. Eventually, Adrian spoke.

'Yes. I know. I tried to call you after I left. I'm sorry I left without saying goodbye. It . . . it was just the way my head was thinking. I'm sorry.'

Rosie didn't answer. She didn't want to explain to him that she'd seen his call that day and left it unanswered. Life had been a little less complicated in recent months without him in it, but he was never far from her thoughts.

'I'm coming to Glasgow tomorrow for a few days. Maybe a week or so.'

'Really? How come? You were saying the last time that your importing business was going well. Are you coming for a break?'

'My friends are getting married. You know, the people I have known for a long time, that settled here in Glasgow.

They love the life, and they invited me to their wedding. So I am coming.'

'That's great,' Rosie said, not really knowing what else to say.

'I . . . er . . . I wanted to invite you to come as my guest at the wedding, Rosie. Would you come? I would like to see you again. Very much.'

Rosie said nothing for a moment. The answer should be no, she thought. But why should it be no? she asked herself immediately. This was one of her greatest friends, he had saved her life. So, they had become lovers in the heat of the moment. But that was in the past.

'Yes. I'd love to,' she heard herself saying.

'Good. The wedding is next week. So maybe we can have dinner. Are you free to do that?'

To do what? Rosie wondered. Was she free? She didn't know. It was a tough question. In her mind and the way she lived her life, Rosie was always free, even when she was involved with someone she loved as much as TJ. Her relationship with him was better than before, because they were not tearing into each other's lives. TJ wasn't constantly reminding her that her job had taken over her life, and that she should look to get out of the newspaper. There were no borders drawn in their relationship, not officially anyway. But there was the understanding that they were together. She saw it that way. So yes, she was free to go to the wedding. But that was all.

'Why don't you give me a call when you get here? I'm working on some very hard stories at the moment.'

'You are always working on hard stories, Rosie. I like that about you.'

Rosie felt her face smiling, looking forward to seeing her old friend.

He hung up, and Rosie pushed out a sigh. Her mobile rang again and it was TJ.

'You home yet, darlin'?'

'On my way. I'll see you at the restaurant in half an hour.'

'Great.' TJ hung up.

She pushed away the twinge of guilt.

CHAPTER FOURTEEN

All Tadi had in his pocket was the ten-pound note O'Dwyer had given him for his part in the robbery. Just looking at it brought back the image of the old couple and their terror, the old man's face bruised and bloody. He would never use it, he'd vowed, no matter how desperate or hungry he was. But now things had changed. He was on the run. He could never go back to the farm. If he stayed, and the police came asking questions about the bodies in the field, anything could happen. One of the other men, who were already jittery, could end up breaking down under questioning, and they'd all be arrested. Or, worse, the O'Dwyers could see how the news was happening and decide to get rid of everyone involved before the police came calling. He had no choice. Deep down he knew he had run out of options the moment he went to work for the O'Dwyers. Now, the only reason he got up every morning was because his wife and son were out there somewhere.

He packed everything he had into his rucksack, took the bus from Lennoxtown to Glasgow, and handed over the ten-pound note to the driver.

Tadi had no idea where he was going as he got off the bus at Buchanan Street, in the city centre. During the months he'd been in Scotland after he'd fled Kosovo as a refugee with his family, they'd lived in a block of flats in the East End of the city, and everything they had was provided either by charity or the city council. He never had any money to take his wife into the town or do anything other than stay at home. Tadi had picked up some small bits of work in a local garage where they paid him peanuts, knowing that he was illegal. And when the time came for him to report back to the authorities and go back to Kosovo, Tadi and his family had fled. They'd used up whatever small savings they had within a week, and it was a priest at a local Catholic church who took them in, when one night, in desperation, cold, wet and hungry, they'd knocked on his door. Now he wished he'd stayed where he was for as long as he could.

Tadi had been talking to some other refugees at one of the local homeless hostels in the East End, and that was where he'd met Finbar O'Dwyer. He'd seemed friendly, and once they'd got talking and Tadi had told him about the mechanical skills he had, Finbar offered him a job and accommodation for his family. He said he didn't pay attention to the laws on immigrants, and as long as they both kept their mouths shut, he could remain in Scotland for as long as he liked. Tadi, in his naivety, fell for it, dreaming that they could live here for perhaps another couple of years before looking to go back to Kosovo. He went back to the church and told his wife to pack everything. The old priest had been sceptical, and asked him to think about it for a day or two. But Tadi was full of excitement about the opportunity that was being presented, plus O'Dwyer told him that he had to move fast or he'd miss the chance. He'd felt guilty because at the time he wouldn't give the name of the new employer to the priest, who'd warned him he shouldn't trust just anyone.

Within a couple of days it was clear that they were not workers – they were slaves. His wife and son were treated a little better, as Ava worked for Mrs O'Dwyer, and she was at least kinder to them. But Ava's workload was huge, cleaning the whole house every day, and washing and ironing for the family. That was why Tadi had devised the plan to leave, which turned out to be his next big mistake. He'd slipped away, just before daybreak. Ava and Jetmir were barely awake as they made their way out of the field to catch the early bus to Lennoxtown. Tadi's plan was to go back to Glasgow, where he would appeal to the priest to take them back. If that failed, he'd go to the authorities and give himself up. But they didn't even get that far. By the time they got off the bus in Glasgow, Finbar was waiting for them in the pickup truck. He said nothing, but he had Timmy with him – mad Timmy, who had slapped him around a few times in the first couple of days because he couldn't understand what he was saying. Finbar told them to get into the truck. They did, terrified to refuse. When they got back to the farm, Tadi was dragged out of the truck, then it drove off with his wife and child. He ran screaming after them, but Timmy caught up with him, and along with O'Dwyer they beat him almost senseless. He was told if he pulled a stunt like that again, he would never see his family again. They didn't allow him to see them for almost two weeks, as he begged for one last chance. If Tadi hadn't been so good at his job, he knew that anything could have happened to him. But finally, they reneged and brought Ava back to see him.

The address written on the piece of paper was a place in Kinning Park. He had no idea where that was.

The bus station was busy with commuters, as well as travellers with rucksacks and luggage. He looked around for someone to ask directions, suspicious of everyone. A couple of uniformed policemen came through the doors to the concourse and Tadi quickly turned his back and walked briskly outside into the busy street. He passed a couple of beggars sitting with signs saying 'No money, no home'. One of them had a tiny puppy, and the owner had the glazed look of a drug addict. Tadi glanced around for someone to ask. Then he saw a smartly dressed young woman coming towards him.

'Excuse me.' He approached her as she was about to pass, and she stopped.

She looked at him as though she was expecting him to ask for money. He pulled out the piece of paper from his trouser pocket.

'Sorry. Can you help me, please? I must find this address.'

The woman's eyes softened and she looked from the paper to him. He felt embarrassed, wondering how he must look to people, in his shabby clothes and unshaven face, his hollow cheeks.

'Kinning Park?' she said. 'You can get a bus from here, but I don't know which bus or anything. It's not that far. You'd be as well walking.' She turned around and faced a long busy street. 'Walk down here, and look for the Jamaica Bridge over the River Clyde.' She raised her eyebrows enquiringly. 'Do you understand?'

'Yes, yes. I understand.'

'Then cross the bridge and walk to the right. That is the area you are looking for. That address is in the tenements along there, about five minutes' walk.'

'Tene-tenement?' he asked, confused.

She smiled.

'Ah. It's flats. Like . . . hard to explain. But it's a long street with flats, old buildings – you'll see what I mean when you get there.'

'Thanks.' Tadi forced a weak smile. 'I will find it.'

'Okay. Good luck to you.'

She surprised him as she stretched out her hand, and he took it, feeling the softness of her touch.

'Thank you so much.'

Then she was gone. He followed her directions, walking down through the city, in the sunshine, really seeing it for the first time, although he'd been here nearly a year. People sat outside in bars or cafes and the streets were busy with traffic and noise. The atmosphere almost made him feel free. But even though he knew he was never going back to the O'Dwyers, he wouldn't be free until he found Ava and Jetmir.

He was at the riverside within a few minutes. He felt thirsty and stopped at a cafe before the bridge and went in, sat in a corner and ordered a coffee and some water. He had no idea what kind of place Ava was in, if she was working for a family or if she was being held like him as a slave. He had to think of a plan. He knew he couldn't just arrive and ring the doorbell. He sat watching out of the window, edgy. The news came on, showing footage of the old woman again and her appeal for the picture. He had the photograph in his wallet. If anyone in this cafe knew that, he would be lynched, and deservedly so. He sighed, trying to put it out of his mind. He had to find Ava and Jetmir, and soon. By this evening, O'Dwyer and his sons would be home, drunk from the market, so he had only until the next morning to act, before they knew he hadn't turned up for work. He finished his coffee, put the water in his rucksack, left the cafe and crossed the bridge, walking in the direction the woman had told him to. Eventually, he saw the road sign for Paisley Road West, and he looked up at the buildings, stone buildings, like something he had seen in Belgrade or in television pictures from Paris. But the buildings looked grubby and some of the windows had grimy curtains or were boarded up. He walked along until he reached the right house. Outside it was a secured entrance, His heart sank. How would he ever get in? He went and sat on a park bench facing the river. He watched as the sun set on the water, his insides feeling like someone was pulling and twisting them. Then he went back towards the building. He watched as a man pressed a buzzer and went in. Then a young woman came along, spoke into the intercom and the door was released. He thought she looked Eastern European. A few minutes later she came out and he followed her.

'Excuse me,' he said when he'd caught up. 'I need to get into this flat here?' He showed her the piece of paper.

She regarded him a little suspiciously, looked him up and down.

'Just ring the bell. One of the girls will answer.'

He didn't know what to think. One of the girls will answer. So Ava wasn't being held there alone. Perhaps there were some other women sharing the flat.

'Who are you looking for?' She narrowed her eyes.

He said nothing, shrugged. She gave him a long look. Then he spoke.

'I . . . I'm looking for Ava.'

The woman's face darkened.

'I don't know anyone of that name.'

'Do you live there?'

'No.' She began to back off. 'I have to go.'

'Do you know some people who live there? A little boy?'

The girl looked suddenly anxious.

'Who are you?'

'I am the husband of Ava.'

The woman closed her eyes and shook her head.

'Then go away. Don't go in there.' She turned. 'I have to go.'

'Please. Wait.' Tadi stepped after her. 'Please. Help me. What is wrong? Is Ava in that house?'

'Go away. Go. Are you stupid? Go!'

She quickened her step until she was almost running down the street. Tadi stood looking after her, bewildered, feeling sick. Ava was in that house, that much he knew from the girl's frightened face, but what kind of house? Who else was there? His head swam with the thought of the danger she was in. He'd heard of people-trafficking where women were taken to work in saunas and night-clubs, but Ava was a woman with a young son. This wasn't a club, but a street at the edge of the city. He looked around him. He had to get out of here, at least for the moment. He crossed the bridge and walked along the riverside, and eventually, exhausted, he sat down on a bench watching the flow of the river, his head in his hands. He looked around him and noticed a building with a large sign over the entrance, *The Post*. He tried to remember the woman's name who had spoken to him in the field. He racked his brain. Rosie. Yes. Rosie. She had said she would help him. But how could she help him? By doing a story in the newspaper, or taking him to the police? He had robbed an old woman of her jewels, money and treasured possessions. He had witnessed a murder and disposed of the body. He had nowhere to go. But he stood up and crossed the busy road, and found himself walking in the revolving doors of the newspaper office. He went to the reception and put his rucksack down, as the woman at the desk looked him up and down and smiled.

'I . . . I like to speak to Rosie. The journalist.'

The receptionist looked at him for a moment.

'Rosie Gilmour?'

'Yes, yes, that's her,' he remembered. 'Can I speak with her?'

She picked up the phone and was about to press the numbers when the lift doors opened, and out walked Rosie. She was with a man, about to walk past, when the receptionist called out.

'Rosie?'

She stopped.

'Someone to see you.'

She turned. Tadi saw the recognition on her face.

'Tadi,' she said, her eyes widening.

They stood looking at each other for a long moment, and Tadi tried to bite back his emotion. She took a step towards him and reached out to touch his arm.

'Tadi. It's okay. Come on. We'll have a cup of tea.' She took his arm and led him to the staff canteen.

CHAPTER FIFTEEN

Rosie showed Tadi to a table, then went out to the reception where Matt was hovering in case he was needed.

'Don't stray too far, Matt. This guy is in a bit of a mess, so I'm going to see what he's got to tell us.'

'I can't believe he actually came to the office. Are you going to be okay with him?'

'Of course. He looks harmless enough. I'll give you a shout in a little while.'

Rosie went over to the counter and ordered two teas and a sandwich. Tadi didn't just look hungry, he looked seriously malnourished. Her mobile shuddered with a text message and she automatically checked it as she put the cups on a tray. It was Adrian, who she was supposed to meet in an hour for dinner. She sent a message back, saying same place, but put the time back an hour. She knew he would understand, and she was looking forward to seeing him, despite the niggle of guilt in her stomach from last night's conversation with TJ. She pushed away the thought. She had work to do.

Rosie walked across with the tray in her hand, glancing around the canteen for somewhere else to sit that was more private, and ushered Tadi to an area that was cordoned off with wooden trellis. She watched as he got up, rake-thin in old jeans and trainers that were worn, with holes on the sides. She motioned him to sit down on the low seats and sat opposite him, sliding a polystyrene cup of steaming tea towards him.

'You should eat something too, Tadi. You look hungry.'

He swallowed. 'I'm hungry, but I feel sick all the time. I . . . I'm so worried. I . . . I need help, but I don't know if I should have come here.'

Rosie looked at him for a couple of beats and said nothing, waiting to see if he would say anything else. He didn't, just picked up the tea and sipped it.

'Tadi.' She half smiled. 'You speak good English, so please listen to me. I hope I can help you. I will do everything I can. But you must just take your time and tell me what has happened to make you come here like this. When I saw you in the field that day, and when you came out from court and those guys took you away, you looked so frightened. But you need to tell me everything.'

He took a breath and seemed to compose himself.

'I come here now, because I am desperate. My wife . . . my son.' He swallowed. 'They are in a house. Prisoners. Like me.'

Rosie scanned his face for a moment.

'Prisoners? Like you? What do you mean?'

'I am from Kosovo.'

'I know. I found that out from the court documents. You stayed longer than you should and you are due for deportation. But it seems the Refugee Council people can't find you.'

He nodded, his eyes cast downward, but said nothing.

'Yes,' Rosie continued. 'I was interested in you after the court, because of the charge, and what was going on with that guy. He was bullying you. I know who they are too. The O'Dwyers. Are you saying you are a prisoner there?'

Tadi looked up. 'Yes. Like a slave. Not only me. Others too.'

Rosie felt a little punch in her gut. Slaves. Modern day slavery was a story that had been thrown around the newspapers a couple of years ago when a nanny told how she was held by a Saudi Arabian family in London and beaten up. She had no escape because she was illegal.

'Are they also immigrants, the others?'

'No. Only one man, from Bulgaria. But the others, they are . . .' He paused. 'One is old man – a frightened old man, I think, maybe . . . I don't know how to say it, but I think his mind maybe slow. He has been there for years. The other two are alcoholics. They came from the hostel. Homeless. Like I was when they found me.'

'When who found you?'

'Finbar – the son of the boss man Rory O'Dwyer. He

come to the hostel and offer me a job, and when I tell him I am married, he says he take my wife and children too, for a good job, a new life.'

'I see,' Rosie said. She took out her notebook. 'Tadi, I want to write everything down you are saying. Maybe not for a story, right now. But I need to be able to have everything you say so I can tell my editor.' She took out her tape recorder. 'Do you mind if I also tape our conversation?'

He shifted nervously in his seat.

'No, please. Are you going to get the police? Please. Let me tell you everything. No police. Please. My wife, my son. They are in danger.'

Rosie put her hand up, as she saw he could easily go into meltdown.

'No. No police. But I need to have everything you say. Don't worry. If you don't want the tape, then no problem. I'll just write it down.'

He eyed the tape recorder and was silent for a moment, then he nodded.

'It's okay. I ask for your help, so I have to trust you.'

'You can trust me. Okay?' She switched on the tape. 'So tell me this, Tadi. It's been niggling me since I saw you in the field that day. Why were you hanging around there? You know there are bodies buried there. Have you seen the news?'

Tadi's eyes seemed to sink even further back in his head as he looked to the ceiling.

'Yes. I saw the news. Is terrible.'

'But why were you there?' Rosie was a little worried that her line of questioning would make him feel threatened. But she had to know why he was up at the field and looked so frightened when she approached him.

'They send me. The O'Dwyers. They said to go up and have a look at what the police were digging up.'

'Why? Is it their land?'

'I don't know.'

'So why were they interested?'

Tadi went silent, then his chin sank to his chest and he shook his head.

'Is so bad, Rosie.' He sniffed. 'So bad what we did.'

Rosie's heart skipped a beat. Surely to Christ he wasn't about to confess to the murder of the students, right here in front of her. He didn't look like a killer, but neither did Boag to the people who had sat next to him in the office for years. Tadi looked up at her.

'They killed Bo. Burned him.'

'Bo? Who's Bo? Who killed him?'

'The O'Dwyers. He ran away, but Finbar and Timmy – he's the brother. Bo was an alcoholic. Homeless, like the other men. He's been there two years. They caught him, and brought him back. They beat him. He said he would go to the police. But then the boss came out and he kicked Bo on the ground til he was nearly dead.' He paused, shaking his head as though he was reliving it. 'Then . . . then they poured petrol on him from the pickup truck, and the boss threw a match.' His hands covered his face. 'Bo was on fire. I hear him screaming. I hear him screaming in my head.'

Rosie was aware that her mouth had dropped open a little with shock. She looked at Tadi, her mind a blur, wondering what the hell she was going to do with this kind of information other than call the police.

'They murdered this man Bo? Is that what you're saying?'

Tadi nodded, sniffing.

'They killed him. Then they told us, take the body to the field and bury it.'

'My God!'

Tadi continued, 'We go with spades and Bo's body in the bucket of the dumper. He was burned, his whole body burned. We took him to the field and we dug a hole and buried him.'

Jesus! Rosie remembered Don's information that they found the remains of a burnt corpse.

'Christ, that's awful!'

'But also, when we dig the hole, we see that there is other bodies there.' He covered his face with his hands again. 'I cannot stop thinking. It was another body. And maybe the skull of a baby, I think. I only saw the shapes for a minute as we put Bo's body in, but the others saw it, I'm sure.'

'You thought it was a woman and baby in the ground?'

'Yes. Is possible.'

'Jesus, Tadi. What? I mean, what did the others say? Did you talk about it? Going to the police?'

He shook his head. 'No. We can't. We know the O'Dwyers would do the same to us. Me and the other men, we say nothing to anyone. Especially me, because my wife and child are somewhere else. They are not in the farm, where they were working for the first two weeks. They took them away.'

'Who? The O'Dwyers?'

'Yes. They took them because after two weeks I know that we are prisoners, and I try to find a way for us to escape. But they caught us, and beat me, and then they took my wife. They say I will not run if they have my wife somewhere. But today I ran, because now it is worse.'

Rosie looked at him, confused, wondering how much worse it could be.

'What do you mean, now it is worse?'

Tadi sat for a moment, gripping the back of his hair, his face grey. Rosie watched as he reached into the pocket of his jeans and brought something out. It looked like an old black and white photograph. He placed it on the table, and Rosie squinted at it, peering to make out the grainy images. Their faces were haunted. A woman stood in the centre, a little boy clinging to her skirt. Rosie's eyes fell on the star of David sewn into their jackets. She looked at Tadi in disbelief.

'Oh Christ, Tadi. The robbery?'

He nodded his head slowly. 'I took it from the safe. Nobody knows I have it. They made me do the robbery. I have no choice. They said that after, I would be free, that I can get my wife and son and go home. But the next day, they laugh in my face.' His voice cracked. 'Please help me.'

Rosie looked at her watch. It was seven thirty. If she was going to talk to the editor she had to do it now. She keyed in his number on her mobile.

CHAPTER SIXTEEN

'Jesus Christ, Rosie! I can't believe what I'm hearing. We need to tell the police. You know that. We have to contact them tonight.' McGuire was pacing the floor of his office.

'But you know exactly what will happen if we do that right now, Mick,' Rosie protested. 'They'll arrest Tadi and lock him up. There is no way they'll go into this softly-softly when there's been such public outrage on the robbery of the Cimmermans. And if he gets arrested, then what about his wife? If Tadi doesn't turn up for work tomorrow, the O'Dwyers will wade right in to where his wife is being held. They've been using her as blackmail for the past few weeks, and if Tadi is telling the truth, they wouldn't have any qualms about getting rid of her. They know if they have her, then he'll have to get in touch with them. And once he does, then it's curtains for him. He's a loose cannon as far as they're concerned. He knows too much. The poor guy is in bits down in the canteen. I've left Matt with him, but we need to work something out, fast.'

The editor stood by the window, arms folded, his heavy eyebrows knitted in concentration and frustration.

'Do you believe him, Gilmour?'

Rosie puffed. 'Jesus, Mick! What's not to believe? Why would he come in here with a story like that? He's got the bloody photograph from the robbery in his hand.'

'By the way, make sure Matt gets a picture of that. And, of course, of him.' He let out a long sigh. 'It's some story to get our hands on. I can see it all over the front page. But it's all happened so fast, and we can't even use it right now. We're duty bound to tell the cops.' He paused, his hands out. 'How do you know he's not a criminal? That he didn't take part in the robbery of his own volition and is now grassing everyone up to save himself?'

Rosie gave a frustrated sigh. 'I'm as sure as I can be that he's not. Criminals don't behave the way he has. I saw him that day being abused by the O'Dwyer guy when he came out of court, and I saw him in the field a couple of days ago. The guy is at his wits' end. He came here as a last resort. We can't turn our backs on him.'

'But what the fuck are we supposed to do? Tell me an alternative to calling the cops.'

Rosie was thinking on her feet. McGuire was right – it was happening too fast.

'Okay. What we do in the next couple of hours is crucial.

If I call my detective contact and explain everything, I'm certain he trusts me enough to understand the situation. But because of the importance of the robbery and Tadi's part in it, plus the bodies that they are trying to identify right now, he can't just keep that information under his hat. The minute he passes it to his bosses, they'll be down here in a flash to arrest Tadi. If they believe his story about his wife being held out in Kinning Park, then they might just batter down the door and rescue her. Tadi might be safe, but who knows what will happen to him once they start questioning him closely. And once he grasses the O'Dwyers up, how do we know they won't just get together and pin everything on him? He's got a photograph that was stolen in a robbery, so that places him at the scene of the crime. If the O'Dwyers have alibis for the night of the robbery, the police might just conclude that Tadi is part of some Eastern European criminal gang.'

McGuire listened, turning the scenario over in his mind. 'You think that's how it could pan out?'

'I honestly don't know, but it's a distinct possibility.'

'So, what's the alternative?'

'Well, just thinking out loud. What if we talk him into going back to work as normal tomorrow, and that buys some time – in that he's not missing – so his wife and kid will be safe. The O'Dwyers will know nothing of his visit here.'

McGuire raised his hands. 'What happens then? Where does that leave him? And us?'

Rosie was silent for a moment.

'Listen, Mick. My friend is in town – you remember Adrian, the Bosnian.'

McGuire looked at her, incredulous.

'Oh fuck, Gilmour!' He waved a finger. 'No! Every time he's around there are bodies everywhere.'

'He's saved my life – more than once. And if it wasn't for him outside my flat a few months ago, that Pakistani would have cut my throat. His presence of mind that night in picking up the knife was key to the police busting the entire family on their fake passport scam. He does things differently from the rest of us.'

'Aye, too bloody right he does – like throwing people down stairwells, and shooting folk.'

'That was self-defence. It was them or us.'

'So what's he doing here?'

'He's going to a friend's wedding. But I'd like to involve him in this.' Rosie rubbed her face with her hands. 'Look, I don't have a plan yet, but I want to have a chat with him and a think. I'm really not keen to hand Tadi over to the cops right now.'

McGuire stood looking at her for a moment, then pushed out a sigh.

'Okay. Here's the deal, Gilmour. I'm going to pretend you haven't told me this, and actually, I'm surprised you *have* told me. Normally I'm the fucking last to know what you're planning. But I want you to go out of here and take a deep breath. Think very carefully what you're going to do. You haven't got a lot of time, so if you want to get the cops involved and get the guy's wife out of wherever the hell she is, then do it now. If you have another plan it's up to you. So make your mind up fast. Talk to the big Bosnian – but don't do anything stupid.'

'Of course not.' Rosie went towards the door. 'I'll call you as soon as I know what's happening.'

'Aye, sure. I won't hold my breath.'

They left his office together – the editor walked to the back bench, and she headed downstairs to the canteen, phoning Adrian's mobile as she went.

Rosie took Tadi to a cafe in Charing Cross where she'd arranged to meet Adrian. She'd told Matt to keep his mobile on. He had already taken a picture of the photograph from the robbery, and a very quick picture of Tadi – so they had something in the bag, given nobody knew what was going to happen next. Tadi was growing more nervous by the minute. On the way to the cafe she explained that they were meeting an old friend of hers from Bosnia, whom she'd met a few years ago when he needed her help. He could trust him, she told him. But what about Ava and my son? Tadi had pleaded. We have to try and make a plan, Rosie told him. We cannot afford to make any mistakes. Rosie watched the door of the cafe, waiting for Adrian to appear, her insides a mix of nerves and excitement, but also worry that she had a huge responsibility, which was growing the longer the clock ticked. She'd explained the basics of Tadi's story to Adrian on the phone, so he would at least know what to expect. The waitress came over and Rosie ordered tea for herself and coffee for Tadi. Then the door opened and there he was. He took a step inside and looked around, and Rosie knew that he'd spotted them straight away, but he was always suspicious and watching for the unexpected. It hadn't occurred to Rosie that anyone could have followed them, but with Adrian, he was always ready. He walked across the room, his expression as deadpan as always, and it was only when she stood up and smiled at him that his lips stretched a little into what passed for a smile. But his eyes now meeting hers were soft and Rosie felt immediately safe and at home when he opened his arms and swept her into a hug. He kissed her on the cheek, and ran a hand over her hair.

'Rosie. Good to see you.'

He kissed her again, but not on the lips, and Rosie chastised herself that right at that moment she longed to feel the softness of his lips on hers. He briefly scanned her hair and face, then his eyes fell on Tadi. Adrian went towards the table, and sat next to him.

'Hello,' Adrian said, as he sat down.

Tadi looked at him.

'Hello. I am Tadi.'

Adrian nodded.

'From Kosovo.'

Adrian lapsed into Bosnian and Tadi's eyes lit up, as they spoke for a moment, then returned to English. 'Where in Kosovo are you from?'

'Near Pristina. Twelve kilometres.'

Adrian nodded. 'I know it. You speak good English?'

'OK. I have been here for over a year. I should be back home. I am illegal now.'

Adrian nodded again, then turned to Rosie.

'So, let's talk about what to do next, my friend.' He put an arm around Tadi's shoulder. 'Don't worry. We must help you. Rosie will help you.'

Tadi's eyes showed his fear.

'My . . . my wife. My son. I . . . I need to find them.'

Adrian took a deep breath and turned to Rosie.

'I know. Rosie, what are your thoughts?'

Rosie explained the scenarios. Either he goes to the police now and puts his trust in them, confesses everything that has happened and hopes for the best, or he goes back to work tomorrow and pretends nothing has happened until they can work out what to do next.

'I cannot go to police, Rosie. I . . .' He glanced at Adrian. 'Is okay if I say?'

Rosie nodded.

'I cannot go to police because they will put me in jail, then my wife . . . my son. No police. Please. Maybe I should just go.' He looked stressed, and shifted as though he was getting to his feet.

'It's okay, Tadi. I understand. If you don't want to, then we won't. Don't worry, my friend. We can think of something,' Adrian said. 'You know if it's a flat or house she is in? What kind of place? Did you see the people in it?'

'No. I was only outside. I think a flat, in a house. Some people went in and out. I talked to one girl, maybe Russian or from Eastern Europe and when I told her I am looking for my wife and her name is Ava, the girl is very frightened. She tell me to go away. So I think Ava is in there. But I don't know. I think it must be dangerous.'

Adrian shrugged and glanced at Rosie.

CHAPTER SEVENTEEN

Rosie hoped she'd made the right decision, but even as they crossed the Jamaica Bridge and headed for Kinning Park, she was still not sure. Trust your gut instinct, she told herself, pushing away the niggle. She faced two choices. If she turned Tadi over to the police – which she knew she should do – things would be out of her control. She'd have betrayed his trust and he would be dragged into custody – and his wife and kid would still be missing. She decided to let Adrian do it his way, which also meant she would lose a lot of control, but he had convinced her that if Tadi's wife and son were in the flat, then he would get them out. She had no reason to doubt him – he had never let her down – even though some of his methods in the past had included a body count. They had convinced Tadi that it was best if he stayed at Adrian's friend's house in Maryhill, where he would be safe. He was in no shape mentally or physically to handle any more stress.

Rosie pulled down the visor and looked at Adrian in the

rear-view mirror as he stared out of the window. His lean face was pale, with the same dark shadows under his eyes Rosie had seen the first day she met him. It was always hard to tell what was going on behind those eyes.

'This is well dodgy, Rosie,' Matt said from the driving seat. 'Have you told McGuire?'

Rosie gave him a sideways glance. 'No. He told me earlier it was up to me how to handle it, so I don't see the point of telling him every move. He'd only pull back anyway.'

'Do we even know who's in this house? Is it a brothel or something?'

'I honestly don't know. I can't imagine why they'd keep her in a flat for any other reason. Maybe this is just where she lives, and she works elsewhere. She hasn't said much to Tadi about what she does – says it was just housework and cooking for some workers.'

'Do you believe that?'

'No.' Rosie checked her notebook. 'Round here, Matt. This is the street. Drive slowly. Try to park outside.'

They pulled up and managed to get a parking space a few feet along from the front door. Rosie gathered her bag over her shoulder.

'You ready, Adrian?' She turned around.

Adrian nodded. He pulled on his khaki jacket, more like an old army jacket, made of heavy cotton with various pockets. Rosie looked at Matt, and she knew they were thinking the same thing – what was in his pockets?

'Okay, good luck, Rosie. But seriously, if there's any hint of shit flying around, get back out here pronto. I'm keeping the engine running.' He managed a smile. 'It reminds me a bit of when we went to that wee pervert's house in Morocco and Adrian came out with him kicking and screaming under his arm.' He paused. 'And look what happened to him . . .'

Rosie half smiled at the memory, even though it ended with the pervert in the bottom of a disused well in the middle of nowhere. Rough justice. That was how Adrian did business.

'Well, let's hope the only thing he's got under his arm this time is that wee kid.' She opened the door. 'Don't go away, pet.'

Rosie glanced up at Adrian as they climbed the steps to the front door of the flats. She pressed a couple of the intercom buzzers in the hope that someone would let them in without identifying themselves, rather than buzz the actual flat, as they would no doubt ask who it was. A few seconds later, the door buzzed open.

As they climbed the stairs to the second floor, Rosie could feel her heart beating faster, and her mouth was dry. The plan was to be quick – Adrian said the surprise would catch everyone off guard.

'You okay, Rosie?' Adrian squeezed her shoulder as they got to the door.

'Yeah.' She grimaced, taking a breath. 'I hope so.'

She rang the bell, with Adrian standing to the side and out of sight, his back tight against the wall. She stood for a moment, feeling the sweat on her hands, and trying to swallow. A few moments later she could hear footsteps on a wooden floor and she glanced up at Adrian.

'Here we go,' she whispered.

The door opened a little, and she could see a blonde woman, heavily made-up, with the glazed eyes of someone who has recently had a hit. She hoped she was spaced out enough not to be concentrating.

'Hi,' Rosie said brightly. 'I'm here to pick up Ava? Finn sent me.' She put her foot in the door.

The woman looked at her sleepily. 'Ava busy right now. Come back a half-hour.'

Rosie caught a glimpse of a little boy toddling around the hallway – he looked up at the door with big wide eyes. She could sense Adrian making the slightest move at her side.

'But Finn says it's urgent . . .'

The woman puffed out a sigh, and was about to turn around and shout something, when Adrian burst past Rosie on the step, almost knocking her off her feet. He grabbed the woman, turned her around and put his hand over her mouth. He motioned Rosie inside, and she stepped over the threshold, taken aback by how swiftly Adrian had moved. He walked along the hallway, and Rosie suddenly saw him reach into his pocket and bring out a revolver.

Christ! She braced herself for one of the doors to burst open any second, but the place was silent.

'Where is Ava? Tell me,' Adrian whispered in the woman's ear as he put the gun to her head.

The terrified woman jerked her head in the direction of a room at the end of the hallway. Adrian walked her along, Rosie behind, her heart thumping in her chest. The little boy stood watching. Then suddenly a door opened and a big, burly guy came out in a tight T-shirt, steroid muscles bulging.

'What the fuck!?'

'Don't move.' Adrian raised the gun and pointed at him.

'Don't fucking worry, pal,' the man said. 'They don't fucking pay me enough money for this shit. What do you want? Take anything you want.'

'Ava. Where is Ava?'

'Ava? The wee man's ma? She's in there, mate.' He put his hands up. 'Listen, mate. I don't want any trouble. I'm only the bouncer in case any of the punters get nasty. Just fucking get on with it. I didn't see anything. You know what I mean, pal?'

He looked beyond Adrian at Rosie.

Adrian jerked his head towards Rosie.

'Go.'

Rose squeezed past him and the gorilla, and went to the door of the room, dreading what was behind it. She pushed open the door and was met by the orange glow from a bedside lamp. A fat naked man stood at the side of the bed as a woman was stripping, taking her bra off and stepping out of her pants.

'Ava!' Rosie said her voice more of a whisper. 'Ava! Quick! We must go. Get dressed. Tadi is waiting for you.'

The woman turned, her face screwed up, bewildered.

'Tadi?'

'I'm helping him. You are in danger. We've come to get you. To take you to him, but you must hurry.' Rosie picked up her clothes and handed them to her.

Ava quickly threw on her T-shirt and skirt, then picked up clothes and stuffed them into a small bag.

'Please. You are not police? You are not going to hurt me? My son. Where is my boy?'

'He's there. In the hallway. Hurry.'

'What the fuck is this?' the naked man spat. 'I paid good money for her. Get fucking back here.'

'You're time's up, pal. If I was you I'd get out of here before the cops come.'

The man's face fell, and he was into his shirt and trousers in a second.

Rosie and Ava came into the hall, and she quickly scooped up the little boy.

'Mama,' he said.

'Come, Jetmir. Quickly. We go to Papa.'

'Go. Hurry.' Adrian still held the gun, pointing it towards the woman and the bruiser with his hands in the air as though he was under arrest.

Rosie opened the door and rushed them downstairs.

'Who are you?' Ava asked as she opened the front door.

'I'll tell you in the car. You're safe now. We're taking you to Tadi.'

'But where is he?'

'Don't worry. Come. Hurry. We have to go.'

Matt's eyes almost popped out of his head when he saw them come down the stairs, and he leapt out and opened the back door.

'Fuck me, Rosie! That was quick. Where's Adrian?'

'He'll be here in a second.'

Rosie got into the passenger seat. Then the front door opened and Adrian came rushing out and climbed into the back seat.

'We must be quick away from here. Maybe they are phoning this man Finn by now.'

Matt put his foot down and they sped out of the street, and were on their way through the town in seconds.

'Jesus, Adrian. What can I say?'

'Was nothing, Rosie. Was easier than I thought.' He stretched out and squeezed Rosie's shoulder.

Ava was sniffing, shocked.

'What is happening? Who are you? Please tell me. Is my Tadi all right?'

'Yes. He's fine. I'm a journalist, Ava. You know, from the newspaper? You understand? My name is Rosie Gilmour.'

She nodded. 'Y-yes, but . . . but how? What has happened?'

'Tadi will tell you everything. He ran away from the farm, and so we had to get you out of there before they discover he is gone. He came to me.'

Ava broke down. 'I want to go home,' she sobbed. 'Please don't tell Tadi what you saw.'

Rosie turned to face her, as she hugged her little boy, a look of bewilderment and concern on his face. She reached over and squeezed her hand.

'Don't worry, Ava. I saw nothing. Don't worry.'

Rosie watched Adrian as he took a long drag on his cigarette and sat back. He looked completely unfazed, as though barging into flats and holding people at gunpoint was all in a day's work. Maybe it was. But she was grateful for his help. They'd come to the bistro close to Charing Cross where they'd spent so many times like this over the past couple of years, when Adrian had been called in to assist. And even when he hadn't, they'd sat like a couple, sharing stories and smiles. Sometimes Rosie came here by herself, just to remember – even though she did question herself about doing that. She downed the remains of her first glass of wine and refilled their glasses. She was drained, but at least Tadi and his wife had been reunited. They had collapsed into each other's arms when Ava arrived at Adrian's friend's flat, finding Tadi sitting in a bedroom, grey with worry. Rosie had told them they were safe now, but to stay in the flat, that they would be looked after until they decided their next move. Rosie glanced at Adrian, suddenly aware that he'd been staring at her.

'You are in another world, Rosie. Like you are dreaming.'

Rosie smiled. 'I'm tired, Adrian. And kind of stumped as to what we do next.'

'They want to go back to Kosovo. Maybe I could help take them there, but I think their passports would cause alarm at the border, because Tadi is illegal here now.'

'I know. He really should go to the police and tell them everything.'

Adrian shrugged. 'Well, he is safe for the moment. My friends will look after him. I will be going back to Bosnia in a few days.'

Rosie sipped her wine and put the glass back on the table. They fell into silence and she could feel the electricity between them.

'Do you have to go back so soon?'

Adrian looked at her, surprised.

'Why?'

'I was going to ask if you could stay and help on the story. I'm not sure what our next move will be, but I think it would be good if you were here. These O'Dwyers are a hard bunch of people. I'd like to have you onside if I go to them.'

Rosie sensed the disappointment in his eyes, and

suspected he'd been hoping she was asking him to stay because she wanted him to.

He looked at her. 'If you need me, Rosie, I will be here. Always.' He reached across and placed his hand over hers, and she squeezed his hand. Her mobile rang on the table and she could see it was TJ.

'I have to take this.' She felt a niggle of guilt as she put the phone to her ear.

'You still working, Rosie? I was thinking if you're not too late, we could go for a beer. I haven't seen you in days.'

'I know, TJ.' She took a breath, could feel Adrian's eyes on her. 'I'm still tied up, though. There's been a few developments in the story, so I'll be late. Sorry. I'll give you a ring tomorrow and we can have dinner.'

'Okay, sweetheart. I miss you.'

'Yeah, me too,' she said, and meant it. She hung up.

Rosie put the phone in her pocket. She felt awkward and guilty and slightly ashamed all at the same time. She took a drink of her wine.

'Your friend,' Adrian said, his eyes locking hers.

'Yes. TJ.' Rosie knew she couldn't avoid his gaze. 'He came back.'

If he was in any way upset, his face showed nothing. He sucked in his lower lip a little and looked at Rosie for a second, then beyond her.

'You are together?'

She knew the answer should have been yes. She was

sleeping in TJ's bed and he in hers. They were spending evenings and some weekends together. Though neither of them had put down any lines, she couldn't deny it was a tacit understanding that they were together. So why couldn't she just say it?

She took a breath sighed. 'I think so. It's hard to say really. But we see a lot of each other. I . . . I . . .' Christ, she was stammering like an idiot.

Adrian waved his hand dismissively, then to her surprise stretched across and held her face.

'I understand, Rosie. You don't have to explain.' He paused, took her hand. 'You will always be my friend. You mean so much to me. Please always know that. Are you happy?'

She took his hand and held it, then gave him a wry smile.

'Happy? I'm not good at happy, Adrian.'

She'd got away with making light of it, but his words were stinging in their sincerity, and she sensed disappointment in his voice. On top of that, she had an overwhelming feeling that she wanted to reach across and kiss him, feel the strength of him in her arms. But it was wrong. Wrong on so many levels for her, for him, and unfair to TJ. Nobody screwed things up like her. Her mobile rang again. It was McGuire.

'What the Christ's going on, Gilmour? I've been waiting for your call? Have you made a decision?'

'Well. Yeah, Mick. I did. Listen, I didn't want to phone

you because it all happened so quick . . . and I knew you'd be busy with the paper tonight.'

'Aye, pull the other one, pal. What have you done?'

'Okay. The subbed version is that Tadi is with his wife Ava and their kid, in a flat in Glasgow. Everything is fine.'

'Fuck me! How did that happen?'

'My friend Adrian helped me. Ava was in a flat. And now she's not. They're safe. Don't worry.'

'Christ! Is anybody dead?'

'Thankfully, no.'

'Well. I need you in here in the morning, because we now seriously have to work out what we do with this guy.'

'I know. I'll be there. But I'll go to the flat first and get pics of Tadi and his family. I'll get Matt to hook up first thing.'

'Fine. But you should have phoned me. You're a pain the arse, Gilmour.' He hung up.

CHAPTER EIGHTEEN

Rory O'Dwyer watched the television news, his guts churning with tension. Of all the fucking things to happen! Weeks could pass down here and you hardly saw a fucking car, and now suddenly it was like a circus with coppers and bastard newspapers and television all over the shop. He'd sensed trouble from the moment they'd started digging around the field, because he knew what was in there. But there was nothing that could ever come back to them with that stupid drunken hoor Bo who he'd put a match to. If they dug him up, he was confident they wouldn't be looking in Rory's direction. The cops would think it was some drug deal or some other shite that had gone wrong, and the body happened to be buried out here. It was the kind of thing that happened from time to time, a body buried in a shallow grave, turned out to be some gangster who had grassed. But now this. Two fucking dead students dug up from the same spot. And their dog. Then more fucking bodies. He knew things might start heating up a bit, but he was confident that the Kosovan guy knew to keep his mouth zipped shut. But the big shock to him was that police had uncovered the remains of a woman and a newborn. Who the fuck would dump a woman and child? A patch of his land was now beginning to look like a fucking burial ground. He could put his hand up to one dead body, not that he ever would, but where the Jesus were the rest of them coming from? On top of everything else, that Tadi bastard had disappeared. He'd got the call last night from the flat where he kept his wife working, telling him that some bastard had come in with a gun and taken her and the kid away. Something was very wrong. Who was this Tadi bastard in tow with? He hadn't turned up this morning, and when he sent Finbar out to his flat in Twechar, everything was gone – clothes, bags, the lot. Bastard had done a runner. The problem was that he knew too much about the robbery and Bo's murder. He had to be found, but Rory knew there was little chance of that. On top of everything, Finn had told him that Timmy was behaving strangely, nervous as shit, and couldn't get a word of sense out of him. He'd been drunk for three days. So he'd summoned both of them to see him. Not for the first time, he wished he'd drowned that halfwit runt at birth. The door opened and Finbar came in with a sheepish-looking Timmy at his back.

'What is wrong with *you*, sir?' He glared at Timmy. 'You

look like a bag of shite. You've been drunk for the past three days. What the fuck's going on?'

Timmy shifted nervously from one foot to another and looked at his brother for support.

'Sit down, for fuck's sake,' O'Dwyer spat. 'You too, Finn.' He looked at Finn first.

'What are we going to do about that cunt Tadi? He could be fucking anywhere. He could be sitting in the fucking police station telling them every bastard thing that's gone on.'

'I know, Da, I can't believe it. The boys have got feelers out all over Glasgow. He must be somewhere. They know a few of the homeless and the immigrants, so hopefully he'll turn up.'

'But what if he goes to the fucking cops?'

'He won't do that. He was part of the robbery, and he got rid of Bo. He'll not go to the cops.'

O'Dwyer let that thought sink in for a moment, then looked at Timmy.

'Right, you. What the fuck's going on? Ever since the cops came round the fields and started digging you've been a nervous wreck. Why are you getting pissed all the time?'

Timmy swallowed and shook his head. He looked jittery from last night's drinking. They sat watching him for a moment, O'Dwyer exchanging glances with his son. Then he got up and crossed the carpet to Timmy and grabbed him by the hair.

'I'll give you two fucking minutes to tell me what's on

your mind, you fucking halfwit. What do you know? What's going on?'

Timmy said nothing. O'Dwyer slapped his face hard, drawing blood from his nose. Finn winced and looked away.

'Have I to fucking beat it out of you?'

He raised his hand to strike him again, and as he did, Timmy put his arms up to protect himself and fell to his knees.

'Oh, Da. Oh please, Da, don't.' He buried his head in his hands. 'I've done something terrible, Da.'

O'Dwyer looked at Finbar, bewildered.

'What the fuck are you talking about?' He grabbed him by the hair again and made him look at him. 'What have you done?'

They watched as Timmy buckled, sobbing now, snot and saliva everywhere. He started to retch.

'Ah, for fuck's sake, boy, what the fuck? You better not be sick here. Get fucking up. You're a fucking man.' He slapped him and pulled him to his feet.

Timmy stood cowering.

'Oh, Da, I'm so sorry. I killed them.'

O'Dwyer glanced at Finbar, frowning in bewilderment.

'What? Killed who? Fuck are you talking about?'

'Them students, Da. I killed them.'

O'Dwyer could feel the colour drain from his face, and his legs felt suddenly weak.

'Aw, Jesus, Mary and fucking Joseph!' He turned to Finn who was standing with his mouth gaping.

O'Dwyer looked at Timmy weeping and writhing, sweat on his forehead, and he had never seen such a pathetic sight. Surely to fuck he was making this up.

'What the fuck are you saying, Timmy? Sit the fuck down and talk to me.'

'Aw, Da, don't hit me any more. Please.'

'Tell me!' He tried to make his voice gentle, but he was seething inside.

'I killed them. I was drunk. I came home that way and saw the tent. And then I saw the dog, digging in the place they buried Bo. I was scared, Da, I was scared. I just stabbed the dog, and I had to do the guy, Da. And her. I had to. What if they'd seen it? I didn't mean to kill them. It just happened.'

O'Dwyer shook his head, not quite believing what he was hearing. For a second he felt light-headed and thought he was going to pass out.

'Holy fucking mother of God, Timmy. You killed them two kids? Jesus wept!' He sat down, his head in his hands.

They went silent but for the sobs and sniffs of Timmy. Then Finbar spoke.

'Timmy,' he said, glancing at his father. 'Timmy. You know the police have found two other corpses in that place. A woman and a baby. You know that, Timmy?'

O'Dwyer took his hands away from his face and looked

up at Finbar. An image suddenly came to him of the Ukrainian girl who worked for them at one stage. Timmy had been following her around like a dog after a bitch in heat. And then she mysteriously disappeared. But that was nearly two years ago. Surely not! Surely to fuck not!

'Aw, Jesus, Timmy! Please tell me that's got nothing to do with you.'

Timmy collapsed on the floor, wailing.

'I'm sorry, Da. I'm sorry. I . . . She was taking money off me all the time. Blackmailing me. Keeping coming back with the baby and asking for money. It was my baby. She said she was going to tell you and Ma. I was scared.'

O'Dwyer rolled his eyes to the ceiling, pacing the room.

'Jesus Christ, man! And you killed her. And her baby? What kind of fucking cunt are you? Why didn't you come to me? It was only a fucking baby.'

'I was scared, Da.'

'So you fucking killed them!' he screamed.

He crossed the room and sank a boot into Timmy's ribs, then another.

'I should have fucking drowned you at birth, you bastard.' He kicked him again and again.

Finbar stepped in and held his father back.

'Please, Da. Stop. Listen to me. Listen. We have to sort this. We have to! Stop!'

O'Dwyer could hardly breathe, sweat trickling down his back, and he could feel his face turning crimson.

'Get out of here, you cunt!' he screamed at Timmy.

Timmy crawled on his hands and knees to the door.

'Sit down, Da. We need to work something out here.'

O'Dwyer sat down. 'What the fuck are we going to work out? It's only a matter of time til the bizzies start asking some serious questions around here. We're the only fucking farm in a few miles, apart from that old bastard woman up the road. They're going to ask questions of everyone here. And what are we going to do with Timmy? He'll just fall on the floor like the gobshite he is and confess.'

'Listen, we'll send Timmy away. We'll work things out. We need to get alibis for the night the students were killed. We'll get the lads down south to do that. Say we were away at a fair or something.'

O'Dwyer said nothing, just stared ahead in disbelief, exhausted.

'And listen, Da. That bastard Tadi. I mean, he's gone missing. Does that not look a bit suspicious to you? He's been here for months and suddenly he's gone – just as they keep digging up bodies? We'll just fucking plug it all on him.'

O'Dwyer looked at him and tried to regulate his breathing as he wiped sweat from his forehead.

'I dunno, Finn. I just don't fucking know. Leave me be for a while now. I need to think.'

Molly O'Dwyer scurried away from the door where she'd been listening when she heard her husband bellow at

Timmy to get out. But she'd heard it all. Even though she'd heard it with her own ears, she still couldn't believe it. She worked around the bedrooms, tidying out drawers and cupboards to keep herself occupied. An image kept coming back into her mind. Elsa, the Ukrainian girl. She was beautiful, blonde with pale blue, sad eyes. Finn had brought her, saying one of his friends asked to give her a job. She wasn't sure how this had come about, but often wondered if Finn had bought these people, even though it had been years before the penny had dropped that the workers had been down-and-outs living in squalor before they came here – and now they were not free to go. Now she'd heard this. She swallowed the lump in her throat. Bo was a harmless, terrified soul, like a bird with a broken wing. And Elsa, the Ukrainian girl, all eager, helping out. But she'd stolen from her once and Molly had set a trap for her, telling her if she did it again, she would tell Finn and she'd be out on her ear. Then she'd mysteriously disappeared. And now this, Timmy saying he'd killed her and the baby girl. His baby. How in the name of Jesus was it possible that Timmy had done this? she asked herself. That he had come out of her womb, and this is what he was. A monster. He was a runt of a child from the word go, had to be revived as he hadn't the lungs to get him through the first few hours. He was slow in his mind too. No point in sending him to school, as he couldn't get anything into that thick head of his. But there was a mean streak to him. She'd seen the badness in him. But what could they do? You couldn't abandon your own flesh and blood, though sometimes she thought that Rory despised him so much that he'd get rid of him. She'd said nothing, as was their way. When you married in their community you got on with your life and that was it. Rory O'Dwyer had been a good-looking young buck among them when they met in Limerick, but he was wild as they come and could knock down men twice his size in a bare-knuckle fight by the time he was sixteen. But it was only when he came over here that she saw the extent of his crimes. Money was coming in and they were getting rich. She never asked where from, because once when she did, she got a slap in the face in front of her sons.

She thought of Tadi and how her husband had said that he'd run away. If Rory had an inkling of what she'd done, he'd kick the living shite out of her. But he never would. As she worked around the bedroom, she thought of Elsa and her young baby. A girl. All Timmy had to do was come and tell her and she'd have talked Rory round somehow, perhaps taken the little one in as their own. A little girl, like the one she never held in her arms, the one that had died at birth. What a bastard Timmy was. What a pure bastard she had produced.

CHAPTER NINETEEN

Rosie woke up, a little groggy from last night's wine. She had the familiar jet-lagged feeling she used to have when constantly travelling on stories, or going from one investigation to another with barely a break, running on adrenalin. It had been like that for the past few months, but it didn't help if she drank too much. Despite the hangover, she was glad that at least she was alone in her bed. She lay with her hands behind her head, reflecting on last night's dinner with Adrian, where they'd drunk much more than she'd intended, and ended up in a bar til well after midnight, reliving some of the scrapes they'd been involved in, glad they'd lived to spend time like this together and be able to laugh about it. Throughout the evening, she couldn't help wondering if Adrian would make a move. She'd promised herself that she wouldn't get involved, no matter what, but the alcohol and the atmosphere, relaxing together like old friends, had made it a distinct possibility. But she wouldn't be the one to make the first move. In the end, Adrian simply walked her home, with his arm around her shoulder. When they got to the door of her flat, he accompanied her inside, and they stood silent in the hallway, a heartbeat away from throwing their arms around each other. She wanted to, and she knew by the look in his eye that he wanted to as well. But they didn't. He held her hair and cupped her face, then kissed her softly on the cheek, saying he'd see her at his friend's house in the morning. Rosie had to admit she was disappointed, as well as a bit ashamed that she was. But now, in the cold light of day, it was for the best. Let's not make life any more complicated than it has to be, she told herself as she threw back the duvet and padded naked down the hallway to the shower.

Her mobile was ringing when she came out of the bathroom, and she picked it up from the hall table, rubbing her hair with a towel. It was Declan.

'Sorry to phone you at home, Rosie, but I thought you should know this.'

'No problem, Dec. I'm getting ready to go to work. I've someone to interview first, then I'll be down to the office. What's up?' She walked into the living room and clicked on her remote control for Sky News.

'I got a call from a copper mate of mine who's in uniform at Pitt Street. He'd overheard something, not sure if it's true, about a witness going missing in the Thomas Boag case.'

'Christ! Really?'

'So he says. My friend's a good guy, and he wouldn't bullshit me. He said it's all being whispered at the moment, but there are arses twitching in high places.'

'There certainly will be, Dec, if they've lost a witness. But they'll be twitching a lot more if Boag's found him first.' Rosie couldn't quite believe what she was hearing, but the way things were going for Strathclyde's finest at the moment, nothing could be ruled out. 'I'll see you shortly. By the way, you should treat your mate to a dinner on expenses. I'll tell the editor it's your shout.'

'Thanks, Rosie.' He hung up.

While Rosie's coffee was percolating, she prepared her usual breakfast of Greek yoghurt, blueberries and oats. It would have been healthy, had she and Adrian not polished off nearly two bottles of red wine last night. She drank a glass of cold water – too little, too late. Look on the bright side, she told herself. You could have woken up with Adrian beside you, then spent your day dealing with your guilt. She keyed in Don's mobile as she sat on the sofa.

'Don, I'm hearing on the grapevine that a witness in the Boag case has gone missing. Is that right?'

'Fuck me, so much for top secret. How did you hear that?'

'If I told you I'd have to kill you. But is it true?'

He sighed. 'Too true, unfortunately. People are crapping themselves up here. We're trying not to think the worst.'

'What – that Boag's got him?'

'Yeah. Fucking mess, Rosie. Epic fail.'

'Who's the missing witness? Can you say?'

'I'll meet you later and fill you in. He's a music teacher though – at Glasgow Academy.'

'Gay?'

'Yep.'

'Oh dear.' Rosie's mind was firing off several scenarios, none of them good. 'So has he just vanished? Done a runner?'

'Christ, Rosie, if only I had answers to one of those questions. We just don't fucking know. But there's a few worried faces up at Serious Crime right now. Listen, I'm going into a briefing. Why don't we meet at O'Brien's later. Around six?'

'Sure. I'll be there.' She hung up, intrigued.

Matt rang her mobile as Rosie got into her car, and she told him she'd wait in the car park so they could go up to Maryhill together and talk to Tadi and his wife. She hoped Tadi hadn't got cold feet now that his wife was back. As she waited for Matt, her mind was suddenly filled with thoughts of Thomas Boag, and her part in his arrest.

It had started with a phone call from a one-foot-in-the-grave junkie hooker contact she occasionally shared a drink with, and paid for information. She'd told Rosie that she knew a rent boy who'd been with the man suspected of being involved in the disappearance of two young men. The rent boy recognised Boag from the photofit the police put out after Jack Mulhearn went missing on a night out with mates, when he had disappeared towards the end of the evening. The newspapers had reported that Jack was the son of the notorious Glasgow gangster Jonjo Mulhearn and was already at university. When Rosie interviewed the rent boy, he told her he'd been with Jack around six months earlier, after he picked him up in a gay bar. He'd said Jack told him he was new to the scene, and that his parents didn't know he was gay. But the rent boy also said he knew a guy called Boag, and that he was a creepy bastard. He told Rosie that the man who matched the police photofit was an IT guy in a credit card company, and he even phoned Rosie back with the name of the firm. She and Declan got to work, using a contact to obtain the names of everyone in the company. They finally found one called Boag who fitted the age profile, and they managed to get a picture of him coming out of the office. When she went back to the rent boy, he confirmed it was the man he knew. Rosie had a splash, and passed her investigation to police. Boag was arrested at his home before the paper hit the streets.

She shuddered, remembering the look he'd given her that morning in court. Half an hour later, he was free. She stared out of the window at the sun attempting to come out. Boag was out there somewhere. Her instinct told him that the music teacher would never be seen again. And if anyone else was on Boag's hit list, it would be her. Maybe she should move out of the flat? Christ! Why was she behaving like this, suddenly paranoid? Too much drink last night and not enough rest for the past few days. Calm down. You'll give yourself more nightmares. She was glad to see Matt's car swinging into the office car park, all smiles, bacon roll in hand. He lowered the window.

'I bought you breakfast. Come on. We'll go in my car.'

She got out of her car and climbed into his.

'Just what I need, a carb and stodge rush. I should really marry you, Matt. We'd be great together.'

'I'm right here, darlin', I'm right here.' He tore off a mouthful of roll and sipped a steaming mug of tea.

'I've just heard some very scary news,' Rosie said.

'What?'

'A witness in the Boag case has gone missing. A gay teacher.'

'Oh fuck! I've just felt a shudder run down my back.'

'Me too, pal, when I heard.' She sipped her tea. 'I mean, it was our investigation that nailed him – basically handed him to the cops.'

'Fuck's sake, Rosie. Let me get my breakfast down. Do you think he's coming after us?' He grinned. 'Well. After *you*, really. I only took his picture.'

'Nah. Don't worry. That only happens in the movies. You'd think he'd be far away from here by now. Why would he hang around when the whole of the UK is after him? I'd say he's abroad by now.'

Matt nudged her. 'Aye, you can't fool me with your bravado, Gilmour. You don't believe a word of that. You're starting to brick it. What if this teacher turns up dead? I think you should look at getting some protection.'

Rosie sighed. 'Yeah, you're right on all counts, but I just don't know. We'll see how the next few days pan out.'

'Aye. Well, don't go home in the dark.'

'Come on. Let's go.'

Rosie was pleased to see Tadi's little boy playing with toys when they stepped into the hallway. Adrian greeted them at the door. The kid looked up, smiled and clapped his hands, seemingly happy with his new surroundings. The resilience of children, Rosie thought, as she clapped her hands back at him. She caught a glimpse of Ava from the living room, giving her a sheepish look.

'Come,' Adrian said, touching Rosie's arm. 'Tadi is in here with his wife. My friends have gone out, so you can talk.'

Tadi got to his feet and came towards her.

'Rosie. Thank you so much for what you've done.'

Rosie put her hands up and shook her head.

'Not me, Tadi.' She looked towards Adrian. 'It was Adrian who did all the hard work.' She smiled. 'But what matters is you're safe now.'

'I will make some tea for you,' Ava said. She glanced at Rosie as she passed her, and she could see the angst in her expression.

'I'll help you,' Rosie said. 'You guys talk among yourselves for a moment.'

She followed Ava into the kitchen and watched as she put the kettle on and took cups from a kitchen cupboard. She could see her hands were shaking, but she said nothing. Ava turned around to face her.

'Rosie. About last night. Thank you so much. You . . . you saved us – I am safe with my husband.' She paused, looking down at the floor for a second and then at Rosie. 'But, please. Will you please not say to Tadi about . . . about the bedroom.'

Rosie put her finger to her lips. 'Of course not.'

'I would die if he knew. I feel so dirty.'

Rosie said nothing, but she saw the shame in Ava's eyes.

'What have you told him about the place? What did you tell him went on there?'

'I told him that people come there when they are brought into the country – and that is true. I say that I cooked for them and did some cleaning. And that is also true. But I didn't tell him about the other . . .' Her voice trailed off and she swallowed. 'I . . . I don't know if he believes me.'

'He will,' Rosie said, because it was what Ava wanted to hear. 'Tadi's only thought right now is that his family is together. So don't worry.'

'But if he knew, he would never want me again.'

'He will never know. So you must try to put it behind you.' Rosie went across to the worktop and placed the mugs on a tray. 'Come on. I want to have a talk with you and Tadi.'

In the living room, Ava carried the tray and placed it on a coffee table. Rosie sat on a chair next to Matt, conscious of Adrian watching her. She cleared her throat and took a breath, looking at Tadi and Ava holding hands on the sofa.

'So how are you? Relieved, no doubt?' She smiled.

Tadi nodded and squeezed Ava's hand.

'Very happy. But, we know it is still many problems. I . . . you know . . . the body, the robbery. I have told Ava about what happened, and the photograph. The old woman. I . . . I don't know what to do now.'

Rosie sighed, not sure what to say next, but she had to talk to McGuire in the next half-hour, and she knew exactly what he would want to do.

She ran a hand over her hair.

'Tadi. Listen. You need to talk to the police. What has happened has really gone too far. It is only a matter of time before the police begin to unravel it. To be honest, you have to go them first.'

He looked worried.

'But how? What can I say to them: that I watched a man being murdered and then I buried him? That I robbed an old man and his wife and stole a photograph of their son? They will put me in jail.'

'You don't have a lot of options at the moment. What would happen if you ran away? Where would you go? None of this is right. You have been placed in this situation and you are innocent, and that's the injustice. But you have to tell the police, before it gets too late.'

Tadi looked at Adrian, his eyes pleading for advice. But he spread his hands a little and sighed.

'Is for you to decide, Tadi. But Rosie is right to say you do not have options. I would take you to Kosovo if I could, but you would be caught when the authorities saw your passport.'

CHAPTER TWENTY

Rory O'Dwyer didn't speak to Finbar at all during the drive back to the house. There had been no emotion or words of farewell when they'd said goodbye to Timmy at Glasgow's Central Station. His cousin Mark would accompany Timmy down to Manchester, where he'd be met by a long-time associate of Rory's who owed him a favour. From there he would simply disappear within the travelling community. The fact that this meant Rory might never see his son again, and that Finbar might never see his brother, was not something that was up for discussion. Needs must. It had to be done. Timmy was toxic. No, he was worse than toxic. He could drag them all down. He couldn't be relied on to keep his stupid mouth zipped.

Deep down, Rory was secretly glad that this idiot was out of his hair at last. He was all the man he would ever be, and would never have amounted to anything – despite the best efforts of him and Finn to include him in the family business, and the devotion of his stupid mother who had treated him like a child for most of his life. Timmy was a waster, and they were well rid of him. He hadn't even protested when Rory told him he would be going away for a long time and not to get in touch under any circumstances. Timmy would just be glad that he wasn't being eliminated altogether, because he would know that his father could have sorted that. Rory had told his wife that her son would be going away for a while, and she knew better than to ask questions. He'd slapped that spirit out of her long ago. You had to treat your women like that, or they'd be all over the place, doing your head in and demanding to know what was going on.

Rory and Finn had gone over the script several times in the event of the police coming calling. They'd taken Jake and the other workers to one of their flats out of the way of the farm until the police activity died down. As Finn now pulled the Jag off the road and into their farmyard, he could see they wouldn't have long to wait.

'The bizzies, Da. Look,' Finn said.

'I know.' He slid down the passenger window and spat. 'Fuckers. They'll be doing the routine house-to-house, so just say as little as possible. You know the drill. Are we clear?'

'Sure, Da.'

Finn pulled up in front of the house and climbed out, walking towards the unmarked car. As they did, two men in suits got out and stood waiting.

'Hello, sir,' the older one said. 'Mr O'Dwyer, my name is Detective Sergeant Malcolm Morrison, Strathclyde Police. We are conducting door-to-door inquiries in the investigation of the bodies recovered from the field nearby. Can we ask you a few questions? I take it you've seen the news?'

Rory glanced to the sergeant and then at the younger detective, but he didn't stretch out a hand in greeting.

'Yeah. But to be honest, myself and my son were away for a few days down south on business, so I only really saw it yesterday.'

'I see,' the DS said, as he turned to the younger cop. 'We'll take some notes here and just ask a couple of questions. You all right with that?'

'Sure. Fire away.'

Rory stood tall, towering over them, legs apart, arms folded, as he answered the few questions the detective asked him. He was in charge here, and he sensed that the cops were being respectful as opposed to probing. The questions were mostly routine – how long they'd lived here, who resided in the house, what kind of work they did. Rory told them and added that now and again they took on some farmhands during the summer months, or if they became busy.

'I understand, sir. Are any of the farmhands around just now so that we could ask a few questions? We're really trying to establish if anyone saw anything suspicious in the area in recent weeks. As you know, the young couple were found murdered in that field.' He waved a hand in the direction of the field. 'But the discovery of the other corpses are just as important. We're looking at three more murders here.'

Rory didn't flinch.

'Of course,' he said. 'As I say, I've only heard snippets. Actually, we don't have any farmhands at the moment. We did have one lad, but he's disappeared over the last few days. He was an odd character, kind of a loner. He was a foreigner.'

'A foreigner?'

'Yeah. He said he was from Kosovo and that he was an asylum-seeker or something, he said he was allowed to do a few hours' work a week. We didn't pay him much, really, just food and bunged him a few quid. He did say he wouldn't be around long. He said he was going back home.'

'Really? When did he disappear?'

Rory was glad that the copper had latched on. Fucking gullible bastard.

'Well, all I can say is he was here when we left five days ago, and when we got back he was gone.'

They stood silent for a moment as the sergeant glanced at the younger cop, who was furiously taking notes in his book. The sergeant glanced over his shoulder and around the yard.

'Did this guy, the Kosovan, not tell you he was leaving?'

'Well, he did say about two months ago that he would be

going soon, but I would have expected him to tell me, you know, or give me a bit of notice. But bugger all.' Rory shrugged. 'Things are a bit quiet for the next few weeks, so it's no great loss to us.'

'Do you have a name for him?'

'All he told us was his name was Tadi. He didn't give us a second name. He was just a guy who turned up one afternoon and asked did we have any work. We sometimes get that, you know, the odd drifter, they come and go. But he seemed a nice enough guy and he was a good worker. Anyway, that's all I can tell you about him.'

The detective raised his eyebrows 'And you think he disappeared in the last five days?'

'Well, he must have – unless he's coming back. But I've been back since yesterday now and he hasn't turned up. My wife says he was here one day, and then the next day he wasn't. That's all I know.'

The detectives glanced at each other.

'Did he stay here? I mean, did you provide accommodation?'

'Not here,' Rory said. 'I have a couple of flats in Twechar I rent out, and I put him up there while he was working. But Finbar, my son here, went to the address yesterday and there was no sign of him.'

The cop looked at Finbar who nodded in agreement.

'That's right. The flat is empty. No clothes or anything lying around, so it looks like he's just buggered off.'

'That's interesting,' the sergeant said. 'But, sir, are you aware that asylum-seekers are not supposed to be working in this country? They are not allowed to earn money.'

Rory managed to look suitably surprised and glanced at Finbar.

'Did you know that, Finn?'

'No, I did not.'

'Me neither,' Rory said. 'Christ, are you going to tell me now I've broken the law? I honestly didn't know that or I wouldn't have employed him. It's the first actual foreigner I've taken on – and it was only a few weeks.'

'Well, yes, actually you shouldn't have had him working here. But anyway, that's not why we're here, so we'll leave that aside for the moment. Could you give us the address he was staying at? And would you be able to give us a description of him?'

'Of course I can.' Rory reeled off the address and the young cop wrote it down. Then Rory looked at Finn. 'He was a tall, skinny kind of fella, wasn't he, Finn?'

'Yeah. Very skinny. Kind of sunken eyes,' Finn said. 'He had light hair, like dirty fair hair, short. That's all really I can think of. Light eyes, I think. He was a strong lad though he was skinny. He worked on the cars a bit for us, and was wiry all right.'

The officer wrote down the information.

'Anything else?'

Finn shook his head, the officers looked at each other and the younger one closed his notebook.

'You'll let me know if there are any signs of him living in my flat, will you? I'd hate to think he's just buggered off from here and is squatting in my house, free, gratis. Asylum-seeker or not – I'm not having that.'

'Yes, quite. Of course, sir. We'll let you know.'

'Anything else I can help you with? Would you like a cup of tea or anything?'

'No thanks. We'll be on our way. Thanks for your help.'

'No problem,' Rory said. 'To be honest, you've got me interested now. I never gave it much thought that your man disappeared, but now that you're here, it's making me think. You never know who you're hiring, do you?'

'No you don't, sir. That's the thing with hiring itinerant workers. You don't know who they are or what their background is.'

Rosie looked up when Don came into the cafe, which was crowded with lunchtime workers. She waved at him and he came across and sat opposite her. He looked as though he hadn't slept for days.

'You need a holiday, pet.' She smiled at him.

'Fat chance. I'll settle for a coffee right now.'

Rosie caught the waitress's eye and waved her across. She ordered a black coffee and a black tea for herself.

'So what's the sketch, Don? I take it there's all sorts of shit on the walls with the witness going missing?'

'And how, pal! What the fuck is it with these guys – they're supposed to be looking after people!'

'Was he on any kind of protection though?'

'Well, not in the real sense, nothing like witness protection or anything. I mean, Boag's only gone missing for the past week, but I think the problem is our guys took their eye off the ball. There'd been such a lot of crap flying around because he escaped that nobody managed to think through what his next move would be. People thought he'd try to get out of the country, so all ports were under surveillance as well as his old haunts – not that he'd chance going back there. But the last thing anyone was expecting was that he'd be digging out a witness. We were still building up a case against him. He'd only just been arrested, so it was going to take time for his case to be fully investigated and be sent to the Crown Office. I'm not even sure how much he knew about the witnesses.'

'Would the missing teacher not have been mentioned by the detectives during interrogation?'

Don nodded. 'Yeah. It's looking like it, but I don't know all the details yet. What I can tell you is that people are twitching in case our witness turns up dead.'

Rosie shook her head. 'What a right mess your boys are making of things these days. You've got to get Boag, before the powers that be send in an outside force.'

'That'll be some red neck for the bosses if that happens.'

'So, what can you tell me about the teacher?'

'You have to be careful how you write this.'

'Don't worry. At the end of the day, I could have been digging this up myself.'

'Yeah, I suppose so. Okay. His name is Charles Dawson, and he's the head of music up at Glasgow Academy. Single, gay, living on his own. Very much the quiet man, didn't mix with any of the other staff, so nobody knows much about his private life.'

'What about family?'

'He has a sister who lives in France. But we've contacted her and they've not spoken in years. So he's very much a loner.'

'Did he come to you about Boag?'

'Yep. But only after he was arrested. In fact, it was the next day.'

'What – he just called the cops and said he knew him?'

'Yes. He phoned HQ and asked to be put through to the incident room. By all accounts, when the boys interviewed him, he was in a right state. He said he felt he should have come forward earlier, like when bits of Jack Mulhearn started turning up and we were going nowhere in our investigation. He said he felt guilty that he could have perhaps prevented the boy's death.'

'How come? Had Boag been violent towards him?'

'That's his evidence. In the beginning it was just a routine pick-up at a gay bar, but then they met again. He said Boag began to get a bit rougher each time and seemed to get some kind of pleasure out of making him afraid. He said he was talking about chopping people up. That was when our man decided he wouldn't see him again. Boag had told him where he worked and stuff and seemed to be quite taken with him. He seemed to become a bit obsessed, but the guy just bailed out and never got in touch again. He didn't return any of his calls and stayed away from the club.'

'I'm wondering how come Boag didn't just do him in, instead of the young boy he picked up.'

'Well, who knows what goes on inside the mind of a psycho. Maybe he was secretly in love with the teacher and didn't want to destroy him at that point, and maybe just snapped with the boy that night.'

Rosie thought about it for a moment.

'That's quite good thinking, Batman. You should maybe get moved to forensic psychology.' She winked at him.

'Aye, or maybe just get moved to psychiatric. I hate cases like this. They really freak me out.'

'You and me both. I keep looking over my shoulder for this bastard, so I wish you'd hurry up and arrest him.'

Don drank his coffee.

'I've told you, Gilmour. You need to get some protection.'

'Yeah, well I'll not be asking the police to do it, that's for sure. Especially if our teacher turns up dead.' She paused. 'Do you think he will?'

'I'd put my house on it.' He drained the coffee and looked at his watch. 'Right. I need to go. We've got a meeting in half an hour. But I'm serious about that protection. You should at least move out of your flat.' He stood up. 'I've got a spare room, you know. Own bathroom.'

Rosie smiled.

'Thanks, Don. But I wouldn't make a great flatmate.'

She had intended on sounding Don out about Tadi, but changed her mind as soon as he sat down. He was so up to his eyes on Boag right now that she was afraid throwing Tadi into the mix might be a big mistake – especially given that the police desperately needed a culprit for at least one of the crimes currently making them look inept.

CHAPTER TWENTY-ONE

Tadi woke to the sound of Ava softly humming from the kitchen, and he could hear the patter of Jetmir's feet as he ran around, playing on the wooden floor in the hallway. It was music to his ears. For weeks, he'd lain desolate in the single bed at night in the dingy, damp flat, unable to sleep, frantic with worry that he would never see his wife and son again. He'd watched the flesh drop off his body, partly from being underfed, but also from the stress of being trapped in this hell. The first night after Ava came back, when they finally went to bed, they'd held each other for a long time until they fell asleep. But he'd sensed a change in her. Outwardly she was glad to be with him, but he could see she was traumatised and afraid. When he asked her why she was sad now that they were together, she told him she was crying because she was happy. Deep down, Tadi knew there was more. He'd never asked her what she did while she was being held in the flat. He didn't want to know. Somewhere in Ava's sad eyes, he could see the answer, but he pushed it away. None of that mattered any more. What's done is done. They were together now, and nothing would keep them apart. He was determined about that, even though there was a niggle in his gut about what Rosie had said – that he should go to the police. He knew she was right, but he needed more time to think. He needed a few more days of this – the sounds from the kitchen, of the aroma of his wife cooking breakfast, and the smile on her face he saw now as he got out of bed and stood by the kitchen door watching her.

'You are more beautiful every day,' he said. 'I wanted to tell you that, Ava. I told you every day in my mind while we were apart and I am going to tell you every day for the rest of our lives.' He went across to the cooker and took her in his arms. 'I am a very lucky man.'

'No,' she said, burying her head in his shoulder. 'It's me who is lucky.'

He held her for a moment, then let go, as she carried on cooking, pushing things around a pan. Tadi went into the living room where the BBC News bulletin was just starting. He stood, gazing at the screen, not paying much attention to some political story. Then he sat bolt upright, listening hard. Had he heard that correctly? The woman was saying that police had revealed this morning that they were looking for a man who may be able to assist with their investigation into the bodies recovered from the field near Lennoxtown.

'The man is believed to be from Kosovo and was working on a nearby farm but hasn't been seen for several days. Detectives are anxious to speak to him and have issued a description of him, as tall, fair and very lean.'

Tadi felt his legs go weak.

'My God! My God!' he whispered.

There was nobody here – no Adrian. He had no way of contacting Rosie Gilmour unless he went to the newspaper offices. But what if the police saw him? He had to keep calm for Ava and Jetmir, but they had to get out of here.

'Tadi,' Ava called. 'Come and get breakfast . . . Jetmir. Come.'

Tadi tried to compose himself. He walked into the kitchen and sat down, but he could see Ava looking at him, bewildered.

'Tadi,' she said. 'What is wrong? You are white. What is it?'

She put a plate of eggs down and poured tea into two mugs. Jetmir was at the table eating toast and scooping up the boiled egg.

Tadi looked at his wife and swallowed.

'Ava. We have to leave here. Now.'

'What? What are you saying, Tadi? We are not safe here? Why you say this so suddenly?'

He took a breath, reached across and held her hand. 'I saw it on the news, Ava. They are saying police are looking for me. Because of the bodies in the field.'

'What? But how? How can they say that? Why?'

'I don't know . . . I don't know how. The presenter just said police were looking for a man who worked in the farm close to where the bodies were found. They said he is missing. That is me, Ava. They said he is from Kosovo, and they describe me.' He could feel himself choke with emotion. 'They are looking for me. The police will come.'

'But . . . but. You must call Rosie. Where is Adrian? We must call someone!'

'We have no phone here. We should go.'

'But why? Nobody knows we are here. Why leave? We can stay here until someone comes, maybe Adrian. Or Rosie.' She pushed the plate towards him. 'Come on. Eat something. We must eat.'

Tadi looked at the plate. His appetite had gone, but he knew he had to eat something.

'I will eat, Ava. But when we finish, we pack our things and we go. We must be calm. We will go to the old priest. Remember him? He will protect us.'

'But . . . but what about Rosie? She said she would help.'

'She wants to take us to the police, but we can't do that now. It's too late. They are looking for me now. They think it is me who killed these people, and that I ran away. Ava, listen. You must trust me. We have to go.'

'Okay, I understand. But can we try to get in touch with the reporter or wait for later? Maybe she will come.'

'No. I want to go this morning. We have to.'

*

Rosie had come to McGuire's office straight from the West End, where she'd been trying to dig up some background on the missing music teacher. Neighbours knew nothing about him, but were shocked that his name had been linked with Thomas Boag. She'd left the street, where he'd lived in an end-of-terrace tenement flat for the past thirty years, and headed to Finnieston where she met with her rent-boy contact. He'd given her more than enough information for a splash tomorrow. He said he'd been with the teacher on two occasions, and remembered him as a gentle, quiet man who took him to his flat and cooked him supper. He felt the teacher was just lonely. The problem Rosie had now was how much they could use in the newspaper, given that Boag was technically innocent til proven guilty, and the teacher was going to be a witness in a future criminal trial, if he was found alive.

'Well, the police have released a statement saying that he's missing, so surely to Christ we can push the envelope a bit further?' McGuire said.

'I hope so, because it's good stuff from the rent boy. We won't be able to use a lot of it – it's only his word. We'll need to talk to Hanlon.'

As she said it, Rosie's mobile rang and she picked it up. It was Adrian.

'Rosie. Can you talk?'

'Of course.'

'Is Tadi with you?'

'No. I'm in the office.'

'He's gone.'

'What? How? How can he be gone? Have you been to the flat?'

'No. But my friend went out for an hour this morning and when they got back he was gone. It must have been recent, because he said that the cooker was still warm. But there is no sign of them in the flat.'

'Oh, Christ almighty!' Rosie put a hand across her forehead. 'I should have had somebody with them all the time.'

'But my friend was there. He just didn't think it was a problem to leave them for a couple of hours because they were asleep when he left.'

Rosie thought for a moment. 'I have to go, Adrian. I'm with the editor. I'll call you in a while.'

McGuire looked at her. 'What's up?'

'The Kosovan – Tadi. He's disappeared.'

'Ah fuck! How?'

'He was in a flat with a Bosnian couple – everything was fine when I left yesterday. I was going up to see him shortly. But something must have happened.'

There was a knock at the door of the editor's office, and Declan put his head around.

'Sorry to butt in, folks, but, Rosie, this is important. Have you seen the news?'

'What news?'

'Cops have issued a statement saying they're anxious to speak to a farmhand who has gone missing. A Kosovan man. They've issued a description. I'm thinking it's your man.'

Rosie slumped back.

'Oh, Christ! You're kidding, Dec. How the hell did that happen? How can they suddenly be looking for Tadi? They don't know anything. I need to talk to my cop pal.'

'Okay,' Declan said. 'I'll get on to one of my mates too. See what the score is.'

'Fucking hell, Gilmour. What is this Kosovan playing at? He's done a runner? I have to tell you, there are alarm bells ringing here. I mean, think about it. He's suddenly gone missing, just as you were going to talk him into going to the police to tell his story. A story that involves bodies being dug up and a robbery of an old couple. Are you sure this guy is as innocent as he says he is?'

'Come on, Mick.'

'I'm serious. And if it looks suspicious to me, it will look a lot worse to the cops. They've got nobody to finger on this, and there's suddenly a missing foreigner who was working in the area.'

'To me that seems all too convenient. There's something rotten at work here, I'm telling you.' Rosie stood up. 'I need to get my detective friend. See what's going on. But I don't like the sound of it.'

'Neither do I. But I'm seeing it from both sides here – unlike you.'

Rosie looked at him for a long moment. 'I'm not naive, Mick. I know what you're thinking – that I know very little about this guy apart from what he's told me. But my instinct tells me this is an innocent man, bullied and beaten beyond belief. I totally believe him. Someone is manipulating this, I'm sure.'

'Well, you'd better go and find out some facts, then. I mean, where the fuck has this guy gone to? And why go so quickly? Why not call you?'

'He doesn't have a phone, and there's no phone in the flat. That's why I was going up now. It's my fault. I should have left a mobile or got Adrian over there earlier.' She paused. 'Maybe he saw the news or found out that the cops were looking for him and he just freaked out.'

McGuire shrugged.

'Listen. I trust your judgement. I think the guy is innocent too, but I want to know more. What makes an innocent man run?'

'The prospect of getting nailed for something he didn't do. That's what makes innocent people run.'

'Well. Go and find him, Gilmour – and quick.'

CHAPTER TWENTY-TWO

Rosie drove towards London Road, cursing herself for the questions she hadn't asked Tadi. When he'd told her that he'd stayed at the home of a priest in the East End of Glasgow, she should have asked the name there and then. It was the basics of reporting – make sure you get everything possible in the first visit, because often you only get one shot. So many times in her career this had proved to be good advice. You wrung all the information out before you let them out of your sight. But she'd been so caught up in Tadi's disturbing story that she'd allowed the minutiae of it to somehow get lost in her list of questions. Stupid. If she knew what Catholic church it was she'd have gone straight there – whether she got through the door or not was another story.

She did have one option. She had to go back to the old priest from her childhood, Father Dunnachie. She'd returned there a couple of years ago after a very long absence, and the old priest had helped her find her mother's grave on a damp winter's day. She'd been given a pauper's burial, but there had been a single handmade cross stuck in the earth to mark the spot. It was only months later, when Rosie's father – who had more or less abandoned her and her mother – suddenly came back into her life, that she realised that it was him who had planted the cross there all those years ago. Going back to see the priest at the church where she used to sit at mass with her mother, where she made her first Holy Communion, took her back down a dark road.

Even now, just driving towards the area, knowing she was going to the old priest to ask for help, all the thoughts came flooding back. The lonely nights and the sadness of her mother pining for the man she loved but who spent a lifetime on the merchant ships, travelling the world, almost always absent from their lives. Then the phone ringing that morning when she'd stood in the hallway, confronted by her mother's body hanging from the staircase. She would never escape that image, no matter how much she pushed it away. It had haunted her dreams all her life, and here she was again, pulling up her car at the old church driveway, knowing this would be sure to feature in her next nightmare.

It was just gone ten thirty, and a handful of congregation were leaving morning mass – the usual collection of pensioners and devout Catholics, who had ridden the storm of sexual abuse scandals that had driven so many of the flock away, in bitterness and anger at the betrayal. Rosie had walked away long before that. But sometimes she would come back to the comfort and familiarity of this chapel and sit in silence, remembering.

She went around to the chapel house and rang the bell, knowing the priest would be able to come in through the sacristy door to his house without going outside. No answer. She rang again and waited. She stood listening to the birdsong in the high sycamore trees, and recalled climbing up there as a little girl for a dare, after her friends coaxed her. The thought made her smile. She turned around when she heard the door open, and Father Dunnachie stood, his blue eyes smiling in the face that had always shown her nothing but kindness.

'Ah, Rosie Gilmour! Look at you! Right here on my doorstep – like an apparition,' he joked in his gentle Irish brogue.

'Hello, Father.' Rosie smiled, suppressing the urge to throw her arms around him.

She could read his face, and she knew he too was remembering the old days. He touched her arm.

'Come on in, Rosie. You look tired.' He looked up at the sunshine. 'In fact, don't come in. Let's have a walk in the garden. Take some sun while we can. You'll have a cup of tea?'

'I wouldn't say no, Father. Black, please, no sugar. As long as it's no bother.'

'Not at all. Never a bother for me if you turn up on my doorstep. You're always welcome here. Hold on a moment.'

He turned and went in to the hall, and she could hear him talking to his housekeeper, asking her to bring some tea out to the garden. He came back out of the door and took her arm.

'Come on, Rosie. I'll show you my horticultural skills that keep me sane in this mad, mad world we live in.'

They walked along the path and through a waist-high hedgerow towards a lawn that looked as though you could play bowls on it. Pink and purple flowers hung on the rhododendrons.

'It's beautiful. So colourful and peaceful, especially lovely on a day like this.'

'You should always take time to smell the flowers, Rosie.'

'I wish.' Rosie smiled.

'I know you never do, though. As I've said to you before, you must take time for yourself. I follow your work and you don't half rattle some cages. I worry about you.' He paused. 'And today, I can see worry in your eyes.' He took her hand in his. 'So tell me. What brings you here? Are you getting married?' His eyes were full of mischief.

'Er . . . no, Father. Afraid not. I don't think I'd be very good at that.'

'You never know til you try.'

'Well, put it this way, it's not high up on my list of priorities.'

He sighed. 'Who knows? You might be right about that. So. What's going on with you?'

Rosie picked at her fingernails.

'I'm trying to find someone, Father. A family I'm helping. A Kosovan man.'

Rosie watched the priest's face for any sign that he knew anything. She saw a flicker in his eyes. He said nothing.

She continued. 'A Kosovan man, who I met a few days ago, told me that a priest down here took him and his wife and child in when he had failed to present himself at the Refugee Council.'

The priest still said nothing.

'You know about him?'

'Why are you looking for him? Because he's illegal? Sure the country's full of illegals, working all over the shop.'

'So you do know who I'm talking about?' Rosie gave him a wry smile.

'I do, yes.'

'Well, the thing is, now he's in serious trouble. He's already told me his story of what happened to him. I believe him. But now the police are looking for him in connection with those dead bodies dug up in the field at Lennoxtown. I know he's got nothing to do with it. Have you seen the news this morning?'

'No, I haven't. But tell me.'

'This man, Tadi. He's in serious trouble. The police want to talk to him. After he left the priest's house, he was being

held a prisoner with a family out in Lennoxtown. A traveller family, settled travellers, but gangsters. They abused
and beat him, and . . .' She stopped. 'Look, I could tell you
a whole lot more, but I don't have a lot of time here, Father.
Tadi doesn't have a lot of time. I had put him up in a friend's
house but he's done a runner. The only thing he told me at
the beginning was about some old priest down in the East
End.' She looked at him. 'I don't suppose it was you?'

He smiled, as he sipped his tea.

'No, it wasn't, but I know who it is. I know who you're
talking about.'

'Great. Can you get me to him? I think maybe he's gone
back to the priest. Do you know if he has?'

'No I don't. I can find out very quickly, but what are you
going to do with him?'

'He needs to talk to the police, before they find him.
Because if they find him, then it might be too late. He
could get banged up while they investigate. He has to talk
to them.'

'You mean turn himself in?'

'Kind of. But I don't believe he's guilty of anything. But
running . . . Well, you know how it looks.'

He nodded, clasped his hands over his paunch.

'What do you think will happen if he talks to the police?'

'I honestly can't say. But it's a whole lot better than them
bursting down doors if they track him to an address.
They've already put out a description of a man they want

to interview, and it doesn't look good if he keeps on running.'

'I see.' He sighed slowly. 'It's very tricky indeed, if he is where I think he is.'

'Can you find out? Please, Father?'

He said nothing for a long moment, then stood up.

'You drink your tea while I go in and make a phone call.'

Rosie drove Father Dunnachie the short distance to St Kilda's church. They pulled into the driveway and got out of the car.

'I'm really grateful you're helping me like this, Father.'

The priest looked at her and touched her arm.

'I understand, Rosie. I know you well, and I think you want to do the right thing by this family. I think you are right, that they need to not hide themselves away here, as it looks suspicious. But it may be difficult to convince them. It was a hard enough job convincing Flaherty to let you near them. So you'll have to be at your most charming to get over this doorstep.'

Rosie smiled, feeling a little punch of adrenalin. She couldn't afford to lose this. She braced herself as Father Dunnachie pushed the doorbell. After a few seconds the door opened and a short, grey-haired woman appeared, wiping her hands on her apron.

'Hello, Father,' she beamed. 'Father Flaherty is expecting you. Come in.' She smiled at Rosie who smiled her hello back.

The polished hall smelled like all the parish houses she'd

ever been in. Pristine, shining and solid. There was an aroma of something baking in the kitchen. It smelled like apples and it filled the house with a warm, welcoming atmosphere.

'I'm baking apple crumble for dessert today, Father, if you're staying for lunch.'

'Oh, I'd love to, Mary, but I've a mountain of things to do.'

'I'll make you a wee bowl to take away then,' she said.

They passed the kitchen, and Father Dunnachie knocked on the door at the end of the hallway. It opened, and a big burly figure appeared, a ruddy complexion topped off by a shock of black and silver wavy hair. He looked like he'd just walked off a mountain, after a bracing hike.

'Hello, Pat. Howsit going? Come in.' He glanced at Rosie, but it wasn't the friendliest of smiles.

'And this will be Her Majesty's press, no doubt,' he said.

'Not quite.' Rosie stood her ground in the face of his sarcasm. She'd seen the way priests manipulated people with their power all her life, and she was never deferential just because of a dog collar. She stretched out her hand.

'Rosie Gilmour, Father. How you doing?'

'I'm well enough, Rosie. Looking after these lovely people.'

He opened the door and they stepped in. Rosie immediately saw Tadi, standing by the window, looking nervous. Ava looked at her and then away, the same sheepish expression in her eyes from before. The little boy was scribbling with some crayons and paper on the floor, unaware of the drama engulfing his family.

'Tadi. Ava.' Rosie crossed the room towards them. 'How are you? Look. I know you are frightened, and that's why you ran away. But we must talk.'

Tadi nodded and swallowed. She could see the Adam's apple move in his thin neck, his face etched with worry. Rosie turned to the priests who were standing watching. She needed to be alone with Tadi. This was not a decision to be made by a committee, and she had the feeling the big priest was less than onside.

'Do you mind if I have some time alone with Tadi and Ava? I need to let them know some things.'

The priest seemed surprised and glanced at Tadi, then at Father Dunnachie who went towards the door.

'Are you okay with that, Tadi?' Father Flaherty asked.

'Yes,' Tadi said softly.

The big priest looked a little crestfallen, but he opened the door, letting Father Dunnachie out first. Then he looked over his shoulder.

'I'm next door if you need me.'

Rosie didn't look in his direction. She waited a moment until the door had closed, then she spoke to Tadi.

'Tadi, Ava, can you sit for a moment. Please?' She motioned them to the sofa, and sat opposite on an armchair by the fireplace.

Rosie let the silence hang for a few moments, waiting to see if Tadi would speak. He did.

'I'm sorry, Rosie. I was so frightened. I saw the news. The

police are looking for me. I . . . I just ran away. I'm sorry. You have been kind.'

'Please, Tadi,' Rosie spread her hands. 'Don't apologise to me. It's not necessary. I know what you must be feeling and how frightened you are. I totally understand you running away. I should have stayed with you.' She paused and took a breath. 'But, you must know that you cannot live like this for ever. You cannot keep running. It's not right.'

Tadi looked at the floor, then his eyes rested on Jetmir.

'Nothing is right, Rosie. It will never be right because of what I did. How can I protect my child, my wife? I can do nothing.' He shook his head. 'I just don't know what to do . . .' His voice trailed off.

There was no other way to say this, Rosie thought, so just say it.

'Tadi. Listen to me. You must go to the police. You must. If you stay here, eventually they will find you and you must know how it will look that you have been hiding. Please believe me. You must go to the police. And you don't have a lot of time.'

'But what can I say? That I saw a man being killed and that I buried his burnt body, and that I robbed an old couple? They will put me in jail. You know they will.'

'If they come in here right now, or in the next few days or weeks, they will definitely put you in jail, Tadi. And it will be much worse. Don't you understand?'

'I am afraid of police. Afraid for my family.'

'Look. I have contacts with the police. I can talk to them and tell them everything that has happened.'

'Why will they believe you?'

'I'm not saying they will believe me. But if I go to them with you, or talk to them first, then it might be better. It won't be easy, but it will be better than them finding you. Believe me, you don't want police coming barging in and arresting you in front of your family.' Rosie looked at Jetmir. 'You have information that could put those O'Dwyers in prison for the rest of their lives, Tadi. The police will listen to you. Trust me on that. They have to listen to you.'

Tadi took Ava's hands, and she looked at him and then Jetmir.

'Tadi. I think we must trust Rosie. I . . . I don't know. But what can we do?'

Tadi took her face in his hands and stroked her hair.

'I don't know. I don't know.' He turned to Rosie. 'So what do we do, Rosie?'

Rosie's heart skipped a little. She wasn't sure herself how the police would react – perhaps they would be furious that she'd withheld information. But her gut told her they would be happier to have some positive leads on at least one of their investigations right now.

'Okay. What we do now, Tadi, is I go outside and telephone a contact of mine who is a detective with Strathclyde Police. I will meet him shortly and tell him everything. Then we will arrange to take you to the police station. I will ask the priest if Ava and Jetmir can stay with him and I'm sure that will be okay. The important thing is for you to come with me once I make the arrangement.'

He looked at Ava for a long time but they said nothing. Then he spoke.

'Okay. I will go to the police.'

'Good. You're doing the right thing. Let me make a phone call.'

Rosie got up and went out of the room, along the hall and outside. She punched in Don's number.

'Rosie,' Don said. 'How you doing? You fancy meeting later?'

'Hi, Don. Now would be a good time.'

'Now? Why?'

'You know the Kosovan guy you're looking for – I saw on the news that the police put a statement out.'

'Yeah. Some drifter who worked at the farm has disappeared. We're all over it.'

'Listen. I've got him.'

'What the fuck?'

'Yeah. I have him. I can bring him to you. But he's done nothing. Look, it's a long story. But I'm not throwing this guy to the wolves. He's completely innocent.'

There was a pause, then Don answered. 'How do you know?'

'I don't know. But I just know.'

'Oh, right. In a Rosie Gilmour way?'

'Never mind that. I can bring this guy to you, but he's terrified, and he's done nothing. So I want to meet you first. Can you come over to Shettleston? I'll meet you in that cafe on the corner of Shettleston Road. Now?'

'Sure. I'm on my way.'

'Please don't say anything to anyone.'

'Course not.'

CHAPTER TWENTY-THREE

Rosie fidgeted with her mobile as she waited in the cafe for Don. She felt tense and edgy, even though she believed she was doing the right thing. She'd already phoned McGuire to let him know she'd tracked Tadi down, and what she planned to do. He told her he was impressed at how swiftly she'd found him, and joked that she must have had him all the time and was just winding him up. He agreed that it was time to call in the police and his parting words were, 'Let's hope for the best.' The best, Rosie thought. It was hard to see what choices poor Tadi had that could ever amount to 'the best'. He'd already fled war in his own country, only to be enslaved by a family of gangsters who involved him in robbery and murder. Was it really best for him to give himself up to the cops? she asked herself. She concluded that of all his shitty options, this was the only real one he had left. She'd also called Adrian to tell him the news. He was just as cautious as Tadi about going to the police, but he also knew there were few choices. She hoped to meet him later when she came out of the police station. Rosie looked up when she heard Don's voice.

'You are totally mental, Gilmour.' He sat down opposite her. 'How the fuck do you get yourself into situations like this?'

'Just lucky, I suppose.' Rosie shrugged.

The waitress came up and she ordered two coffees.

'So tell me about it, Rosie. Have you really got this Kosovan guy?'

Rosie nodded. 'Yeah. Well, as long as he's not done another runner. I had him for a couple of days, then he went missing this morning. But I managed to find him.'

'Why the fuck are you only telling me this now, Rosie?'

Rosie looked at him and raised her eyebrows.

'How was I to know you were looking for this particular guy? First I hear of it is on the news.'

Don sighed. 'It was just a line we had to put out. I mean, for fuck's sake. How was I to know you were already dealing with him?'

'Anyway,' Rosie said, 'I have him. I met him in one of the fields near where you were digging, and he looked like a poor soul. But the thing is, do you know who this guy is?'

'Nope. How the fuck would I know?'

'Remember that day in the High Court, when Boag escaped?'

'Like I'll ever forget it.'

'Well. Remember outside, the guy who was in court for trying to trap the seagull?'

Don looked puzzled for a moment, then the penny dropped.

'Oh fuck. It's not him, is it?'

'Yep. Remember, we saw him getting huckled by the bloke in the car and you took the number plate and checked it for me?'

Don looked at Rosie, his mouth dropping a little.

'Fuck me! O'Dwyer? That bastard O'Dwyer family. He was staying with them? Was he working for them?'

'Not working, Don. Imprisoned. A slave. Held there against his will, and the shit beaten out of him on a regular basis. Not just him, other guys too. That's what these bastards do. They keep slaves.'

'Fuck's sake. That's far-fetched. I know they're gangsters, but who keeps slaves in this day and age?'

'You mean apart from the sex slaves in the brothels all over the city?'

'Well. You know what I mean. Apart from that.'

'That's what he was. A slave. And he's told me everything. What he's done. It's really serious. The guy's terrified. To be honest, I'm shitting myself handing him over, but there's no other way.'

'What has he done?'

Rosie took a breath and said nothing for a long moment.

'You know the bodies you dug up? The burnt guy?'

'Yeah. We've got an ID on him now, from dental records. Robert Bowman, a drunk down-and-out. Went by the name of Bo.'

Rosie's eyes lit up.

'Bo? That confirms Tadi's telling me the truth.'

'How?'

'He told me he and some other guys held at the farm were forced to watch as O'Dwyer kicked this Bo guy to within an inch of his life. Then O'Dwyer's boy poured petrol over him and O'Dwyer threw a match onto him.'

Don's face dropped.

'For fuck's sake!'

'Yeah. Then they made Tadi and the others take him to the field and bury him.' Rosie paused, watching Don. 'That was when Tadi found out there were other bodies in the field. He felt the spade hit something, and there they were. He thought it might be a mother and a baby.'

'Oh fuck! And this guy can tell us all this?'

'Yeah.'

'What if he's lying to cover his tracks?'

'Why would a guy on the run from Kosovo suddenly start doing things like that?'

Don shrugged and said nothing.

'But there's more. Hold onto your pants for this.'

The waitress arrived and placed the coffees on the table. Don drank some of his and put the cup down, eyes wide.

'It was the O'Dwyers who did the robbery of the old Jewish couple – the Cimmermans.'

'What?'

'Yep. They made Tadi go with them. He was in the house. He was disgusted by what he saw them do.'

'Fucking hell. He's told you all this?'

'Yeah. And, wait for it, he has that photograph the old woman was talking about. He took it out of the safe. O'Dwyer ordered him to empty the safe and the picture was there, but for some reason he doesn't even know himself, he stuck it in his shirt pocket.'

'He has that picture?'

'Yep. This guy is an innocent man. I'd stake my life on it.'

'Where is he?'

'Close by. But just hold on a minute. I want to bring him in my car. You can come behind in your car, or get some help, but he goes with me.'

'Rosie. I'll get my arse kicked for that.'

'Don. Tell your boss you do it my way, or not at all.'

He puffed out a frustrated sigh, then took his mobile out.

'You'll have to come in as well, Rosie. They'll want a statement.'

'Sure. As long as they let me back out,' Rosie joked, but she could see Don wasn't smiling.

Tadi had been silent in the back seat of the car as Rosie drove Father Dunnachie back to his home, on their way to the police. Don's car followed close behind, and she could see in her rear-view mirror that he had a passenger – probably one of the detectives he worked alongside. Behind Don's car, a police panda car was following at a discreet distance. It was clear that Tadi was going nowhere. Rosie had to keep telling herself that she was doing the right thing, but at this moment, she felt that things were slipping away from her, even though they weren't – well, not yet. She and Father Dunnachie had stood in the hallway while Tadi said his goodbyes to Ava and Jetmir. Father Flaherty had said very little, but his face had distrust and betrayal written all over it. Rosie hoped she'd prove him wrong, and that Tadi would be back soon enough. The priest had embraced him before he left, and Tadi swallowed hard as he came into the hall and they headed for the door.

They pulled into the back car park of the Pitt Street station, as Don instructed, and an operative on the entrance lifted the bar to let their car through. Rosie parked and got out of the car, opening the door for Tadi, who came out of the back seat and stood beside her. She could see his hands were shaking. Don pulled up and jumped out of the car along with the other detective.

'My name is Detective Sergeant Don Elliot, Tadi.' He didn't shake hands. Then he turned to Rosie.

'Rosie, we'll take it from here. But you're to come upstairs with us, as they want to have a chat with you.'

'Who wants to have a chat?'

'Not sure. But it'll be okay. I've told them what you told me. So obviously you feature in this story. You fine with that?'

'Yeah.' Rosie shrugged, but she wasn't really fine. Nerves fluttered across her stomach. She wasn't in the mood to take any crap from any cops who might want to give her a hard time. 'Let's go then.' She smiled at Tadi.

Once they got inside the building, they were met by a female plain-clothes officer and another, older male detective. The older man approached Rosie.

'I'm Detective Inspector James Morton, Rosie. This is DC Janice Forsyth. If you'll come with us please?'

'Sure,' Rosie said, feeling a sudden sense of foreboding. 'I'm just going to bell my editor and let him know. He's been trying to get me.'

The officers looked at each other but said nothing, and they walked on ahead as Rosie punched in McGuire's private line.

'Mick, it's me. I'm up at Pitt Street. They want a chat with me.'

'What kind of chat, Gilmour? They're not going to fucking arrest you, are they?'

'Er . . . I hope not. Hard to say at the moment. Look, I can't talk long, but just wanted to let you know.' She hoped she was conveying her sense of unease.

'I've got a bad feeling about this, Rosie. I hope it's not all going to go tits up. I'm going to alert Hanlon anyway, just in case you end up in the pokey. If I don't hear from you in an hour, I'm sending him up there.'

'Might not be a bad idea,' Rosie said as she walked behind the officers along a corridor on the second floor. 'Talk later. I have to go.'

'Don't be taking any shit . . . But don't be making trouble either.'

'Thank you, Henry Kissinger,' Rosie said as she hung up.

The officers directed Rosie into a small room. It looked suspiciously like the kind of room where they interview suspects, and similar to the one she was taken to a couple of years back when the police tried to frame her for cocaine possession. Despite their bullying tactics then as she investigated corruption at top level in the police, despite them planting cocaine in her flat, she was still able to bring down the Chief Constable and one of his cohorts. This was a bit different, she hoped. DI Morton looked at his watch, then went out of the room, leaving her with the detective constable, who stood with her hands clasped in front of her.

'So, what happens now?' Rosie asked as soon as the door was closed.

The detective gave her a look that said you should know better than to ask that. 'Er, I think you probably know that I won't be able to comment.'

Rosie shrugged. There was no point in trying to strike up a friendship here.

'Just wondered who was coming to talk to me.'

The officer looked at her and then beyond her out of the window, where the sky was turning grey.

'Looks like we're in for some heavy rain,' she said.

Rosie couldn't help but smile. They didn't half turn them out these days to despise the press – especially the tabloids. The officer straightened up suddenly at the sound of the door handle being turned. It opened and DI Morton breezed in. He flicked a glance at Rosie and she looked up and met his steely grey eyes staring back at her with what she could only describe as contempt. This was not looking good.

He crossed the room and stretched his hand out.

'I'm in charge of this inquiry, Miss Gilmour.' He gave her a firm handshake and held it a second longer than necessary. 'Just so we are clear about that.'

There was no way to answer that, Rosie decided, other than to say your boys were not exactly performing well, so she bit her tongue, saying instead, 'How're you doing?' and watching him as he went round behind the desk so that he was sitting opposite her.

Another officer, younger and obviously dressed by the same tailor, pulled up a chair and sat alongside his boss. Rosie waited and watched as the DI placed a sheaf of papers on the desk and took a pen out of his inside pocket. He looked at the desk for a long moment, then up at her. Again with the fixed stare. On another face it might have been attractive, Rosie thought, but along with the general demeanour that he was putting out, she braced herself for trouble.

'I might as well get to the point,' he began. 'Firstly, we're obviously grateful that you got in touch to bring us the man we've been looking for over the past couple of days. We think he may be crucial to our investigation. So we do appreciate your help.' He paused, looking at Rosie, as though he was expecting her to smile coyly. She didn't. She just stared back. 'But the fact of the matter is, you have been in possession of this information for the past few days. Let me put it another way. If this man turns out to be a suspect in any part of our investigations – and from what I hear, he has made a full confession to you – then you, Rosie Gilmour, have been harbouring a suspect.' Another pause. 'That is a criminal offence. But I'm sure you know that.'

He waited and Rosie felt she'd better say something.

'I think that's putting it a bit rough, Inspector. The man came to me for help. I was aware that it was the police he should be talking to, but he was frightened.'

'Well, if he's witnessed a murder, buried a body and taken part in a vicious robbery, then he's every right to be frightened of the police.'

'All of which was done against his will.'

'Yes, so he says. But if you don't mind, we'll be the ones investigating whether he's telling the truth. And right now, we're several days behind – thanks to you. What were you trying to prove? That you could do all this yourself?'

'Don't be ridiculous,' Rosie snapped. 'I told you. The guy was terrified. He's a foreigner, living as a slave in a foreign country, his wife held somewhere else. If you guys were doing your job it would be the bloody O'Dwyers and the likes of them you'd be looking at.'

'Don't tell me how we should do our job. It's not smart – sitting where you're sitting.' He sat back. 'Listen. I know your reputation goes before you, Rosie, and you'll get a bit of respect for that from this side of the table, but this is a serious criminal investigation. It's not for the tabloids to decide when to get the police involved. In my opinion, you've been allowed to get away with this crap too often. And I'll tell you this – it's about to change now that I'm running the show here.'

Rosie glanced from the inspector to his detective, who was sitting staring at the desk, avoiding her eyes. She should take the heat out of this by being civil, but she couldn't resist it.

'Fine. I'll remember that the next time I'm able to deliver a serial killer to you – who then manages to escape from custody. Oh, and the next time I bring a poor bastard refugee to you, who actually got murdered while in police protection.' She felt her face burn. 'Listen, Inspector. Don't try to monster me. If every story or investigation I did was a straightforward case of passing information on to the police, then my job would be easy. But I'm a journalist, not a cop, so I have a job to do too.'

She could see the colour rise in the chief's face as she spoke, but now it was calming down. He clicked his pen, knuckles white.

'Okay, Rosie. I think we're quite clear here on who should be doing what. But right now, this Kosovan man is in custody, helping police with inquiries, and it will stay that way until we can eliminate him. So we'll need a full statement from you. Then we can make a decision regarding your part in this.'

'What do you mean?'

'I mean whether or not you will face charges of harbouring a suspect.'

'Aw, for Christ's sake!'

'Is that the start of your statement, Rosie?' There was something resembling amusement behind his eyes, and she realised he was toying with her.

'Yeah. It is. Make that the start of my statement. And, I have to phone my editor. I'm not making a statement without my lawyer present.'

'Sure. Go ahead.' The inspector stood up. 'I'll be back in ten minutes.' He turned to the other officer. 'Get Rosie a coffee, will you?'

She sat fuming, filled with disbelief and worry over what they were doing to Tadi. She scrolled down to McGuire's number.

CHAPTER TWENTY-FOUR

Rosie finished her coffee as she watched Sky News, where a Strathclyde Police inspector from the public relations department was trying to say as little as possible about the fact that a Kosovan man was helping them with their inquiries.

'Does this mean you are following a direct line of inquiry, Inspector?' asked one reporter.

'It means we are currently interviewing this man as part of our investigation.'

'Is he a suspect?'

'I cannot comment further at the moment. All I can say is what we put out in the statement earlier – that we are questioning a man who worked in the area,' the inspector replied.

'I understand he disappeared while police were digging the field. Is that true?'

'I cannot comment,' he said wearily.

'Inspector. One last question,' said another hack. 'Is it true that police are also questioning a newspaper reporter regarding withholding information?'

The inspector looked at the reporter and sighed. 'No comment. Now if you don't mind, we'll keep you informed of any developments.'

'Bastard,' Rosie said out loud. She recognised the voice asking the last question as the big reporter from the *Sun* newspaper, who was always at least four steps behind her on every story. But he obviously had contacts somewhere inside the police who had dropped him the titbit that Rosie had been quizzed last night. It wasn't an important part of the investigation from where anyone was sitting, but it was always a good ploy to get the boot into the opposition. And now that he'd said it on camera in front of the rest of the media, they would push the police for a proper answer. She cursed again and got up, taking her cup to the kitchen and running the tap on it. She came into the living room and stood at her balcony window, gazing at the traffic and the movement of people starting their day. She thought of Tadi – wondered what kind of night he'd had. Don had called her last night to say that Tadi was being held overnight, because he had confessed to the robbery. He was in trouble over that, Don had said. But he got the impression that the detectives interviewing him, including DI Morton, believed his story. He told her not to get her knickers in a twist, and that Tadi was being looked after. But he was being held as much for his own protection as the investigation. They were also going to be looking at the O'Dwyers today. They'd previously been interviewed by a couple of plods in plain clothes that they'd managed to deceive, but the gloves were off now. Rosie told Don they'd be lucky if the O'Dwyers were still there, but he said that Rory O'Dwyer would brazen it out, because he was that pig-headed and cocky. He believed he was untouchable.

But even with all of Tadi's information about the farm and the man he saw being murdered, nothing shed any light on the young couple and the mother and baby who were also in the grave. They were no further forward on that. Rosie made her mind up to go down to the farm at some stage today, and see if she could get a chance to talk to O'Dwyer's wife. Tadi had said she was kind to him, so this just might be the way in. She picked up her bag, and as she was heading down the hallway, her front doorbell rang. When she opened it, the postman stood there with a package.

'Recorded delivery. Needs a signature.'

Rosie smiled at him but got no response. Nothing like an all-singing, all-dancing postman to start your day.

'Cheers.' She took the package and signed his clipboard.

She closed the door and examined the postmark, but it was smudged and she couldn't make it out. It felt quite heavy. She wasn't expecting anything, so she looked at the large brown box with suspicion. Old habits died hard. What if it was a bomb from the UVF – a parting gift for her big drugs mule exposé on them last year? She would take it to the office and open it, she decided. She put it under her arm, went downstairs and sat it on the passenger seat of her car.

The editorial floor was already busy with early shift reporters at their desks, mostly chatting and answering phones – nobody had really started serious work yet. The news editors were glued to their screens. She could see McGuire at the back bench, sitting with his feet up on the desk sipping coffee, chatting to one of the artists. He looked up, shook his head and smiled as he saw her. She hadn't come into the office after Hanlon got her sprung from the police last night. She'd called him to say she was free, and he'd joked about starting a petition to release her. She put the package on the desk and greeted Declan who was about to pick up his phone.

'You made it then, Rosie? I thought they'd try to do you on withholding information.'

'I think they'd love to. But I honestly don't think it would fly. Anyway, the good news from my contact is that the cops believe Tadi's story – so far anyway. So at least he's not getting charged – well, not right now.'

Rosie lifted the package.

'This came in the post to my house this morning. So I

thought I'd bring it down here – in case it's a bomb.' She smiled at Declan.

'Cheers for that,' he said, putting the receiver back down. 'I might just get out of the way while you open it.'

'Don't be daft. It'll be all right.'

'Do you think you should open it? I mean, really? What if it is a bomb?'

'Don't worry. It'll be some mail order crap that I can't remember ordering.'

Rosie took the scalpel she used for sharpening her pencils from her drawer and cut it open carefully around the tape. Inside, bubble wrap covered a box. The box had a clown's face on the lid, and she tore away at the bubble wrap until the box was unwrapped.

'Maybe it's a jack-in-the-box. Like Jack jumps out and stabs you in the eye?' Declan said as he stood back a little.

'Look at you, shitting yourself,' Rosie joked.

Then she sliced the tape from the lid and eased it off.

'Oh, fuck!'

Rosie gasped and staggered backwards, the shock almost knocking her off her feet. Inside the box was the severed head of what looked like a woman. Perfectly preserved. Bloody at the neck where it had been hacked off, long hair matted with blood. Suddenly the whole room was swimming and she steadied herself on the desk and slumped onto her seat. Her hand went to her mouth.

'I think I'm going to be sick. Fuck! Declan. It's a head. Oh, Jesus Christ!'

Declan stepped forward and looked inside.

'What? Oh, fuck! Fuck's sake, Rosie! Oh my God!'

The editor looked up, his eyes narrowing. Then he saw Rosie, jumped to his feet and rushed across the few yards to her desk.

'What the fuck's going on?'

Rosie looked up at him.

'Shit, Mick. It's a head. A severed head. A woman.'

McGuire looked at her, incredulous, then glanced in the box and stood back, aghast.

'Aw, for fuck's sake! Call the cops! Quick! Fucking Christ almighty! What the fuck is going on?'

Declan was standing at the box again, his face ashen.

'Rosie. That's . . . That's Jenny Cassidy, if I'm not mistaken. You know, the downstairs neighbour of Boag? The woman who's been missing for months? I recognise her from her picture. I'm sure it's her. Look. There's a bit of paper stuffed in her mouth.'

'Oh, Christ!' Rosie looked up at McGuire. 'It's Boag, Mick. He sent this to me. It came to my bloody house. I've carted it all the way down here in the passenger seat of my car. Jesus wept!' She stood up. 'I need to go to the loo.'

'Dec. Phone security,' the editor said. 'I want someone here til the cops come. Keep people away from these desks.' He spread a hand indicating the immediate three desks, where some reporters stood dumbstruck. 'And put the fucking lid back on before I bring up my kippers.'

Rosie rushed to the toilet and promptly vomited up her breakfast. She sat on the toilet afterwards, shaking, her face sweaty from retching. Every nerve in her body was on edge. Boag knew where she lived. He had sent a severed head to her home. *To her home.* Christ almighty! The toilet door opened and one of the young reporters came in.

'You all right? The editor says to come into his office when you're ready. The cops are on their way. Fucking hell, Rosie. This is right off the scale.'

Rosie was somewhere between hysteria and disbelief as she sat in the editor's office. She sipped from a mug of sweet tea Marion had put into her hand. Judging by the grim look on McGuire's face, he was as stunned as her.

'It doesn't get much more serious than this, Rosie.'

She nodded, a sudden choking in her throat with the realisation that nothing would be the same from now on. It wasn't just the image of the head. Boag had sent this to her home. Had he been watching her? Following her every move? Maybe he had even been in her flat. She shivered.

'I'm scared, Mick.' She picked at her fingernails.

McGuire rushed to the sofa and sat beside her. He put a comforting arm around her shoulder.

'I know, sweetheart,' he said, pulling her a little closer and patting her hair. 'I know.'

They sat that way for a long moment, Rosie allowing herself to be held. McGuire's phone rang on his desk and he let go.

'That'll be the cops.' He took her by the shoulders. 'You okay?'

Rosie nodded, pulling in a breath and puffing hard.

'Yes. It's just the shock. I'll be fine in a little while.'

McGuire went to his desk and lifted the receiver.

'Okay, Marion. Send them in.'

His door opened and Rosie looked up as the tall figure of Detective Inspector James Morton came in, his face a mask of concern. A younger detective was behind him and they both looked from Rosie to the editor.

'Chaps,' McGuire said. 'Some fucking turn-up for the books this, is it not?'

'That's one way of putting it.' The chief strode across to the editor and stretched out a hand. 'Detective Inspector James Morton.' He jerked his head behind him. 'This is Detective Sergeant Alan Mason.'

McGuire looked across at Rosie and was about to introduce them.

'We've already met.' The DI looked at Rosie, his expression softening a little. 'Christ, Rosie. Can you not give us plods a bit of peace?'

Rosie smiled thinly. 'Yeah. Just attention-seeking, Inspector.'

'Jim.'

His demeanour was completely different from the con-frontational figure she'd encountered yesterday, when he was flexing his muscles.

The inspector turned to the editor. 'Rosie and I had a chat yesterday after she brought the Kosovan to our office. Well, more of a run-in than a chat.'

'Good. So what do you think, Jim?' McGuire asked. He motioned them to sit. 'Take a seat, lads, I'll get some tea. What happens now?' McGuire went to the door and told Marion to bring some tea.

'Right now, we've arrived with a full team. Forensics, the whole shooting match. We'll get the box out of your way as soon as we can, Mr McGuire. But it's a bit of a process with forensics. They'll be checking everything in case there are any fibres or stuff they can trace.' He turned to Rosie. 'It came to your house then? Can you talk us through it, Rosie? And listen, I know this is hard and you'll be in shock. So just take your time. You okay with that?'

'Sure. I'm a bit better now. I just about passed out though, when I opened the box. I've seen some stuff in my life, but that's just right out the park. My nightmares will be a bit special now.'

Rosie was trying to tough it out. She couldn't cope with the sympathy in the room right now, or she'd break down in front of everyone, and that just wouldn't do. She described her morning and how she'd met the postman. The DS took notes as she told them how she had carried it to her car and brought it to the office. She suddenly burst out laughing,

'I still can't believe I drove down here with a woman's head on the passenger seat. I mean, really. You couldn't make this up!'

'That's for sure,' he said. 'Forensics will need to go through your car, and your house, I'm afraid. Everywhere you put the box down.'

Rosie nodded and they sat for a moment in silence.

'He's following me, isn't he? What was that stuffed in her mouth? A note?'

The DI looked at the editor, then at Rosie. Marion came in with a tray with cups of tea and put it on the table in front of them.

'It was.'

'Is it from Boag?'

'It would appear to be.'

'Have you read it?'

The DI nodded. He went into his inside pocket and took out a clear polythene evidence bag. Everyone watched as he put rubber gloves on and eased it out. Rosie could feel her heart beating faster.

'I can tell you what it says, Rosie. But if you don't want to, we can leave it.'

'I want to know,' Rosie said a little too quickly. 'I . . . I need to know.' She put her hand to her lip to stop it trembling.

'Rosie.' McGuire frowned at her.

'Mick, I need to know what I'm dealing with here. This bastard's delivering a head to my door, I need to know what he's saying.'

'Have you ever met Boag, Rosie?' The DI asked.

'No. Course not. Well, not to my knowledge anyway. Why?'

'Well, he hints that he knows you.'

Rosie felt her stomach lurch.

'Can you read me the note, please?'

He glanced at the DS, then cleared his throat as he began.

'"This is what happens when you ask too many questions, Rosie Gilmour. I'm watching you. You're not that clever. You don't see me, but I see you. Petrol stations are lonely places at night."'

A chill ran through Rosie and she visibly shuddered.

'Jesus! Bastard is following me!'

'That bit about the petrol station. When were you last at a petrol station at night?'

For a few seconds Rosie's mind went blank. All she could see was herself looking over her shoulder every moment of the day. She heard the DI's question in the distance. Then she remembered.

'Oh, Christ!' She looked from Mick to the chief. 'I was in the petrol station three nights ago, on the way home. About half ten. The one up off Byres Road.'

'Great. We can check the CCTV. I don't suppose you noticed anyone. Was it busy?'

'No. I don't think so. Actually, I don't even remember. Sorry. To be honest my head has been all over the place the last few days. Snowed under with work, and I can't even remember where I was coming from the other night. You know what it's like. You go in, get petrol and you barely look at the guy on the til. I'm sure everyone's the same.' She shook her head. 'Do you think he could have been in there? Maybe even behind me or something?' Rosie lifted her cup, but feeling her hands shaking, she put it back down. She could see McGuire clocking it.

'We need to get you some protection, Rosie. Proper protection this time.'

She didn't protest.

'We can take care of that, Mick. In fact, we'll be taking care of it from here on in, Rosie. You should move out of the house, and we'll put you somewhere safe.'

'But I'm working. I'm in the middle of an investigation. I'm on the story about Tadi and his family, and the O'Dwyers. I want to do that. What's happening to Tadi, by the way?'

'Don't worry about him at the moment. He's not going to face charges, but we have to hold onto him. Leave that for the moment. Can you think of any other places you've been to lately where there might be CCTV?'

Rosie considered for a moment.

'Maybe in the street? I had dinner at a bistro the other night with a friend. I was at the supermarket. I can give you some details of where I was in the past week if I can get time to think. But what if he's been watching me for a while – maybe even before he was arrested? What if he was reading my stories before the cops moved in? Jesus! It could have been my head in that box.'

'Well, we're not going to allow that to happen,' the DI said. 'Look. I'm going back out there for a bit to talk to the lads. You have a think and relax a bit, then we'll make some plans for you. But listen, try not to worry. I know that's all right coming from me, but you'll be protected, Rosie. We'll have someone with you twenty-four seven.'

He stood up, his DS also got to his feet and they left the room.

Rosie looked at McGuire.

'This is serious, isn't it, Mick?'

'Yeah. But you'll be fine. Let's work out where you want to go. You can still work, but you need to be somewhere safe.'

'I don't want cops with me all the time. Not in my face, anyway. I can stay in my house. The cops can watch me from there.' She paused. 'I have my friend here.'

'Who?'

'Adrian's here. I can ask him to stay a while longer.'

'The big Bosnian? Great. If ever there's a man for punching somebody's ticket it's him. Call him.' He looked at her.

'And maybe you should take the rest of the day off. Just relax while we work out where to put you.'

'No. I've got stuff to do. I don't want to be sitting around, letting things multiply in my mind.'

'Fair enough.'

Rosie got up and walked towards the door, conscious that the editor was watching her as she left.

CHAPTER TWENTY-FIVE

Adrian was leaning on Rosie's car, smoking a cigarette, as she left the office and headed for the car park. She had asked him to come with her to have a look at O'Dwyer's place to see what they could pick up. When she'd phoned him, struggling to get the words out about what had just happened, he told her he'd be at the office in fifteen minutes. As he saw her coming towards him, she could see him studying her face, waiting for her to break down. He squeezed her arm.

'You are all right, Rosie?'

'Yes. I'm okay. Come on, let's go. I've got things to talk to you about on the way.'

By the time they were on the outskirts of Lennoxtown, Adrian had agreed to stay on in Glasgow for the next few weeks to make sure she was safe. He didn't trust the police to do the job, and she told him that she didn't want a policeman living in her house, which she knew would be what they would suggest. She couldn't have Adrian living in her house either, she told him. And she didn't want to have TJ there all the time. TJ meant the world to her and she knew he would happily move in so she wouldn't be alone, but Rosie knew it wouldn't work. She needed her own space – always had – and that was one of the reasons she had not taken things further with TJ. She sometimes wished she wasn't so afraid of commitment. Adrian agreed to be with her any time she needed him, and for the moment that made her feel safe. The conversation was professional, which seemed ridiculous, given that a few months ago he'd been sharing her bed. She didn't address the subject, but it was the elephant in the room. Rosie decided she would talk to him about it in a more relaxed way when they went for a bite to eat in the next couple of days. But right now, there were more pressing matters. As they drove past the O'Dwyers' property there were none of the usual pickup trucks or big cars in the yard. Only a small red car parked next to the house. There was no sign of any workers around the place and she wondered if O'Dwyer had let them go, or if they'd met the same fate as poor Bo. He wouldn't just turn them free – they knew too much. But there was a sinister emptiness about the place as Rosie drove into the yard. The only sounds were the dogs barking behind a high wire fence, screening off what looked like a scrapyard.

'If you wait in the car, Adrian, I'll give the door a knock.'

She walked round to where the car was parked, which seemed to be the back door of the house. She waited for a second, listening to hear if there was any activity inside. Then she saw a television blaring in the corner of the room. There was no buzzer, so she gave the door a firm knock, then glanced in the kitchen. She waited a few seconds. Nothing. She knocked again, this time a little harder. Eventually she heard a door being opened and she peered in the window to see a woman coming into the kitchen. She looked about the right age to be O'Dwyer's wife, and she walked towards the door, glancing out of the kitchen window to where Rosie was on the doorstep. Then she opened the door. It was the black eye that Rosie saw first, bruised and slightly swollen. Recent, by the look of it. Her short hair was in an old-fashioned style that made her face look even plumper than it was. The eye that wasn't swollen was pale and bloodshot, and the woman looked worn out. Her lips were full, but pale, with no trace of make-up, and she was dressed casually in a baggy top and loose-fitting trousers. She looked at Rosie, waiting for her to speak.

'Mrs O'Dwyer?'

'Yes. Who are you, please?'

'Is Mr O'Dwyer home at the moment?'

'No, he's not. He's out on a bit of business.'

Rosie detected an accent, a trace of Irish.

'My name is Rosie Gilmour, Mrs O'Dwyer. I'm from the *Post* newspaper.'

The woman sighed and took a step back. 'Aw, now look! I'm not wanting any reporters around here. We've had them over the last day or so, people poking around. But my husband made it clear to them we've nothing to say.'

'Okay,' Rosie said. 'I take it the reporters were here because of that Kosovan man who went missing? The police were looking for him. It was a very strange turn for the story to take, so that's why you'd have the press calling down here asking questions.'

Mrs O'Dwyer said nothing. Rosie chanced it.

'Did you know the Kosovan man very well, Mrs O'Dwyer? I understand he'd worked here for a few months. With the cars and things.'

She looked over Rosie's shoulder into the yard. 'So they found him then?'

'Tadi? Is that who you mean?'

Mary nodded.

'Yes. They say he's helping with their inquiries. They're very suspicious because of the circumstances he left in. You know, with the bodies being dug up. One minute he's been working here a few months, and the next he's done a runner. You can imagine how that looks.'

'He wouldn't do anything like that, the Kosovan fella. He was quiet. Hard-working. A family man.'

'Do you know where his family is? A wife and son, I

believe.' Rosie was trying to draw her, and as long as the door wasn't getting slammed in her face she was winning.

'I've no idea. But I hope he's not in any trouble. He was all right, you know.'

'Have you been watching the news about the bodies they found up there?'

'Well, it's never off the telly, is it? Hard to avoid. That poor young couple out camping . . .' She shook her head and her lips tightened.

'Yes,' Rosie said. 'A real tragedy. The police are no further with finding out who did that. But the other thing was the body of the woman and the baby. That was just awful. A little one in its mother's arms . . .'

Rosie let her voice trail off, because she could see something in Mrs O'Dwyer's eyes that looked as though she was remembering. Her lips quivered a little.

'The child was only four weeks old, according to what I hear,' Rosie continued. 'Somebody must have killed her and then dumped her there. What kind of monster does that?'

Rosie had no idea who had killed the woman and child, but she could see that the image was resonating with Mrs O'Dwyer. Because now her eyes were filling with tears and suddenly she stepped back.

'I have to go,' she said. 'Now, go away. You people aren't helping coming around here. You can't help that poor woman now, with her wee babba, and you can't help that young couple, God love them. I can't talk to you, you'll only make it worse.'

'Make what worse?' Rosie persisted.

'Everything.' She lightly touched her bruised eye. 'Just go away. I can't say anything. It's all a mess. The police up and down here, and aw, Jesus, those poor people.'

She looked like she was about to go into meltdown, but Rosie couldn't bring herself to walk away. She was hiding something, and she had to try to tease it out. Tadi had told her that she'd helped him – that it was her who told him to leave. She knew about the robbery, and it was only a matter of time until the police knocked on her door and took her in as a witness in their investigation. She was a lot more aware of her husband's criminal activities than she dared admit, but that was the problem. Her black eye was probably the result of her saying something out of turn to big O'Dwyer. Rosie tried to press on.

'Mrs O'Dwyer – Molly. Listen. I know that you helped Tadi, the Kosovan.'

Rosie let the words hang there, then put her hand up when she didn't answer.

'Don't worry. Nobody knows that I know this, except Tadi and you. He's spoken to me. He came to see me at the newspaper. He's told me everything.'

'Tadi?' She looked shocked. 'Is he all right? Is he in the jail? He didn't kill those people.'

'I know he didn't,' Rosie said. 'I know he also took part in the robbery of the old Jewish couple, along with your husband, your son Finn, and some others. You know that, don't you?'

Molly's mouth dropped open a little and she stood back.

'Go away from here. Go away and never come back and never come here when my husband is in and say what you've just said to me. I'm warning you. Go away now, while you can. My husband will be back in the next hour or two. You don't want to be here asking questions when he comes in.'

She was closing the door, but Rosie put her foot firmly in it and gave it one last shot.

'Tadi has told me about Bo, and what Rory O'Dwyer did, Molly. The police will get him eventually. You'll be part of that cover-up if you hide things for him. Look after yourself.' She let her glance linger on her bust eye. 'From where I'm standing, it looks like you have to.'

The door slammed shut and Rosie stood for a moment in the eerie silence. One thing she was sure of was that Molly knew a lot more about O'Dwyer than just the robberies and murder of Bo. Perhaps it was wishful thinking, but Rosie felt that despite Molly's protests, her heart wasn't in defending her husband much longer.

Later, exhaustion hit Rosie like a train. By mid afternoon she was feeling light-headed. McGuire told her he could see she was only half listening to anything he was saying, as they planned where to go next on the story of Tadi. Now that he was with the police, the media was speculating on whether he was a suspect, trying to dig up any background on him. The *Daily Mail*'s line was that immigrants brought more trouble than they contributed, and should all be sent home. No surprise there, as the right-wing tabloid had a xenophobic streak a mile wide. McGuire was as frustrated as Rosie that they couldn't publish the real story about Tadi – because the bottom line was there was no proof. Plus the fact that the police were asking them to hang fire as they continued their investigation. It was out of her hands for the moment, but at least Tadi was safe, and hopefully so were Ava and the little boy. The editor told Rosie to go home and relax, as she wasn't much good to anyone walking around like a zombie. The other newspapers and media were in a frenzy over the delivery of the severed head to Rosie's home, and the editor's phone was red hot with requests for interviews. Not today, he'd told all of them. The story had been confirmed by the police, so they'd have to go on what they had. Rosie was glad, and agreed to go home. McGuire only allowed her to go to her own flat because DI Morton had telephoned him to say there would be a twenty-four-hour police presence outside her house for the foreseeable future. There would also be a police car follow-ing her wherever she went. She didn't expect to feel glad about that, but she was, and as she drove up to her flat she could see the unmarked car pull out of the *Post* car park behind her. There was another car outside the flats when she arrived. She gave them a cursory nod, as two officers got out of the car and followed her up to the front door, then went in after her. It felt really strange, but comforting at the same time. She let herself inside the door of her flat.

'We'll do a quick check of the place, Rosie, if that's okay.'

'Sure,' she said, standing in the hallway.

A couple of minutes later, they returned.

'It's all fine. We've been out there the whole time anyway, but we're to check just in case.'

'Thanks,' Rosie said as she led them to the door. 'I really appreciate it – even if it does feel a little weird.'

They didn't answer, and left.

She locked up and stood with her back to the door, letting out a long sigh. The choking emotion that had come after the head-in-the-box incident had gone. Now it all felt surreal, but the most overwhelming feeling was tiredness. Before she did anything else, she made a quick check of her bedroom, in all the wardrobes and even under the bed – just in case. Then she ran a hot bath, kicked off her clothes, and made a cup of tea. It was too early to drink wine. Two hours later, Rosie woke up on the top of her bed, still in her bathrobe, as the phone rang beside her. She opened one eye. It was TJ. She hadn't told him what had happened.

'Hey, you. Still working?'

'No.' Rosie yawned. 'Just woke up.'

'What? It's five o'clock. How come you're asleep?'

'I got the afternoon off. I was knackered, so I had a bath and crashed out. I didn't mean to sleep so long.'

'What's going on that you're sloping off to bed in the afternoon, sweetheart?'

'I'll tell you when I see you.'

'You've not been sacked, have you?'

Rosie chuckled. It was good to hear his voice. 'No. Not yet. Something happened today, and it took the feet from under me.'

'You in trouble? Tell me.'

She yawned again. 'You wouldn't believe it if I did. So let's save it for the first gin and tonic. I'll see you at the La Trevi.'

'I can't wait. Will I come and meet you at the flat?'

'No, I'll walk up.'

She hung up. She hadn't seen TJ for nearly a week and had been looking forward to tonight. But everything had changed now because of Boag. Somehow this bastard had avoided the entire police force of Scotland, yet he was managing to stalk her. That could mean that TJ was also in danger. The newspapers would be full of the severed head story by tomorrow, so she had to tell him about it first.

TJ listened, his expression somewhere between fear and disbelief, as she told him about the grisly delivery from Boag.

'I'm totally speechless, Rosie.' He shook his head and refilled their wine glasses. 'This is like a horror movie.' He reached across and covered her hand with his. 'You must be scared out of your wits. This . . . I mean . . . Christ, I don't know what to say. Maybe you should leave the country for a while. The newspaper would pay for that, wouldn't they?'

'Of course,' Rosie said. 'But I can't, TJ. I'm in the middle of this massive story on the Kosovan and the O'Dwyers I told you about, as well as this Boag situation.'

'Situation? It's a bit more than a situation. This bastard sent the head of one of his victims to your front fucking door. With a warning note. It's way past a situation.'

Rosie managed a half-smile. 'I know. Bit of an understatement. But you know how it is. I'm not going to do a runner in the middle of this.' She took a long drink of her wine, feeling more relaxed now due to the large gin she'd downed when they came in. 'Maybe this is the drink talking, but I hope not. Listen, TJ, I'm not going to let Boag terrorise me. Okay, that's not quite true, because he's already terrorising me. Big time. But if I run, he's won, and I bloody won't let him win. This is personal now. But believe me, I'm looking over my shoulder all the time. I'm jumpy as hell. If a door bangs I just about go through the roof. But running away to some restful beach isn't going to make that any better. Look. The cops will get him. He'll slip up.'

'But what if he doesn't? He's more or less said you're next on his hit list.'

She sighed. 'I've got a police tail on me twenty-four seven. They're outside the restaurant now. I saw them parking. They're at my flat all the time I'm there. The only reason they're not in the flat is because I won't let them. They wanted to put me up somewhere, but I refused. The compromise is that they come into the flat with me every night, check all the rooms and make sure the locks are working. Then they sit in shifts outside. When I'm leaving, I've to phone them and they follow me. I walked up here and they were close behind me, more or less kerb crawling. I'm scared, yes. But there are a lot of people protecting me.'

TJ was silent for a moment, staring beyond her as the restaurant began to empty.

'The thing is, Rosie, I'm supposed to be going down to London for a couple of weeks. I was going to tell you tonight – it's just been confirmed.'

'Really?' Rosie was surprised. This came from nowhere.

'Yeah. These guys I'm working with up at the Blue Note are session musicians, and they are old friends of some guy who's making an album, and he invited them down to work on the backing. He needs a sax player and they suggested me. It's only for a couple of weeks. But I think I'll cancel it. I can move in with you. Or you could move in with me.'

Rosie put her hand up. 'No, no, TJ. Go. I want you to go.'

'What?' He looked hurt.

'Don't be daft. I don't want you to go, but I think you should. Because right now, I'm worried that you might also be in danger. Remember the other night when we were out and then I said I wanted an early night?'

'Yeah.'

'Well, I went for petrol, and in the letter that was stuffed into that poor woman's mouth, Boag mentioned the petrol station – so I think he might have been there that night. Maybe he saw us in the restaurant? How do I know he hasn't got his eye on you in order to get at me?'

'Christ, you're giving me the creeps.' He laughed, but it wasn't very convincing.

Rosie smiled. 'I mean it, TJ. He's a twisted bastard. Who knows what he's planning? I think you should just slip out of the picture for a couple of weeks. By that time, I hope the cops will have got him.'

He puffed out a sigh. 'I dunno, Rosie. I don't like it. Why not come with me to London?'

'I'm working. I can't just swan off. I won't.'

Rosie hoped this was not going to become a row.

'Okay. I understand. But I don't think it's me he's coming after. It's you. I just don't want to leave you.' He touched her cheek with the back of his hand.

'Don't worry. I'll still be here when you come back.' Rosie paused, trying to find the right words. 'You know how I told you Adrian was here, helping with the Tadi story and stuff? Well, the editor said we should keep him on as extra protection.' Rosie watched him, and saw a flicker of resentment.

'You mean . . . staying in your flat?'

Rosie sighed. 'No, TJ. Come on. Don't be daft.'

He said nothing for a few moments. Then he drained his glass.

'Okay. But I'll miss you, and I'll be worried sick.'

'I'll be fine. Honestly.' Rosie tried to keep it light, but inside she was terrified. She glanced out of the window. It was dark now and she just wanted to go home. She hoped the police car was outside. How nuts was that?

'You know what I'd love to do?' She took TJ's hand. 'Sometimes I wish I could turn the clock back . . . Go to that crazy bar we went to – you know, when we first got together – and get drunk on tequila. I'd love that. But I can't, because I have to work.'

'We could go for an hour.'

'No we can't. An hour will end up being all night. Let's go home. We'll have a police escort all the way.'

TJ waved at the waiter and paid the bill. When they got up to leave he took her face in his hands and kissed her on the lips.

'You're a mad bastard, Rosie Gilmour. I wish I didn't like you so much.'

CHAPTER TWENTY-SIX

The sound of Rosie's front door closing woke her as though an electric shock had surged through her. She slid her hand across the bed, but TJ wasn't there. Shit. He'd closed the wooden shutters on her window before they went to bed, so she lay there in the darkness, barely breathing. She listened for any sign of activity in the kitchen in case he was up preparing breakfast, but the house was deadly silent. He probably left early and didn't want to wake her. But he never did that. Calm down, she told herself. She reached across the bedside table to her phone. It was eight thirty. Shit! 'Get a grip, Gilmour,' she whispered. 'You're cracking up.' She slipped out of bed and quietly pulled open the shutters. The pale grey sky gave a small, not very promising light. Then she tiptoed down the hall, half expecting a dead body and blood on the walls. Of course, it was ridiculous. She had three locks on the front door and a police car watching her flat, yet the crazed part of her mind still entertained the notion that Boag had somehow got in here and killed TJ. She was about to phone him from her mobile when she saw a note on the kitchen worktop.

Had to bail out early, sweetheart. Meeting with the guys about the London gig at eight, and didn't want to wake you up. You had one of your nightmares again. Try to relax. Talk later. Love you. Xxx.

She sighed and shook her head, filled a glass of water and thought of the nightmare. Normally she would remember the moment that she had woken up crying, but she hadn't this time. Then the image flashed through her mind of a nightclub. It was all men, dancing under strobe lights. Some weird guy sitting at the bar watching everyone. She was there too in the distance, and saw him watching her. Christ! She blinked the image away, made herself breakfast, then showered and sat at the open balcony doors, hoping the sun would come through. Her mobile rang and she picked it up. She recognised the number of Declan's desk.

'Rosie. It's me. The editor said to phone you.'

'He's in already?'

'Yeah. He's got a meeting. But he said to phone you, because there's been some incident with an old priest out in the East End. He says it might be a guy you know? Apparently you were there yesterday? A Father Dunnachie.'

'What?' Rosie's stomach dropped. 'What's happened? Yes. I do know him. What's happened?'

'He's been attacked in the parish house. Stabbed. Pretty bad. And . . . his attacker tried to cut off his hand. Cops say he's not going to make it.'

'Aw, Christ, Dec! Don't tell me – Boag?' she said, choked.

Silence for two beats, then Dec said, 'They're not saying. Could be anything. But nothing was stolen, so it's not a robbery.'

'It's Boag. I know it. I was with the old priest yesterday. It was him who took me to find Tadi. Boag must have been following us. The bastard has done this to get to me. Christ almighty! Father Dunnachie is an innocent man in his seventies, who never did anything but good in his life. How can anyone hurt him?' She heard her voice crack and stopped.

'I'm sorry, Rosie.'

They stayed on the phone, not saying anything. Then Rosie found the strength to speak.

'Which hospital is he in?'

'The Royal.'

'When did it happen?'

'Must have been the middle of the night. His housekeeper was away at her sister's overnight, and only came in at seven this morning. She found him in a pool of blood. Amazing that he's still alive. Poor old guy.'

'I can't believe this is happening, Dec. What a fucking monster!'

'I know. The editor wanted you to know. He says to come in as soon as you can.'

'Can you tell Mick that I'm going up to the hospital to see the priest first? If he's really bad he might not last much longer. I . . . I need to see him.' She swallowed. 'I feel so responsible. It's my fault.'

'No it's not, Rosie. Don't think that way. Boag's a psycho. This is not your fault. You can't be like that. I'll tell McGuire you'll be in later.'

'Thanks,' she managed to say before hanging up.

She stood clutching her phone, looking down at the early traffic snaking up Charing Cross. An icy shiver ran through her.

On the way up to the hospital, her mobile rang. It was Don.

'Rosie. I've got bad news.'

'I already know, Don. Father Dunnachie. Please don't tell me he's dead. I'm on my way to the Royal.'

'He's still alive. But only just. He's lost a lot of blood.'

'This is my fault, Don. If I hadn't asked him to take me to Tadi, he'd be alive. He didn't even know that Tadi was at his friend's house until he phoned him on my behalf. He had nothing to do with this. His only connection was me. It was me who pulled him into this. I . . . I feel—'

'Rosie. Calm down, pal. Listen. Stop thinking like that. This fucker Boag. If this was him, he's trying to get to you. But we don't know for sure if it is him. But it's looking that way. The fact that he's following you, and that the old priest's hand was nearly hacked off, is pointing to it being the work of this twisted fucker.'

'Killing a poor old priest who never did anyone any harm. Jesus, Don! You guys have to get this bastard. How come he's walking around Glasgow able to go into somebody's house in the middle of the night to do that?'

'We didn't put a watch on the priest's house. It never even occurred to us. Before you ask, we've already been to the other priest's house and taken Tadi's wife and kid out. We've got them somewhere safe, so don't worry.'

'Good. I'll come and see them later. Can you arrange that?'

'I'll see what I can do.'

'Can you get me into the Royal? You know what they're like up there.'

'Yeah. Don't worry, I'll make a call and sort it. Listen, just take it easy, Rosie. Don't let this fucker get to you. That's the most important thing right now. We'll get him. I'll call you later and we can meet if you're free.'

'I need to go. I'm almost at the Royal.'

'Okay. I'll make the call now. Just give it five minutes.'

There was a female uniformed police officer at the door of the ward, and she watched Rosie as she came out of the lift towards her.

'Are you Rosie Gilmour?'

'Yes. I've come to see Father Dunnachie. Is that okay?'

'Yes. It's been arranged. Follow me, please.'

Rosie walked behind her through the swing doors, the officer's shoes squeaking on the polished floors. She glanced into a couple of wards where nurses were attending to patients. The humid atmosphere made her feel nauseous. Memories came flooding back of the last time she was in a hospital, there to see her own father, holding his hand as he slipped away. The fact that she was there to see the old priest who had married her parents caught Rosie's throat, and she swallowed hard as they approached a room at the end of the corridor. The ward sister came out and closed the door softly.

'He's very weak.'

Rosie nodded, unable to speak.

'I'll be out here.'

In the room there were two priests, one about the same age as Father Dunnachie, the other, Father Flaherty. He glared at Rosie as she came in. She looked at Father Dunnachie on the bed. He had suddenly aged since yesterday, his face deathly pale. He clutched rosary beads in his uninjured hand.

'He's been saying your name. Maybe dreaming or something,' Father Flaherty said.

The other one stood silent, praying.

'He's had the last rites,' Father Flaherty went on. 'He doesn't have much time now. Do you want us to be with you? He's drifting in and out of consciousness, but we think he can hear us. He was praying with us a while ago.'

Rosie glanced at both of them. 'It's up to you.'

'We'll leave you alone. We'll be outside.' They left the room.

Rosie stood for a while staring at the old priest, her chest tight. Nothing could have prepared her for a moment like this. How could she ever have imagined that the priest she'd known all her life would be lying here like this, hack marks on his arms and chest, his wrist bandaged where Boag had tried to sever it? This was the priest who gave her her first Holy Communion, who heard her first confession, who chided her from time to time because she seldom appeared at church. For some reason, he could see her better than a lot of people she had known all her life, and she could never explain that to herself. It reinforced her feeling that there must be something in there, something spiritual, that made them choose to live the life they did, which was often lonely. Perhaps there was a depth to men like him that ordinary people couldn't grasp. She went across to the bed and leaned across and touched his hand. It felt warm, the skin papery and thin.

'Father. It's Rosie.'

For a moment there was nothing. Then a flicker of his eyelids and he opened one eye slightly. There was a hint of the smile that he always had for her.

'Rosie.' He squeezed her hands. 'Dear Rosie.'

She choked back tears. 'I'm so sorry, Father.'

He shook his head. 'Sssh. It's my time, Rosie. I'll never be far away. My body is weak. I'm not afraid.'

'Oh, Father. I—'

'Sssh, Rosie. Listen to me. You were doing the best for them. You must never feel bad, never blame yourself. This is God's will.'

'B-but how? How can it be?'

'Don't be a stranger to Him, Rosie. Listen to Him. Open your heart. Always. You are a good woman – like your mother. And with your father's anger inside too.'

'Will I get the other priests back in?'

'Yes. I'm going to sleep now. The long sleep. I'm ready . . .' His breathing laboured.

'Father . . . I—'

He squeezed her hand tight and held it, his knuckles white. She wanted to ask him if he had any idea who did this to him, but she couldn't bring herself to.

'Don't let them win, Rosie. Never let them win.' His chest heaved, and his grip released as his hand dropped on the bed.

She went over to the door, and opened it. When the priests saw the look on her face they rushed in.

The older priest with the stole on his neck began praying over Father Dunnachie, his breath shortening. The other priest joined him and they prayed together.

'Take our brother James to your heart, Lord. Keep him safe . . .'

Rosie watched while they prayed, as Father Dunnachie's face seemed to relax, his mouth opened a little, his features came to rest. The nurse came in. Rosie went past her, nodding her thanks. She walked briskly down the corridor and out of the hospital. She clocked the police officers in the car parked next to hers. She'd forgotten to phone them, so Don must have told them where she was. She almost ran to her car. When she got inside she locked the door and let her tears come.

CHAPTER TWENTY-SEVEN

Rosie was going through her copy on the murder of Father Dunnachie for the final time, glued to the screen, when her desktop phone rang. She picked it up.

'I'd like to talk to Rosie Gilmour, please.'

The voice was gravelly, hard-bitten, but businesslike in tone.

'You're talking to her.'

'Rosie. This is Jonjo Mulhearn.'

She stopped in mid breath, waited two beats.

'Jonjo Mulhearn?' She glanced across her desk at Declan, whose eyes popped.

'Aye. I'd like to talk to you. Are you free any time?'

'I . . . I thought you were in—'

'I'm out. Few days ago,' he cut in.

'Oh, right. Sure,' Rosie said quickly. It didn't matter what he wanted to talk to her about. If Jonjo Mulhearn wanted to talk, she was ready. She'd tried to interview the family enough times to know that if she went back, she might lose at least two of her teeth. 'I'll be glad to talk to you, Jonjo. Any time, any place.'

'Right. Can you meet me in the Crown bar today? At three. You know where it is?'

He wasn't going to spend much time on small talk.

'Yes. I'll see you there.'

'Just you. Nobody else. All right?'

'Yeah. That's fine.'

'I'll see you then. Thanks.'

He hung up.

'Jonjo Mulhearn? Was that really him?' Dec asked.

'So he said. I think so, but I'll not know until I go. I've to meet him at three today.'

'Fuck's sake! You haven't duffed him up over the years, have you?'

'Not that I can remember. He was up and down to London a lot, and in jail for the past nine years. So whatever he did was before my time. I'm not expecting to get shot.'

'Famous last words,' Dec said, sinking his teeth into his bacon roll.

McGuire had insisted that a photographer be somewhere to snatch a picture of Mulhearn – purely for the sake of it, he said. You never know when he might fuck up again, and it was always good to have a fresh pic. It's not as though you could hang around outside his house, or any of the

pubs or restaurants he frequented, as he was always sur-
rounded by minders. Rosie had also phoned Adrian to
come along with her – to be in the background, just in case.
Matt had been tasked with the photography job, and had
phoned Rosie from the roof of one of the buildings opposite the pub in Glassford Street to say that Jonjo was in the
bag. He'd snapped him as he got out of a car with some fat
bloke and went into the Crown. Matt was going back to the
office in case anyone clocked him. The fact that he'd been
there made Rosie a little edgy as she and Adrian got out of
her car and headed for the Crown. She glanced around to
see if there were any minders watching. There weren't. She
stopped, took a deep breath and braced herself.

As she pushed open the swing doors, it felt a bit like
walking into a bar in an old Western. Four or five punters
stood at the bar, and immediately stopped talking and
glared at her. She noted that there were mirrors low down
on the gantry, presumably to see below the tables in case
anyone pulled out a gun. The last time she'd seen mirrors
like that was on the Shankill Road – and somebody did
pull a gun that day.

The Crown wasn't a bar that people like her normally
went to unaccompanied. Lawyers sometimes used it, but
they were always mob handed, and usually in the company
of some of the gangsters or hard men who were the main
clientele. She could see a little snug at the far end, and a fat
bloke emerged and came towards her. He looked a bit like

pictures she'd seen of Jonjo at his son's funeral, but it wasn't him. Then she suddenly remembered he had a brother, Tony.

'Rosie Gilmour?' the guy asked quietly, casting a brief glance at Adrian.

She nodded. 'Tony?'

He looked surprised and impressed, jerked his head and walked away. She followed, nodding to Adrian to wait at the bar.

At the end of the bar in the snug, Jonjo sat at a small round mahogany table, a mug of tea in his hand. She stood for a moment taking in the scene, the man sitting below a painting of Argyle Street in the old days of trams. He was wearing a pale blue shirt, open at the neck, and jeans. He stood up, taller than he looked in the archive photos. His hair was close cropped and mostly grey, but despite the broken nose, she could see he'd been a handsome man in his day. Word was he'd almost gone to pieces when his son was murdered, and the way he was murdered had ripped the heart from him. But there was no sign of that right now as his pale eyes locked hers.

'Rosie.' He reached out his hand. 'Thanks for coming.' He looked over her shoulder at Adrian. 'Who's the big fella? Your minder?'

'That's Adrian. A friend,' said Rosie, hoping Mulhearn wouldn't make an issue of it. He didn't.

Mulhearn looked more like a retired army major, smart

and in command, than a Glasgow hard man. But he was a hard man. They must have taught him manners in Shotts.

Often when she met a gangster, unless it was someone she'd known for a long time, there was a lot of posturing. Usually they made some sexist remark, to which Rosie would come back with an even smarter put-down, to establish her position. But this guy, jailed for killing two thugs who'd threatened his turf, seemed almost benign.

He motioned for her to sit down.

'Drink?' He lifted his mug. 'Being too long inside ruined my drinking habits.' He almost smiled.

'I'll have some tea if that's all right. Contrary to what you might hear, we're not all drunks in my profession.'

He motioned to his brother to bring some tea.

'Most of the ones I knew growing up were.'

'Well, it's a bit different these days.' Rosie was glad of the small talk to break the ice. 'It was a bit wild when I first started, but nowadays you'd be hard pushed to find a reporter in a pub during the day. It's all quiet now, and instead of afternoon punch-ups on the editorial floor, the only sound is the gentle hum of computers.'

'Better or worse?'

'Better for the liver and the head, I'd say. But we do get out to play now and again.'

He gave her a slight smile, then grew serious.

'I heard you were out at my house after Jack . . .' His voice trailed off as though he couldn't say it. For the first time he looked vulnerable.

The direct question startled Rosie.

'Yes,' she said, spreading her hands. 'I'll be honest with you, Jonjo. I hate doing these kinds of things – having to knock on the door of someone who's lost a loved one. But that's part of my job.' She paused, conscious he was studying her face. 'I'm so sorry about Jack, for your loss. I can only imagine—'

'You can't imagine.' He cut her off, his eyes dropping to the table for a second, then back to her. 'I couldn't have imagined it myself until it happened. Then you're just . . . well . . . your life is just what it is after that – which is really nothing.'

They sat in silence, Rosie listening to the swing door opening and shutting and the ping of the til. She wished he would say something. He didn't.

'Anyway.' She couldn't take the silence any longer. 'I fully understand that nobody wanted to talk. But we had to try. I honestly didn't push it too much, but I was left having been told in no uncertain terms that nobody would give an interview.'

'My wife wanted to talk, but the boys wouldn't let her – my brother. They said I would explode. They asked me afterwards, and I said to say nothing.'

Rosie wasn't quite sure where this was going, but she smelled a story. Was she really going to get a sensational sit-down with Jonjo Mulhearn talking about his grief for his boy?

'Of course. I understand that. But if you or your wife ever want to talk, I'd be glad to do that.' She waited. Nothing. 'Jack seemed such a promising young man. University and everything all ahead of him. That bastard Boag has a lot to answer for.'

She watched as Jonjo took a long breath and held it, seemingly to control himself. He let it out slowly through his nostrils. His knuckles went white as he picked up his mug. For a second she thought he was going to hurl it at the wall in anger, frustration, grief, because whatever he was feeling right now was still raw and it was written all over his face.

'Well. Maybe another time, my wife will talk. But that's not why I asked you here.'

Rosie said nothing, just looked at him, waiting.

'It's about Boag.' He examined the table, fiddling with a beer mat. 'Listen. I'm wondering something. A reporter in your position, I presume you talk to cops and stuff.'

Rosie shrugged. 'Sometimes. I have some contacts.'

He looked through her.

'So do I, Rosie. Some more cooperative than others. But I still can't trust them. When I was growing up anyone could be bought.'

'I do remember the stories. I did one myself a couple of years ago. Brought down the boss – Gavin Fox. Chief Constable.'

'Foxy. That greedy bastard. Bad lot. So were his cronies who got done with them – and that one who topped himself. I knew them all. Chancers.'

Rosie wondered again where this was going. He hadn't brought her here to reminisce about corruption in Glasgow's finest. It was about Boag. He'd already made that clear.

He looked at her as though sensing her curiosity.

'I know a lot about you, Rosie.'

She kept her face straight, didn't respond.

'I know you're a good reporter – that much I'm sure of. In the nick, you get a lot of time to peruse the newspapers at your leisure – all the ins and outs. I digested all that. I can see that you're at the frontline a lot in what you do. You've had a couple of slappings in the process. That fucker Tam Dunn. Him! I saw he roughed you up a bit. He was a polecat from when he was a teenager. I grew up with that mob. He got what was coming to him. If I hadn't been in jail, I'd have made sure he got it. And Big Jake.'

'Oh, him.'

This time he did smile. 'He doesn't like you. You're not on his Christmas list.'

'I'll try not to worry about that.'

'Anyway. What I mean is: Boag. I want to ask you one thing.' He sat back, stretched his legs. 'Okay, you don't know me, or even if you can trust me. You might even be afraid of me.'

'I'm not afraid of you, Jonjo,' Rosie said quickly and meant it.

'Good. I'd never harm you. I admire you, I mean that. I'm a criminal. It's what I am, but I'm not a bad bastard who cuts people up, or a smack dealer who made his fortune filling kids with heroin, so that they end up stealing from old women for their next fix. I hate all that shit.'

'You used to deal in heroin if we're to believe what we hear.'

It was risky to throw this in, and she knew it.

'Not heroin. It was cannabis. It was a very long time ago, Rosie. I didn't like it, and I wasn't top dog in the crew then, so as soon as I carved my way to the top, I got out of it. I'm in property now. Bars and restaurants.'

'The cops call it money laundering, Jonjo.'

She knew it would irritate him, but she wanted to assert herself.

He shrugged, a little irked. 'Listen. I'm not here to go to confession. Can you hear me out?'

'Of course.'

'Okay. I've seen your stories in the last few days on Boag. He cut someone's head off and sent you it. Jesus Christ! Sick bastard.'

'Yeah,' Rosie said. 'It was a bit disturbing.'

'I bet it was.' He sat forward, pushing his mug to the side so he was leaning across the table. 'So I wanted to ask you if you ever got anywhere near Thomas Boag before the police, would you do something for me.'

Rosie stared at him. She knew what was coming. She waited.

He swallowed. 'I just want one thing, Rosie. I want to have two minutes with him. Alone.' His lips were tight and she could see the determination in his clenched jaw. 'That's all I ask. An evil fucker like that doesn't deserve jail or the justice of a trial. He's butchered innocent people. Not just my boy. My Jack . . .' He shook his head. For a second Rosie thought he was going to tear up. But he swallowed it back, his face set in anger. 'I'll tell you something – and you can take this as gospel – Boag was never going to make it to his trial. It was all planned as soon as he hit the Bar-L on remand. He should have been dead by now. I had promises from my boys. Your story the next morning would have been Boag's death.'

'Really?'

'Yes.'

'Well, I can't say it would have been a bad thing. One bastard off the face of the earth.'

'Exactly. So would you give me the chance if it ever comes to that? I mean, if you find out where he is? Anywhere. Even at five minutes' notice. I'll be ready. Just tell me.'

Rosie took a breath and blew out a long sigh. 'You're asking a lot, Jonjo. This is something that may never happen anyway. The way Boag looked at me in court, I'll be glad when they pick him up.'

'Or I get him first,' he interrupted. 'I'd be doing you a favour.'

Rosie half smiled. 'Whatever. Truth is, you'd be doing the world a favour.'

'So will you help me, Rosie? That's all I'm asking.' He paused. 'And if you ever need any help for anything – I mean anything at all – I'll always be in your debt.'

They sat in silence as Rosie nursed her mug of tea. She should help him, because in her gut it was the right thing to do, but it was wrong on so many levels. Right now, if she could tell Jonjo Mulhearn where Boag was, she would. And the retribution he sought would be swift. She'd even celebrate once he got him. But she was not a gangster who lived in that world. She was a journalist. How would society function if people like her didn't work within the law? She sat for a moment, watching him. Behind the tough, angry exterior she could see how broken he was. She took out her mobile.

'Can you give me your phone number, Jonjo?' He took his mobile out and they swapped numbers. Rosie looked at her watch.

'I need to move. I'm still working on this story.'

She stood up, and he followed.

'Do we have a deal?' He stretched out his hand.

Rosie looked at his face, felt the strength of his hand in hers.

'It was really good to meet you, Jonjo. I hope we can talk again.'

He raised his chin in acknowledgement, and she could feel his eyes on her as she walked away from the snug and out the main bar towards the swing doors.

CHAPTER TWENTY-EIGHT

Rosie followed Molly O'Dwyer's car all the way from the farm until she took the motorway junction for Glasgow city centre. She'd managed to stay far enough away on the farm road, parking up on one of the side roads so that her car would be out of sight when Molly drove out of the yard. Rosie was trying to keep a low profile, which wasn't easy when a car with two detectives went with her everywhere. She didn't like the idea of having to phone them every morning to tell them where she was going, but these days part of her was glad that the police weren't far away. She wasn't expecting Boag to jump out of some dark corner and attack her. He was much more sinister than that, but just knowing that he might be watching sent shivers through her.

The biggest shock was when her mobile had rung on the way back to the office yesterday, after she'd sat with Father Dunnachie. It was the first time she'd heard his voice, but he didn't have to say who he was. She knew. She heard heavy breathing, then he spoke.

'The old priest wasn't on the agenda, Rosie. That was just a wee personal thing. From me to you. To let you know how easy this is. You see, I'm smarter than them all. That's why I'm where I am now, and you're all over the place. Scary, isn't it? See you, Rosie.'

When she reached the top of the stairs on to the editorial floor, she had to sit at her desk taking deep breaths to recover. Then she went into McGuire and told him. Within minutes, a posse of detectives were down at her office, one taking her phone apart and attaching it to some contraption. But there was no trace. Boag was too smart for that. When she told Adrian, in the evening, he'd offered to come down and sleep in the spare room. Rosie declined. She had just said goodbye to TJ, and it felt wrong to have Adrian in her house. Not that she was planning to do anything with him, but she wasn't sure she could trust herself.

Now she followed Molly O'Dwyer's car into the car park next to St Enoch Square, waited for her to get out and then walked after her. Adrian had insisted on coming with her, even though she felt safer in the busy city centre. She knew the police were only a few yards behind her, somewhere. As she walked up Buchanan Street, the precinct full of shoppers, buskers and lunchtime sandwich runs, she wondered what it was like to have an ordinary life, go home and leave your work behind, and actually fall asleep when you went to bed at night.

She watched as Molly went into the House of Fraser department store. Rosie kept herself in the background while Molly shopped in the designer areas for tops and a jacket, then went into the lingerie department where she bought some rather risqué underwear that didn't quite match the impression Rosie had of her. Perhaps she was having an affair. She couldn't blame her with the brute of a husband she was tied to. Then Molly went up the steps to the cafeteria, ordered tea and a sandwich and found a seat at the back. She examined her purchases, then took out her mobile phone and began texting furiously. Rosie waited until she was almost finished with her sandwich and then went to the counter and bought a cup of tea. Adrian waited at the other side of the cafeteria with a coffee. There were few customers, but Rosie crossed the room and sat at the table next to Molly. She didn't look up immediately, but when she did, she looked startled.

'Molly. Can I talk to you for a moment?'

Molly glanced around the room. 'Are you following me?'

Rosie stared at her for a moment. 'Well. Yes, I am, actually. Look. Please listen to me. I could see you were upset the other day, and I think you know something . . . about what happened. I think you know a whole lot more.'

Molly interrupted. 'So why are you following me? Do you think I'm going to tell you?'

'I think you want to. But you're scared.'

'Bloody right I'm scared. Don't you know anything about my husband? He could tear you limb from limb with his bare hands. Everyone who knows him is aware of that.'

'He killed that poor man Bo, Molly.'

She didn't answer, and her face showed only a glimmer of reaction.

'And maybe he killed the woman and her child. What kind of man does that? You keep slaves at your farm, Molly. How can you reconcile yourself with that? How can you sleep at night?' Rosie hoped to provoke a reaction.

'You think I have a choice? Are you naive or just stupid?'

Rosie let it go.

'Did your husband kill that woman and child?'

Rosie could see her lip trembling a little.

'He didn't do that.'

'How do you know?'

'It wasn't him.'

For a moment there was nothing, just the heavy tension in the air and the feeling that she was about to crack. Molly shook her head.

'How could I have given birth to someone who could do that?' she muttered.

'What?'

'I'm going away from here, Rosie Gilmour. I'm leaving. I'm not going to the police to tell them what I know, I'm leaving and I'll never come back here ever again.'

'Where are you going?'

'Away. Abroad. I've lived my life here and I've tried my best, but I . . . I can't do it any more.'

'Talk to me, Molly.'

'You can't help me. Why would I do that?'

'I can help put your man in jail for what he did, for the murder of Bo, for the robbery, for enslaving those poor men . . . What about the young couple found in the grave? Did he kill them too? And the woman and the baby? I can help take him away from you, if you do the right thing—'

'It wasn't him who did that,' she interrupted. 'He didn't kill the woman and baby.' Then her face crumpled. 'It was our Timmy.'

Rosie couldn't believe what she was saying.

'Timmy? Your son? He killed them?'

She nodded, covered her face with her hands. 'May God forgive the bastard for what he did. I don't know where he came from. In God's name we'll never know where he came from.'

'Why would he kill them? How do you know this?'

They sat in heavy silence, then Molly shook her head in despair. 'God help us! I don't know for sure. I overheard them talking, and Timmy confessed. It was last week when they found the bodies and police were asking questions. Timmy was behaving strangely. Then he told Rory and Finn in the living room. The door was closed, but I heard everything. It was like a sword going through my heart.

That girl. She worked here with us. A Ukrainian girl – lovely wee thing. Then she suddenly left. I heard Timmy telling his father that she'd been blackmailing him because he got her pregnant. So the bastard killed her and her baby.' She shook her head. 'All he had to do was tell me about it and we would have taken both of them in. Mother of God, I would have done anything for it not to happen. If only he'd told me . . .'

'My God!' Rosie said.

'That's not all.' Molly shook her head in despair as she looked down at the table. 'He killed that young couple too. The students.'

'What? Timmy killed them?'

Molly nodded. 'I heard him say it. He killed them and buried them in the same grave. That was the moment I decided I can't live with the lies any more. So I've made my plan. I know where I'm going and I'm not coming back. No police, nothing. I can't help that wee girl now, or Bo, or those poor young students, but I helped Tadi get away. At least I did that. I'm going tomorrow. When Rory and Finn are away for the day. When they come back I'll not be there.'

'Are you going abroad?

'Yes. Spain. I . . . I have a friend there. A man I've known who's been my friend for years, every time I go there we meet. He's been more of a friend to me than that bastard Rory ever was.'

'You're having an affair?'

'Call it what you like. He makes me happy. No . . . He can't make me happy because I can never be happy, especially not now. But I can't be a part of Rory's lies any more. I'm sick to my stomach.'

'Molly. Come with me and talk to the police. You can put him away.'

'No. No police. Not interested. I've told you what I know. You can do what you like with it.'

'So where is Timmy? Did Rory send him away when he confessed? Can you at least tell me that?'

'Yes. He's down south with some traveller friends. Somebody owed Rory a big favour. We'll never see him again. Rory could have had him killed, but he couldn't do that to his own flesh and blood. Unlike Timmy, who killed his own baby . . . my grandchild.' She sniffed. 'I lost my own daughter when she was eight months old, and my heart has never healed. And he goes out there, makes a woman pregnant and kills her. Burying her like a dog in the field. I'll never be free. But at least I won't have to be sitting in that house every day, knowing that she was buried just there, knowing that my grandchild is buried and I didn't even get to see her. I can't even discuss this with Rory because his only worry was about Timmy getting found out. That's the kind of selfish bastard he is. So he just got rid of Timmy. But I can't live with it any longer.'

'Molly,' Rosie said. 'Where exactly is Timmy? What friends is he with?'

She sat for a long moment, then spoke. 'He's with Paddy McMahon's crew in Blackpool. Paddy's da was the king of the gypsies. His son is not half the man he was, but he is a bad bastard. He can fight like a demon and will defend his family and crew with every inch of his life. You think you can turn up there and ask for an interview? Rosie, listen to me. Take a step back from this. You want to tell the police the address, I'll give you it. Let them go and bring Timmy in. I'll gladly see him locked up for what he did, but if you turn up there, that mob will rip your arms off. Even the women fight like men, I'm telling you.'

They sat for few moments, Rosie processing the information, wondering if there was a small chance that Molly would talk to the police.

'Molly. Once you get to Spain, all going well, Timmy gets arrested along with your husband and Finn. Will you testify against them?'

She shook her head. 'I didn't see anything, so I can't.' She paused and looked away. 'I only overheard the conversation.'

'You'd still be a crucial witness – about the slaves and the beatings – even just to confirm that the Ukrainian girl did stay at your house.'

She sighed. 'I don't know.' She gathered her bags. 'Look, Rosie, I'm leaving here now. If I ever want to contact you I will, but if you alert the police to the fact that I'm leaving, I'll make you out the biggest liar and fantasist that ever was. Do you understand me?' Her face hardened.

Rosie looked at her as she stood up. 'Can I use what you've already told me?'

Molly thought for a moment. 'When I'm out of the country, you can say what you like. Nobody will find me unless I want to be found.'

Rosie stood up stretched out her hand. 'Good luck, Molly. Thanks.'

'Aye. Good luck to you too. And remember what I said about the McMahons. Don't be a hero.'

Rosie watched as she made her way through the tables and towards the stairs at the top of the cafe. She never looked back.

CHAPTER TWENTY-NINE

Rosie knew McGuire would not be impressed by her plan, so it was no surprise that he was pacing up and down in front of his desk, ranting.

'Honest to Christ, Rosie! Are you not in enough danger with this nutcase Boag stalking you? Why would you want to walk into some kind of travellers' enclave and put yourself at risk? What do you think they do in these places? Sit around reading cups and smoking pipes, spinning yarns about the good old days making clothes pegs for a living? There are criminal bastards among them who would cut your head off. You're crazy even to suggest it.'

'But, Mick,' Rosie protested, 'we wouldn't be diving right in among them. We would be watching Timmy over a couple of days and seeing what he's about, getting pictures of him – things we wouldn't be able to do if we just phoned the cops and told them what Molly O'Dwyer told me. Once they know that, they'll arrest him and that's the last we'll get.'

'Don't tell me you're going all that way and then not planning to approach Timmy? Don't bullshit me, Gilmour.'

Rosie couldn't help the smile that came to her lips.
McGuire in this kind of mood was hard to deal with, but it
was entertaining.

'Well, if I did approach him, I wouldn't just be barging
in. I'd wait til the time was right. Maybe if we could get
him on his own somewhere. Matt's looked at the area
online and it's at the edge of Blackpool, not that far from
the town. I also talked to a contact in the local paper about
the traveller site and she said that the travellers are well
known in the area. She said her paper tried to investigate
claims that they run organised dogfights, but they got
nowhere. They're into this illegal bare-knuckle boxing too,
but it's all hush-hush. So I'm not expecting to waltz in
there and get anything. I'm aware of the dangers. I don't
even know if Timmy will definitely be there, but I'm sure
if he is, we'll find him. And we'll have Adrian with us for
back-up. Honestly, I'm sure we can be in and out quickly
and come back with something great. This Timmy character is key to the investigation up in that field. His mother
told me she overheard him confessing to his father that
he killed the young couple, and also the woman and
baby. If we do get to him and he bursts, then we'll get the
father and the other son for the murder of Bo. It's too good
not to try.'

'And too dangerous.'

'Come on, Mick. It's more dangerous for me in bloody Glasgow right now, with Boag skulking around, ready to cut my head off. I'm a nervous wreck and that's the truth. I'll be glad to get out of the place.'

The editor gave her a long look and let out a heavy sigh as he sat down behind his desk.

'Right. Okay, Gilmour. Here's the deal. You can go, but two days is all you're getting. If you sense any kind of shit about to kick off, or have any suspicion they are onto you, I want you back into the car and right on the motorway. And if you do get anywhere, then I want you to call the cops immediately and bring them in. Are we clear about that?'

'Of course.' Rosie smiled. 'I'll bring you back a stick of rock.'

'Yeah, right. Now get out of here before I change my mind. By the way, you'll have to tell the cops protecting you that you're going out of town on a secret assignment, otherwise they'll be tailing you all the way.'

Rosie stood up. 'Sure. I'll sort it with the cops.'

It was early evening by the time Rosie, Matt and Adrian arrived in Blackpool. They drove along the seafront, taking in the view of holidaymakers and day-trippers making their way off the beach and heading to cars, buses or cafes. A raft of teenage memories ran through Rosie's mind as she recalled her first summer holiday down here from

Glasgow, on a bus run with the relatives she'd been staying with after running away from the children's home. It had been a week of abandon, being able to go to bars and discos, unbridled kissing against walls with horny sixteen-year-old boys from the north of England. The headiness of teenage years, growing up, believing anything was possible. She'd considered hiding and not going back on the bus, back to the mundane, unsafe Glasgow tenement where nobody was ever happy, and every day was more like an existence than living. It was her first taste of being away from whatever passed for home at that age, and looking back, she decided it was there and then that she must have made up her mind that she had to get out.

Marion had managed to get them rooms above a pub at the edge of town, where they wouldn't look out of place among the salesmen or travellers. Matt had established – from chatting up the barmaid – that the open street market was tomorrow, which was the busiest day of the week in the town. She'd told him it was popular with people from outlying villages and the odd tourist, but there were sometimes problems in the evening because a rough crowd from the travelling site nearby came in and spent the afternoon at the market and the evening carousing in the pubs. It usually ended in a punch-up. She moaned that when she grew up here it had been an idyllic little place, but now it had been ruined by the travellers and all they brought with them.

Once they'd eaten in the bar, the three of them walked down to one of the pubs close to the North Pier.

'I've always liked this town,' Matt said. 'It speaks to me of crazy teenage years on bus runs from Glasgow.'

Rosie turned to him and smiled.

'Really? You too? Must have been a rite of passage for any self-respecting Glasgow kid to go to Blackpool, get drunk in the Bier Keller on the promenade, and snogged in the dance hall.'

'Yep. That was me. But I liked it so much I came back about three years running. Before I discovered Benidorm.'

Rosie chortled. 'Yeah. Blackpool – Benidorm with rain.'

Adrian smiled, not really knowing what they were talking about as he watched the door and studied the men who'd just walked in.

'The men who've come in, Rosie. Do they look like locals or maybe from the traveller site? What do you think?'

Rosie glanced up. Three big bruisers, one with at least two bellies under his shirt and the other two built like fridges. They were talking loudly and one of them slapped the other on the back, a bit too hard, as they ordered a drink. Rosie listened to their voices. She could detect the accent of the traveller.

'I'd say they were travellers all right.'

She watched as the men stood at the bar, knocking back

half of their pints in long deep chugs. A few minutes later, the door opened and a tall skinny man came in and went across to them. One of the men turned around and shouted at him.

'Timmy, you cunt! What the fuck took you so long?' He was joking and the others laughed. He turned to the barman and ordered another pint.

Timmy walked to the bar. He wiped his mouth with the back of his hand and picked up his pint from the bar.

'Took me ages to find the fucking place. Then I'd to wait for the cunts to turn up.'

'Did you drop the dogs?'

The man lowered his voice. Timmy nodded, without taking his mouth from the pint.

Rosie, Matt and Adrian exchanged glances.

'Shit,' Matt said. 'That's got to be him.'

'Looks like it. But we've no real way of knowing, as I don't have a picture of him. We'll just have to wait and see.'

Adrian finished his drink and got up. 'I'll go to the bar and buy the drinks. Maybe I can hear what they are saying for a moment.'

Rosie looked at Matt.

'Sure.'

She didn't have to tell Adrian to be discreet.

Rosie and Matt watched as Adrian went across to the bar. He stood next to the men. He had that way about him that men would never say to him he was in their space because, by instinct, they could sense the danger in him. She noticed one of the men glance at him and then look at his mate as Adrian stood at the bar. He ordered the drinks and lit up a cigarette.

'Awright, big man?' One of the men turned to him. 'Not from around here, are you?'

Adrian looked down at the shorter man for a moment, then shook his head. 'No.'

The other three of them glanced at him, then at each other. Adrian put his cigarette down on the ashtray and carried drinks over to Rosie and Matt. He came back to the bar and took a drink from his pint.

'Where you from, big man?'

Adrian looked at him and said nothing.

'Your accent, I mean. I heard your accent. You foreign?'

Adrian turned to them squarely. 'I am from Bosnia.'

'Oh, right,' said one of the men. 'One of them refugee blokes?'

Adrian looked at them and said nothing.

The other man piped up. 'You don't say much, do you?'

Rosie could see that Adrian's pale face was deadpan.

'My English is not good. I am learning.'

'So where you headed?'

Adrian shrugged. 'Not sure.'

'You with them people? That your bird?'

Adrian didn't look across at the table.

'No. I only met them earlier.'

'You looking for work?'

Adrian shrugged. 'What work?'

'Bit of labouring.'

One of them reached out and touched Adrian's shoulder.

'Looks like you're built for hard work, mate.' Adrian flinched but half smiled.

'I used to box. Back in Bosnia.'

The three men looked at each other and their eyes brightened.

'Seriously, mate? You a fighter? A man like you could make a shed load of money. Fuck that working lark. How long you here for?'

'Not sure. Maybe couple of days. Maybe more.'

Adrian picked up his pint and stubbed out his cigarette.

'I go back to my friends now.'

The man touched his shoulder again.

'Hey, listen, mate. Here's my number. If you're interested in a bit of work, let me know. By the way, I'm Pat, this is Johnny and Martin. And this skinny cunt is Timmy. He's a Jock. If you want a drink, come and join us later.'

'Thank you,' Adrian said, putting the piece of paper in his jeans pocket.

He came back to the table and sat down.

'Okay,' he said quietly. 'We must not look like we are big friends. Did you see me talking to them? They ask me if

I was with you, and I said I only met you a little while ago here.'

'Good,' Rosie said. 'I heard some of what they were saying. You were great, Adrian. Did I hear you say you were a boxer? Christ! Did that just come out of the air?'

His lips moved a little to a smile.

'It was like the light going off in my head. I just said it to see what happened. They are interested in me. Offered me some work.'

'Aye, but they might want to put you in a bare-knuckle fight. Imagine being in some brawl with one of them fat bastards up there. What if they sat on you?'

'They are not fighters. Maybe they were one time. But now they are fat. Strong, but fat. Easy meat for a fighter.'

'Adrian,' Rosie said. 'Listen. Let's not get ahead of ourselves here. If these people are who we think they are, then let's not get involved. It's good that I think we've established that Timmy is there, so what we need is a picture of him and then we can see.'

'They said he was a Jock. That means Scottish, doesn't it?'

'Yes,' Rosie replied.

'This Timmy,' Adrian said, his eyes growing dark. 'He is the one who killed the woman and the little baby?'

'Yes. So his mother says.'

Adrian nodded and was quiet for a moment.

'What do you think will happen if the police get him?'

'I don't know. Maybe he'll confess and grass up his father and brother. His mother says he's a bad lot.'

Adrian looked at Rosie, then down at the table.

'How did he kill the mother and baby? Do you know?'

'The mother was killed by a blow to the head, from what the police told me. Same for the baby. Evil bastard.'

Adrian said nothing more and they sat silently watching as the men at the bar ordered more pints with whisky chasers.

After an hour and one more drink, Rosie could see the men at the bar getting more and more drunk and pushing each other, laughing. The bar was also getting busier.

'I think we should hit the road soon,' she said. 'I don't want to be around here too long in case these plonkers come over and start talking to us.'

Adrian nodded. 'I think when you and Matt go, I stay for one more drink as I don't want to leave with you. I told them I am alone . . . I'll see what else I can get from them, then I'll come to the bar in the place we stay in about half an hour. Maybe I can find out a bit more about this Timmy. Make sure he is who we are looking for.'

Rosie could see by Adrian's face that this wasn't up for discussion. He knew what he was doing, and if anyone could gather more information in a situation like this, it was him.

'Okay. Good plan.' She got up. 'Come on, Matt. You can

buy me a nightcap in our place. Put it down as a pull,' she joked.

'Sure, boss. Let's do it.' He turned to Adrian. 'But if you get into a fight, Adrian, don't be bragging you've got a mate who'll come down and sort these guys out. Get my drift?'

Adrian almost smiled, but not quite.

CHAPTER THIRTY

Rosie sat in the passenger seat as Matt drove them out towards the traveller site on the outskirts of Blackpool. They passed the North Pier, the rows of terraced B&B houses that used to pack in Scottish holidaymakers during the summer. Now some had been turned into flats and bedsits, and the town looked tired and run-down. The site wasn't hard to find, stuck on the edge of a field with rows of caravans, and some static bungalow houses – kit jobs with apex roofs, made of fibreglass or metal. Kids played among tied-up ponies, and acrid black smoke rose from a bonfire. A couple of older men sat outside their caravans smoking, but most of the others were either arriving in pickups or leaving.

Adrian's decision to hang around the bar the previous night proved to be useful. As the travellers proceeded to get increasingly drunk, they'd become slack-mouthed and asked him if he fancied coming to a dogfight the next night. He said he wasn't sure, but would think about it. They offered him a bare-knuckle fight – a hundred quid to knock a man out, but he declined. Another time, he told them. But the dog-fight was where the money was made, and betting men came from around the area – not just travellers but punt-ers and gangsters. It was well protected. Rosie had seen the television documentaries before, and attempts by journal-ists to get close to it, so she didn't expect, or even want to be any closer than she needed. But it would be a bonus if they could get a picture while they were trying to snatch one of Timmy. They hadn't seen him around this morning, so their only hope was that he would be around the town in the afternoon, once the market kicked off.

Her mobile rang and Don's name came up.

'Rosie. Where are you? The guys told me you slipped your leash.'

'Hey, Don. I was going to phone you, I just said to the guys that it was a top-secret job I'm on. I should be back tomorrow. And if I get lucky, I'll have some great informa-tion for you.'

'I hope you're not doing anything daft.'

'No. Well, not yet.'

'Are you in Scotland?'

'No. Down south. Looking for someone. What's happen-ing back there?'

She heard him sigh. 'It's all getting worse by the day.

They're talking about bringing an outside force in to help in the hunt for this fucker Boag. I can't believe we haven't had a sniff of him. I mean you've been the bloody closest to him – he's even fucking phoned you on your mobile, yet we can't get near him.' He paused. 'You're not there tracking him, are you? Because that would be totally stupid.'

'No, course not. I'm looking for someone else. I know how frustrating it must be for you guys with Boag running around there. He's a clever bastard, he really is. But he'll make a mistake – I just hope it's soon, because to be honest, I'm scared witless now every time I go out of my house in Glasgow – and even when I'm in my bloody house. Have the press got hold of the outside force line yet?'

'No. It might not happen. The bosses are trying to resist it. I know it looks bad from our point of view, but to be honest, I don't give a shit who comes in. We really need to find this guy before he does anyone else in.'

'Exactly. Listen, I have to go. But I'm serious about what I'm doing. It might be big information for you, if it works out.'

Silence.

'Rosie. If you're doing anything like that, you really should have given us the tip first. Christ's sake! You need to watch yourself.'

'I'm okay. I've got back-up.'

Don was quiet for a moment as he registered the information.

'Not sure I like the sound of that. Call me as soon as you can.'

'Sure.' Rosie hung up.

By the time they got back, the town was beginning to fill with people. Stalls were being set up along the main drag, and traffic was building in the car parks. Rosie had spoken to her local paper contact who gave her an idea where the dogfights were, at a piece of waste ground close to the town centre, in a disused scrapyard. They took Adrian with them to do a recce of the yard, but it was padlocked.

They sat outside a coffee shop watching the bustle of the town. Rosie felt a wave of exhaustion. She was listening to Matt and Adrian talking, but was miles away.

'Rosie,' Adrian said. 'You are daydreaming?'

She glanced at him from behind her dark glasses and met his eyes smiling, and for a moment wished they were here together just the two of them, relaxing over coffee on a trip without any strings or problems. But life wasn't like that. She snapped back to the moment.

'I'm a bit tired. I never sleep much when I'm on jobs like this. Kind of like being fired on adrenalin all the time. There comes a time when I'm running on empty, but don't worry, I'm not quite there yet. Right. So let's think of a plan? We can't really do much til we see if these guys come back into town.'

'I think they will. They go to the markets in the

morning, do some business, and they told me they would be in that bar again by late afternoon.'

'What if they invite you to the dogfight, Adrian?'

He shrugged. 'Then I should go.'

'Will they invite us? You could say we are your new friends, and we're heading away in the morning. That we're not a threat or anything.'

He thought for a moment. 'Maybe. We'll see.'

'If that Timmy is with them today, then I need to snatch a pic of him,' Matt said.

'Yeah,' Rosie agreed. 'But I don't see much chance of getting any kind of word with him without being lynched, so we might have to settle for a picture.'

By late afternoon, Rosie and Matt were packed up and heading to join Adrian in the bar where they'd been last night. They'd decided that whatever happened, they had to be ready to leave town tonight. There wasn't much point in hanging around for another night if they could get a picture of Timmy. It wasn't what she'd hoped for, she'd hoped there was a chance she could get hold of him without getting lynched, but that wasn't going to happen in the kind of company he kept. McGuire had already been on the phone telling her to get it done and head for home.

When they got into the bar, Adrian was on his own, drinking tea.

'I saw one of the men from last night,' he said quietly.

'They are coming for a drink. They said they were going to a cafe for some fish and chips and then coming here. He offered me some work again. So I said we could meet for a drink, but I was seeing my friends before they went away tomorrow.'

'Good stuff, Adrian,' Rosie said, as she waved the waitress over. 'I'm well impressed by the way you can convince people.'

'I think the less that is said, the better. If you don't say too much, you don't give the game away.'

Rosie smiled, glanced at him.

'Yes, we noticed.'

'I get scared when you go all silent, Adrian,' Matt said.

Adrian sniffed. 'You're a funny guy, Matt. Always saying you are scared, but you are not. You are very brave. I remember Morocco and Kosovo.'

'I was shitting myself all the time,' Matt replied.

'Maybe. But you didn't give up. You got your pictures. Always.'

Rosie looked up as the waitress came with their tea and saw the guys coming in through the door. Timmy was with them.

'Your mates have arrived, Adrian.'

The bar was already busy with late afternoon diners, tables being wiped and a constant flow of food. Rosie and Matt ordered burgers and chips; Adrian said he'd eaten a sandwich earlier. One of the big men noticed him and called him over. He said nothing, just got up and went across to the bar. Rosie turned to Matt.

'We need to get a picture of Timmy, but it's going to be difficult in here.'

Matt stood up. 'I'm going to the car to get set up with my camera stuff. I'll put the secret one on my jacket and go up to the bar for a drink, but I'll also need to get a better one. So I might try something.'

'Try what?'

'Not sure yet. I'll let you know.'

Rosie watched the conversation at the bar as Matt left and she hoped Adrian wasn't getting himself in too deep. She knew he would push things to the limit, believing he could handle himself, but these were hard men. For the moment the conversation seemed good-natured and every now and then the man who seemed to be the leader of the pack leaned in conspiratorially. Matt came back and sat down.

'Right, here's the plan, Rosie.'

She looked at him, waiting.

'Okay. You're my girlfriend and I'm going to take some pictures of you and you can take one or two of me, while we're sitting here. We'll just act all lovey-dovey and stuff. So don't be flinching at anything I might do in the next few minutes. In fact, you might even enjoy it.'

'Aye, right, Matt. Just don't get all cocky.'

'Give me your hand.'

Rosie couldn't help smiling as she held out her hand. He pulled his chair closer to her and ran his hand through her hair. Rosie glanced up and could see Adrian clock the movement. Then Matt let her go and leaned back, taking pictures one after the other. He handed her the camera.

'Now you take a couple of me.'

Rosie got up and took some pictures. This went on, one of him, of her.

'Okay, now I want you to stand up where the light is coming in the window. If you're in the right place then I can also get a pic where Timmy is in the edge of it. We'll only have one shot at this, so we have to be fast.'

Rosie got up and stood nearer the window. He took the picture and she sat down. The travellers at the bar didn't seem any the wiser, but Adrian was watching every move.

'Got him,' Matt said as she sat down. 'It's not the best image in the world, but it'll do if we don't get anything else. In fact, I'm going to leave here as soon as we finish eating, stake this place out from across the road and get him when he leaves.'

'Good idea. I'll come with you and we'll leave Adrian to it. We can see him when he comes out.'

It was nearly an hour later when Adrian came out of the bar first, the others following him except for the leader. She could see Adrian taking his mobile out of his pocket and making a call as he moved down the street a little and out of their sight. His number came up on her mobile.

'Rosie. Listen. They have invited me to the dogfight, so I am going to go with them. I will go in their pickup truck, so you and Matt can follow me. But be careful.'

'Do you think that's a good idea, Adrian? I mean, just like that? So quickly? We don't know how safe it is.'

'It's not safe. But I will be okay. I talked to the boy Timmy, and he told me the dogfight is exciting and lots of people win money. He holds the money when the betting starts. He talks like a big man, but he is shaking and sweating all the time.'

'But we won't be able to get into the dogfight, surely?'

'No. Best not to. Just wait at the edge of it. Park the car somewhere close, so that when I come out we can drive away fast.'

Rosie suddenly thought.

'Listen. Can we stick a camera on you and you can video it?'

'Yes, but you will have to be fast, because we are going soon.'

Rosie rang Matt and told him. He was at Adrian's side in two minutes, and hid a camera in the pocket of Adrian's shirt flap.

'Okay, mate. Hope that works,' he said.

Adrian backed away.

'Okay. Watch where I go. Don't come after me, no matter what happens. But be ready to go.'

*

Half an hour had passed since Adrian had disappeared behind the big steel gates, dragged shut by two bouncers. From what they could see inside, it was a scrapyard with a huge barn. Rosie and Matt sat about fifty yards away in a lay-by and got out of the car, so that they could see cars going up and people arriving, the gates opening and closing. For something as secret as dogfighting it seemed to be fairly open, and Rosie assumed that unless you were one of their own, you wouldn't dare turn up. As darkness began to fall, they could hear the shouts and roars from within, and the snarling and yelping of dogs and people roaring – cheering for whatever dog they'd backed.

'I hope Adrian's getting this on camera,' Matt said.

'I'm sure he will. But I hope he's all right.'

Now and again the gates opened and a punter came out, then they closed again. Rosie's mobile rang. It was Adrian.

'Rosie. Be ready in five minutes. Okay? I'll be outside. We need to be quick.'

Rosie turned to Matt. 'It's Adrian. He said to be ready, to be outside. Do you think it's safe to take the car down there?'

'We have to. As long as we're sitting there ready to go, with the engine running. Come on. Let's go.'

They drove the car with the headlights off until they got outside the high gates. Inside, they could hear snarling and shouting, and shrieks from the punters. Then the gates suddenly opened a little and Adrian appeared, Timmy behind him. Adrian walked to the left a little as though to point something out to him. When Timmy followed, Adrian suddenly turned to him, quick as lightning, and punched him hard in the face. Then another two rapid blows, and Timmy collapsed. He'd been carrying a bag of something, and Adrian grabbed it and threw it away as he bent down and scooped Timmy up. He walked towards their car with the limp body of Timmy under his arm like a package.

'Open the boot of your car, Matt.'

'What? Fuck me, Adrian!'

'Hurry. We don't have time.'

Rosie sat open-mouthed.

'Hurry, Matt. Open it.'

'Oh fuck!' Matt said as the boot clicked open.

They glanced at each other, wide-eyed, as they heard Timmy being clattered into the boot. Then the back door opened and Adrian threw himself in.

'Let's go. Quickly. Before they notice.'

'Christ almighty, Adrian!' Rosie said. 'What we going to do with him? You're kidnapping him.'

'Is no problem. He is an evil man.'

Rosie looked at Matt and knew they were both thinking the same thing – of the pervert in Morocco filming children for porn films. He too was bundled into the boot of a car by Adrian and he ended up at the foot of a very deep well in the scrubland. No great loss to the world. But this wasn't Morocco – this was Blackpool. Jesus.

As Matt's wheels screeched in the dust and they took off, Rosie could see in the mirror the bag full of money, notes tumbling out, carried off in the breeze.

CHAPTER THIRTY-ONE

By the time they were half an hour up the M6, there was no sign of anyone trying to pursue them. Matt kept his foot to the floor, and they were suddenly conscious that the loud banging from the boot had stopped.

'Do you think he's dead?' Rosie said.

'Don't know,' Matt said.

'What the hell do we do now?' Rosie turned to Adrian.

'You are the boss. I thought you wanted to talk to him.'

'Yes I do, but I wasn't planning on kidnapping him.' She was looking out of the windscreen at the landscape to see where they were. 'How about we stop somewhere in the countryside and have a look at him?'

'You planning to interview him?' Matt asked.

'Well, yes. If I can. But I also want to get him to Glasgow as soon as possible, and get the cops. They can deal with him.' She saw a sign for Kendal. 'Look, let's pull off here.

Maybe go a few miles into the Lake District. There are bound to be some quiet roads.'

Matt took the exit and they drove on the slip road towards Kendal. After a few miles of twists and turns they were deep into the country. There was a clearing on a side road and he drove up and parked the car.

'This secluded enough?'

'Yeah,' Rosie replied, opening her door. 'Let's get him out of the boot and see what happens.'

As Matt pinged the boot open from the driver's seat, Adrian and Rosie stood at the back of the car. When the hatch lifted, Timmy O'Dwyer shrank back, terror all over his bruised face.

'Wha-what the fuck! What is this? Listen. Don't kill me! Please . . . My da's got money. He'll pay whatever you want.'

Rosie watched him squirm, trying to find a place in the boot to hide. Adrian reached across to him and he whimpered.

'I haven't done anything.'

Rosie took a step forward and switched on her tape recorder.

'That's not true, Timmy.'

'What?' He glanced up at her, his eyes wild, terrified. 'Who the fuck are you?'

'Never mind that just now. But it's not true to say you haven't done anything, is it?'

'What? What are you talking about?'

'Those people in the grave at the field. That was you, wasn't it? The woman and the baby. You killed your own baby, Timmy O'Dwyer. Your own child, you murderer.'

His mouth dropped open. 'Aw fuck! Are you cops?'

'No. Not cops.' Rosie went closer. 'You stink, Timmy. You stink of fear and badness. How could you kill your own baby?'

'I . . . I didn't.'

Adrian reached in and grabbed him by the neck, almost choking him as he lifted him out of the boot. Timmy's legs buckled, but Adrian pushed him to his feet and punched him against the car. He punched him hard again in the face and Timmy spat blood as his body buckled. Adrian raised his hand to punch him again, but Rosie reached over and touched his arm as she met his eyes, full of anger. He stopped, mid blow.

'Timmy.' Rosie turned to him. 'Look. We know all about you. The cops are about to come and get you, so there's no point in lying. You're finished. You'll not see the outside of a jail cell for the next twenty years. I know what you've done and I know you told your father and your brother Finbar about the murder of Elsa and her baby.'

Timmy suddenly perked up.

'The fuckers!' he muttered. 'They grassed me up! My own family. I knew it when they sent me away. I knew they'd grass me.'

Rosie knew she should stop right now and call the cops, but she couldn't resist it.

'Why did you do it? Why did you kill them?'

He stood for a moment, his eyes wild, as though he was being confronted by an image he had tried to banish.

'Ah fuck! She wanted money, so she did. I gave her some and she wanted more. She was blackmailing me, the cunt. Said she was going to tell me da and he would go mental.'

'So you just killed her? And your baby?'

His face began to break. 'I . . . I didn't mean to. I . . . I was drunk. Then – she pushed and pushed and I went crazy – I . . . I didn't mean to.'

'You killed them both. How can you say you didn't mean to?'

'Once I hit her and she fell down and banged her head, I had to do something to hide it all. What could I do? I couldn't tell my da. I just went black. It was like everything went black. But I always knew they were there. It followed me around every day.'

'What followed you? Are you saying you felt guilty? Ashamed?'

'I don't know. Just scared. I . . . I drink too much and I can't control myself.' He shook his head.

'So is that what happened when you killed the young couple? The kids who were camping? Were you scared they'd got too close to your grave, scared they would find your secret?'

Timmy started to whimper. 'Oh please, I'm sorry. I . . . They . . . I just went mad. I was coming back from the pub and I saw the dog was digging. I only meant to kill the fucking dog, and then the guy comes out and I just kept hitting him. And then the girl.'

'Christ!'

Adrian dragged him away from the car.

'Adrian. What are you doing?'

He stopped. 'Rosie. Let me deal with him.'

She went after him.

'Adrian! No. You can't! We have to get the cops!'

'He should not be alive, in prison, after what he did. He killed his own baby.' He was choking Timmy, whose face was turning blue.

'Adrian, stop!' Rosie pulled his arm. 'Please! Don't do this! It's not the answer! You cannot keep doing this! It won't make it any better for you . . . Please, Adrian.'

Timmy was on the verge of passing out, his eyes bulging, when Adrian let him drop to the ground. He looked at Rosie, his eyes full of anger, then turned away and walked towards the car. Rosie and Matt watched as Timmy lay on the ground, grunting and clutching his neck. She went over to Adrian where he stood lighting up a cigarette and drawing it deeply. He looked down at her.

'I'm sorry, Rosie.'

Rosie held his arm and squeezed it.

'Come on. Let's get him back in the boot. We'll take him

to Glasgow and hand him over. That's all we have to do. Anything else is just wrong.'

He looked at her for a long moment, his eyes hard and far away.

'Everything is wrong, Rosie. All of it. Nothing will ever be right again.'

'It will be as right as it can be, Adrian. We do the best we can, that's all. Come on.'

They stood for a moment, then Matt got into the car and started the engine. Adrian looked down at Timmy then lifted him up like a rag doll. He dumped him into the boot and slammed it shut.

As soon as Rosie saw the sign for Abingdon she punched in McGuire's mobile number. She'd rejected his calls earlier, and knew that by this time he'd be ranting. He answered straight away.

'Gilmour, I've been trying to bloody phone you.'

'I know, Mick. Bad area. But I'm nearly home now.'

'My arse, Gilmour. What's happening?'

'We had to get out fast – as per your instructions.'

'What happened? Did you see that Timmy bastard?'

'We did. And we've got an interview. Well, a sort of inter-view.' She was conscious of Matt stifling a chuckle.

'So where is he? Is he still in Blackpool?'

'Er, no. He's with us.'

'What? He agreed to come to Glasgow? Did he admit anything?'

'Everything. I'm going to phone the cops now, so that they're ready to take him in.'

'You mean he's actually sitting in the car beside you?'

'Not quite. He's in the boot.'

'Oh fuck! You kidnapped him? Christ, Gilmour! Are you kidding me?'

'Who's going to believe we kidnapped him, Mick? Seriously. He's just confessed on tape to me that he killed his baby and its mother. And – wait for it – he also did the camper couple.'

'What! You are fucking joking.'

'Nope. He's confessed to it.'

'Just like that?'

'Well. We kind of trapped him into it. I told him I knew he confessed to his da and brother, and he assumed that they stuck him in. He's as thick as pig shit. But he's a bad bastard. Put it this way: he's very lucky to be alive.'

'Does that mean the big Bosnian got his hands on him?'

'Just a bit.' She paused. 'Listen, Mick. It might get a bit dodgy when the cops get involved, given the circumstances of us bringing him in. So can you have Hanlon standing by? I'm taking him to Pitt Street. We'll be there in an hour.'

'I'll phone him. Well done, Gilmour. But I'm a bit edgy about this.'

'Me too. Talk later.' She hung up.

As they passed Lesmahagow and the sign for Glasgow, Rosie breathed a sigh of relief. They were almost home. But this was far from over. She called Don.

'Rosie. How you?'

'Listen, Don. How can I say this . . . There's been a significant development in the bodies in the grave story. I'm heading to Glasgow right now . . . with the guy who did it.'

Silence.

'Shit!'

'I have Timmy O'Dwyer in the car. He's admitted everything on tape. I'll explain it all later. But if I were you, I'd be out at O'Dwyer's farm picking up his father and brother Finbar. Because he's named them too – in the death of Bo – just as Tadi told you. And the robbery.'

'Fuck me! And he's with you?'

'Yeah. His father sent him away into hiding, to traveller mates down south. He knows he's done for. He's a bit knocked about.'

'What happened?'

'Never mind. All that matters is he's admitting everything – even the murder of the young campers. He did it. He told me he was drunk and on his way home. He went past the field, saw the couple's tent near the grave, and got freaked out.'

'Christ almighty! I'd better get the boss.'

'I'll be at Pitt Street in half an hour.' She paused. 'And Don, I don't want any heavy stuff from your bosses over how this has come about. So can you explain that?'

'I'll do my best, Rosie.' He hung up.

CHAPTER THIRTY-TWO

Rosie pulled down her visor to look at Timmy in the back seat. He sat still as a mouse, staring straight ahead, one of his eyes beginning to swell. They'd taken him out of the boot a few miles back and Adrian had told him that if he moved a muscle, he would kill him. Timmy knew he meant it. Adrian caught Rosie's eye but there was the same lack of expression she had seen on him so many times over the years, when he'd kind of zoned out. What was going on behind those eyes right now, she didn't know. But there was no triumph or happiness that he was bringing this killer in. Rosie knew he'd have preferred to mete out his own justice to this piece of shit – to make up for all the people who had been on the receiving end of bastards like him. She partly understood it. Unless you had been where people like Adrian had been, among the violated and butchered innocents in your homeland, you really knew nothing of pain. But whatever was going on in his head, it was clear that Adrian was not making progress with coming to terms with his past. Rosie flipped up the visor. That was for another day.

'Rosie.' Adrian leaned forward. 'Before you meet with your police, I will go. You understand?'

'Sure,' Rosie replied. She turned around and could see something like hope register in Timmy's eyes.

Adrian grabbed his upper arm and squeezed it until Timmy squeaked in pain.

'But you don't move. If you try to get out of the car, I will be close by and I will be watching you. Believe me. Is better if you go with the police than be found by me.'

Timmy said nothing.

Rosie phoned Don.

'Don, can you be outside the office in two minutes? At the back entrance?'

'We're on our way down. I'll get the lads to open the gates.'

Matt pulled up just yards from the police station.

'Is here okay, Adrian?'

'Yes. Thank you.' He squeezed Rosie's shoulder as he opened the door. 'I call you later.'

She turned her body around and they faced each other in silence for a long moment.

'Thanks, Adrian. Be careful.'

He squeezed her shoulder a second time.

'You be careful, my friend.'

Then he was gone, walking briskly away from the car and up Bath Street as they turned into the police station. Timmy sat, his hands on his knees, his face sweating. Rosie could see four uniformed officers coming out of the back door towards her car, and a second later Don, along with DI Morton. Matt stopped the car, they both got out and he locked the door. By the time Don and the DI were at the car, Timmy was banging hysterically on the windows.

'Let me out! Please! They kidnapped me! Help! Police! Help!'

Everyone looked at Rosie and she looked at Matt, then turned to the car.

'Don't listen to the shit he's talking. He's a bad bastard, guys. He killed four people. He's told me all about it, in front of Matt.'

The DI gave her a long look, then said to Matt, 'Can you unlock the door please?' He nodded to the uniformed officers to move forward.

As the door opened, Timmy frantically struggled to get out, but he was met by a six-foot heavyweight plod who grabbed him and turned him around quickly, pushing him into the car with his arms behind his back. The other officer cuffed him.

'It's a set-up, officer. These bastards kidnapped me. I've done nothing.'

Rosie looked at the DI and Don.

'He's a liar,' she said quietly. 'But as you'll find, not a very good one. He's thick as pig shit.'

The DI gestured to Rosie to come away from the car and she and Matt followed him and Don.

'Rosie. Did you kidnap this man? Because if you did, his defence lawyer will drive right through any case we try to build.'

'He's guilty,' Rosie snapped. 'He told me he murdered his own baby daughter, buried her and the mother in that shallow grave, Inspector. I've got the full interview on tape. Don't listen to a word he says. He killed that young couple too.'

'Rosie, I believe you. I believe he told you that. But look at the state of him. What happened? Did someone rough him up?'

Rosie stood her hands on her hips.

'Yes.'

'Who?'

Rosie glanced at Don, who looked at her and then the ground.

'A friend of mine. But he's gone now. Look, none of this matters in the great scheme of things. He's a murderer. I'm leaving that up to you guys now. I've brought him to you, so I can't do any more.' She paused. 'I have to go back to my office. See how we want to play this.'

'Do you have the tape of his confession?'

Rosie looked at him for a moment but didn't speak.

'Yes.'

She glanced at Matt, grateful that he had suggested that they take ten minutes before they hit the road to transfer the tape onto one of his gadgets so that she had a copy. He had been afraid they would have to hand it over, but in the drama of the moment, Rosie had forgotten. Now she went into her bag and pulled out the copy. She handed it to the DI.

'There you go. No charge.'

He took a long breath and shook his head slowly, an expression somewhere between incredulousness and gratitude spreading over his face.

'We'll need you to make a statement. Can you come with us? Let's go up to my office.'

Rose put her hands up. 'I will make a statement, no problem. But not right now. I have to get back to the office. Do you understand?'

'Yes, Rosie. But we have a job to do.'

'I'm sorry. But the statement will have to wait.' She glanced at Timmy, face down on the bonnet of the car. 'I'd say you'll have enough on your hands getting your own confession from that piece of shit.'

The DI grimaced. 'If we don't get a confession, he'll say your confession was beaten out of him.'

Rosie smiled defiantly as she pulled her bag on her shoulder.

'Well, look on the bright side. At least it wasn't *you* who beat it out of him. So you're in the clear, pal.' She paused. 'Now please, I have to go, if it's okay. But I'll be available at the *Post* in the morning.'

The officers stood still, as though they didn't know how to react.

'Your protection guys are outside, Rosie. Wait there while we tell them you're on your way out of here. Okay?' Don said.

'Okay,' Rosie said and turned towards the gate where a car, with two plain-clothes officers inside, drove in.

Adrian was already in the all-night cafe in Woodlands Road when Rosie walked in. She'd called him as soon as they left the police station, after she'd spoken to McGuire. Instead of coming to the office at this time of night, the editor had told her to go home and get some sleep. The tape could wait til tomorrow morning. He was just glad that she hadn't been arrested for kidnapping. But Rosie was too wound up to go to bed and the thought of going back to the empty flat filled her with dread. That had been happening more often in the past few days. She felt threatened by the silence that she normally craved, and the loneliness that she had always felt comfortable with now closed in on her. What was happening to her? She brushed the thought aside as she told Matt to take her to the cafe, then go home and get some sleep. She knew Adrian would be there for her. He always was.

'Rosie? You are okay?' He stood up when she came towards him.

She nodded. 'Yes. What about you?'

Adrian made a so-what face, and gave her a peck on the cheek.

'Are your policemen still watching you?'

'Yes. They're outside. They must think I'm some raging insomniac. But I don't feel tired yet.'

'I'm the same. I won't sleep if I go to my friend's house, so I'm happy to sit here with you.'

The waitress came over and Rosie ordered a decaf tea, and Adrian some mineral water.

'Insomniacs together. But I need my sleep, Adrian. I'll be wrecked in the morning, and I've got so much to do.'

They sat in silence for a moment, comfortable in each other's company. Then Rosie looked at Adrian.

'Did you think at any point in that dogfight that you were going to get rumbled – caught, I mean?'

'Always a little bit of me is ready in case it happens. It would have been bad in that place if something went wrong. These people are very different from you and me. Different from a lot of people I know – even violent men I have known. They have their own, how do you say, code and way they do things. They would have torn me apart. Maybe throw me to the dogs.' He sipped his water. 'But I am here.' He paused. 'Do you think the police will get a confession out of Timmy?'

Rosie nodded. 'I think so. Don called me and said they'd picked up the father and brother, so no doubt a lawyer will have been called by now. If the cops do their jobs right tonight, they will get enough to hold them in custody for a couple of days.'

Adrian was looking beyond Rosie into the street.

'I keep thinking of the mother and the little baby he killed.' He brought his gaze back to Rosie. 'You know why I was so out of control earlier, don't you?'

She reached across and touched his hand.

'Of course. And I understand.'

Adrian's mouth tightened.

'I wanted to punish him. Stupid, I know. I cannot punish the man who killed my child. I wanted to punish someone who killed another innocent mother and child. I have tried not to be like this.' He shook his head.

'I understand.'

Then Adrian changed the subject. 'How long do you want me to stay here? I mean, in Glasgow, to help you?'

She looked at him curiously. 'Do you want to go home?'

He shook his head. 'No. Of course, I will stay as long as you need me. Always. I will stay until the police catch this man, Boag. Because I think he is someone who is cleverer than a lot of people. He is your real danger now – not the gypsy people.'

'I know. Don't make me any more scared.'

He half smiled and leaned across and touched her hair.

'I miss you sometimes, when I'm back in Bosnia, Rosie. Like that time when you were over, in hiding. I think a lot of those days and the good times.'

Rosie didn't know what to say. It had been a desperate time, and she'd run to him when she should have gone to TJ. But it was in the past. It had to be, if she stood any chance of having any kind of normal relationship with TJ.

'Me too. I think of those times. Good memories.'

There was a slight awkwardness in the moment. In the past, Rosie would have allowed the conversation to develop and they would perhaps have ended up together tonight, in the quiet of the bedroom, as lovers and friends. But she said nothing, and they sat listening to the noises of the city and the hiss of the coffee machine behind the counter.

CHAPTER THIRTY-THREE

McGuire listened to the tape, playing it again and again, wincing and frowning at Rosie sitting opposite him in his office.

'He sounds a bit under pressure, Gilmour – like he doesn't have a choice.'

'I know what you mean,' Rosie said. 'But he did have a choice. He could've said nothing. He was still going to the cops whether he confessed or not.'

'But was your man terrorising him?'

Rosie folded her arms.

'It's fair to say he got a going-over, Mick. But we're not the cops, we don't have to play by their rules.'

McGuire frowned. 'We don't beat stories out of people, Gilmour, you know that. But apart from anything else, you might be called as a witness if this goes to trial. What's it going to look like if a reporter is seen to be –' he made an inverted-comma gesture with his fingers – ' "coercing" a confession from a guy by having him beaten up?'

'The beating was in self-defence, is what I would say. I would say that my friend got a bit of a hiding too in order to get out of the place and bring Timmy with him. And at the end of the day, Timmy didn't have to go into the detail he did about how he killed those people. Nobody was more surprised than me when he confessed to killing the young couple. He wasn't coerced into that. He just opened his trap and let it all spill out. He's that reckless.' She paused. 'And anyway, I'd bet my house on it not going to trial. He'll plead guilty. The cops have already picked up Rory O'Dwyer and Finbar, and they'll be all over the farm looking for forensic evidence. Maybe they'll even find a weapon. This case is only going in one direction – towards jailing these three bastards. Plus the cops have got Tadi's testimony about the robbery and how they put him up to it. Guaranteed they'll all plead guilty. They're going down for a long time. I'm not even worried about it.'

McGuire stood up and walked across the room, past the wall adorned with pictures of historic front pages of the *Post*. He stood at the window with his back to Rosie. Then he turned around.

'Then in that case, I think we need to use what we've got before the police start charging everyone and closing us down. What can we use?'

Rosie sat back with her hands clasped behind her head.

This was what she'd hoped for. McGuire liked to push it as much as she did.

'The police and Crown Office will go nuts. But basically, I can sit down and pretty much put a full story together of the whole investigation – from the bodies in the grave right up to the O'Dwyers being arrested.'

'I want to use Timmy's confession.'

'We'll need to get the lawyers in. It's dodgy. But it's not a confession to the police. It's a confession to a reporter – a claim by him that he's killed four people.'

'I want to use it. I can't resist it. Write it as he says it. Straight quotes.'

'Okay. Then I'll put everything down in the next couple of hours – just tell it as it was told to me and write up our investigation, how we went down to Blackpool to track him down and found him in the midst of a dogfight. Adrian got some footage from inside one of the fights.'

'Brilliant! I want to see the pics as soon as possible.'

'Good. Matt has them now. If I get the copy done early enough, we can talk to the lawyers in the afternoon and pray that the cops don't charge anyone in the next twenty-four hours.' She stood up. 'But tomorrow is Father Dunnachie's funeral, so I want to go and pay my respects.' She sighed. 'I still can't believe it's happened. Imagine going through your whole life as a priest in a difficult community, and then some psycho from nowhere bursts into your home and murders you. It's just so . . .' Her voice trailed off. 'I feel so responsible.'

McGuire came back to his desk.

'I know you do. But listen, you made your peace with him before he died, and he told you that you weren't to blame. So you need to stop beating yourself up and get on with it – really, you owe that to him. Go to the funeral, and then you need to put it behind you.'

Rosie knew he was right but there was still a heaviness in her heart because Father Dunnachie was one of the last remnants of her early life, someone she could talk to. One of the few people who really understood why she was the way she was.

'Okay. I'll go and get started.'

Rosie woke up to the sound of rain on her bedroom window. She lay staring at the ceiling, still tired despite her early night. Yesterday had been a long day, putting her piece together by early afternoon, then spending the rest of the day going through it with Hanlon and the boss of the legal firm. They'd made all the usual noises about the consequences of using the story in all its graphic detail, and were particularly concerned about the taped confession. But in the end it was the editor's call, and McGuire decided to publish. When she'd left the office last night, she could see the front page on the screen with the massive headline: I CONFESS. Then a smaller headline below:

'SHALLOW GRAVE' KILLER UNMASKED. Rosie's story led with the first paragraph.

A man has confessed to the murder of the young students stabbed to death and buried in a shallow grave near Lennoxtown. And in his astonishing admission of guilt, he also admits to killing the woman and her small baby, which he claims is his, whose bodies were found in the same grave. Today, the Post *can reveal the grisly details of Timmy O'Dwyer's dark secret after he got a Ukrainian girl pregnant, and we can tell the story behind the burnt body of Robert 'Bo' Bowman, the down-and-out whose body was also in the grave.*

It would be one of the most historic front pages the *Post* had ever seen, and the paper would be flying off the shelves today. But there'd be some almighty fallout from the police by the time it hit the streets. Rosie braced herself and kicked back the duvet. She showered and had breakfast watching the rain coming down in sheets across Charing Cross and the slow snake of traffic. She picked out black jeans and a white shirt, then her navy raincoat, and headed out of the house for the funeral. She picked Adrian up as arranged outside her flat where he stood in the rain wearing his canvas bomber jacket. She stopped by the police protection car and as they lowered the window, she told them where she was going. Then, just after nine, she headed out with them behind her, towards the East End of

Glasgow, past the rows of tenements and shops beginning to wake up to a new day.

There was already a crowd filing into St Gregory's church, and pupils from the local primary and secondary schools were lining up to take their seats. Rosie went inside and sat in the back pew with Adrian. Just coming into the place, the smell of incense and candles, brought a lump to her throat. The last time she'd been here was to ask the old priest about her mother's grave. Father Dunnachie had helped her find it, and he even went with her to see it. Now his oak coffin sat on a pedestal at the front of the church, where it had been taken last night during a service. A few priests came in from the front door, and she saw the Archbishop of Glasgow arriving and walking down the aisle towards the sacristy where they would dress for the requiem mass. A few minutes later, the strains of the organ brought everyone to their feet, as the choir led in the parade of priests. The singing began.

I, the Lord of sea and sky, I have heard my people cry.
All who dwell in dark and sin, my hand will save . . .

And then the chorus.

Here I am, Lord. Is it I, Lord?
I have heard you calling in the night.
I will go, Lord, if you lead me.
I will hold your people in my heart . . .

Rosie managed to swallow the lump in her throat until Adrian put his hand on hers, then tears spilled over. She felt embarrassed, burying her face in a tissue. What was going on here? Was she weeping for the priest, or for herself, for the miserable memories of her early life, because at times like this it all came flooding back. The congregation sat down and she managed to compose herself, grateful that Adrian was holding her hand.

When the service was over, Rosie watched outside as they slid the priest's coffin into the back of the hearse. She caught the eye of Father Flaherty and he gave her a sympathetic smile.

'The cemetery is a couple of miles away, Adrian,' she said. 'We'll go there.'

'Are you sure?'

'Yes. I want to.'

He didn't question her and they headed for her car.

They joined the line of people filing into the cemetery, along the narrow paths between graves old and new. Rosie stood on the hillside, gazing at the trees and the city ahead. She scanned the crowd, and saw Don and a few other police officers she recognised. Sometimes they would go to a funeral of a murder victim, in the unlikely event that the killer turned up. A burst of heavy rain broke through the grey clouds, and people stood under umbrellas as the priests made their way to the grave ahead of the coffin. She watched as Father Dunnachie was lowered into the ground and the young curate began a decade of the rosary. Suddenly, Adrian grabbed hold of Rosie's arm.

'Rosie,' he whispered, 'don't look now, but I can see Boag in the crowd.'

Rosie felt as though she'd been punched in the gut.

'Oh, Christ! Where?'

'Over there on the brow of the hill. Where you left the car. Can you see him?'

Rosie was glad of her dark glasses, despite the rain, and she scanned the crowd. Then she saw him. He was standing, wearing a black overcoat, his hair lank and wet. It was him.

'I have to call the cops.'

'He is watching you, Rosie. Don't do anything. Let's quietly slip away in the crowd. We'll walk towards him as though we haven't seen him.'

'Then what?' she said as they walked away. 'We need to get the cops.'

'We will. I just want to see where he goes.'

They slipped through the crowd, Adrian keeping his eye on Boag. Rosie took out her mobile and called Don.

'Don. It's me. Listen. Boag's here.'

'Fuck! Where?'

'On the brow of the hill. I'm walking there now.'

'I can't see you.'

Rosie scanned the skyline.

'The top of the hill, above where the cars are parked.'

Silence.

'Fuck! I see him.' He hung up.

Rosie and Adrian sidled through the crowd, closer and closer to Boag, then, when they were only a few yards away, he turned and looked Rosie in the eye. He sprinted down the hill.

'Hurry,' Adrian said. 'I'm going after him. Best if you wait.'

'No,' Rosie said. 'I've called the police. They saw him and they'll go after him. Leave it to them.'

'I'm going, Rosie. I can see him getting into a car. Can you give me your keys, please?'

Rosie looked at him.

'I'm coming too. You drive.'

CHAPTER THIRTY-FOUR

Adrian drove out of the cemetery and followed the small dark blue car they'd seen Boag get into.

'We're sure it's him, aren't we?' Rosie felt stupid for even asking, but her head had been so all over the place the last few days that she was beginning to question herself.

'It's him. He was looking at you. It's what I noticed first. I'm watching the crowd and everyone is concentrating on the coffin and the priests, but this man was staring in your direction. Then, suddenly, I know who he is. I can't believe he comes to the funeral.'

There were three cars in front, heading for the south side of the city, and Boag's was in the middle.

'Do you think he knows we're following? I mean, do you think he wants us to follow him?' Even saying it gave Rosie the creeps.

Adrian shot her a sideways glance.

'Yes. I think he wants us to follow him. Listen to me,

Rosie. I think I should drop you here, and let me go after him. I can get him. I *want* to get him. No police, just me and him. I can finish this today.'

Rosie's gut was in knots. She was terrified of what she was doing, and all her instincts told her to stop the car and get out now. But she couldn't help herself.

'No. I'm coming. I can't let him win.'

Her mobile rang, and she saw Don's name on the screen.

'Rosie. We're about four cars behind you. Is he ahead of you?'

'Yes. There's three cars in front of us, and he's the second one. A small, dark blue car. Looks like a Ford Fiesta or something. We can see him.'

'Good. I'm going to get some help. We'll get him cut off at the top of the road. What the fuck is he playing at? Trying to get you to follow him?'

'I don't know. I think so.'

'Who's with you?'

'My friend.'

'The Bosnian?'

'Yes.'

'Listen, Rosie. I want you to get out of the car now and leave this to us. Do you hear me?'

'Yes, I hear you, Don. But I'm not going to do anything stupid.'

Suddenly there was a ferocious bang behind their car, and Don's phone went dead.

'Christ! What was that?' Rosie turned around to look out of the back window. From the angle, it looked as though a lorry had come out of a side street and smashed into two cars from the side. She could see one of them overturn and land on its roof.

'Is a crash.' Adrian kept one eye on his rear-view mirror.

'Shit. I think it's the cop car. Or the one in front. I can't see. My friend's phone cut off.' She tried to phone Don back, but it rang out.

'We keep going. I can see him. He is turning off the main road.'

Boag's car turned the corner, and Adrian slowed a few seconds before he also took the turn. They were leaving the main part of the Southside, and Rosie knew this road would take them out towards the countryside. They drove past some old buildings and a derelict boatyard, then up the rise of the hill where the steep embankment led down into a small stream.

'Where's he going?' Rosie said. 'There's nothing much up here, except a few storage places and lock-ups. There's the old sewerage works up there near the park.'

Adrian said nothing and kept driving behind him. Rosie began to feel more uneasy now that they were getting further from the city, with no protection from the police. She tried Don's phone again, but it went to voicemail. He would have called back if he could. He must have been in the crash. She prayed he wasn't seriously injured, and maybe his phone was just knocked out of service. They should turn back.

'Adrian.' She touched his arm. 'We should leave it.'

'Rosie.' He slowed down a fraction, looked her in the eye. 'Please. Let me stop and you can get out. I am staying with him. It finishes today.'

Rosie had seen that look in Adrian's eye before. She couldn't leave him to go on his own. She rang Don's number again. Nothing. Then she dialled 999. A woman's voice announced, 'Fire police ambulance?'

'Hello. My name is Rosie Gilmour. I'm a journalist with the *Post*. Thomas Boag, the serial killer, is in the Southside of Glasgow. I am behind him in my car. The police were behind me but there's been an accident.'

'Where exactly are you, madam?'

Rosie looked around as Adrian drove up the winding road past some tall trees, away from the housing. Her mind was a blur. She couldn't see Boag's car in front any more. It was eerily quiet.

'I came off Pollokshaws Road and now we're going up the high road between trees . . . You know, where there's a small stream running along the bottom of a steep bank. It's . . . I think it's close to the old sewerage works . . . I—'

'Rosie,' Adrian interrupted. 'You should call Mulhearn. Maybe the police won't come.'

She glanced at him, and saw a look as close to fear as she'd ever seen in his eyes. She scrolled down her phone.

She put the operator on hold and dialled Jonjo's number.

'Jonjo. It's me, Rosie. I need your help. I—'

'Where are you?' Jonjo broke in.

'I . . . I'm not sure. I'm chasing Boag, with my friend Adrian. We drove off Pollokshaws Road and we're heading along that high road up towards the old sewerage works, I think. I can see tall trees, an embankment and a small stream. I think it's a trap. We followed Boag from the old priest's funeral. We're at the top of the hill, close to the lock-ups. But I can't see his car any more.'

'I'm on my way. Don't worry, Rosie. Keep your mobile free.'

He hung up.

Suddenly, there was a heavy thud and the back window shattered. Rosie dropped her mobile as the car thrust forward, her knees bashing against the bottom of the dashboard. She glanced at Adrian in time to see the second his head hit the windscreen in what seemed like slow motion. What the hell had happened? She grabbed Adrian's arm. He was conscious, but bleeding from the head. Then there was a shadow at her side window, and she felt the door handle being yanked. She looked up and her blood ran cold. It was Boag. She bent down to pick up her mobile, the 999 call woman's voice still on the line, saying 'Hello? Are you there?'

Boag stood there, his lips drawn back in a snarl, his face

sweating. He had a machete in his hand. He snatched her mobile and threw it over his shoulder, down the embankment. Rosie shrank back as he opened the door wide and reached in. Then he grabbed her arm and hauled her out of the car, beating the back of her legs with the machete as she struggled. But even though she could feel it cutting her flesh, there was no pain – just icy cold fear. As she fell to the ground, she could see that Adrian still looked woozy, but he made to open his door. In a flash, Boag leaned in the car, hacking wildly with the machete. Adrian moved away in time for it to miss his head, but the full force of it scythed into his leg. Rosie pulled herself up to her knees and gasped as she saw Adrian's thigh opened up in a gaping gash, blood spurting everywhere. Adrian groaned, but couldn't move. Then Boag turned to her and raised the machete above his head. She froze, unable to move, waiting to die. Nobody was coming. Not Mulhearn. Not the police. This was it. Then Boag grabbed her by the hair and spun her around. He placed his hand on her neck and squeezed so hard she almost passed out. As he dragged her backwards, she could see the shock on Adrian's face, etched in pain as he tried to move but couldn't. He tried to stem the blood pumping out of his leg.

'Mulhearn will come, Adrian. He will. Hold on. Please . . . Please. Let me go.' Rosie could hear her own muffled voice.

But Boag was silent as he dragged her away. She could see a doorway into a lock-up that was part of five similar storage places joined together. Boag kicked open the door and pulled her into the darkness. Then she heard the door closing. Where the hell was she? Then she felt a heavy blow to her head and blacked out.

When Rosie came to, she was lying on a wooden pallet on her back. Her legs were stiff and bruised, but she could feel stinging, torn flesh. Christ! If Boag had wanted to, he could have chopped through to the bone, but he'd been beating her with the machete to stop her struggling as he'd dragged her away. When she tried to move, she found her hands were tied above her head. She tugged at them, but her wrists hurt. She moved her legs a little but there was rope around her ankles tying her to the pallet. It was pitch black. She lay trying to catch her breath, the panic rising in her chest, trying to work out where she was. As her eyes began to adjust to the dark, she could see she was in some kind of pit. There was a strange, sweet, sickly smell. Then the reality of the familiar stench hit her – dead bodies, rotting corpses. As she peered into the darkness, she could feel water around her feet, but she couldn't see where it was coming from. What if it got deeper and deeper and she drowned here, like this? She heard herself whimper. 'Oh, God, help me,' she whispered. Then there was the sound of sniggering.

'God can't help you now, Rosie Gilmour. It's too late for God.'

Rosie turned, but she couldn't see him. It was too dark to make out anything other than a shadow.

'Please don't do this,' she pleaded. 'They *will* find you. I called the police. They know where I am. They'll be here soon.'

Silence.

'Oh, the police? They'll never find me. I've been all over this city. In shops, cafes, pubs. I've been under their noses and they still couldn't find me. They're not clever enough. And neither are you.'

'Why are you doing this? How many people have you killed? What kind of monster does the things you do?'

Nothing. Then suddenly she was hit on the legs with some kind of metal rod.

'Please! Stop! My legs! Help me!'

Silence. Just the sound of him breathing. Then he spoke.

'I'm not going to help you, Rosie. This is the end for you. All that work, all those stories you did, exposing people. You think you and your stupid newspaper run the world. But you're nothing down here. I'm in charge.'

'Fuck you, Boag! My investigation got you in jail. You butchered two innocent young men, you twisted bastard! And you murdered your neighbour. You're sick.'

Again the sniggering.

'Aye. But look at you now.' He suddenly thrust something in front of her. In the darkness she could see it was a piece of limb, a leg. She shrank back.

'You know who this is?'

She shook her head. 'Get away!'

'It's her.' Boag grinned. 'The head I sent you? These are the other parts of her. I just took them out of the freezer yesterday, so you could see. She thought she was clever too – watching me, sneaking around that flat below me, trying to find out what I was doing. But that wasn't clever. Interfering bitch.'

'You're a bloody psycho.'

'Aye. But what does that make you? You came after me! I knew you would. Because you might be clever, but you are also stupid.'

In the passenger seat of his blacked-out Range Rover, Jonjo carefully loaded six bullets into his revolver. But the bullets were only for use if things got really out of hand. He wasn't planning on shooting Thomas Boag. No. That twisted cunt wasn't going to get an easy path out of this world. He reached down into the sock above his desert boots, pulled out the leather pouch, and took out his open razor, unfolded it, touched the blade, then folded it back and returned it to the pouch. He could see Danny, his driver, glance out of the corner of his eye as they sped over the Kingston Bridge, and off the slip road onto Kilmarnock Road. Jonjo pushed the pouch back into his sock and secured it.

'You boys sorted in the back there?' Jonjo half turned to Geordie and Aldo.

'Yep. Doing it now, boss.'

He watched as Geordie took a revolver out of the silver attaché case and handed it to Aldo, then put together a sawn-off shotgun. Geordie worked expertly, the way he'd done since they were lads on the rob, teenage tearaways, right until the big heists, the payrolls and bank jobs. Aldo caressed the revolver, opened and checked the chamber, clicked it back. He stared out of the window, his dark heavy Italian features always showing the same expression whether he was happy or sad. You never knew what he was thinking. Deep as the ocean, was Aldo Jaconelli. He kept his anger contained and always appeared passive. The perfect hitman for any job. He would give his life for Jonjo, the bond sealed from when they were teenagers, when Jonjo saved him from certain death after bullies in their housing scheme hung him by the feet out of a window. Aldo loved him like a brother. It wasn't up for discussion, though; Boag was Jonjo's. But right now, they had to work out where the fuck the psycho was.

'Where exactly do you think this reporter bird was, Jonjo?'

'Trying to work it out, mate. I know the old sewerage works, so let's make for that. I used to go up there as a kid and she did describe the road up to it. So let's just keep going.'

On the road ahead they could see flashing lights and a line of traffic.

'Fuck! It's a crash. Fire brigade are there. Cops. And two ambulances.'

'Shit! We've no time to sit in this. Take the next left out of this before we get near them.'

They could hear the police helicopter whirring overhead.

'They're everywhere. Do you think she phoned the cops as well?'

'I don't know. But let's get as far away from them as possible.'

They drove up Pollokshaws Road, conscious of one or two patrol cars, then up towards the quieter road and the tall trees Rosie had described. Jonjo tried to phone her, but it was ringing out. In the distance he could see the top of the old sewerage works as they climbed the hill. He rang the phone again, but nothing. Then, at the top of the road, they turned into a lock-up area and he spotted a car shunted to the side of the road with the rear windscreen smashed. Someone was moving inside it.

'Get close to that car, Danny. I think it might be Rosie's.'

They drove up to the car, and Jonjo saw Adrian. He'd only met him once before, with Rosie. He barely recognised him he was so pale, but it was definitely him.

'Christ. It's the big Bosnian. Stop. Let me out. Keep me covered in case it's a trap.'

Jonjo got out of the Range Rover and slowly went around the back of the car.

'Adrian! Big man! It's me. Jonjo.'

He saw Adrian's head wobble a little and he heard groaning.

'Jonjo! He took Rosie.'

Jonjo was at the side of the car and opened the door. He could see Adrian's leg, the torn flesh, some of the blood had congealed, but it was bleeding through his fingers where he had applied pressure to the wound. It looked bad, as though he'd severed an artery. His face was also covered in blood from a head injury.

'Oh fuck, man! What happened?'

Adrian tried to pull one leg out.

'Quick. Get me out of here. I lose a lot of blood. Do you have any medical things? Bandage or something.'

Jonjo looked over his shoulder and motioned for the boys to come and they all piled out of the car.

'You're all right, big yin. We'll get you sorted. I've got some kind of medical kit in the car, I think. Can you move your leg?'

'Yes. But is bad cut. A machete. Boag. He took Rosie.'

'Bastard. When?'

'She was on the phone to you. Then he rammed the car. He grabbed her. I was dizzy from the crash – I hit my head. Then he slashed my leg. I don't know where he is. He dragged her away.'

'Fuck,' Jonjo spat, looking around. There was an eerie silence except for the sound of the stream.

Danny and Aldo took hold of Adrian by his arms and

helped him onto his feet. When he put his foot down, more blood pumped out.

'Jesus,' Aldo says. 'He needs to go to a hospital, Jonjo.'

'No.' Adrian glared at him. 'No hospital. Just take me to your car. I can clean it. I can fix it if you have things.'

Danny gave Jonjo a surprised look.

'Whatever you say, pal. Come on. Into the car.'

They got him in the car and Danny handed him a hip flask from the glove compartment and told him to drink it. Then he went to the boot and took out the medical kit. He unfolded it on the seat and pulled out bandages, pins, tapes.

'Did you see him go anywhere at all, Adrian?' Jonjo asked. He poured some alcohol from the hip flask over Adrian's leg. 'Sorry, man,' he said as Adrian winced in pain.

'I'm not sure. But he dragged her backwards, and the only place to go from the car is these things, like garages. You see them?'

Jonjo looked across at the lock-up units – they were the kind of places people used to store drugs and stolen goods before police got wise to it. He counted five of them. Take your pick. He walked over to them, Aldo at his side, his eyes on the ground.

'Check the dust, Jonjo, see if there are any marks of her being dragged. You'd see her shoes or footprints or something maybe.'

'Good shout, wee man.'

They studied the ground. Four lock-ups. Two looking like they'd not been opened for years, rusting, another one, new bright blue, then the black one at the end.

'Look,' Danny said. 'Drag marks. Like someone being huckled in there.' They walked closer to it. 'And fresh footprints.'

Jonjo looked at him and almost smiled.

'Cheers, Tonto. I knew all them mornings watching *Lone Ranger* would pay off.'

CHAPTER THIRTY-FIVE

Rosie was drifting in and out of consciousness. She'd been hit on the side of the head and could feel caked blood there, and that the area around her eye was swollen. A sudden draught of air came from somewhere, and daylight spread into the room. She glanced around. There was nobody here. She focused now that she could see properly. She was in what looked like a pit mechanics used in garages, only deeper. Perhaps this place had been a workshop before. She turned her head and saw that the light was coming from what looked like a concrete door that had opened a little. The door was built into the wall of the pit, as though it opened into a crawl space. Above the pit she could make out some tools and equipment. On the wall there was a spade, hammers and a long-handled axe. She tried to move her arms a little and could feel the rope. But suddenly, when she tugged at one of them, it felt quite slack. Then she manoeuvred it again. It felt slacker. Had Boag really made a mistake and not tied her properly? Had he loosened it while she was passed out? Perhaps it was a trap. She left it in case he came in. Her mind was firing on a surge of adrenalin. Where the hell was he? Had he opened the trapdoor and just gone off and left her here? She raised her head and felt a thumping pain as she looked around. There were a couple of old glass bottles, and a small overturned stool. She could see two big butcher's knives, lying too far away from her to do anything with them. She lay back, tugged at the wrist tie again, but she was too afraid to try to untie herself in case he came in – that's if he wasn't up there watching her. She wriggled on the pallet, feeling her blouse soaked with sweat. She was weak from shock and pain, and the desperate prospect that she had no way out of here. But her mind was working overtime. She closed her eyes, then opened them again, peering up. Then she saw Boag. He was standing at the edge of the pit, a shaft of light falling on his face, dark shadows under his eyes.

'Why are you doing this?' Rosie could hear her voice echo a little in the pit. 'Why are you torturing me like this?'

He said nothing, but she could see him still standing staring down at her. She waited for a long moment, hoping he would answer, hoping that maybe she could have some dialogue with him. She remembered reading somewhere that kidnap victims would try to strike up some kind of relationship with their captors as a form of self-preservation.

But in her gut, she knew there was nothing she could say to this monster that would reach him. She had to try, though. At least to buy herself some time.

'Thomas,' she heard herself saying. 'Who made you like this? Who did this to you, that you would kill and torture people like this? Tell me. You're going to kill me anyway. So just tell me.'

Silence.

'You've done terrible things, Thomas. But you can't always have been like this. There must have been a time when you were a little boy. What happened, Thomas?'

Christ, Rosie thought. I'm sounding like a bloody shrink, asking him this, as if he'll even be taking it in.

He said nothing. Then after a few moments, he spoke. 'They all did it,' he muttered.

Rosie lay stunned that he had even answered, not sure what to say next, but knowing she had to say something. She could hear her heartbeat.

'Who did it?'

He said nothing, and Rosie held her breath, waiting.

'School. The boys. Beating me, punching me every day, laughing. Bastards.' His voice trailed off, and she could hear him breathing. Then he spoke again, this time sounding agitated. 'You think it's funny for someone to pee in your school bag, in your lunch, and make you eat your sandwiches, all soaking wet in pee? In front of everyone? Laughing. Always laughing. Fuck!'

'I'm sorry that happened to you, Thomas.'

'Shut up!' he shouted. 'Shut up! You're not sorry. Nobody is sorry. Nobody was ever sorry.'

'Did you tell your parents? Could they not go to the school? Make them stop?'

'Shut up. *I* made them stop. You know how? I went to Joe Black's house one night – he was the worst bastard – and I broke in when they were sleeping. They had this dog . . .' He seemed to snigger a little. 'A white poodle. Charly won all the prizes in stupid dog shows. No more prizes for Charly after that. I cut its throat and left it on the kitchen table . . .'

Jesus! Rosie didn't know what to say next, but she tried. 'What happened? Did they know it was you?'

'They knew it was me all right, but they were too scared to say anything when I went to school the next day and asked Joe how Charly was. Nobody ever hit me again.'

Rosie wasn't equipped to take this kind of conversation any further. She didn't know if whatever she said would make him even more crazed, but she couldn't just leave it like this.

'Thomas, you need help.' Rosie wasn't even sure if she believed that herself. If someone came in here right now and shot him, she'd feel a lot better. 'Listen. There are doctors and psychiatrists who could help you understand the terrible things you've done. And maybe why you did them. People were bad to you. Please. You've killed enough people. Please stop it now. Let me go. Give yourself up to the police.'

She could see him standing with his hands over his ears, shaking his head, vigorously, then slowly. He sighed. Then, to her horror, he picked up a ladder and put it to the edge of the pit, lowering it down. Christ! He was coming down, a knife in his hand. As he began to step down the ladder, he was shouting.

'You don't know anything. You don't understand. I like it, Rosie Gilmour. I like killing people. They make a fool of me . . . everywhere . . .' He was on the ground now, and standing over Rosie.

'At work, they called me weird – smelly. That teacher. I liked him in the beginning. But he thought he was superior.' He slapped his head with his hands. 'And those boys. They didn't like the rough stuff. I saw them scared. Like you now. Scared.'

He took a step closer to Rosie, and crouched down. She caught his rancid sweat as he leaned over and pressed the point of the knife into her forehead. She could feel him pushing it on her skin, and it stung as he twisted it a little.

'Do you like the rough stuff?'

He traced the point of the knife, from her forehead along her cheek and down to her chin. She could feel the pressure of the knife, but it wasn't deep enough to cut her. But now on her neck, he pushed it harder. She could feel the pulse in her neck thumping. A cold sweat broke out all over her and she could hardly breathe. She kept looking up at him, hoping her eyes were pleading for mercy. He pulled the knife from her neck and traced it across her bare chest where the button had come undone in her struggle with him earlier. She felt the knife going in. He had cut her. Pain surged through her and she suppressed the urge to scream as he dragged the knife along, cutting her but not stabbing her. She could feel the warm blood trickling on her chest. Then he stopped.

'It's over, Rosie Gilmour. I'm finished here.' He pulled the knife away and turned towards the ladder.

Rosie held her breath, terrified to speak, as she watched him climb the ladder, then when he got to the top, he pulled the ladder up. He didn't look back at her, didn't utter a sound.

Then she heard a door open upstairs and close again, and the click of it being locked from the outside. She waited a few moments, but there was no sound. She tugged again at her wrist and it was slack enough for her to pull her arm out of the ligature. She managed to twist herself so that she could reach the other wrist, and after a few seconds of trying and cursing, it came away in her hand. She breathed a sigh somewhere between panic and relief and as she pulled herself up, her hand went to her chest where she could feel the fresh warm blood. It was still bleeding, but not gushing.

She sat up stiffly and stretched her back, then leaned forward, and without much effort managed to untie the rope binding her feet. She pulled up her trouser legs and winced at the cuts and bruises to her calves. She sat for a moment, trying to work out why Boag would leave her like this, able to untie herself so easily. Perhaps he'd thought she'd be too scared to move. Or maybe he just thought there was no point in her untying herself, because even if she could move, there was no place to go. Rosie rolled over and stood up, a little unsteady on her feet. She looked around, trying to get some bearing on what this was. Her eyes fell on the trapdoor in the wall, where the water seemed to be trickling in. It had to lead somewhere. She went slowly towards it and peered through. She could see daylight in the distance. She looked at the walls to see if there was any way she could climb up out of the pit, but there was not a chance. He'd taken the ladder, and even if she'd placed the pallet against the wall, she'd still be several feet short of the top, with nothing to grip onto. She sat back down, her heart sinking. She was trapped – afraid to open the door wide in case there was more water, and also scared to pull it and go through because she had no clear idea where it led. Boag didn't need to butcher her like his other victims. He could just leave her here. She knew Adrian was up there somewhere, and she could guarantee that despite his injuries, he would have managed to get some help by now, but they wouldn't know where she was. All she could remember was being dragged backwards up a small lane and then into this blackness. Where were the cops? She'd dialled 999, but there was not a siren or a helicopter in hearing distance. Probably too busy with the pile-up further back, and chances were the 999 call hadn't been responded to yet because she didn't give enough information. She was trapped. Then she looked again at the trapdoor. It had to lead somewhere, and no matter where it was, it had to be better than being stuck in here. She didn't have a lot of choice. That's exactly how Boag had planned it.

'Help!' she shouted, listening to her cry echo up the pit and down again. 'Help! Please! Help me, somebody! I'm trapped! Is anybody there? Boag, you twisted bastard! Where are you?' She slumped against the wall and sank down. 'Oh Christ, Mum, I'm going to die here.' She started to cry. The filthy water stung her bloodied calves. She bent down and looked in the trapdoor again. She could see a light in the distance. She took a deep breath and took hold of the metal ring on the trapdoor and pulled it with all the strength she could muster. It opened enough for her to get through. She braced herself, crouched down, and crawled in. She stayed crouched as she made her way into the tunnel, her heart pounding. Cockroaches scuttled along the walls. A rat swam towards her and she froze as it slithered past her hand. The water was shallow and she moved on, almost zombie-like, towards the light. Then her eyes focused on what looked like a rusting metal gate. Christ! It was a dead end. She pushed herself towards the gate, and as she gripped it, she could see outside, the grass, the embankment, a narrow stream, which must be where the water was coming from. But there was no escape. The penny suddenly dropped. This is what Boag had wanted. She had to get back fast. She scrambled and turned round in the narrow tunnel. Then, as she'd crawled a few yards, she heard the sound of the heavy concrete door being scraped along the ground. It was closing. Jesus! Caught, like a rat in a trap.

'Wait! Please!' she heard herself shouting.

'I knew you would do that. In the sewers where you belong, with the rats.'

She heard the door close.

Rosie opened her mouth to scream, but nothing came out. The water wasn't flooding in, but the longer she was here, the deeper it might get. Then she peered at things lying in the muddy sludge. Christ! It was body parts – a leg, an arm. How long did she have? It would be over soon.

'Help!' she screamed, so loud she felt dizzy. 'Help! Please! Somebody help me! I'm drowning! Help!'

Aldo was carefully picking his way down the embankment in the direction where Adrian said Boag had thrown Rosie's phone before he dragged her off. Jonjo told him to take a quick look in case it was there because, you never know, maybe this mad bastard Boag would phone it. He could hear it ringing in the long grass, and crept around to see where it was coming from. Then he saw it vibrating under some twigs. He picked it up, and was about to dash back up, when he thought he heard someone shouting down at the foot of the hill. He looked around. Nothing. Then he heard it again but there was nobody there. The mobile rang again and he saw Jonjo's name on the screen.

'Jonjo! I've got it! Listen, man, there's somebody screaming for help down here, but I don't know where it's coming from. Somewhere along the path at the bottom. There's a wee kind of stream. Can you get down here pronto?'

The line went dead, and in a few moments, Jonjo and Danny appeared at the top of the hill and scaled their way down.

'What's happening? Where's the sound coming from?'

They all stood in silence, listening. Again the shouting. 'Help!' It was definitely a woman's desperate cries.

'Fuck! It's coming from down there. What the fuck!'

All three of them rushed down, slipping and sliding, and eventually they reached the muddy water. They could see a metal fence that looked as though it had been built as some kind of gateway. They got down on their hunkers and stayed close to it. Then it happened again.

'Please! Somebody help me! I'm trapped! Help!'

'Fuck! That's Rosie.'

Jonjo clambered down along the path of the water and pressed his face against the fence.

'Rosie! Rosie Gilmour! Is that you?'

Nothing.

'Rosie! Is that you? It's me! It's Jonjo, Rosie!'

Silence. Then a plaintive wail.

'Jonjo! Yes. It's me! Boag's trapped me! Christ, Jonjo! Please get me out of here . . .' The voice trailed off.

'Rosie. Listen to me, sweetheart. Don't worry. We'll get you out. Just hang on. Try to keep calm. Can you remember what happened?'

'A lock-up, then a pit, like a mechanic's pit, he threw me in there. There was a trapdoor, and I went through thinking I could escape, but there's a gate here and I can't go any further. He came back and closed the door – a big concrete door, and I can't get back in. I don't know where he is. Hurry! There's rats . . . and bits of dead bodies . . . Aw, Jesus! Hurry! And there's water coming in.'

'Bastard. Don't worry, just hang fire. Don't worry about the water. It's only a little bit and it's not flowing fast. Keep calm. We'll get you out.'

'What about Adrian? Is he all right?'

Jonjo didn't answer. He turned to Aldo. 'You stay here, Aldo. Keep talking to her. Keep her calm. We'll go back up and blast our way into that fucking lock-up.'

They quickly climbed their way up the embankment and back to the lock-up where Adrian was standing leaning against the wall to take the weight off his leg. Geordie was standing by Jonjo's car.

'We found her, Adrian. She's trapped in some kind of fucking tunnel that led from the lock-up.'

Jonjo noticed Adrian's eyes light up and suddenly he was off the wall and standing full stretch.

'Is this lock-up, you think?'

'I don't know. But looks like it might be our best option.'

'Let's go.'

'Stand back,' Jonjo said.

He turned to Danny and jerked his head towards the door. Danny blasted it with his gun and the padlock flew off.

They pulled it open and went inside, blinking in the darkness. Jonjo glanced around the room in dismay at the bloodstained workbench, a discarded chainsaw . . . and body parts strewn on the floor.

'Fuck me! What the fuck is this place! Christ almighty!'

They stood over the pit.

'It must be down here.' He turned to Danny. 'Get that ladder, Danny. I'm going down.'

'I go.' Adrian stepped forward.

Jonjo stood up to him.

'Not with that fucking leg, man. You wait here. I'm going down.'

Then suddenly they heard Danny groan and they turned around to see his shocked expression as he fell to the floor. Behind them, Boag had stuck a knife between Danny's shoulder blades. Then he pulled a gun and stood facing them, pointing at Danny's head.

'Are you the cavalry, by any chance? Bit late, boys. Why

don't you go back about your business before I have to put you on my workbench.'

Jonjo felt a red-hot rage burn in him so fast that he could feel the room swimming. This was the cunt who butchered his only son. He was standing two feet away from him. One of his best mates was bleeding out on the floor, and he could do nothing. Fucking nothing. Just like he could do nothing for his son. His head felt like it was going to burst wide open. Then suddenly there was a gunshot, and he blinked, waiting for one of them to fall to the ground. But it was Boag who dropped, groaning, blood spouting from his side. Adrian stood with a small revolver in his hand. He limped towards him and pointed the gun to Boag's head, kicking his gun out of his hand.

'No!' Jonjo said. 'Leave him, Adrian! He's mine. And he doesn't get a bullet in the head. Leave him! I'm going to get Rosie. So you stay here with that fucker. And don't do anything to him til I get here. Please promise me that, big man.'

Adrian blinked in acknowledgement, and kept the gun to Boag's head as he lay writhing.

Jonjo dragged the ladder over and dropped it, securing it at the top of the pit. He climbed down with agility, glad of the training regime he'd kept up at the prison gym. Then he saw the trapdoor. He went across and grabbed the rope handle. It was heavy concrete and he dragged it across until it opened.

'Rosie! Rosie! Where are you?'

He pushed himself into the tunnel and moved along. Fucking rats and cockroaches everywhere. He froze as his hand touched a limb lying in the sludge. Christ almighty! What a fucking scheming nutter Boag was. He must have dug up the floor of the lock-up to build this death pit with a trapdoor leading nowhere. God knows how many people had been tortured and butchered in this dungeon, or how many body parts had ended up down here.

'Rosie. It's Jonjo.'

'Here! I'm here!'

He edged his way towards the voice. Then he saw her, the terror in her face – not the face he'd seen the first time he met her in the bar, with that swagger to her movement, her hair shimmering in the light. This was the face of someone waiting to die, pale, sunken eyes, panic. He barely recognised her. She was staring at him, but she wasn't moving towards him.

'Rosie. Listen, it's me. It's okay. Come on! We need to get out of here fast.'

He moved towards her but she flinched.

Then her face crumpled and she started to cry.

'You're all right, sweetheart. Come on. Hold my hand. You're safe now. Come on. Hold on. We're nearly there.'

He crawled along as Rosie clutched his hand tight. He got to the door and pushed his way through, pulling her behind him. He pulled Rosie to her feet, took her by the shoulders and shook her.

'Rosie. Listen. You're safe now. But we need to get up this ladder. Only a few steps. Adrian's up there. Come on. You go first. I'm right behind you.'

She said nothing, but seemed to compose herself, sniffing as she took the bottom rung, gingerly balancing as he held the ladder. He watched as she climbed, her legs like jelly. She was halfway. Once she was at the top he saw her crawl and fall onto the ground. He took the steps one at a time, the ladder moving in the slime and water on the floor. The ladder slid, unsteady as he climbed, and he had to concentrate every step. The fact that Boag was sitting up there pushed him on with the scent of revenge. When he got to the top, Rosie was on her hands and knees, trying to get to her feet. He pulled her up. She looked at Adrian with the gun to Boag's head. Her face suddenly turned red, and she hobbled across towards them. She kicked Boag in the face, knocking him on his back.

'You bastard!' she spat.

'Come on, Rosie.' Adrian grabbed her and pulled her towards him with one arm. 'Sssh. It's okay. You are safe now.'

'Oh, God, Adrian! I thought you were dead.'

She passed out.

'How's Danny?' Jonjo said.

'He needs a hospital. Lost a lot of blood. He needs a hospital, quick.'

Jonjo looked at Geordie, still standing with his sawn-off shotgun.

'Okay. Geordie, can you help take them to my car? I'll deal with this piece of shit.'

Adrian stood for a moment, then eased Rosie to her feet as she blinked and looked around.

Jonjo stood for a moment in the stillness. He scanned the room, wondering if any of the bloodied equipment had been used on his son. He looked at Boag – this evil bastard who had picked up his innocent laddie.

'You don't know me.' Jonjo stood over Boag.

He waited as Boag looked up and said nothing.

'I'm Jack Mulhearn's da. The boy you murdered. You cut my boy's fucking head off, you evil cunt!'

Boag lip curled somewhere between a snarl and a grin.

'Oh, that boy. Sweet one, him!'

Jonjo, in one seamless movement, reached into his sock and pulled out the razor. He made three lightning slashes in Boag's face, opening up fine lines, oozing blood, covering his face in seconds. Boag grinned, blood running into his mouth.

'All those people you killed. You would have been dead before the morning in Bar-L. You were never going to trial, you fucker.'

Boag didn't answer, just stared straight back at him.

Outside, Adrian and Geordie were helping Danny into the Range Rover, where Aldo was already in the driving seat. Rosie stood shivering, as Jonjo came towards them.

'Thank you, Jonjo. You saved my life,' she said through tears.

'Come on. Let's get you out of here.' He took her arm and helped her into the back seat. 'Listen. You need to make some calls. Police, whatever. I'm going to drop you somewhere, then I'm out of here. I can't be seen anywhere near this. You understand?'

'Yes. Neither can Adrian.'

'Okay. We'll drop you at the hospital gate. Make your phone calls.'

Rosie took her phone and punched in McGuire's number.

'Mick. You need to help me.'

CHAPTER THIRTY-SIX

Rosie was on the sofa in McGuire's office as she recounted the past few hours of her ordeal, while he sat dumbfounded, at times shaking his head in disbelief. He'd sent Declan up to the Victoria Infirmary to pick her up when she'd insisted she was not staying in hospital, despite the doctor's orders. The cuts from the machete and the knife were minor and only needed butterfly stitches up, and she had no other injuries apart from bruising to her face, as well as an angry bump on the side of her head. But the doctors were concerned she was suffering from severe shock. That was putting it mildly, Rosie had felt like telling the young medic. She'd be seeing that rat-infested tunnel in her nightmares for the rest of her life. They'd taken blood samples and given her a course of antibiotics because she'd been exposed to contaminated water, and she was told to come straight back at the first sign of illness, as there was a real risk of infection in her wounds. Declan had taken her to her flat where she stood in a steaming hot shower for ten minutes, scrubbing her body til it hurt, not really sure if any of this was real or if it was all part of one of her feverish nightmares. McGuire told her to take the day off and he'd come up to see her, but she couldn't bear to be on her own. The only place that felt like home right now was the *Post*. But the tiredness was beginning to hit her, and she rubbed her face. McGuire sat looking at her, full of concern, but Rosie could see he was thinking ahead.

'Jesus, Rosie. I honestly don't know how you're sitting here right now. But I'm thankful that you are.' He shook his head and pushed out a sigh. 'I know this isn't the moment to give you a hard time, but did you really need to go after that psycho when you saw him at the funeral?'

'It was instinct, Mick. Pure instinct. Adrian spotted him in the crowd and he was going himself, then without thinking I said I was going with him. But I did phone the cops. So I didn't feel as if I was going straight into a dangerous situation by myself. The police were right behind us – until the bloody crash.' Suddenly she stopped. 'Shit! The crash. I need to phone Don again. I've tried to call his mobile but it's going straight to answer machine. He must have been in the crash.'

She thought she saw a flicker of something in McGuire's eyes, but he started talking.

'You should have stopped then. Turned back and left it to them.'

'Adrian was going it alone if I did that. I had to be there. I know now it was reckless and I shouldn't have done it, but I just acted on instinct.'

McGuire made a steeple with his fingers as he sat forward.

'We'll need to work out what we tell the cops. From what Declan is hearing on the police grapevine, Boag wasn't there by the time the cops arrived. So you're going to be questioned very closely on that.'

Rosie's mind flashed back to the moment Adrian pulled her towards the Range Rover.

'It all happened really quickly, once Jonjo got me out of that pit. But I can't go telling the cops any of that – about Jonjo Mulhearn rescuing me. Because when I left, he was still with Boag. I mean he's just out of jail. The very fact that he was involved in this would get him straight back in there. Look, I don't give a monkey's that he's a career criminal just out of jail for murder. If he hadn't come and got me, I'd be dead. Simple as that. I'm not sticking him in for anything.'

McGuire spread his hands.

'I understand that. I'd feel the same in your shoes. But we're talking about the law here. You know what the police are like.' He paused. 'Did you actually see anything going on with Boag and Mulhearn?'

Rosie took a moment to remember. Everything, all the bad things, would be etched in her mind for ever, but the last few moments were a blur.

'Okay. Here's what I can remember, and I'm telling *you* the truth. But I'll not be saying this to the cops.' She took a breath. 'I was at the point of collapse when I got to the top and Adrian grabbed hold of me and then I was being pulled out of the lock-up. Jonjo was on the phone, and asking for someone to come to the place, and he told his mate to drive me to the Victoria. I heard him say they would take Danny somewhere. But I can only vaguely remember some guy lying with blood pouring out of him. I do remember Boag, though, his face staring at me. I'll never forget that. But all I can tell the police is that my Bosnian friend was at the top of the pit with some others who I didn't know or recognise, and then he pulled me away. He told me not to look back. I distinctly remember Adrian telling me that if I didn't look back then I wouldn't see anything, so if I was questioned on what I did see, I wouldn't be lying.'

'And did you look back?' McGuire asked, his heavy eyebrows raised.

Rosie puffed.

'Well, yes.'

'Christ! Why am I not surprised by that!'

'I couldn't help it. I just turned around for a moment.'

'And what did you see?'

'I heard Jonjo telling Boag who he was, that it was his son he butchered. Then Boag said something, but I don't remember what. Then suddenly Jonjo slashed him. I mean, real expert stuff. Like criss-crosses all over his face – he's obviously not new to slashing faces.'

'You can't tell the cops that without naming who the guy was.'

'I can't tell them anything, other than Boag was at the top of the pit, and there were some heavy-looking guys who I didn't recognise.'

'They're going to ask you why they would be rescuing you. And you're going to look like you're lying through your teeth when you say you've no idea. Do you realise that?'

'Yes. I know.' She sighed. 'But what else can I do?'

The door opened and Hanlon came in, his stiff QC's collar straight out of a High Court murder trial.

'Fuck me, Rosie!' He came across and bent to hug her. 'I've heard all sorts of horror stories. Jesus Christ! Are you sure you're still alive?'

Rosie tried a smile.

'Not really. I keep thinking I'm going to wake up in a cold sweat and it's all a nightmare, and I'm actually dead. My head is all over the place.'

McGuire interrupted. 'Tom, as I was saying on the phone, the dilemma is what she's going to say to the cops. They'll be down here shortly, and she needs to get her story right.'

He lifted the teapot and poured himself a cup.

'You tell them fuck all, that's what.'

'But they're going to want to know how she got there,' McGuire said.

'Yes, I know. That bit's all right. You tell them exactly what happened, about following him. You can say this big Bosnian friend of yours was with you. Tell them everything right up until you get rescued. But that's where you have to go all vague.'

'I am a bit vague on it anyway.'

Hanlon eyed her and smiled wryly.

'Good. You're doing well, Gilmour.'

'No. Seriously.'

'Right. The thing is, Boag is nowhere to be seen. So your big mate Jonjo, the superhero, must have arranged to take him somewhere so he could have his revenge.'

Rosie nodded. 'I think so. He could have killed him there and then and tossed him into the pit of water, then got off his mark. But he wanted to make him suffer.'

'Well, that's up to him,' said Hanlon. 'And I can't say I blame him. If the cops aren't as stupid as they look sometimes, they'd be wise just to let this disappear. Put it this way: there's less chance of Boag doing a runner if he's in the company of Jonjo Mulhearn than if he's in police custody. He's already proved that. I'd put my house on Boag being hacked to bits as we speak.' He lifted a biscuit and broke it in half. 'The cops won't bust our arses over this – trust me.'

'Do you know that for sure?' McGuire asked.

'No, not for sure. But I talked to one of the DIs on this murder trial I'm on, and he seems to have heard a lot of the story about Boag and you, and the fact that when the cops

turned up he's nowhere to be seen. The preliminary statement you gave to the cops at the hospital – about some
guys being out there at the right time, is not bad. They'll
know it's bullshit, but I'll be surprised if they have you on
any charge for it.'

Rosie let out a sigh.

'Well, that's a relief. I really hope I don't have to fight
with the cops. I'm knackered. Frazzled and knackered.'

'You need to see a doctor, Rosie. You can't just walk out
of here and go home as if nothing happened. You should
talk to a professional – a counsellor or something.'

She was silent for a moment, aware that McGuire and
Hanlon were looking at her with well-meaning expressions.
She felt a lump come to her chest and she swallowed hard.

'I know,' she said.

TJ was back in Glasgow, and only vaguely aware that
she'd been in some trouble. He was coming to meet her in
an hour at the office. Right now, he was the only counsel-
ling she wanted. She wondered where Adrian had got to.
She hadn't even phoned him to ask about his leg.

McGuire went back behind his desk and picked up some
papers.

'I've got a conference in ten minutes. I've had a couple of
calls from other papers as the news has filtered out that
you've been kidnapped by Boag. So we'll need to think
about how we handle this, Rosie.'

Hanlon looked at her.

'Would you be up for an interview? A press conference?'

Rosie shook her head. Right now she couldn't trust herself to speak in front of anyone without breaking down.

'I don't know. I don't think so right now. To be honest, I'd rather just sit down and write it for us. We could put it in the paper and let the rest of them lift it. If anyone wants to talk to me tomorrow, I might be in better shape.'

McGuire smiled. 'I was hoping you would say that. But you realise it is going to look a bit vague when you write that you were rescued by someone you don't know.'

'I know.'

'But once you say it, and it goes in the paper, you have to stick to that line. You have to believe it yourself,' Hanlon said, then he grinned. 'The truth, the whole truth, and nothing like the truth, as we say.'

'I know. I'm convincing myself right now.'

'I'm starving,' Hanlon said. 'Come on down to the canteen with me and we can sit for a while.'

Rosie got up as he did and they both headed towards the door. She turned to McGuire.

'I'll get a bite to eat, then go to my office and just write it, Mick. I'll let it run and run. Get it off my chest. Maybe I'll feel better.'

McGuire winked at her. 'That's the spirit.'

They had just finished drinking their coffees when Rosie's mobile rang: it was Marion to say that the cops had arrived to talk to her. As they headed upstairs, Rosie rang Don's mobile again, but still no answer. Big DI Morton was already in McGuire's office, accompanied by a female detective. The DI shook her hand and McGuire motioned them all to sit down. She couldn't quite work out why the DI looked so grim-faced, and hoped he wasn't about to tell her she was getting arrested.

'How are you, Rosie?' he said, his eyes fixing hers.

'I'm shattered,' she replied. 'But I'm alive.'

There followed an awkward silence and Rosie looked from the cops to McGuire, who was as grim-faced as them.

'Listen, Rosie,' the DI said. 'I've got some bad news for you.' He cleared his throat. 'We lost a detective today. In a car crash. He was following you, when you were in pursuit of Boag. I believe he's a friend of yours. Detective Sergeant Don Elliot.'

Rosie's stomach dropped. Christ almighty, not Don.

'Oh God!' she murmured, both hands to her mouth. 'Oh my God! I've been trying to phone him. Jesus! I thought maybe his phone was busted. I . . . I . . . It was my fault. I phoned him from the graveside to tell him Boag was there. Oh, Christ! Don was a really good friend. I've known him a long time.'

She shook her head. Inside she was choking to say how close they'd been for years; that he was one of the best, most caring friends she'd ever had; that he was always there when she needed him, kindred spirits sometimes brought together by a shared loneliness which they laughed off over a few drinks and banter. The fact that he was one of her most crucial contacts who helped her with information when all the doors were closed didn't matter a damn right now. She was never going to see Don again.

The DI sighed. 'I gathered that. I'm sorry for your loss. He was a good man and a fine detective. He was being moved up to detective inspector in the next few months, but he hadn't been told yet.'

Rosie managed a half-smile. She imagined how Don would have loved that. How they'd have celebrated, got drunk together, and enjoyed his big moment.

'He'd have been so proud of that, Inspector. I know he was a good detective. He cared about people. Was he . . .' She paused, an image flashing up of the crashed cars she'd seen through her visor mirror. 'Was he killed outright?' She couldn't bear the thought of him suffering.

The DI nodded. 'He was. The paramedics pronounced him dead at the scene.' He paused. 'So, at least he didn't suffer. It was a massive head injury when the car overturned.'

She wondered if there had been a second before he died, when he realised it was happening, and if he raged against it, or if he quietly accepted death. She hoped he had found a moment of peace.

She looked at the cop and then at McGuire, who gave her an understanding grimace.

'I'm sorry, Rosie.'

She swallowed hard. She needed to get this interview over with and get out of here.

'Can we start my statement, please? I have to put my piece together from today for tomorrow's paper.'

Rosie walked alone along the corridor off the editorial floor and went into her office, after the interview was over. She was so numbed from the shock of Don's death that everything that happened to her today didn't feel import-ant any more. She knew it would, though, and it would come back to haunt her again and again. But right now she needed to be by herself. She closed the office door and shut the vertical blinds. She went behind her desk and pulled up a blank document on the screen, then sat back, staring at it, not sure where to start. How do you put the cold fear of death into words? How do you tell that for a second it crossed your mind that death would be a relief; that per-haps you'd finally see the people you loved and lost, who visit you in your dreams, instead of the constant void left behind by them? Rosie swallowed back her tears, picturing herself up to her neck in the pit of water, choking and try-ing to breathe. You never, ever give up, she told herself. You do it for them, because they cannot be here. She began to write, her fingers trembling on the keys, cold sweat on her back.

I have no right to be alive to tell this story. But I am . . .

When she finished she sat back and read it quickly, recalling every terrifying moment. Then she pinged it to McGuire and swung her feet onto the desk. Her mobile rang. It was TJ.

'Rosie. I'm outside. Sweet Jesus! I'm hearing terrible things. Are you okay?'

'I don't know,' she said, choked. 'I . . . I just want to go home.'

'Come on then.'

CHAPTER THIRTY-SEVEN

When Rosie awoke she was curled into a ball in her bed, arms and legs stiff as though she'd been holding onto them all night. She turned onto her back and looked out at the pale grey morning sky, her first thought of Don and the realisation that she'd never see him again. Sadness washed over her and she closed her eyes for a second. He would want her to tough this out, and he'd have told her as much over a couple of gins at O'Brien's. She swung her legs out of the bed. The aroma of coffee floated through the open bedroom door, and she could hear cutlery and plates being rattled in the kitchen. The familiar sounds she often woke up with that meant TJ had stayed over. He'd be making breakfast and he would kid her about keeping him awake all night, or they'd talk about where they'd been the night before, how they'd drunk too much. It would be as though nothing had changed. But it had. Last night, when they got home, they'd shared a bottle of red wine while eating a takeaway, which she picked at. She'd talked animatedly of the whole story, of her rescue, told every cough and splutter of it as he sat mesmerised, shaking his head. She knew he'd wanted to say that this was enough, that now, if ever there was a time to call it a day, this was it. The way their relationship was these days, he didn't nag her about her job the way he used to. But this was different. Whatever she did next, whatever investigation or story she uncovered or reported, she would surely never come this close to death again, and a horrible death such as the one she'd just been spared. TJ didn't need to say it. She knew it herself. She should be getting out. But in the same moment she could hear herself saying it inside her head, she knew she couldn't. There was nowhere else to go. Sure, she could fill her life no problem, travel the world, write a book, sit on a beach. But this was who she was. She had to find a way through, and she would.

Her mobile rang and it was Adrian.

'Adrian. How are you? I meant to phone last night, but it all got a bit—'

'I'm fine. No problem. But you, Rosie. Are you all right? I was so worried about you, but didn't want to phone.'

'I'm okay. Your leg?'

'Is fixed. A doctor friend of Jonjo fixed it. And the other man, Danny. He fixed him, but he was in a bad way.'

'So where are you?'

'I'm at my friend's house. Will I see you?'

'Yes. Do you know what happened to Boag?'

Silence.

'No. Not really.'

'Did Jonjo take him?'

'Yes. But better if we don't know.'

Rosie said nothing. Best to leave it.

'Adrian, I have to go to work, but I'll call you later and we can meet.'

'Okay. Is good. Be careful.'

'Boag is gone, I hope. I won't be so frightened.'

She hung up. Rosie knew it was bravado. There was a nervous knot in her stomach, like an aftershock. She pushed it away.

Rosie stood at the kitchen door for a few seconds, watching TJ make French toast, shaking the bread in the pan. He turned around, as though sensing her presence. He pushed the pan off the gas and came towards her.

'Hey, you.' He put his arms around her and she caught a whiff of his freshly showered body and felt the softness of his face. 'How are you feeling? If that's not a stupid question?'

'Glad to be here having breakfast with you, if that's not a stupid answer.' She hugged him. 'I'm all right – I think.' She pulled away from him and scanned his face, knowing he was studying her, knowing he was looking at the shadows under her eyes. He caressed her hair.

'You'll be all right, darling.'

'I'll have a quick shower,' Rosie said. 'I'll need to turn up at work quite soon.'

'You could take the morning off,' he said. Then he glanced at Sky News blaring in the living room. 'Though judging by the news you're a major celebrity, so I don't suppose you'll get much peace today.'

Rosie turned to watch it. She winced at Boag's face on the screen, and an image flashed back to her of his pasty face crouched over her, knife in hand. She blinked it away. She was glad the volume on the television was low. She didn't want to hear it right now.

'I'll probably have to give some kind of interview,' she said. 'But I don't want to do it in the public glare, because I'm not telling the truth about everything.'

'You don't have to lie. Just be economical with the truth.'

She smiled at the thought, but her mind was far away.

'Yep, that's it.' She turned and went down the hall and into the bathroom.

She stood in the shower with her eyes closed as the warm water rained down on her, feeling it sting a little at first on the back of her hacked legs and the wound in her chest. Then it felt good. She was grateful to be alive and doing this simple thing.

The day had flown past in a whirlwind of more meetings with police, and two interviews – one for television that would be shared with other media, and one with the Press Association. Rosie knew both reporters well, and she knew they would hate being this side of the interview as much as she did, but she had to get it over with.

She was glad to get out of the office and walk to the end of the road where she'd arranged to meet Adrian, but as soon as she walked outside into the drizzle, the knot came back to her stomach like a punch. Shit. Deal with it, she told herself. These moments had happened before, usually after a trauma. It was like a kind of grim reaper nudging her along, saying that no matter how much bravado you have, your nerves are in shreds, and they will jump up and bite you at a time of their choosing. She'd been twitchy this morning even going into the office. And now, outside in the traffic, she was glad of the walk, glad to feel the rain on her face. But suddenly the drone of the traffic seemed louder. A horn honked and she jumped. She was just tired, she told herself. Then she felt nauseous and had a sudden urge to run back inside, to the safety of the walls. She glanced over her shoulder at the *Post* building, thought about walking back. What the Christ? A panic attack. Step on it right now, Gilmour. You have to. But as she walked on, she could hardly catch a breath and felt light-headed. She could see the cafe in the distance, and she quickened her step. Just a hundred yards. She wanted to run, but her legs felt like lead. Calm down. She looked over her shoulder. Someone was following her. But there was nobody. Once she reached the cafe, she slumped against the window, eyes closed, her heart pounding. Suddenly the door opened and she felt a hand on her. She jumped. It was Adrian.

'Rosie.' He looked startled and worried. 'What? Are you sick?'

He caught her just before she buckled.

'I'm so sorry, Adrian. I . . . I . . . Oh Christ!' She slumped into his arms.

'Come on. Inside. Have some tea and sit down. It's just the shock.'

Rosie allowed him to lead her inside. She was beginning to feel the attack subside. She'd had them before, and they always made her feel like she was going to die. Of course, nobody died of a panic attack, but when they gripped her like that, it felt as though there was no way out. She sat down, and Adrian went to the counter and ordered tea, then sat opposite, watching her, holding her hand as the waitress brought the tea over. She eyed Rosie as though she knew her from somewhere. The news was blaring on the television mounted on the wall, and Rosie saw the girl going back behind the counter and talking to the woman, then pointing to the television.

'I'm okay, now. Sorry about that, Adrian. It was . . . it was . . .' She shook her head. 'It's happened before, but not outside like that. I mean, it just overwhelms me.' She took a breath. 'Then yesterday, the police told me that Don, my detective friend, was killed in that car crash.

Remember the car behind us? They were following us, and we saw it.'

He nodded, shocked.

'That's bad, Rosie. I'm so sorry.'

'We'd been friends for years. He died chasing after me trying to get Boag. I feel a bit responsible . . . a lot responsible.'

'You must not feel bad like that. He is a policeman. He was doing his job. He would have been after Boag if he'd have seen him first. It is not your fault.'

'I suppose not,' Rosie sighed. 'I think that's why it all got on top of me and the panic came just there.'

He nodded. 'I know these things. You are not alone. When . . . After my wife . . . After the war, I had times like that. Many times. Like I am afraid, but I know I am not afraid. I had no control.'

She looked at him, surprised that he suffered them, but more surprised that a man who played his cards so close to his chest would admit it.

'Really? You had them too? It's hard to imagine you feeling like that. You're always so . . . so in control, strong.'

'Yes. And I am strong. But there were times when I felt like you just now. But you must know it is nothing. It will pass.'

'It's passing already. I didn't sleep much last night, so I'm frazzled with exhaustion, apart from everything that happened.'

'You will feel better soon. Would be good if you could have a holiday.' He rubbed Rosie's hand. 'I'm going back in a couple of days. Come with me, Rosie. Come to Sarajevo. Like . . . like before, we can relax. You like the place . . . I . . . I mean . . . I know not like before, but for you to rest. To put yesterday behind you.'

He sounded so enthusiastic, as though he'd been thinking about it all night, that Rosie felt choked.

'Oh, Adrian! I . . . I don't know. When I'm like this, sometimes it's best just to work through it. Keep busy.'

'But you must have a rest. Not just three or four days. Would be good to be far away. Nobody can touch you in Sarajevo.'

She reached across and touched his face, felt the urge to kiss him.

'I know. I know. I'll have to wait a couple of days and see how it is. I still have the other story I'm working on – Tadi and the O'Dwyers. I need to see it through.'

Adrian nodded, a little crestfallen. 'I understand. But know that I am here. Always. In Sarajevo or anywhere. My friend. Like from the very beginning. We have seen many things together.' He shook his head as though he barely believed it himself.

Rosie smiled.

'I know. So many things. You are always there for me. Especially right now when I nearly passed out. I'm so grateful to you, Adrian.'

They were silent for a long moment. Then he looked at her and sat back, pushing his hand through his hair.

'I wanted Jonjo to leave Boag to me, but I think he wanted revenge.'

Rosie nodded. 'I won't be surprised if his body is found any day now.'

They sat, saying nothing, drinking their tea, holding hands. It felt so natural. But part of Rosie felt guilty, because if TJ had walked in, he would think the worst. But he'd be wrong, because whatever had gone on in the past with Adrian, whatever feeling she had now – that if she was honest with herself was not just physical but a deep love and trust – she knew that this was all it could ever be. Like this. She felt safe and protected, and loved.

CHAPTER THIRTY-EIGHT

Rosie sat at the bar in O'Brien's sipping a gin and tonic. She'd made her mind up before she left the office that she'd go there tonight, just for one drink. Call it a homage to Don, but in an odd way, this was where she felt closer to him. So many shared moments, stories, swapping information, had gone on at this bar, that she had to come back and have one last drink and raise a glass to her old friend. She felt like throwing it back quickly, followed by a second. On another day, when a story she'd busted her gut on had made it onto the front page, the first two drinks wouldn't have touched the sides. But the thought of waking up with a hangover, or worse, waking in the middle of the night alone, during one of her fevered nightmares, forced her to take it easy. She was sitting here in the bar doing the usual things, going through the motions of watching the early evening punters downing champagne, but right now, she felt she was looking at it from a different place. She hoped it would pass, this feeling in the pit of her stomach that made her think that nothing would ever be the same again. It wouldn't be. But life had to go on. It had to. She didn't want big changes in her life. Losing Don had brought a deep sadness to it, but she also didn't want to become this jumpy, nervous wreck that she was right now. It would pass, she told herself, as she took another sip. Life goes on. The rules were this: you might sit for a time on the sidelines feeling overwhelmed and paralysed by it all. But sooner or later you picked yourself up and got on with it, or you were left behind. She'd known that from an early age, and even her experience of yesterday wasn't going to change that. She wished Father Dunnachie was still alive, then she might have knocked on his door and told him how she was feeling. A lump came to her throat and she tightened her lips.

The silver-haired barman from Donegal watched her from further down the bar as she finished her drink, then came up with another gin and tonic for her. He slid it across the bar.

'On the house, Rosie. From Don.' He winked, pouring himself a small whisky. 'I'm sorry you lost your friend. I saw it on television last night. I used to enjoy the craic between the two of you.' He raised a glass. 'Let's drink to him. He would have liked that.'

Rosie smiled, swallowing the lump in her throat.

'Here's looking at you, Don.' She knocked back a good slug of her drink, as the barman did the same.

Molly O'Dwyer sat in the waiting room of Barlinnie Prison, looking around her at the young women, dolled up to the nines to meet their men inside. Some had young children on their laps, visiting the fathers they'd probably grow up emulating because there was little chance of them seeing anything different in the shabby housing schemes, where crime lords ran the show, and ordinary families didn't stand a chance. Molly asked herself how she had come to this. Where had she gone wrong? she'd asked herself again and again. She'd gone wrong from the moment she married Rory O'Dwyer, she'd concluded. Her whole life had been about doing what she was told without protest. And if she did rear up, she was slapped down without mercy. She'd put up with his bullying and brutality, keeping quiet about his crimes over the years, but what she'd overheard that day in the kitchen had sent her over the edge. He had covered for Timmy when he knew he had murdered his own flesh and blood. She could never forgive him. Now that she was out, she was terrified, but there was a liberating feeling too, that she'd never felt in her entire life. Where she came from, as a teenage girl, you were married off to your first real boyfriend and it was him who determined how you led your life. She had never been free before. And now she was. Since she'd bailed out of the house a few days ago and gone to Spain, Molly agonised over what her son had done, the reporter's words ringing in her ears. She finally found the confidence to come back, now that Rory, Finn and Timmy were being held by police. But she knew she wouldn't have long, because their lawyers were shit hot, and had bailed them out so many times before. She didn't want to see Rory's face ever again. Or Finbar's. She was here to see Timmy and that was all. She looked at her watch. Her flight back to Alicante was at eight this evening, so as soon as this was over she'd head straight to the airport and get out for all time.

The big prison warden came in, scanned the room, and told people to follow him through the security checks. She watched the others, used to the routine, as they went through the door into some kind of locker room where they were met by officers. They took their handbags off them, searched them and stored them in a locker. She didn't want to give hers up as her passport was in it, but she had no choice. She was horrified when the prison officer asked her to open her mouth so he could examine inside in case she was smuggling drugs.

She waited in the room, sat at a table just a few feet away from the other families, and looked up as the prisoners were led in. Then she saw Timmy, his face grey with worry but the eyes still with that dark, mad look they always had. She felt nothing. No twinge of sadness. Only anger and disgust. He began to crumple when he saw her, and he went towards her with his arms outstretched.

'Don't!' she spat. 'Don't touch me!'

'But, Ma! Look at the state of me! They beat the shit out of me. They kidnapped me and they forced me to confess to something I didn't do. My head was all over the place. I can't believe they did this.'

'Shut up!'

'Ma!'

'Shut up!' She leaned closer to him, lowered her voice. 'You listen to me, Timmy O'Dwyer, and listen good. Don't give me your shite. I never want to see your face again, in or out of here. I know what you did. You're despicable. I heard you telling your father and Finn that afternoon what you did. That poor girl . . .' She began to fill up and bit back tears. 'You're evil.'

'But, Ma!'

'Don't you "but Ma" me! How could you? How could you kill your own flesh and blood?'

'I couldn't help it, Ma! I got scared. Da would have gone mental.'

'You bastard! I would have taken the baby in, no problem. I would have loved her. You killed your own daughter. You should roast in hell, you demented fucker.'

'Ma, I didn't mean it.'

'It doesn't matter. And you killed that poor young student couple. Two people on the threshold of their lives. Two innocent people. Do you seriously think you are going to get away with that?'

'Da's got lawyers.'

'Lawyers? A lawyer will not absolve your rotten stinking soul for what you've done. You should roast in hell. You listen to me, if you've got a scrap of decency in that sick twisted mind of yours, then you'll do the only good thing you've ever done in your life and make a full confession to the police.'

'Aw, Ma!'

'What do you think is going to happen to you? You have no place anywhere because of what you did. You can't help these poor people you murdered now. It's too late. But you can at least admit to the police that you did it. God knows it might give a scrap of comfort to the poor families, though I don't think so.'

They sat in silence.

'Ma, I'm sorry. I really am. I just lost my head . . . I—'

'Shut up!' She looked around at the prison officer, then glared at her son. Her insides were churning but she was driven by her anger and disgust. 'I have nothing more to say to you.' She stood up. 'Do as I say. And may you roast in hell, and let the last faces you see be that little baby and her mother.' She turned and walked away. She was almost buckling as she tried to hold back the tears, making her way through security, until she got all the way out of the prison gates. Then she broke down.

CHAPTER THIRTY-NINE

Rosie was walking in the front door of the *Post*'s office when her mobile rang in her jacket pocket. She fished it out and saw there was no name on the screen. She pressed the phone to her ear and could hear breathing.

'Hello?' she said.

'Is that Rosie Gilmour?'

'Who's speaking? No name came up.'

'Listen. Is that Rosie? I've got a message from Jonjo.'

Rosie stopped at the top of the stairs for a second, then walked towards her desk.

'Yes. This is Rosie.'

'Okay. Right. Listen, I'm going to tell you where to go if you want to find Boag.'

Rosie's heart jumped.

'Is he alive?'

'No.'

She breathed a sigh of relief. 'Okay, I'm listening.'

'If you go up to Drumchapel and head into the Bluebell Woods, you'll find him there.'

Rosie sat down, conscious of Declan watching her. She took out her notebook, phone still pressed to her ear.

'But that's a big place.'

'Go a hundred yards in, and you'll see a wee shed thing. It used to be a gatehouse but it's disused now.' He paused. 'He's in there.'

Rosie let it sink in for a moment. What if it was a trap again? No. It couldn't be. Whoever was calling was doing it on behalf of Jonjo.

'Listen. Why didn't Jonjo phone me himself? He has my number.'

'He said he'll phone you once you get there.'

'Is he going to meet me?'

'No. Just go there if you want to find Boag. That's all I was told to say. All right?'

'Okay. I'll go right away.'

'Right. Don't hang about. He's been there for a few days already.'

He hung up. Rosie sat back and shook her head. She let out a sigh.

'Jesus, Dec! That was a call telling me where to find Boag's body.'

'Shit! Seriously?'

'Yep.' She stood up. 'I'd better tell McGuire.'

As she was walking to her office, she saw Matt at the picture desk and waved him over.

'Listen,' she said, walking him into a corner, 'I've just had a call from someone saying Jonjo told him to phone me. He's told me where I can find Boag's body.'

'Fucking hell!' Matt looked over his shoulder. 'I'll get my gear.'

'Don't say anything to the picture editor yet. I'm going to see Mick first. Let me tell him. We need to keep this tight.'

Matt nodded. 'I'll be here waiting for you.'

Marion was at her desk and Rosie nodded her head towards the editor's open door.

'Yeah, he's in.'

She knocked on the door and walked in. McGuire looked up as she approached.

'Gilmour. How you doing? You look a bit more rested. Did you get a night's sleep?'

'Yeah, thanks. I feel a bit better today. But listen, Mick, I've just had a call from someone on behalf of Jonjo Mulhearn. He's told me where I can find Boag's body.'

'Oh fuck! Is it genuine?'

'It has to be. The caller wouldn't give his name, but phoned my mobile and said Jonjo told him to call.'

'Why didn't he phone himself?'

'I asked that myself. He said Jonjo told him he would call me when I get there.'

'Holy fuck! I'm loving this. Best news is that the bastard is dead. I really hope it's genuine. So where is it?'

'Up in Bluebell Woods, Drumchapel. It's a big place, but he's been quite specific.'

The editor stood up and came out from behind his desk.

'We're going to have to call the cops.'

'I know, but I want to get five minutes before they get there so Matt can get a picture. Once they're in, the whole place will be sealed off.'

McGuire rubbed his chin.

'Right. We should really phone them now, in case it's some kind of trap.'

'How can it be a trap?'

'I don't know. But I don't want you walking into some death trap. I can't cope with much more of that.'

'Aye, cheers, Mick. I'm having a few sleepless nights myself.' Rosie couldn't help but smile.

'You know what I mean.' Mick grinned.

'Tell you what. I'll call the cops in plenty of time. I'll phone and see if I can speak to that big DI Morton. He seems all right.' She shook her head. 'This is when I miss Don. I could have phoned him and he'd have dealt with it and brought the troops up with him. But I don't have any history with this DI, apart from pissing him off a bit when I handed Tadi over.' She took out her mobile and dialled the police HQ, letting it ring as she turned to McGuire. 'With a bit of cooperation from him, he'll let me and Matt be in the woods no longer than a couple of minutes before they come in. Matt won't take long to bag a few pics.'

'It's dodgy. But what I'd give to get a pic of that twisted bastard strung up. I hope they've chopped him up.'

'I'm not sure I want to see that; it will be good enough for me if he's off the face of the earth.'

She turned to go.

'Phone me as soon as you see what's what.' He pointed his finger. 'Do you hear me?'

'Yeah. I hear you. I will, no problem. I'll call your mobile.'

She turned and left the room, joined Matt at the top of the stairs, and they walked briskly to his car.

They had already driven up to Drumchapel and were heading for the Bluebell Woods area, when Rosie became aware that she and Matt had barely spoken. He suddenly glanced at her and touched her knee.

'How you feeling, Rosie? I didn't get a chance to talk to you yesterday with everything that was going on. I couldn't sleep last night thinking about all that shit you went through, after I saw your story.'

Rosie sighed, gazing out of the windscreen. She hadn't really wanted to revisit those moments right now, but Matt was one of her closest friends, and they'd been through so much together, so he knew how she would feel.

'I'm getting through it. Day by day – hour by hour, if I'm honest. I actually slept last night, but I'm not sure the real trauma has sunk in yet. It's one of these things that will come back to haunt me again and again, and pop up any time. You know what it's like. I had a bit of a panic attack meltdown yesterday. I was with Adrian, and thank God I was, because he was really supportive.'

'Yeah. Well he's been through a lot himself.'

'He was great. And it's good to talk about it, I suppose, but I'm trying right now to concentrate on this. I don't know what I'll feel like if Boag is actually there.'

'Well, I'll be doing cartwheels to get a picture exclusive. Sorry to be so crass, but what a result it would be.'

Rosie's mobile rang but there was no name on the mobile number that came up.

'Hello, Rosie? DI Jim Morton. Sorry I missed your call. I was in a meeting. How are you doing?'

'I'm all right, Jim. Thanks for getting back.' She'd left a message for him at Pitt Street earlier. 'Look. I've got some really good information here from a contact telling me where to find Boag.'

'Seriously? Where is he?'

'Well, the thing is, Jim, I want to ask you if you could possibly maybe turn the other way for a couple of minutes so I can get in there with my photographer to get a picture of him – that's if Boag is really there.'

Silence. Rosie waited.

'Rosie. Listen to me. I want to be clear here. I know you had a friendship with Don, and I respect that. I'm an old-fashioned cop in many ways and I think there should be a bit of come and go with reporters like yourself. But as you were told when you handed over that Kosovan lad to us: you are not running the show here – we are. So really, you have to tell me where you're going, as I presume you are on your way there now?'

'Yes. I am. But I just want a couple of minutes—'

'You're not listening, Rosie. You don't even know what you're walking into. It could be a trap.'

'I'm sure it's not. Look, it's only two minutes. I'll phone this number just before I get to the place so you can be on your way. By the time I get into the spot where I'm told Boag is, you'll be almost outside.'

'Christ almighty! You can't dictate to us.'

'I'm not dictating. I'm leading you to where you will find the body. Come on. There has to be a bit of give and take. It's only fair.'

'Christ! Right. What area is it in? You need to tell me that.'

'It's up in Drumchapel.'

'Fine. If you're heading there now, how far away are you from the spot?'

'About five minutes.'

'I expect a phone call in less than ten minutes. I'm on my way to Drumchapel now. But this is really bang out of order, Rosie. And you need to know that. We need to have a serious talk when this is over. You're lucky you've not been charged – so far.'

Rosie could hear the frustration in his voice, but she knew she'd won him over.

'Of course. I'll be happy to do that. I'll call you as soon as I can.'

'Make sure you do.'

Matt pulled his car onto the dirt track road that led into the Bluebell Woods. It stopped after a hundred yards and the rest would be on foot. It was a well-known haunt for kids and teenagers, and there were remains of beer cans and areas where there had been fires lit. As they got out of the car, the sun disappeared behind the trees, and suddenly it was dark and eerie as they looked at the narrow path stretching into the woods. Rosie got out of the car and pressed the DI's number.

'I'm at the Bluebell Woods, Jim. The main entrance. There's a gatehouse about a hundred yards in. That's where I'm told Boag is.'

'Fine. I'll be there in less than five minutes. Be careful. You're off your bloody head.' He hung up.

'It's a bit creepy-looking,' Rosie said as they started to walk in. 'Do you know this place, Matt?'

'I remember I used to come to my cousin's some Sundays in Drumchapel and we came up here. I know the place you're talking about – that old gatehouse thing. I remember it. The caller was right, it's only a hundred yards or so.'

Rosie looked over her shoulder and a shiver ran through her.

'It's a bit scary going up here. I'm feeling a bit jittery.'

'You'll be fine,' Matt said. 'The cops will be here in a minute. Do you want me to go by myself? You wait here?'

'No. I'll be fine.'

She took a deep breath and a tentative step into the shadows. Her heart was going like an engine as they picked up their feet and she was consciously counting the yards . . . sixty, seventy . . . They could see the shack up ahead. The sun came out from behind the clouds and it was light again, and the path seemed clearer. They could hear sirens in the distance.

'Cops are on their way, we'd better hurry.'

Matt walked a little faster, and Rosie quickened her step to keep up. She looked around her over her shoulder and watched for any movement in the woods. She felt sweat on her neck and back. They came up to the gatehouse. Matt turned to her. The sirens were getting closer.

'You wait a second, Rosie. I'll go in.'

She nodded and stood where she was, watching the woods, eyes everywhere. Her heart was hammering in her chest. She watched as Matt pulled back the half-open door and stepped inside. He was only in there for a couple of seconds when she heard him.

'Fuck me!'

'Matt, are you all right?'

She rushed forward, but was relieved when he appeared back out, his face white.

'Jesus!'

'Is he there?'

Matt took a breath and tried to push it out as though to stop himself retching. He bent over.

'Aw, Christ! I think so. Well. I don't know. It's in bits.'

'A body?'

Matt's face was pale.

'Head off, arms chopped! Christ almighty! And the foxes have been at it.'

'Jesus!'

Rosie knew she didn't have to go in there. Matt's pictures would be enough. But she couldn't help it. She moved towards the gate and Matt.

'Are you sure about this, Rosie? You don't have to.'

She looked at him, gritted her teeth.

'I do, Matt. I have to see it for myself. I have to know that he's in there. I don't care if he's in bits. I have to see it. Maybe it'll help me.'

The sirens were blaring now, and Rosie knew they were at the edge of the woods.

'Quick. In and out, Matt.'

Matt went in, snapping everything in sight as he did, the location, the doorway, then inside. Rosie followed him, and the smell hit her first, that sweet sickly smell of decaying human flesh. She put her hand up to cover her nose and mouth. She stepped forward. There he was in the corner, a pile of limbs and torso, legs and bones, a bloodied mass like something from a bombing. But the head lay there, the eyes staring at her the way they had that morning in court, and the same way they had when she looked up as he was dragging the knife across her chest, and the same face that stared at her when Adrian pulled her away from the lock-up. That was all he was now. A pile of rotting, half-eaten flesh. Fuck him! He couldn't harm her any more. She kept her eyes on him, and her heart stopped for a moment, then she turned and left. Outside, she could see the cops rushing up to the scene.

'Hurry, Matt. The cops are here.'

She could hear Matt fire off a few more snaps, then he came out behind her, snapping the approaching police as he did.

'Hey. Get that fucking camera away,' one of the cops shouted.

'Shit,' Matt said. 'We're going to get our arses felt by the plods.'

'It's my tip-off, so they'd better not kick my arse.'

Matt put his hands up, as he and Rosie walked out of the area and onto the path. Half a dozen uniformed officers rushed past them, radios blaring. She looked up and could see the DI stepping briskly towards her. He gave her a look and shook his head.

'Christ almighty, Rosie Gilmour! You need to get out more.' He almost smiled. 'Is it him?'

Rosie nodded. 'What's left of him. The foxes have been at him. But it's Boag all right.'

'Excellent.'

Rosie and Matt were about to walk away.

'Rosie,' the DI said. 'Listen. Don't go anywhere. We need to talk about how you knew about this. This isn't over yet.'

'It was a tip-off.'

'Anonymous?'

'Kind of.'

'I'd like you to hang around for a moment, if you don't mind.' He looked her in the eye. 'And, I appreciate your tip, by the way. I owe you a drink – if I don't bloody arrest you.'

'Sure.' Rosie smiled, and punched McGuire's number in.

'It's Boag. They carved him up. Cops are all over it now.'

'What a fucking result. Pictures?'

'Yeah. Matt's got plenty.'

'Brilliant. How do you feel, Gilmour – I mean, seeing him?'

Rosie hesitated for a moment.

'I feel good, Mick. And that's the truth. He can't touch me any more.'

'That's the stuff. Get back here as soon as you can.'

As they were walking towards Matt's car, Rosie's mobile rang. It was Jonjo.

'Did you see him?'

'I did.'

'Can you meet me for a chat? Same place as the last time. In half an hour?'

'Sure.'

He hung up.

CHAPTER FORTY

Rosie drove her car to the bar where she'd arranged to meet Jonjo. The police protection guys assigned to her had been told to stand down now that Boag's remains had been found. There was something liberating about it, she thought, as she drove back into the city, her radio blaring, the sun bursting through giving the city an upbeat feel. She shouldn't really feel this good, given what she'd been through, and she wondered if another panic attack was just around the corner. But she pushed the thought away. Time would take care of that. In a few months she'd be back to as normal as she could achieve. She found herself looking forward to seeing Jonjo, which wasn't right, because whatever else he was, he was a murderer. She shouldn't forget that.

When she walked into the bar, the same barman who'd been there last week raised his chin as a hello and nodded towards the snug at the back. As she was making her way there, one of the men she vaguely remembered from the other day came towards her. She wondered if the squat, fat Italian was the same man who had phoned her this morning. Jonjo got to his feet and took a long look at her when she came face to face with him.

'Rosie. Thanks for coming.'

Rosie stood a little awkwardly. She wanted to gush and say no, thank *you*, Jonjo, because I wouldn't be here right now if you hadn't saved my life. She wanted to tell him she'd be eternally grateful to him. But that was not what you did with a guy like this. He was no hero, he'd just been in the right place at the right time, though he'd been a hero to her. She looked him in the eye.

'Jonjo . . .' She hesitated, feeling herself blush. 'Before you say anything else, I just want to thank you for saving my life. I'll never be able to repay you for what you did. I know that if it wasn't for you, I'd have died in that shithole.' She swallowed. 'So, thanks.' There, keep it simple and honest.

He stood looking at her, then glanced beyond her as though he was taking in the moment.

'You owe me nothing, Rosie. You know that you could have told the plods chapter and verse of what happened the other day and who was there. But you kept quiet. You have more guts than many of the men I've worked with in my life.'

Rosie felt a little embarrassed – being praised by one of

the biggest crime figures in Glasgow felt odd. He motioned her to sit down.

'Drink?'

'What's that you've got?'

'Tea. Black.'

'I'll have the same.'

He looked at the other man. 'Aldo, sort it will you?' Aldo disappeared to the bar.

'He was there the other day, I think?'

'Yeah. It was Aldo who heard you screaming. I sent him to look for your mobile after your big pal Adrian said Boag threw it down the embankment. While he was there he heard the screaming. Good man, is Aldo. He's my right-hand man. All my life.'

'I have to thank him too.'

Jonjo shook his head. 'He was glad to help. That's his style. A real gentleman in so many ways.' He raised his eyebrows in emphasis. 'But you wouldn't want to cross him.'

Rosie nodded. She wondered if Aldo had played a part in the trussed-up remains of Boag. They sat now with their mugs of tea; she waited to see what he was going to say.

'So you got your pictures then?'

'Yes.' She looked across at him. 'It wasn't a pretty sight.'

He nodded and said nothing for a long moment. Then Rosie spoke. 'Can I ask you, Jonjo, did Boag say anything? I mean, anything to you, about your son, or about what he had done? Did he even express a scrap of remorse?'

Jonjo shook his head, his face tight.

'No. Nothing. He's the most evil fucker I've come across, and I've seen them all. This was worse than evil. He could have been killing people for years, you know.' He sipped his tea. 'Well, he'll not kill any more innocent laddies.'

Rosie let that hang in the air for a moment and she could see from his face that he was picturing his son, perhaps in his final moments. But even though she knew she would never be writing up this interview for the newspaper, her journalist mind was riven with curiosity. She wanted to know details. She felt a bit ashamed of that, but it's how she was.

'Did you do it yourself?'

He looked at her, a little surprised and a glint of suspicion.

'I'm not going to talk to the police, Jonjo. Not now, not ever. I should, but I won't.'

He waited a moment.

'I have people who dispose of garbage like Boag. I've had them up from London hanging around here for a fortnight. I knew we would find him. It was only a matter of time.'

Another silence. The door opened and Rosie heard the sound of traffic.

'So you didn't play any part in it? Even the "eye for an eye" justice?' Rosie couldn't believe she was having this kind of conversation with a man who had been part of what could only be described as a gruesome murder.

Eventually, Jonjo nodded. 'I cut him so I could watch him bleed. But it was going to take a while. Let me put it this way. The idea was that he would feel the first of his limbs being severed.'

Rosie felt a little light-headed picturing the scene.

'Jesus!'

'Aye. He squealed like a stuck pig. The good thing is that he knew what was going to happen to him. Of course, he would know from the minute I picked him up from that lock-up that he was finished. But it was important to me that he knew it wouldn't be quick. It was important that he went the same way as the others he had done. The woman from downstairs, the music teacher . . . my laddie and maybe that other poor boy they haven't found yet. But not one word of remorse did he utter.'

Rosie blinked away the sudden flashback of the woman's severed head that Boag had sent to her in a box. Christ! It seemed like ages ago. No wonder she was having the odd meltdown. She nodded in agreement, not just because she was sitting in front of him, but because she absolutely believed what he was saying. It was and would always be a dilemma for her. Where do I go from here? she thought. I'm sitting opposite the man who kidnapped and helped murder a serial killer – a man who effectively did the world a favour – but he had operated outside the law. She could hear McGuire and Hanlon saying as much, and that was why she knew she could never write this story, any more than she could walk out of here now and tell the police what she knew. It was up to them to arrest people and it was up to the courts to convict and jail the offender. Jonjo Mulhearn didn't live by those rules, but *she* did. Yet here she was, as though she was part of the secret, part of the plot. She didn't know what to say.

Suddenly, Jonjo broke the silence.

'Anyway. I just wanted to clear things with you, to see that you were all right about what happened to you, and to tell you about Boag. But that's not the only reason I needed to see you.'

Rosie looked at him, not knowing what to expect.

'The O'Dwyers. Those fuckers.'

'Oh, right.' Rosie had almost forgotten that she'd asked for his help to see if he could put feelers out on the street and find out who took part in the robbery of the Cimmermans.

'I said I would help you and I have. Here's the sketch. One of the men involved in the robbery is handing himself into the cops as we speak. He's in London Road police station at the moment, grassing them all up. He can talk about the Kosovo guy who was there, back up his story, and spill his guts on Rory O'Dwyer and those two prick sons of his. So the O'Dwyers are fucked, as of now.'

For a second, Rosie didn't know what to say.

'Christ! I have to say, I'm wondering how you managed to achieve that.'

Jonjo gave her a long look.

'If you live long enough in this game, you get to call in the favours you've done for people over the years; the people you've saved from the grubber, the lives you've rescued, families you helped. The guys you gave a leg-up to. People deliver for you.'

'So what will happen to the man who sticks them in?'

He shrugged. 'Don't know. They'll do him on a lesser charge. Maybe even get him acquitted. The cops might look after him, but who knows. If they let him go, he'll have to get off his mark, because the O'Dwyers have a lot of friends. So someone will be out for him.' He paused. 'But he's done his bit. I thought it was important to sort that out.'

They sat for a few moments, and Rosie looked at her watch.

'I'll have to go. I haven't been back to see the editor since this morning, and I know he'll be going nuts over the pictures of Boag.' She paused. 'But in terms of a story, I won't be able to tell the truth of everything over the last few days, of Boag's body today and how it got there . . .'

'How does that sit with you?'

Rosie waited a few seconds before answering. 'Sometimes that's how it happens. It's not right though, not by the book. But what happened to Boag, however bloody and primitive, was justice. I believe that. Completely. So I'm going to have to live with the truth bit.'

Jonjo sighed. 'What is it they say about newspapers? They'll be eating chips out of it tomorrow?'

Rosie smiled at the old saying – it had been a great leveller for journalists who'd got puffed up with their own importance after they broke a major story.

'Yeah. Makes me wonder sometimes why we take ourselves so seriously. Here today, gone tomorrow.' She stood up, pulled her bag onto her shoulder.

'But you're different, I can see that.' He looked up at her.

Rosie sighed. Despite what Jonjo was, what he'd done, how he'd led his life – she liked him. She felt safer with him than a posse of cops. She reached out her hand as he got to his feet.

'Thanks again, Jonjo. I mean it.'

'I hope I see you again some time, Rosie. You be careful now.'

Rosie drove back to the office, her mind in turmoil. She was betraying everything she believed in, that the pursuit of truth was the be-all and end-all of her psyche. But she didn't feel guilty. Boag had killed innocent people and ruined families and lives. One of her best friends had died in a car crash chasing after him. Why did we have to give a fair trial to people like that? Did this mean she wasn't a good journalist any more? She wasn't sure right at this moment. She was ready to go back and write the story of the tip-off, but it wouldn't be the whole story, and other hacks out there would know it. They would perhaps judge her, but they would *never* know the truth. Perhaps that made her no better than the villains or criminals who lived outside the law, because today she was playing by *their* rules, not hers. She would talk to McGuire about it, but her mind was already made up. Her mobile rang on the passenger seat, and glancing over, she recognised the DI's number from earlier.

'Rosie. I thought you might want to know of a development in the O'Dwyer story – about the robbery at the Cimmermans.'

Rosie was so surprised to get a friendly phone call from the big cop that she didn't quite know how to react.

'Of course, Jim,' she managed. 'I'm all ears. And I appreciate you phoning.'

'Well. You were helpful to us, so as I told you, I'm an old-fashioned cop, and that works both ways – as long as you don't abuse it.'

'Course not. What's happened?'

'One of the robbers from the old Jewish couple's house, who was with the O'Dwyers that night, has given himself up.'

A smile spread across Rosie's face.

'No way!'

'Yep. He's just walked into London Road a half-hour ago, and is sticking every one of them in. And he remembers the foreign guy being there too.'

'Christ. That's amazing. Your boys must be doing cartwheels.'

'They are. Nobody can understand it.'

'So our Kosovan friend Tadi is off the hook – on all counts?'

'He will be. Once we tied up some loose ends, he will be deported back to Kosovo – he wants to go home anyway. Oh, and by the way, he said to tell you thank you for helping his family. For your kindness.' He paused. 'We'll maybe one day find out how this all came about.'

'Well,' Rosie said, thinking of Jonjo's words about calling in favours. Pressure must have been put on this guy. 'There's a lot we can't understand, so the best thing is just to take it when it's going, and celebrate. The O'Dwyers will be banged up for a long time.'

'You bet. Will Boag's body be all over the paper tomorrow?'

'Oh yes. Well, as much as we can publish so as not to put our readers off their breakfast.'

'Are you saying who did it?'

'How would I know who did it? And does it even matter?'

'It does, Rosie. It should.'

Rosie wanted to ask if it mattered to him. She knew it wouldn't have mattered to Don, but she didn't know this guy well enough to ask questions like that.

'Yeah. It should. But that's not really how life is.'

'Aye. I'll buy you that drink some time, and you can tell me how you'd put the world to rights.'

Rosie smiled.

'I'd like that, Jim. Give me a call any time.'

'I'll see what your paper says tomorrow first.'

He hung up, and Rosie pulled into the car park of the *Post*, stood outside and looked up at the four-storey building, where so much of her life had been invested. Bad times, hard days and sad ones too. Today, she may have crossed a line. But it still felt like one of the good days.

ACKNOWLEDGEMENTS

A great deal of my life is spent writing, or thinking about writing, or agonising about writing. So much so, that I rarely get time to thank the people around me who support me and enrich my life.

So thanks to my sister Sadie, who has always been with me every step of the way. And cheers to Christopher Costello and Matthew Costello who are always throwing in ideas for stories and characters, and to Kat Campbell for thinking outside the box to take my novels further. Also thanks to my huge family including my brothers, nephews nieces, great-nieces and great-nephews, and cousins. You all know who you are and the part you play in my life. Thanks to Alice and Debbie for the hospitality and curries shared in London, and Ann Marie.

The Motherwell Smiths, for some great times together in Dingle, and also my cousins Helen and Irene.

Thanks also to my great friends, Eileen, Mag, Annie, Liz, Mary and Phil, Helen, Barbara, Donna, Jan, Louise.

And my journalist pals for the laughs when we look back on the good times – Simon and Lynn, Keith and Maureen, Mark, Thomas, Brian, Gordon and Janetta and Jimmy, Ross, Peter, Alex and Gerda, Ronnie.

In Spain, thanks to Lisa, Lillias and Nat, Mara, Wendy, Yvonne, Jean, Sarah, Fran, Davina and Billy, Sally, Jean and Dave.

In Ireland my pals Mary and Paud, Sioban and Martin, Cristin, Sean Brendain and Christiana.

All at Quercus, especially Jane Wood my mentor, Therese Keating, and the team.